Praise for

Double Exposure

This smart, propulsive novel is a thrill, with rich characters full of humor and heart. Sacken knows this world, and she portrays it with a masterful touch of suspense and surprise.

Steven Wright, author of *The Coyotes of Carthage*

Jeannée Sacken follows her excellent debut novel, *Behind The Lens*, with another superbly written story. The protagonist of both books, Annie Hawkins Green, is without a doubt currently my favorite badass woman. She is smart, strong, gutsy, and kind, but at the same time flawed, with emotions (and lingering PTSD) that cause some of her decisions to take her into situations that range from mildly upsetting to life-threateningly dangerous. In *Double Exposure*, Sacken carries on where she left off in the first. Once again, the reader is carried deeply into the dust and danger of real life in this war-plagued country. The action is fast-moving, unpredictable, and at times heart-stopping. Sacken's prose is brilliant. I can't wait to see what comes next.

Patricia Sands, author of the best-selling Love in Provence series

A superbly crafted and thrilling sequel with enough twists and turns to keep you riveted right up to the tension-filled finale. Jeannée Sacken captures the beauty and complexity of Afghanistan through the eyes and lens of Annie Hawkins—always with a tough, yet tender touch.

Debra Thomas, Sarton Award winner of *Luz*

Sacken has done it again! Captivating, fast-paced, and unsettling, *Double Exposure* is a story of strength, love, perseverance, and resilience. Chock-full of raw emotion and visceral pain, it made me weep then rage at the plight of females in Afghanistan. A must-read for women and those who love them.

Laurie Buchanan, author of the Sean McPherson novels

Double Exposure is the sequel to Jeannée Sacken's first novel, *Behind the Lens*. Where *Behind the Lens* was a successful women's fiction novel with some romance, *Double Exposure* thrusts the reader into full-out romantic suspense. Not only is the tension high and the immersion visceral, but the romance is deeply emotional (I fell hard for Cerelli). *Double Exposure* stands alone. You can enjoy it without reading the first novel. But why would you? They are both so good. I believe I called Sacken's first novel "unputdownable." This new novel is not only unputdownable, it's unforgettable. I predict *Double Exposure* will win more awards than the last one.

Jennifer Trethewey, author of historical romance

With smart narration, nuanced characters, and thought-provoking situations reminiscent of Hosseini's *A Thousand Splendid Suns*, Sacken brilliantly explores the story of Annie Hawkins, a photo-journalist torn between the needs of her teenage daughter back home and her own deep-seated desire to change the lives of the women in a small Afghan village. This topical tale is laced with empathy, insight, and authenticity as Hawkins fights against centuries-old traditions, political and professional intrigue, and her own need to advance her career, all while juggling a burgeoning love affair and searching for a kidnapped girl. Your heart will race when you reach the propulsive climax.

Maggie Smith, author of *Truth and Other Lies*

Jeannée Sacken has done it again. A well-researched story and intriguing suspense that grips you till the end.

Kathryn Gauci, best-selling author of *The Secret of the Grand Hôtel du Lac*

Sacken brilliantly funnels readers right back into each of her characters' lives once again as the independent and ever-so resilient photojournalist, Annie Hawkins, returns to politically, religiously, and culturally charged Afghanistan. True to the historically diverse cultures and religions influencing Afghani life today, Sacken's vividly descriptive storytelling is full of suspense, humor, tragedy, edginess, and irony, triggering feelings of sadness, anger, love, and determination. This is an intense read that focuses on the inner strength of women, the power of profound friendships, the love that aids survival during the hardest moments in life, and appreciation for one another despite cultural and religious divides. Sacken develops characters that have an awesome sense of compassion for humanity and willingness to appreciate and respect one another's differences. Hopefully, the saga of war photojournalist Annie continues beyond *Double Exposure*.

Heba Elkobaitry, Muslim Cultural Advisement Consultant

Praise for

Behind the Lens

A gripping Afghan tale starring a strong hero wielding a camera.

Kirkus Reviews

A powerful, heartbreaking story of an American woman seeking redemption after exploiting a photographic moment in an Afghani village. Jeannée Sacken's artistic gaze is unflinching as Annie Hawkins' tale plays out against the perilous background of the war in Afghanistan.

Shauna Singh Baldwin, author of *What the Body Remembers,* *The Tiger Claw,* **and** *The Selector of Souls*

Behind the Lens is a stunning debut novel ultimately about friendship and family set amidst cultural upheaval.

Lisa J. Lickel, Wisconsin Writers Association

2022 Hawthorne Prize, American Writing Awards

2021 Book of the Year – Fiction, 2021 Best Women's Fiction, 2021 Best Mystery/Suspense, American Writing Awards

2021 Notable Book of the Year, *Shelf Unbound*

2021 Best Debut Fiction, Winner Women's Fiction, Winner Suspense, Firebird Book Awards

Also by Jeannée Sacken

Behind the Lens

DOUBLE EXPOSURE

JEANNÉE SACKEN

www.ten16press.com - Waukesha, WI

For information, please contact:

www.ten16press.com
Waukesha, WI

Cover design by Kaeley Dunteman
Editing and interior design by Lauren Blue
Chapter image design by Josh McFarlane
Author photo © Agnieszka Tropiło

For Roi Solberg

and

*for the girls in Afghanistan
whose schools have been shuttered*

October, 2015
Doha, Qatar

ANOTHER AIRPORT. ANOTHER DELAY. I stand rooted in the middle of the jostling crowd, staring at the international departures board for a full minute after the ON TIME posting for my flight to Dulles disappears. The agent at the gate tells me they're waiting for a new crew. It could take hours. As a war photographer, I'm used to delays. But after three months on assignment in Saudi Arabia and Yemen, I want to get back to the States. First, to D.C. and a few heavenly days with U.S. Navy SEAL Captain Finn Cerelli. Then, home to Milwaukee for some long-overdue time with my sixteen-year-old daughter Mel. I can only hope she'll put whoever her current boyfriend is on hold to spend time with me. Probably not a realistic expectation for a noncustodial mother who drops into her life once in a while, but I can always hope. For now, I've got to find a comfortable place to hole up and wait.

I shoulder my Lowepro camera pack and trudge back into

the main terminal of Hamad International Airport. Strolling past glitzy stores—the likes of Gucci and Burberry, Bulgari and Tiffany—rarified places where I can't afford to shop, I make my way to the Oryx Lounge, one of my favorite spots in any airport.

Crossing the room to an empty and dimly lit corner, I recognize a few other photogs and journalists. Some are staring glassy-eyed at their cell phones, decompressing, clearly on their way home. Others are chatting and laughing, stoked on adrenaline, about to head out on assignment. I avoid eye contact, grateful to be alone. Claiming two club chairs, I slip off my pack onto one of them—my way of making sure no one joins me.

Nursing a double Maker's neat, I relish the smooth nuttiness that warms all the way down. I also power on my cell, determined to make the most of the first reliable Wi-Fi in months to catch up on my text messages. Hundreds to get through, but there are three people I need to contact first. I alert Mel that I'll be arriving sometime this coming weekend, just in case she has plans involving a boyfriend in my no-boys-allowed apartment. Not a rule she tends to obey when I'm out of the country, which drives me to distraction. I should probably confiscate her key, except she needs a place to retreat to when she's not getting along with her father, or more typically, her stepmother. Things got pretty dicey between them five months ago—the last time I was in Afghanistan.

I swirl the bourbon in the glass. Maybe I need to think about renegotiating the custody arrangement? Mel would love that. A long sip. But how the hell could I ever make it work? My job has me out of country for months at a time. I tuck the thought away for consideration at some future—and unspecified—date.

Then, I let my boss know I'll check in with him as soon as I get to D.C.

I save Cerelli for last, warning him that I'll be later than expected. I'm savoring my bourbon and thinking of the man himself, working myself into glorious anticipation, when my phone buzzes in a new message.

My body is mine,
But my Beloved drinks me like rare, red wine.

I smile at the *landay*. Cerelli is rugged and fearless and all military. He also composes the most romantic poems I've ever read. Kind of ironic since *landays* are traditionally composed by young Afghan women for lovers their parents will never allow them to marry. My heart quickens as I read the poem again. Damn, I've missed him. Even though he seriously complicates my life. Not for the first time, I wish I carried a picture of him. But *No pictures!* is his constant refrain. Nothing that could possibly link me to him should terrorists ever kidnap me. No matter. The image I carry in my mind's eye is much better. His silvering hair, military short now, not the ponytail he wore when I first met him nine years ago. Brown eyes that melt when he sees me, making me want to swim into them and take up residence. And his arms, so strong they could break a person in two, but they make me feel safe.

I take another look at the *landay* and exhale my disappointment. Not from Cerelli. It's from someone called Rahila. No last name. Rahila? As in Rachel. My middle name. Seema's, too. Seema—the girl I love second to my own daughter. The girl who disappeared months ago.

My fingers tighten on the phone. Could this really be from Seema? Could she be calling herself Rahila now? Good God, if she wrote this, that means she's alive.

Just that quickly, I'm back in the quiet, sleepy village of Wad
Qol, tucked halfway up the peaceful Panjshir Valley in the shadows
of the Hindu Kush Mountains. Not the Shangri-La that Darya,
my best friend—and Seema's mother—had promised, but close
to it. A welcome relief considering the violence plaguing the rest
of Afghanistan. I was there to teach a photography workshop at
Darya's secondary school for girls. And almost as soon as I arrived,
Seema started acting strangely, spouting one lie after another. *No,
Auntie, I don't have a boyfriend.* And later, *I'm sorry, Auntie, I can't
go with you; I have to study.* Nothing like the girl I used to know.

Damn it. How could I have let myself believe her? Then again,
Darya didn't pick up on the lying, and she didn't think there was a
serious problem, just that Seema was probably tired from studying
too hard for graduation exams. I was pretty sure there was more to it
than that. My instincts were telling me that there was a guy hanging
around—a potentially serious problem in Afghanistan where the
whole boyfriend/girlfriend thing is very different from the U.S. I
didn't say anything to Darya because I wanted to be sure. Except, by
the time I *was* sure, it was too late. Way too late. Dar was lying dead
in the schoolyard, killed by Seema's boyfriend Awalmir. According
to the teachers, he laughed when he shot her, laughed while he
burned down the school. And Seema was . . . gone. Kidnapped? Or,
could she actually have been part of what happened, then run away
with her boyfriend? Her *Taliban* boyfriend.

As quickly as that thought surfaces, I shut it down. It's been five
months, and I still don't want to believe that Seema, sweet princess
Seema, would do such a horrific thing.

I swallow hard and read the poem again.

My Beloved. Does Seema or Rahila or whatever she's calling
herself even know her 'Beloved' killed her mother? And where

the hell *is* she? I study the phone number. The area code—I'm pretty sure it's Afghanistan. Looking over my shoulder toward the information desk, I see the line has thinned down to one person. I'm over there in a flash.

In his charcoal-gray suit, the clerk is darkly handsome with a smile intended to make knees go weak. Mine included.

"Is there..." I stumble over my words. *Get real,* I chastise myself. *I'm almost old enough to be his mother. Besides, I've got Cerelli waiting for me.* I snort a laugh. If Cerelli were here and the clerk were a gorgeous woman, I have no doubt he'd take a moment or thirty to appreciate the scenery. I clear my throat. "Is there, uh, any way you could tell me where this phone number is from?" I hold up my cell so he can see the number.

He reaches for a list of country codes. "It is Afghanistan." Another breathtaking smile.

"Can you tell me which city? Kabul? Or Kandahar?"

His gaze drifts down to the text. "I'm sure there's a code embedded in the number, but I don't know the different cities. Sorry." He flashes yet another smile, his perfect white teeth nearly blinding me.

"Thanks anyway."

I retreat to my corner. So, if this *is* from Seema, it's a good bet she's in Afghanistan. And here I sit in Doha. Not all that far. If I could just figure out where she is . . . I could do what? Go search for her? Right. The chances of finding her are next to nil. And if I do, then what? Would she wrap her arms around me and beg me to take her back to the States?

I read the poem for the umpteenth time. As much as I don't want to believe it, she sounds happy. Almost gleeful. Like she's throwing her joy in my face. Or her parents' faces. My heart sinks as I force myself to face reality. Whoever wrote this doesn't sound like she's been kidnapped. Is that why she sent me this text? To let me know she's happy? That I don't need to look for her?

I toss back the rest of my bourbon and signal for another. Something's off with this *landay,* only I can't figure out what. I know Afghan teens are writing these poems and calling them in to talk radio shows, using just their first names—a secret and safer way for boys and girls to pass messages back and forth. As long as their parents or older brothers or uncles don't find out. It's not only families that don't approve, but the Taliban. And ISIS. They don't want girls writing or reading at all. And certainly not composing poems that express secret, forbidden love. Which brings dishonor to girls and their families. In other words, they *kill* girls for things like this. Honor killings.

That's what's bothering me. There's no way Awalmir would approve of Seema writing this. And the Seema I last saw wouldn't go against him. So, why did she write it? What's she really trying to tell me? And bottom line: why send it to *me?* Something to discuss with Cerelli when I get to D.C.

"Annie? Annie Hawkins Green?"

I recognize the Aussie accent and look up at a man I'd just as soon leave buried in the past. The black eye patch takes me by surprise. "Josh." I raise my phone a little higher and do my best to appear busy.

He nods at the unoccupied chair. "Mind if I join you?" Not waiting for an answer, he moves my Lowepro to the floor and sits. "Crikey, that's heavy. But then, you always did carry a shitload of camera gear."

I focus on my texts.

"It's been a while." He waves for a beer.

"It has." But not long enough.

He clears his throat. "Since Masum Ghar."

"Let's not go there, okay?"

"Look, Annie, I came by to say sorry. It was crook what we did, hazing you."

I slam my phone down on the table. "Then why'd you do it?" My voice is sharp and a notch too loud. Around us, people stop their quiet chatter and stare. Josh looks surprised. What? He's expecting me to be all sweetness and light and tell him everything is long forgotten?

"You must've realized it was mainly Nic's idea. Dan and I—"

"Didn't do a damn thing to stop it. In fact, I remember you riding off with them, leaving me to fend for myself in the worst sandstorm of the season." I take a breath and admonish myself to lower my voice. "I could've fucking died out there. Then, I had to 'explain myself' to the CO, who was decent enough not to ship me home." I don't tell him the rest of what happened. The ambush at the small, run-down village of Khakwali. The deaths of my Marine escorts and Malalai, the ten-year-old Pashtun girl who was too feisty and way too smart for her own good. The military scrubbed the entire incident, not to mention the village. I don't need to be the source of any journalist digging back into it.

His beer arrives. He takes a long pull and sets down the bottle on the gorgeously grained wood side table between our chairs. Without a coaster. "Look. You were a star for not giving us up. Had us by the balls. I've had a lot of time to think about that day. I was a total arsehole. I'm sorry." He does sound upset. Sincerely sorry.

Oh, hell. Even though I like letting him twist in the wind, what's the point? It sure won't bring back Murphy or Lopez or Malalai. But if I can stop him from hazing one other female journalist . . .

I stab my index finger against the table. "Don't do it again. To anyone. Next time, I won't stay quiet."

He nods his contrition. I believe him. And hope now that he's said his piece, he'll move on to some other corner.

He takes another pull of beer. "Word is your crew just got back from Yemen. Any advice about getting in?"

Our crew actually spent more time in Saudi Arabia, waiting to cross the border, than we did in Yemen. Being as the Saudis don't want any eyewitnesses to their proxy war, they have an annoying embargo on the news media entering Yemen. We finally resorted to getting ourselves smuggled over the border late one moonless night—thanks to our producer and senior correspondent calling in a lot of favors. Getting out again and to Qatar was almost as tough. I'm not about to hand over that information. Let him call in his own favors.

I look around as if I'm about to impart a seriously important and top-secret strategy. "Patience. A lot of patience. Who are you with now anyway?"

"Al Shabakat." He gives me a pointed look like he knows what I'm about to say.

I don't let him down. "Funny how I keep running into you people."

"Yeah, Piera McNeil mentioned you two had a great time in Afghanistan."

"Piera does have a way of misrepresenting things." I shake my head and sigh to drive home my point. The journalist I call the Piranha made my life miserable in Afghanistan.

He leans forward but doesn't lower his voice. "She also says you're off the market."

I raise an eyebrow. "What's that supposed to mean?"

He smirks. "No more bed-hopping."

His words shove me back in my chair. "She. Said. What?" For obvious reasons, Cerelli and I keep our relationship under the radar. SEALs put themselves in freaking dangerous situations all the time, and Cerelli's no exception. What really worries them is the *tangoes*—Navy speak for terrorists and militants—finding out about their families and lovers and going after them.

He leans closer. "She said you and Nic hooked up in Kabul. More than hooked up. That you two are an item."

"Nic? Are we talking about Nic Parker Lowe?" Leave it to Piera to screw that up, too. I let out the breath I've been holding. "Sorry to disappoint."

Josh quirks a grin. "Nic doesn't deny it."

What happened between Nic and me in Kabul was that he came out of the closet. And made it very clear I was to tell no one. So, now I'm his cover? Well, that could work both ways. I shrug. "Actually, I did see Nic in Kabul. Dinner that included a *very nice* apology on his part." I blush. On cue. That should give Nic some cover. Because the minute I walk out of the lounge, Josh will be rushing to confirm the rumors.

On the side table, my phone buzzes. Finally! The out I need. I pull up my texts and pretend to read what comes up on the screen. "I'm boarding!" I push myself up from the chair and shoulder my Lowepro. "Nice running into you, Josh. And like I said before, patience is the key to getting into Yemen." I turn my back and head toward the door. Halfway there, I stop and retrace my steps. "It's 'Annie Hawkins' now. I dropped the 'Green.'"

Out in the terminal, I power walk toward my gate, stopping a moment to admire my favorite piece of public artwork anywhere—a gigantic wooden sculpture called *The Lie*. A marionette with his peg of a nose, slumped forward just before the woodcarver, Geppetto, wishes him to life. I've always liked the idea of an artist being able to make artwork real. To have that kind of impact.

People hurrying past, chattering on cell phones, quickly end my moment of contemplation and get me walking again. I also take a look at my latest text for real. It's definitely not a boarding call. It's not from Cerelli either. Which has me wondering why he's suddenly gone quiet. This message is from my boss:

My office. Tomorrow. 4 p.m. sharp.

Washington, D.C.

I CHARGE OUT OF DULLES Airport's international terminal at 3:45 p.m., Lowepro on my back, duffel in hand, and just manage to catch the Silver Line Express shuttle. There's no way I'm going to make a four o'clock meeting in the city. I fire off a text, telling my boss the best I can do is 5:00 p.m. Which isn't going to make him happy.

Checking the rest of my texts, I find one from Cerelli. *Come when you can. I'll be here.* My heart skips a beat.

Nothing from Mel. Typical. I send another. *Hey, sweetie. Back in the U.S. Spending a few days with Cerelli. Home Sunday. Can't wait to see you!*

At Reston, I catch the Metrorail into D.C., then jog the three blocks from Union Station to the TNN building. The security guard scans me through. The elevator lets me off on the fifth floor, and I jog to my boss's office, skidding to a stop in front of his assistant's desk. Kevin. He started here the same time I did. He's my touchstone.

"You're late." Kevin looks pointedly over his shoulder at the clock, which reads 5:15.

"Yeah, well. My flight got in just over an hour ago. I feel like I ran all the way from Dulles."

"Hate to say it, girlfriend, you look like it, too. And those jeans certainly make a statement."

I glance down at my black jeans—ripped at the knees. And no longer black, more of a dusty gray. My dirt-caked army boots. And, of course, the bulky, many-times-patched copper sweater my grammy knit for me decades ago. Definitely not what I should be wearing for a meeting with the boss. Even if it *is* Chris Cardona—a really good guy who couldn't care less what I show up in. But this will test even his good nature.

Kevin nods toward my pack and duffel. "Leave your stuff here with me. It'll make a better impression." Then, he lowers his voice. "They're all waiting for you."

I'm already pushing open the door before I fully process what he just said. 'They're *all* waiting for you.' Who the hell is in there? Chris didn't say anything about other people.

Door open, I slip inside. Kevin was right. Besides Chris, there are two VPs I've gone drinking with a few times, the director of Human Resources, and a gray business-suited man I've never seen before—all seated around the long rectangular conference table. Every last one of them looks solemn. 'Grim' might be more accurate. There's one empty chair. At the end of the table.

"Sorry," I mutter, sitting down as unobtrusively as possible. "Yemen. Qatar. Just landed. Dulles."

Chris nods curtly as if this makes all the sense in the world. Actually, in the news business, we all understand this kind of shorthand. Foreign correspondents are always coming in from or going off to somewhere. Damn, he looks upset. His hands are resting on the table, clenched so tightly his knuckles are white. The tiny black hairs on the back of his fingers are standing on end. "Glad you could finally join us." He coughs out the words. "You know everyone here, except for Marcus Johnson."

I start to smile 'hello,' when Chris adds, "Marcus is a member of our legal team."

My smile falters. Everyone's back to looking at me. Might be nice if they clued me in. Instead, they let me squirm—for a full minute. Brutal.

Finally, Chris clears his throat and unclasps his hands, placing them flat on the table. "A situation has been brought to our attention."

A situation? I look up sharply and see the concern etched across his face. Obviously, he's waiting for me to speak. To explain. "I don't understand."

The impeccably dressed HR director leans forward. "Just so we're following protocol—Annie, would you like to have a personal representative present?"

All I can do is stare at the woman's small gold hoop earrings. I'm caked in dry sweat and completely exhausted. My brain isn't functioning well enough to process what a personal representative is, much less why I might want one here and now. Other than something bad is about to come down. Totally bewildered, I shrug. "You tell me."

"Annie, this has to do with your trip to Afghanistan last May." Chris looks down at his hands. "It's serious." He points toward the video monitor, which I notice for the first time is front and center for easy entertainment viewing. Something tells me what we're about to see won't be all that entertaining. Especially for me.

Time to get my act together. Slapping my palms flat on the
table, I lean forward and do my best to keep my voice steady,
controlled. "I've just gotten off a fourteen-hour flight from Qatar.
Before that, I was in Yemen for a month, which is the equivalent of
a hellhole for those of you who haven't been there." Which means
everyone in the room except me. A dig I probably shouldn't have
allowed myself. "And Saudi for eight weeks before that. So, no. I
have no idea what any of this is about."

Chris slides off his glasses and pinches the bridge of his nose.

Oh, this is really bad. The last time I saw that move was just
before he told the crew about our former producer's death by sniper
fire in Kabul. Oh, fuck. Who now?

Before I can carry that thought any further, Chris picks up the
remote and clicks on the monitor. Instantly, a wide-eyed woman's
face fills the screen. She looks drawn, hollowed empty by a horror
she won't be able to comprehend for a long time. Maybe not ever.
Her wild red curls are escaping from under her black *hijab*. There's
no mistaking who she is.

"Get. Away. From. Me!" she yells, two-handing a semi-
automatic handgun, pointing it first at the camera, then at someone
offscreen. There's a bobble in the video feed as if the cameraman
scrambled to get out of the line of fire. The film keeps rolling.

A second woman, a reporter from another cable news network,
mic in hand, steps into the frame. The intrepid Piera McNeil from
Al Shabakat. "What about her daughter?" Her voice is gentle, her
tone oozing concern. Not exactly the way I remember it. Her mic
is right in the face of the red-haired woman, so close it could knock
out a few teeth. "Seema, right? Where is she? Was she killed in the
fire?" I stare at her lips, slightly out of sync with her voice.

On the TV monitor, thick smoke envelops the two women,

all but screening them from view, and a blast erupts off-camera. Probably one of the kerosene containers stored in the Wad Qol Secondary School for Girls, which is fiercely burning. Flames shoot high above the building, completely engulfing it. The smoke clears, and the charred remains of a once-white Toyota pickup are just visible—embedded in the front classroom. Off to one side, Tariq Ghafoor kneels next to the body of his wife, Darya Faludi. My best friend. Women in black *burqas* and headscarves cluster together, a respectful distance away, waiting to put Dar's body into the flatbed of the waiting truck.

Another kerosene container explodes.

Next to me, the Vice President for Digital Coverage jumps in his seat. He clears his throat nervously, a sure sign he hasn't been in a war zone anytime recently. If ever.

Back on the screen, a man's arm clad in a nubby sports jacket wraps around the gun-toting woman from behind, ready to pull her out of the shot. Or to keep her from shooting.

But not before the red-haired woman speaks again, her voice bordering on hysterical, her hands tightening on the pistol grip. "Try me." Wait. Didn't Piera say something else before I pulled the gun out of my pack? I try hard to reconstruct what happened but come up blank.

Piera finally sees the gun and smiles. Such an oddly self-satisfied smile.

Another bobble in the video feed. Then, the screen fades to black.

On my other side, the VP for News exhales a sigh of relief, as if she's worried the red-haired woman might actually have shot Piera. As if she doesn't know what happened next. Which is pretty disingenuous, given that I'm sure everyone in this room has watched the video clip at least a dozen times. Everyone, that is, except me. This is my first time seeing the video.

But I lived it.

I'm the woman training the gun on Piera McNeil. In my defense, Piera stepped way over the line of human decency a couple hours after the Taliban had killed Dar and burned the school to the ground. As I learned firsthand, she'd do anything to get a story. That said, pulling the Sig Saur wasn't my finest moment. I was wrong. Dead wrong. Full stop.

I stare at the monitor. Numb. Unable to move. Fighting hard to keep the blank screen from sucking me into it. Into the hellacious oblivion that I left behind me in Afghanistan. I clasp the armrests of my chair, struggling to stay in the here and now. Oh, God, the hair on the back of my neck is prickling. Sweat is pooling between my breasts.

"Annie? Annie!"

I jerk my eyes away from the monitor and look at Chris, who's busy massaging his forehead. He clearly doesn't want to be in this room, saying what he has to say. Yeah, well, I don't want to be here either.

"Please tell me the gun wasn't loaded."

Loaded? Was it loaded? I honestly don't remember. I also couldn't say if I had the safety on or off. Cerelli would kill me if he knew, but I don't generally do guns, so I have a hard time keeping up with all the minutiae. Not to mention that everything was crazy horrible that day.

I slowly shake my head, unable to answer.

Attorney Marcus Johnson leans forward, nearly sprawling across the table. "Ms. Hawkins—" A deep, resonant voice, authoritative. All attorney.

"Annie, please," I say before realizing I probably shouldn't interrupt.

"Okay, Annie. There are a few questions I've got to ask."

I nod.

"Is that you in the video?"

I nod again.

"And you're holding a gun?"

This is agony. I close my eyes. "Yes."

"Thank you. Now, let me be very clear." Marcus Johnson's voice could easily lull me into a false sense of security—it's that comforting. Except there's no way I can forget he's an attorney. That alone keeps any comfort far at bay. "Whether or not the gun was loaded is irrelevant. What *is* relevant is that the plaintiff swears she was afraid you were going to kill her."

"Piera says I tried to *kill* her?" I bury my face in my hands. But the fury radiating throughout my body won't let me sit. Shoving back my chair, I stand, then pace the room for a few minutes just to give the adrenaline a chance to subside. I've got to hand it to the attorney and everyone else. They let me work it out.

I sit again and place my palms gently on the table, splaying my fingers in what will probably be a futile attempt to keep myself from making a fist and pounding the arm of my chair. "I wanted her to back off. Taliban were all over the place. They'd just killed Darya Faludi." I choke out her name, as if saying it somehow makes it real, even after all this time. "She was the school director, my best friend. And her daughter—Seema—was missing. We didn't know if she was in that—" I wave my hand at the monitor as if the burning school were still there. "Or if she'd gone home. Or if they'd kidnapped her. The Taliban."

"Fuck." Chris has heard most of the story. Off the record. He's buddies with Cerelli and knows there are parts of what happened, big parts, that the Pentagon will never allow to be released. Not to anyone, especially not to Al Shabakat. Because it involved a long-running black op. Which is way more secret than a special op. What Chris doesn't know for certain, I'm sure he's guessed. I'm also sure this is the last thing he wants to deal with.

"Piera wouldn't back off. She had to get a story, no matter how much she was hurting other people." I look at each person in the room. "You all know what she's like. Venomous. Toxic. Anything is fair game." My voice gets louder.

"Here's the problem, Annie," says Marcus calmly. "Anyone watching this video, what they see is Piera talking to you in what most people would say is a completely reasonable way. Some might say she sounds kind and compassionate. And you come off as unprovoked and a little crazed." He raises his hand to fend off my protest. "I'm not saying she isn't a first-class bitch. Hell, I've heard stories about her that would curl"—he looks at my hair—"in your case, straighten, your hair. But this is about what the video shows and what each of you says."

I slump in my chair.

"Why did you have a gun?"

"Are you kidding?" I snort out a laugh. "I was in Afghanistan. It's a frigging dangerous place. Everyone has a gun. Or a knife."

"It's a fair question, Annie. You're not known for carrying." Chris is looking at me, clearly asking if I can tell the attorney about the origin of the Sig Saur. The gun that Cerelli insisted on, that Darya herself thought was a good idea. I sure can't tell him that Darya was more than the director of the girls' school. That she and Tariq were deep-cover operatives for the U.S., reporting to Cerelli.

I look at the monitor. Blank. No help there. Then back at Chris. I shake my head. I'm not giving up Cerelli. I say his name, and Al Shabakat will out him on all their broadcasts by tomorrow. No, sooner. I'd be as good as ending his career. And probably his life.

"Wait!" says one of the VPs, looking at Chris. "Are you telling me that correspondents—*our* correspondents—carry weapons when they're in the field?"

Chris shrugs, somewhat disingenuously. "As far as I know, they don't."

The VPs frown. The director of Human Resources looks slightly green.

"What does that mean?" says Marcus.

Chris goes back to massaging his forehead. "You people have no idea what it's like in a war zone. I'm sending correspondents, videographers, and photogs into hell. And they're risking their lives every minute they're in-country. You expect me to tell them to protect themselves with notepads and cameras? What we've got is a kind of 'don't ask, don't tell' policy. I don't ask them whether they're packing. Hell, Annie here was one of the few who was vocal about *never* carrying a weapon. I can't tell you the number of times I've heard her say, 'I shoot cameras, not guns.'"

Marcus turns toward me. "Is that accurate? What Chris just said about you?"

"It is. I hate guns."

"Then, what changed?"

I look down at my hands, clenched into fists in my lap.

"Annie, I need you to tell me why you were carrying a gun. And not just any gun. A Sig Saur, which I believe is the weapon of choice for U.S. Navy SEALs?"

I'm not sure if that last bit was a question or not. I opt for not and don't answer. Instead, I try to steer things in a new direction. "I wasn't in Afghanistan for TNN."

Marcus blinks in surprise. "This is news to me. Why were you there?" Which sounds for all the world like, *Who the hell would go to Afghanistan if they didn't have to?*

I tell him. A sanitized version of what happened back in '06. "During my embed, I took a photograph of a village girl who was killed. Later, when I won the Pulitzer, I vowed to go back to help Afghan girls get an education. About the same time, my friend, Darya, bought a dilapidated building, and I helped pay to convert it into a school for girls. We came up with the idea of me giving a photography workshop." When I say it that way, it sounds simple and not nearly as complicated as it really was. "I left my press pass home. Intentionally. If anything happened, I didn't want to involve the company. And since this wasn't an official assignment, I thought it would be unethical to use my affiliation."

We all look at Marcus. Does this change anything? No one needs to ask the question. We wait, holding our collective breath while he ponders this new piece of information.

The tap of his pen against the table calls us back to order. "We could probably make a reasonable case to sever the two parties. Since Annie wasn't on assignment, the company likely has no legal liability."

"Liability?" As soon as I say the word, I cringe. Why can't I just keep my mouth shut?

"Liability," he repeats. "Piera McNeil and Al Shabakat want TNN and you held liable for this incident. As I said before, they're saying attempted murder, which, of course, could not be prosecuted in this country. Their attorneys know that as well as I do."

"So, what does this mean?"

"They're suing. Claiming severe mental distress. They've thrown some numbers around. I must say, Piera McNeil really has it in for you. You sure you didn't do anything else to this woman?"

She said you and Nic hooked up in Kabul. More than hooked up. That you two are an item. I hear Josh sharing the latest Piera-perpetuated rumor back at the Oryx Lounge.

I shake my head in frustration and disbelief. "She thinks I did. But as always, she got it wrong."

Chris shoots me a stern look. "Please share."

"It's too ridiculous for words. There were three of us in Kabul, at the InterContinental, for a few days. Besides Piera, Nic Parker Lowe was there."

"The BBC correspondent," Chris clarifies for Marcus. "And?"

"And Piera kept trying to get in his bed. He wasn't having it, and I ended up as his cover."

"His *cover?*"

Damn, I almost let out that Nic's gay. "Look, he didn't want to sleep with Piera. He let her believe he'd hooked up with me. Which wasn't true. Then, later, in Wad Qol" —I point to the monitor—"Nic was there, too, trying to help me get away from her. Apparently, she bought it, and now she's pissed. I heard about it yesterday in Doha."

"I take it that was Nic Lowe's arm around you in the video clip?" This, from Marcus.

"Yes. Tariq Ghafoor, my friend Darya's husband, asked Nic and me to check back at the house—to see if Seema was there." I swallow hard. "It was a bad scene. And that's when Piera showed up and tried to block us."

"Is there anything to the story?" Chris says.

"What?"

"You and Nic look pretty chummy in that clip." He has the grace to look abashed. Probably for Cerelli's sake.

"Does it matter?" I shoot back.

"It does not," says the attorney, ending my squabble with Chris.

"So, where are we?" Chris sounds weary. I know him pretty well, and it's clear he doesn't want to kick me to the wolves.

"For now, we keep the cases together, and we play hardball. Strictly speaking, we could argue that the company doesn't have legal liability, but the optics could kill us. Pulitzer Prize-winning photographer returns to Afghanistan to teach at the girls' school she helped build. I think the best thing for all concerned is for me to put our insurance carrier on notice." For the first time since the meeting began, Marcus grins. In fact, he sounds almost gleeful, as if he's looking forward to the fight. "I'll talk to counsel at Al Shabakat and also to Nic Lowe. You sure there's nothing else you need to add about your 'relationship' with Mr. Lowe?"

"I don't have a relationship with Nic Parker Lowe. We're casual friends who run into each other in the field once every nine years."

"Is there anyone else I need to talk to?" Marcus glances at me, then at Chris. He clearly wants to know the origin of the Sig.

I clench my fists tighter. "No. No one."

Chris briefly shuts his eyes.

"Okay then." Marcus pushes back his chair.

I exhale. Maybe there's some hope that this clusterfuck, as Cerelli would call it, will get resolved. Without me getting fired or having to go to court or paying Piera the little bit of money I've managed to save over the years.

"Annie? You going to be in D.C. for a while?" This, from Marcus.

"A few days. Then, I'm going home to Milwaukee. I've got a couple weeks off until we head out on the next assignment."

He nods. "We'll talk again soon."

Chris, though, is shaking his head. "One more thing." He looks at me, sad but resigned. I have a pretty good idea what he's about to say, and I don't want to hear it. Out of the corner of my eye, I see the VPs and the Human Resources director all nodding in agreement. "Annie, pending the resolution of this situation, you're officially suspended."

3

SUSPENDED. THE THOUGHT KEEPS me paralyzed in my seat on the Metro. Neither Chris nor Marcus could give me a time frame for getting this 'situation' resolved. Assuming they *can* get it resolved. What if they can't? What if I end up on the losing end of the lawsuit? Owing big bucks to Piera McNeil? Even with a nondisclosure agreement, this is the kind of thing that'll leak out. Which means if TNN cuts me loose, no one's going to touch me. At least they're still paying me. For now. But what am I going to do if I end up jobless?

By the time I get to Cerelli's condo in Alexandria, my brain is scrambled, and I'm ready to drop. He opens the door and gathers me into his arms. I settle against his cashmere-sweatered chest, bury my face in his shoulder, and promptly burst into tears. Not exactly the homecoming I'd had in mind.

He tightens his hold and kisses the side of my head. "Sweetheart."

I cry harder. Bizarre for me, and Cerelli knows it. He's seen me at my worst, and the only time he's ever experienced me crying was on the phone right after Darya died.

He walks me to the extra-deep, black leather sofa—the perfect vantage point to watch the lights of the D.C. metro area twinkling in the night sky. "Talk to me."

I can't. Not yet. I shift the focus to him. "I'm amazed at how well you're walking." I choke out the words.

He pours me a glass of bourbon. Double, neat. Smart man, anticipating my need to unwind. I recognize the bottle of Blanton's with its signature pewter horse and jockey. Liquid gold. The man is even smarter than I thought.

Picking up his scotch, he follows my conversational lead. For now. "A lot of PT." He grins, but I can see a whole lot of concern harbored in his eyes.

"What's that thing you've got on?" It looks like a hands-free black steel crutch that he kneels on. Buckles are holding it across his stump and around his thigh. When I left, he was using forearm crutches. This thing sure gives him a lot more mobility.

"This contraption is called an iWALK. My new best friend."

"When do you get fitted for the prosthesis?"

"I got it while you were away. Two, actually. One for running. One for walking."

"How about you get another for dancing?"

He laughs. "I've never been able to dance. A prosthesis isn't going to help."

"Jeez, Cerelli. You lost your left leg. You lead with your right. Just take some lessons."

He presses his forehead against mine. "I'm glad you're not coddling me."

"I promised you I wouldn't. There's not a fiber of pity in my body. In fact, I'm determined to be downright merciless." Which isn't true in the least. "So, if you've got the prosthesis, why are you wearing this thing?"

"To give my leg a rest. By the end of the day, I need it."

"Pain?" I remember the phantom pain that was plaguing him before I left.

"More that the muscle is contracting. The leg gets loose and starts rubbing, which can lead to sores. In other words, bad news. It should sort out in about a year. Once it does, I'm in line for a bionic leg."

A year? How can he be so matter-of-fact about it? Just knowing that the man I love has to watch his incredibly powerful leg lose muscle and get smaller and weaker—it's all but gutting me. Not to mention that this happened because of me. Because he went back to Afghanistan to get me out and took a bullet in the leg. Even though he told me it wasn't my fault, I know it was. Just thinking about it gets my tears welling again.

A moment later, a sudden sharp rap on the front door has me jumping off the sofa. *A knock on the door,* I tell myself as I gulp for air. *Not a bullet. Cerelli's apartment. I'm safe.*

"That's probably the pizza delivery." Cerelli's voice is calm, firm. Nice of him not to comment on my jumpiness. "You mind getting it?"

"No problem." Okay, maybe he didn't notice that I'm kind of on edge. Yeah, right. A minute later, I'm back, putting the box on the table, then off to the kitchen in search of napkins. I open every drawer. Then decide we need plates, too. Anything to avoid Cerelli asking me what's wrong.

"Annie? You coming back?"

I make my way to the living room. "Am I that obvious?"

He takes the napkins and plates and puts them next to the pizza box. Then pulls me into his arms. "You ready to talk?"

I take a deep breath and blink my eyes furiously, doing my best to dry up the tears. The last thing he'll want to hear is that I'm crying over his leg. Then there's that little episode of PTSD he just witnessed. He probably *does* want to talk about that. He'll also want to hear that I'm doing something about it. As in therapy. Which I'm not—yet. I move on to the other thing that's got me upset. "That. Goddamn. Sig." I angrily spit out the words.

"What?" Clearly not what he was expecting. He leans away from me, just a few inches, and pushes my now-damp hair off my face.

"Back in Wad Qol, when Darya was k-k-killed." I stutter on the word. "I told you, remember? That frigging bitch Piera McNeil? I pulled the Sig on her."

Cerelli tucks a hank of hair behind my ear. "I remember."

"Apparently, all these months later, Piera has decided to object to having a gun pointed at her."

He twines his fingers around mine. "The bottom line?"

"As far as I can tell, she thinks I stole Nic Parker Lowe from her. At least, that's what she's telling everyone."

"You've got to be fucking kidding me."

"I wish I were."

"He's gay." Cerelli doesn't look the least bit concerned that I might possibly have been screwing Nic. After all, Nic was straight once upon a time. Or at least, he has an ex-wife. But Cerelli trusts me. And that is extremely comforting right now.

"I know that. And you know that. The rest of the world doesn't. While I was in Doha, I ran into one of the assholes who hazed me back in '06. He works at Al Shabakat now and had lots to say about

Piera's theory on Nic and me." I take a deep breath. "This would be a whole lot easier if Nic would just come out of the closet."

Cerelli hugs me hard. "Okay, now tell me the real bottom line."

"You mean the part where I'm suspended pending further investigation?"

A wave of pain sweeps his face. Phantom pain? Or feeling bad for me? "Why?"

"Me pulling the Sig. It seems they have it on tape. I saw the video today. Pretty damning. As the lawyer kindly pointed out, I come off like a crazed lunatic and Piera looks like the soul of caring concern."

"Is that true?"

"If you can ignore Darya's body lying in the dirt and the school burning in the background, I guess you could interpret it that way."

He cradles me against his chest, his cheek resting on the top of my head. "The clusterfuck that keeps on giving."

"Indeed."

"What aren't you telling me?"

Unbelievable. How can this man possibly know I'm holding back? "What do you mean?" I whisper. Except I know exactly what he means. He's always been able to see through me, which is disconcerting as hell and, at times like these, drives me nuts.

"Annie. Don't give me that."

I bite my lower lip. No. I can't possibly tell him that Chris and Marcus suspect Cerelli gave me the gun. They absolutely cannot find out that I'm seeing Cerelli. In the most intimate way. No Navy SEAL wants that kind of information made public.

"Tell me." He presses his lips against my hair again, then lifts my chin.

Pursuing the offered diversion, my lips find his.

He answers my kiss. Deepens it. Then slides my Grammy sweater off my shoulders. I whip off my long-sleeved T-shirt while he unzips my jeans. "Would you mind terribly taking off the rest of your clothes?"

Such a lovely invitation. Exactly what I need right now. Even though this is just a temporary reprieve. Cerelli hasn't given up on finding out the rest of what happened. Far from it. He probably thinks he can seduce it out of me. He probably can.

"First, a shower. I'm filthy, and I smell awful." I push myself off his chest.

He pulls me back. "You smell perfect."

LATER, AS WE SNUGGLE together under the duvet I brought in from the bedroom, he whispers in my ear, "You going to answer my question?"

I prop myself up on his chest and gaze down at him, trying my best to look like I have no idea what he's talking about.

"Don't give me that, Annie. Pulling a gun in Afghanistan—it happens all the time."

I shake my head. He's right. I can't begin to count the number of times when I was out drinking, and one of the guys got way too pissed. Guns came out. Knives, too. But that's not exactly the same thing as me holding the Sig on Piera.

"What's really going on?" Cerelli's voice hardens. "Why did Piera wait five months to pull out this video? And now what? She's gonna run it on-air? That's blackmail, and the TNN attorneys know it as well as I do."

"Marcus Johnson is handling things," I say softly.

"Good."

"He said something about 'putting the insurance carrier on notice'?"

"Which means Al Shabakat and Piera are going after deep pockets." He shakes his head. "None of this feels right."

Somehow, I'd forgotten Cerelli went to law school and worked as a lawyer for the Navy before becoming a SEAL. He does a mean interrogation. Terrifying, in fact. Years ago, I was on the receiving end of a brutal questioning, and I'd seriously rather not have this homecoming devolve into a repeat.

"Talk to me." His voice is quiet. Steel. There's no way he's giving up until I tell all.

So, I do. Even though telling him is going to cause problems. Big-time. "Marcus and Chris want to know where I got the gun. Chris knows I'm not the biggest fan of—"

"Believe me. I know all about you and guns." Hands on my waist, he repositions me lower onto his hips.

I look away. Then whisper, "They both noticed it wasn't just any gun, but a Sig. As they said, 'The weapon of choice for Navy SEALs.' Not the gun a journalist would carry—if a journalist was going to have a gun." I look back at him, his brown eyes riveting me in place. "Holy shit."

"What?"

"She *smiled*—like she was really into the fact that I was holding a Sig. The 'weapon of choice for a highly classified operative.' I'm sure that's what she said. Although that got edited out of the video clip. At least, the clip I saw today. Last May, she was after me to say who I was working for. She said something about the CIA. Now she's saying she was scared I was trying to kill her?"

"Ah. That's the game she's playing."

"Game?"

"Piera isn't after you, sweetheart. She's got her sights on someone else. Probably me. It's not the first time. Al Shabakat likes to out U.S. operatives. And Piera's had me in her sights for a while."

"I didn't tell them you gave me the gun."

He scowls and jams his fingers into his hair, which is a little longer than I remember. We both know telling Chris and Marcus that Cerelli gave me the Sig will end up with the outside counsel and Al Shabakat. And *they* can't be trusted to keep this under wraps, especially not with a 'classified, top secret' label pasted across the whole mess. If Cerelli says anything, his face and name will be streaming on every cable news show around the world, starting in places like Saudi and Qatar, Afghanistan and Pakistan. Places where a lot of insurgents—and probably some government types— already have him on their hit lists.

I see the light of realization dawn in his eyes. "Took you long enough," I whisper.

He gathers me against his chest. "I'll talk to Chris Cardona tomorrow. See what we can work out."

"Cerelli! No! Don't you dare." I push back from him. "You say anything to Chris about this, and I'll—"

"You'll what?"

"I'll—oh, hell, I don't know what I'll do. Just let *me* deal with my own mess."

I FIGHT MY WAY OUT of my usual nightmare—hunkered down in the stable in Afghanistan, waiting for the Taliban to come after me. Finally waking, I'm nestled against Cerelli's chest. His arm rests along my back, keeping me warm. No matter that there's just the one duvet, the man is a wonderful, pulsing furnace. Slowly, taking care not to wake him, I lift my head just enough to look out the wall of glass. It's dark, probably after midnight, and the distant city lights are still twinkling across the horizon. There are hours to go before I should be waking up.

Cerelli's arm crawls back to my shoulder. "You're awake."

"Sorry I woke you."

"I'm always on alert."

"Huh? Well, yeah, in the field. This is your *home*."

"It's the training."

I know this about him. Cerelli is always on. Nothing escapes his attention. And as I'm learning, he barely gets any sleep. Ever. Despite that, he's an amazingly nice man, even if he always has to be in control. Me, on the other hand, I go too long without sleep, I turn into a total bitch.

He squeezes my shoulder. "You okay?" He knows all too well that only nightmares and hallucinations would wake me.

"Jet lag, I guess."

"You told me you don't do jet lag."

"You caught me. I don't. Can't. Not with my travel schedule." I kiss his chest. So warm.

He raises my chin and lowers his lips to mine. A kiss that takes my breath away and is clearly searching for the answer to what woke me. "What's bothering you?"

"I don't like being suspended." I sigh, wishing we wouldn't talk about what happened yesterday afternoon, wishing he'd just kiss me again. I lean forward.

His index finger presses gently against my lips. "I told you that I'll call Chris."

"And I told you no." I know he's only trying to help, but I can't let him put his own career—hell, his *life*—on the line. For me. Again.

"Annie. Let me do this. I'm responsible—"

"You're not responsible for me."

"I strong-armed you into taking that Sig."

"I could have said no." I feel the rumble in his chest. It takes a few moments for me to realize he's laughing. "What?"

"Then, why didn't you? Say no, that is."

"I felt bad for you. There you were, being such a nice guy, trying to help, and I was being—well, not very nice."

He laughs harder. "That's the trick to getting you to do what I want?"

I exhale my exasperation. "Cerelli."

"Then tell me what we're going to do about this 'situation.'"

That makes me smile. I know it's my problem, caused by my losing control, at least mostly, but I like the 'we.' He's got my back, and that feels good. But I stand my ground. "*We* are not going to do anything."

"You care to elaborate on that?" His finger is back at my lips, tracing them.

I do my best to sound confident, even though I'm not. "Marcus and the other lawyer will take care of it. A couple weeks. At most. Then, I'll be back at work."

"Marcus is good. The entire legal staff is. I'm sure the insurance attorneys are, too. But not that good. It could take them a lot longer—months—to bring Al Shabakat around. Sounds like they're standing firm behind Piera."

"The Piranha."

"From what I've seen of her on television, it's an appropriate name. It still doesn't change the fact that her network is looking for blood. Yours. And possibly mine."

That sobers me. "You think they might win?" The wobble in my voice betrays me.

His other arm circles around me. "Honestly, no. But this could take a while to resolve."

"So, I'll spend some time with Mel. It's been way too long." Right. School's in session. She's in rehearsal for her winter dance recital. And like any sixteen-year-old, she'd rather hang out with her friends. I can't just drop in when it suits my schedule and expect her to free up her life.

"What's your plan B?"

"Maybe you and I—?"

He shakes his head. "Great for me. Boring for you. I'm back on the job and putting in long hours every day with PT."

PT, I get. I know he's determined to walk normally again. And run. And do everything he's used to doing. That takes a hell of a lot of commitment, and Cerelli's definitely up for the challenge. Always a SEAL. But he's back working? How the hell is he up to that? I raise my eyebrow. "Seriously? When were you going to tell me?"

"It's not what you think, sweetheart. I'm behind a desk. At least, for now."

Oh, God. I can't begin to imagine Cerelli with a desk job. This must be killing him.

He's quiet for a long thirty seconds. I can tell he's trying to figure out the best possible way to broach the ticklish subject of my seeing a therapist. He finally goes for the direct assault, but gently. "This might be a good time for you to work on those nightmares and hallucinations." He doesn't say what we both suspect: that I'm dealing with PTSD. The result of my horrendous experiences in Afghanistan that refuse to stay in Afghanistan. For no good reason, I keep putting off what I know I should do. Call it denial. He's right, and I know it. This would be the perfect time.

"I'll consider it." I do my best to sound like I'm making a sincere promise, except this isn't the first time I've said it. Clearly, I've got a lot of resistance to all the deep digging and mucking around that working with a therapist would entail.

"You do that." I hear the tiny note of pleading in his voice. Which tells me he's reasonably certain there's no therapist in my immediate future.

THE NEXT TIME I WAKE up, the sun is streaming through the windows. Lying naked under a duvet on the sofa in very broad daylight, I become embarrassingly aware of the way the building curves in a gigantic crescent. Cerelli's condo sits at the northern end with a great view into the floor-to-ceiling windows of the condos at the southern tip. Which means the people there can see us, too. At least he has shades. Black shades that are transparent at night—all but invisible. During the day, they're a bit more shade-like. Tonight, I'll suggest we use the bed. No need to put on a show for the neighbors.

In front of me on the coffee table, our two cell phones are lined up next to each other. One of them buzzes the arrival of an incoming text. Grabbing mine, I swipe it on and tap my way into my messages. Mel. Typical, taking a day—or three—to get back to me.

I've got a really cool fundraiser on Sunday at the lakefront. See you then. Have fun with Captain Cerelli! HA!

Fundraiser??? I text, then deposit my cell back onto the table. If I know my daughter, I'll be home before she answers.

I let my thoughts drift to Cerelli and me. Last night. Fun, indeed. Not that I want to discuss my 'fun' with my sixteen-year-old daughter. Wrapping the duvet around me, I head toward the bedroom in search of the man. And find him in the master bathroom that no longer has a jetted tub. Instead, he's in one of the largest showers I've ever seen. With two rain heads. You could fit an army in here. Check that, a navy. I do a double take when I realize he's sitting on a stool. His stump on full display. A pair of crutches leaning against the glass door within reach. That stops me short. I'm getting used to his having only half a leg, but the stool absolutely kills me. And I don't recover before he sees me.

"Good. You get to see the complete package on display." His voice rescues me.

I drop the duvet to the floor and step into the shower with him. "And so do you."

He throws back his head and laughs. "I've seen you in the shower before. A real pleasure, as I well remember."

I turn on the second showerhead and step under it. "Don't tell me you've got a video feed set up in *this* bathroom, too?" I haven't forgotten my stay last May in the surveilled room at the Kabul InterContinental. Thanks to Cerelli's handiwork.

"Hey, that was all in the name of much-needed security. They'd had some very nasty Taliban visitors the year before."

"Yeah, Taliban. There was no reason to stick *me* in that room. I hardly looked like a serious threat to the hotel."

"I disagree. You are a very dangerous woman." His voice sends shivers charging up my spine. Given that right now I probably look like a drowned rat, I appreciate his admiring gaze.

Standing under the shower, I prop my hands flat against the cool tiles and welcome the warm water as it runs down my back, sluicing off days of sweat and grime. "Oh, yes!" I moan. "This is beyond fabulous. I could seriously live in this shower."

"Did you just moan?"

"Oh, yeah."

"Glad my shower excites you."

I turn off the water, borrow his shampoo, and lather up my hair. "You can't possibly imagine how wonderful this feels. It's been a long time since I've had a proper shower. A bucket of cool, highly questionable water and a tin cup don't exactly do it for me." Water back on, I rinse, then look for conditioner.

"Conditioner?" He runs his fingers through his silvering hair. "You're kidding."

I'm not about to go search through my duffel. I'll just have to

comb through the knots. I turn off the shower and am working my
fingers through my hair when I catch Cerelli studying me. Intently.
"What?" I can feel myself blushing.

"Nothing. I'm just surprised. Four minutes. Almost a Navy
shower."

"Thank you. I think."

"That was most definitely a compliment. Now, I want you to do
something for me." He twists around and grabs a mirror from the
niche in the tiled wall.

My blush deepens.

He laughs. "It's not what you're thinking. One of the joys for
amputees is making sure the stump stays healthy. Every day, I get
to check it over. Orders from my physical therapist. No nicks.
No cuts. No bumps. Nothing that could get infected. It can be
challenging to see everything." He lifts up the mirror to emphasize
his point. "Care to help?"

"I thought you'd never ask." Which is how I come to be kneeling
naked in front of a seated and very naked Cerelli. "You're positive
there's no camera in here? I'd hate to be filmed like this."

"Sweetheart, you look great from every angle."

I take a deep breath, then before I can overthink my first time
touching it, I take his stump in hand and scrutinize it. Every quarter
inch. With great care. Nothing, and I mean nothing, is getting past
me. That's when I see the little red spot. A sore. Tiny. But it's there.

"You found something."

"Sorry. Yeah, I did. It's really small, though. Hardly noticeable."

"Infection is a serious risk. I'll run it by my PT today. For now,
it means I can't wear the leg."

I sit back on my heels, feeling absolutely miserable, like I've
failed him. I really wanted to give him a clean bill of health. For

today. He leans forward and cups a hand on each side of my face so that I have to look at him. "You did good. I missed that. Something I can't afford to do. Or I'll end up in deep shit."

"GOOD CATCH." THE PHYSICAL therapist at Bethesda Naval Hospital nods at me.

Sitting on the end of a treatment table, his stump on display, Cerelli looks proud of me until the PT turns to him. "I expected better than this, Captain. You should've seen that. You've been making phenomenal progress up till now. Something like this could send you in the wrong direction. Fast."

Cerelli scowls. "Yeah, well—"

"Sorry, sir, but there's no 'well' about it. You take care of what's left of this leg or you'll lose it."

"Now, you just wait a minute!" Turning toward the big and hunky-as-hell PT, I clench my fists. "That is the tiniest sore, and it's up under that ridge of skin. What kind of orthopedic surgeon leaves a fold like that anyway? Besides which, it's impossible to see anything with that thing you call a mirror. What he needs is a scoping mirror. With a built-in light."

Cerelli hoists himself onto his crutches. "Fighting my battles, are you now?"

"And you!" Whirling toward him, I jab my finger against his chest. "You of all people should've known that mirror was worthless."

"Need some help, Captain?" A third big-and-hunky guy wheels up in his chair. "You want me to take care of this babe for you?"

I throw up my hands in surrender. "Uncle. I'm surrounded."

"Thanks, Moose. I've got her." Cerelli quirks an eyebrow in my direction.

Moose. Now there's a nickname I understand. Even in a chair, this guy is most definitely a moose.

"If the lady is done"—the PT bows in my direction—"let's get to work."

For the next hour, I watch from my corner as Cerelli is put through the ringer. Upper body work to start. He straight-arms himself on the parallel bars, walking with his hands. His U.S. Navy T-shirt stretches taut across his chest, shoulders, and biceps. The man has muscles—even bigger than I remember and toned to within an inch of his life.

For a few seconds, I'm back on the USS *Bataan*, nearly nine years ago. Cerelli is putting me through the grinder, accusing me of all kinds of insane things, including screwing a Marine and collaborating with the Taliban. I haul off and slap him across the face. He subdues me with one hand.

One hand. That day on the ship was the only time I've ever felt the full strength in that hand. I blink and look at him heaving his body along the parallel bars, working like his life depends on it. I bet his hands are stronger now.

Thirty seconds to regroup, then he's on the mat, doing leg lifts and sit-ups. Next, the PT is sitting on Cerelli's good leg while the man himself lifts what's left of his other leg. Sweat is pouring off him. I can't imagine.

Another thirty seconds to rest, and Cerelli is working on his balance. One-legged.

"Usually, he's got the iWALK on for this and he's on the plank. The Captain's able to balance on it like nobody else." This is from Moose, who's parked his chair next to me. I wonder what he feels like, confined to a chair, no lower legs, watching Cerelli fight to walk again. And run. Sometimes life is just fucking unfair. "He's a good man."

"Yeah, he is."

"He'll never tell you this: he's the reason I'm sitting here today."

I turn and stare at him.

"That didn't come out right. I was on his team in '06. Near Kandahar. In fact, I was there when we rescued you." He grins. "You were one brave lady, running all that way, never complaining."

"Thanks. Only I sure don't remember feeling brave."

"Believe me. You were. Impressed the hell out of all of us. Especially the Captain." He pats my thigh, leaving his hand there a little too long.

I want his hand gone but don't want to embarrass him. Finally, I cross my legs, and his hand retreats.

"Six months later, we were back in Afghanistan. Farther west, near Herat. It was night. We were on the move, and I stepped on a fucking IED."

I suck in my breath.

"He carried me out. Saved my life. Not that I've always wanted to live. Stuck in a chair. A lot of the time, it just plain sucks." He nods toward Cerelli. "Nothing gets to that man. Even losing a leg. The Captain's doing great. Watch him walk, and you wouldn't know he's a leg down. As far as I know, he's got only one weakness, and I'm looking at her."

What can I possibly say?

Instead, I turn back to watch Cerelli powering through rep after rep of one-legged push-ups. How can he do that?

"I owe him. So, you remember." Moose's hand is back on my thigh. One brief pat. "You hurt him, I'll come after you."

5

CERELLI'S IN THE LOCKER ROOM when my cell phone rings. Chris Cardona. Not the person I really want to talk to. Didn't he dump enough on me yesterday? More than enough. But I know better than to avoid taking the call.

"Chris."

"Annie. Look, something's come up. Can you meet in my office in, say, an hour?"

Shit. It's been less than a day. What could possibly have come up? Unless . . . Unless TNN has decided I'm not worth the megabucks it's going to cost them in lawyers' fees to sort out the mess I've landed them in. "You mind clueing me in?"

"Not over the phone. We've got to talk about this in person."

I know that tone of voice. Resigned. Somber. He's going to cut me loose. Fire me. A deep breath to keep from throwing up, then I do what I can to keep my voice steady. "I'm in Bethesda with Cerelli. Rehab. I'll get there when I can, but it may take me a little longer than an hour."

He draws a long breath. "You with Finn right now?"

"He's in the locker room."

I can almost hear the gears turning in Chris's head. "Tell him you have to sign some paperwork."

In other words: my exit interview.

"SWEETHEART."

I glance up from my phone to see Cerelli dressed in crisp khakis, his left leg strapped onto the iWALK. His smile doesn't extend to his voice. For a moment, I wonder if he overheard Chris's call. But that's impossible, even for a man with Cerelli's powers of observation.

"I'm sorry." He actually looks close to miserable. "I just got summoned to the office. Could be a long afternoon. Will you be okay on your own?"

"I just got called into the office, too." I swallow hard.

Cerelli is quick on the draw. "Why?"

"Don't know. All Chris would say was there's some paperwork I need to sign."

He gives me a sidelong look. "What do you think?"

"I think he's going to fire me." My voice catches.

"Let me talk to him. They've got to know the full story—that I gave you the Sig. Insisted you take it."

I shake my head. "I can't let you do that. You know as well as I do it's too dangerous for you to be part of this. Piera will out you for sure."

"Annie—"

"It's my problem. I'll deal with it."

He clomps a step closer and drapes his arm around my shoulders. "You look like you're heading toward your execution."

"I think I am."

"Come on. They've sent a driver for me. I'll drop you off." He kisses the side of my head. "Call me. No matter what."

AS ALWAYS, KEVIN IS SITTING sentinel outside Chris's office. His smile takes me aback. A great smile, but considering the circumstances, it feels off.

"He's waiting for you."

"You going to tell me what's going on?"

He stops smiling. "Sorry, girlfriend. No can do."

"Traitor," I hiss as I walk past him.

Shouldering open the door, I see the long conference table now empty, the chairs squared up to the edge. The video monitor is pushed back flush to the wall. Chris sits behind his desk, on the phone. As soon as he catches sight of me, he ends the call. "Close the door, will you?"

Just like every other one-on-one meeting I've had with him over the years, I drag over a chair, positioning it at the corner of his desk. Something tells me he's not going to be offering me a shot of bourbon from the secret stash in the bottom drawer. Then again, maybe he'll take pity on me after he delivers the news.

He leans back in his chair. "You doing okay?"

"I've been better. Last night was a bit—much."

"Yeah. Sorry about that. But there've been some developments."

"The Piranha finally told the truth?"

He smiles, sadly it seems to me, then shakes his head. "No such luck. And that investigation will continue. But I've got an assignment for you, and I've been authorized to reinstate your position."

Not fired? I gape. "Excuse me?"

"This is completely confidential. You tell no one. Your daughter, your ex, Finn. Especially not Finn Cerelli."

"Details."

"I need you to go to Afghanistan."

The pit in my stomach yawns wide open. "Why?"

"The Afghans are starting negotiations with the Taliban. I need you on the crew that covers the opening session."

I think about that for all of ten seconds. There's something wrong with this picture. Negotiations between the elected government and the Taliban. Every news organization will be all over this story. No need for secrecy. I cross my arms and study him for a long minute until he takes off his glasses and pinches the bridge of his nose. "What aren't you telling me?"

"Damn it, Annie. I'm throwing you a lifeline here."

"Why do I feel like your lifeline has me dangling over a pit of vipers?"

Behind me, I hear a throat-clearing cough. Turning, I see Nic Parker Lowe, ankles crossed, leaning against the windows overlooking the Mall and the Washington Monument. "Hello, old thing. Like I've always said, you do have a way with words."

"What the hell are you doing here?" And how did I miss seeing him when I came in?

He laughs, then, crossing the room, grabs a chair and positions it by the other corner of Chris's desk. "Shall I tell her?"

Chris stops pinching the bridge of his nose and leans forward, elbows on his desk. "I take it no introductions are necessary?" He looks at me. "We've landed a major coup. Not only has Nic left the BBC and signed on with us, the Taliban have offered our crew two days of exclusive access to a few of their major officials and absolute protection in Chimtal District." Now, he's grinning—all the way to his eyes. So is Nic.

"Seriously?" This is the kind of story journalists dream about. Hell, I have colleagues who'd kill to get this assignment. Bottom line: the Taliban are getting media savvy. They know it's only a matter of time before they're back in control and want to show themselves in a positive light. Chris was right when he called it a coup.

"You in?" Chris's tone is all business now. What he's really saying: do you agree to complete confidentiality? Which means no telling Mel, Todd, and definitely not Cerelli.

"Two questions. Why me?"

"You know Afghanistan. You speak Dari and Pashto."

"A little Pashto." I narrow my eyes. There's something else Chris isn't telling me.

"The Taliban approved you being on the crew. They were very particular about who they'd accept. There are only four of you, by the way. Besides Nic and you, Nazir will film. And Mahamadou will produce."

"Great crew." And I mean it. These guys are some of the best in the business.

Chris nods.

Nic coughs again. "What he hasn't told you is that I insisted on working with you."

Okay, then. We get to the real reason. Nic Parker Lowe, TNN's new star talent, wants to make amends for the hazing he subjected me to back in 2006. To be more accurate, he's paying me back for not giving him up to the base CO, who thought I'd snuck outside the wire to meet up with the enemy. One word from me, Nic would've been toast—packed out of Afghanistan on the next plane and quite possibly fired by the BBC. Nic is paying his debt. He's saving my career. I wonder if Chris knows.

"Thanks."

"Pleasure."

"You said you had two questions?" This is from Chris.

"What happens with the investigation?"

He doesn't bat an eye. "It continues."

Of course it does. I swallow hard.

"You're in?"

"I'm in. Except—"

Chris sighs. "What?"

"You know Cerelli. I've got to tell him something."

Chris sits back in his chair. "You can tell him you're part of the crew going to cover the negotiations. But you tell him nothing, and I mean nothing, about the Chimtal meeting."

Will Cerelli let me get away with a partial truth? The man can sniff out a lie or a misdirection like nobody else. And what about when the interviews air? Oh, God, there will be hell to pay. But this is my career. And my decision. "When do we go?"

Chris smiles. "Six weeks. In Kabul by December 1st. Kevin will make all your travel and hotel arrangements."

"And when do we go to Chimtal?"

Nic leans forward. "I'd like to know that as well."

"Still being decided."

Despite the adrenaline rush, my stomach clenches. Yeah, the Taliban are pledging complete security, but I'm well aware of the danger. Still, it's nothing I haven't done before. Many times. Most recently two weeks ago with the Houthi rebels in Yemen. I can see why Chris is adamant that I not tell Cerelli. He'd be apoplectic. And it's not like he tells me about his assignments—all of which are secret and scary as hell.

6

"I FIGURED AS MUCH," says Cerelli after I tell him about my meeting with Chris. Not a word about the secret Chimtal interviews, just the public coverage of the Afghan government's talks with the Taliban.

"Give me a break! How could you possibly have known?"

"No mystery. In fact, when I was briefed about the upcoming negotiations, I expected they'd offer you the job."

"Seriously?"

"Sweetheart, you know Afghanistan better than most photographers. TNN would've been stupid not to give you the assignment. And Chris isn't stupid."

I heave a sigh of relief. So far, he doesn't suspect there's anything more involved.

"What did you tell him?"

I glance down at the tiled kitchen floor—anything to avoid his eyes while I all but lie to him. "I told him I'd go. No choice really. Not if I want to keep my job. Nic Parker Lowe's going, too. He just signed with TNN."

A curt nod. The muscle at the corner of his eye pulses for just a moment, then eases up. "What happens with the investigation?"

I shake my head. "It continues."

"They're squeezing every drop of blood out of you."

"Don't I know it." Then, I bury the secret Taliban meeting as deeply as I possibly can, so I won't be tempted to say anything or even think about it.

CERELLI AND I LAZE TOGETHER on the sofa, his arm heavy on my shoulders, my legs draped across his stump. I'm honestly getting used to his leg being only half there. He's nursing a double shot of scotch. I'm working on a double bourbon. In front of us, lights twinkle in the dark sky. A stunning panorama.

"Happy?" he asks, his lips against my ear.

"Very. You?"

"You don't need to ask. But I am."

I smile into my bourbon. And remember that I haven't yet shown him the text from Rahila. Do I really want to spoil this romantic moment? Of course not. As often happens, though, all I have to do is think something, and Cerelli knows it.

"Talk to me." He takes the heavy glass from my hand and puts it safely out of reach on the coffee table.

"You're worried I'm going to attack you with that?"

He smiles. "The thought has crossed my mind."

"Jeez. I thought you trusted me."

"Oh, I do. Most of the time. Tell me what's going on." He traces the outline of my ear.

I shudder with pleasure. *Do not say anything about that text!*

Sure enough, before I can stop myself, I'm reaching for my cell and pulling up the text from Rahila.

Cerelli helps himself to my phone. "Is this from Seema?"

"Possibly."

He reads it out loud.

My body is mine,
But my Beloved drinks me like rare, red wine.

Damn, he has such a great voice for reading love poetry.

I'm replaying his reading of the *landay* when he turns to me. "The first line's a bit forced, almost trite, but the second isn't bad. It doesn't work in Dari, though. Or Pashto. Not enough syllables, and the rhyme's off."

"Now you're a critic?"

"Just making an observation. This was definitely written in English. By someone who doesn't know the genre as well as she should. Does that sound like Seema?"

I point out the name. "Rahila. Which is Arabic for Rachel— Seema's middle name."

"Named for you."

I start to question how he knows this but give up. Thanks to his investigation back in 2006, he knows nearly everything about me. Which can be annoying as hell.

"Darya told me," he says in answer to the question I haven't asked.

"Oh." How can he say her name so easily? Then his hand tightens on my shoulder, and I realize it's not all that easy for him either.

"What are you thinking?"

Best not tell him my real thoughts. "I don't recognize the number."

He takes a look. "Zero-three-zero. The code for Kandahar. Which is where Awalmir's family lives. That only means someone bought the phone there. As far as I know, Seema isn't there."

I lean my head against his chest so I can see the number on the screen. "How do you know that?"

"Sawyer's been checking out Kandahar."

"You've been looking for Seema?" I had no idea. We argued about this very thing a few months ago. Cerelli was adamant that he didn't want me searching for her.

"Also looking for Awalmir. There's no sign of either one anywhere around Kandahar. Sawyer thinks they could be farther west, maybe in Herat." He's back to studying the *landay*. "When did you get this?"

"Don't know. I saw it when I was catching up on texts at the airport in Doha. Why?"

"I got one, too. A few weeks ago." He reaches for his phone and holds it up for me to see. I read it aloud.

My body is sweet like ripe mulberries:
Purple outside, inside raw meat.

I suck in my breath.

"Your turn to analyze." He raises an eyebrow.

I exhale. "I don't believe Seema or Rahila or whatever she's calling herself wrote this. English is her first language. Not so for this writer. Plus, it just doesn't have the same girlie and lyrical lilt as her others I've read."

"Agreed. But they want us to think Seema wrote it."

"You care to elaborate on that theory?"

He sets the phone back on the table. "Someone over there knows we're looking. Likely Awalmir himself. Or he figures that we *will* look if we get a good enough idea where to search. He's leaving a trail of bread crumbs for us to follow."

"That doesn't make any sense. Why would he want you to find them?"

"Think about it."

I come up blank. "Sorry."

"It's a trap. To draw me out."

"Then why send anything to me?"

"Same thing."

"Come on. They can't possibly know about us. There's no way."

"How can you be sure?"

Suddenly, I'm not so sure. I'm back in Wad Qol, my first night there. Dar and Tariq are long asleep, but I'm not. Voices from the courtyard drift in through the open window of my tiny bedroom, keeping me awake. When I head to the lounge and the kitchen at the front of the house to investigate, I find Seema, my Lowepro pack clutched to her chest, a headscarf draped around her neck. She's clearly been outside, probably with a boy, even though she denies it. She says my phone woke her. The ringtone, a romantic song by Nasrat Parsa that Cerelli himself programmed.

"Oh my God! Seema and Awalmir had access to my pack. And the sat phone. At the time, I was worried about the Sig, but what if Awalmir wasn't interested in the gun? What if he bugged the phone? He could've kept track of me. And I led him straight to you."

Before I can finish explaining, Cerelli has pulled up Sawyer's number and placed the call to Afghanistan.

Barely fifteen seconds later, Sawyer's voice fills the room. "Captain?"

"You have that sat phone Annie used last May?"

"Should."

"Check it out."

"On it."

Cerelli ends the call. It's unbelievable how attuned these two men are to each other. Neither one said more than a couple words.

In just a few minutes, Sawyer calls back with the news. "Affirmative."

Cerelli's quiet for a minute, obviously considering his options. "Dismantle." That's when it occurs to me that they're speaking like this in case someone is listening in, someone they don't want hearing what's going on. Not that I'm paranoid.

"Roger." Then, faster than I thought possible, he's back on the line. "Done. Say, Finn, you got Annie there with you?"

I wave at the phone. "Sawyer. It's been a while."

"Take care of him, will you?"

The image of Cerelli doing all those one-leg push-ups flashes in front of me. "Oh, he's coming along just fine." Cerelli runs a finger down my cheek. Then my neck. I grab his hand to keep it from going lower. Jeez, all the man has to do is touch me, and I quiver. Holding fast to Cerelli's wandering hand, I manage to keep my train of thought. "You watch your back. Okay?" I seriously don't like him being in Afghanistan without Cerelli.

"No worries." Then he's gone.

I study Cerelli's face. He's clearly considering the ramifications of a bug having been planted in the sat phone I was using, a bug that neither he nor Sawyer installed. "So?" I finally ask.

"Just thinking back over our conversations last spring."

Really great phone sex. I flush from my chest on up to my neck and my cheeks.

He laughs. "Yeah, that, too. Definitely enough to put the two of us together. I was remembering when we talked about 'Operation Seema.' Your words. If someone was listening, they clued in to the plan you and Darya and Tariq came up with to get Seema out."

"What exactly did we say?"

He studies me for a moment, then shakes his head. "It doesn't matter."

Which tells me that it does. I think hard and finally hear myself telling Cerelli every last detail of getting Seema to Kabul, then onto a plane and—drugged—to a deprogramming facility in California. If Awalmir heard that . . .

"Sweetheart, don't go there."

"I as good as told Awalmir and Seema what we were going to do."

Cerelli's arms are around me in an instant, holding me fast. "Listen to me. I was the other half of that conversation. We didn't know. None of us. And we don't know for sure what Seema and Awalmir were doing then or what they're up to now."

"I left my pack where they had access to it. That's obviously when they put in the bug. Which means I set everything in motion. That means I—" The force of the realization slams me back against the sofa and sucks the air from my lungs.

"You are *not* responsible for Darya's death. This is on Awalmir and Ghazan. And probably Seema."

Tears welling, I bury my face against his chest. Darya. My best friend. No matter what he says, my guilt is wrapping its sinews around me tighter, burrowing deeper. "You think Seema was in on it?" I choke out the words.

"It's getting harder and harder to think she wasn't."

CERELLI'S PHONE IS RINGING again. I don't miss the strange look that crosses his face when he reads the caller ID. He glances at me, back at the cell, then swipes his finger across the screen. "Finn Cerelli."

"Todd Green here." My ex-husband sounds tentative and a little worried. "I'm trying to get in touch with Annie? She's not returning my calls, and now her voice mail is full. It's probably nothing, but you know the places she goes. I can't remember if she said Iraq this trip. Or Syria. Anything could've happened. Any chance you've heard from her?"

"She's fine. Just back in the U.S. She stopped off in D.C. for some meetings and probably hasn't had a chance to call." Cerelli speaks quietly and slowly, his psychologist voice, and inch by inch talks Todd off the ledge.

"Do you have another number I could try?"

"As a matter of fact, I'm expecting to hear from her any minute. I'll have her call you."

"Thanks. Appreciate it."

Cerelli ends the call and turns to me. "You catch that?"

"Kind of hard not to."

He shakes his head. "I don't mean what he said. I mean the tone. That man's got feelings for you."

"Feelings? No way. He just can't get over the fact that I'm not at his beck and call. Besides, he's married to a gorgeous woman who stays home and caters to his every fantasy."

"Sex is one thing. Okay, sex is big. But love is something else. I know." He drops a kiss on my forehead, then snags my phone off the coffee table and hands it to me. "Put the man out of his misery."

I do. "Todd."

"Annie." The relief in his voice is palpable.

Okay, maybe the man does have feelings for me. "Sorry I haven't called. It's been busy here."

"You're okay?"

"I'm fine."

"I take it you're with that Navy captain?"

Exactly how that's any of his business, I don't know, but I'm determined to keep my tone casual and upbeat. "I am. So, what's up?"

"It's Mel."

Casual and upbeat go right out the window. "Is she all right?"

"Catherine Elizabeth and I can't figure out what's going on with her. Suddenly, she's best friends with this Muslim girl."

I wait for him to explain, except he doesn't say anything else. It dawns on me that, in his mind, being friends with a Muslim girl *is* the problem. Or, Todd's using this as an excuse to call me. A quick glance at Cerelli's raised eyebrow confirms my suspicion. "And?"

"Come on, Annie. You can't already have forgotten what happened to Darya and Seema."

I close my eyes. "Believe me, I will never forget. But I'm not seeing the connection."

"The girl is *Muslim*. From Afghanistan. She and her mother even wear those head coverings." He sounds exasperated by my apparent stupidity.

"So?"

"That's a problem." He pauses for a moment, probably trying to figure out what he can say to turn me to his way of thinking. "Look, you said you want to discuss issues of importance concerning Mel. That's what I'm trying to do."

"I'm sure I'll meet this girl when I get home. And I'll talk to Mel."

"That's all I'm asking. When will you be back?"

"Soon."

"Any way you could make it tomorrow? We've got to put a stop to this. Mel and this girl are working with her mosque on a fundraiser to rebuild Darya's school. She says you gave her the idea and that you'll take the money when you go over there to find Seema."

Beneath me, I feel every muscle in Cerelli's body tighten.

This is news to me. But if I say that, I'm pretty much telling Todd that Mel has been lying. Something I don't want to accuse my daughter of doing, especially when it sounds like she's trying to do something good.

"I'll talk to her. And I'll text you when I get home." I put down the phone and turn to Cerelli.

His face is a study in immobility except for the muscle that's pulsing next to his eye. "Annie." There's nothing intimate or wistful about his voice. "We've talked about this. Going to Kabul is bad enough, but at least you'll be with your crew. And a local fixer. But looking for Seema? It's too damn dangerous. Hell, why do you think I've got Sawyer searching?"

How do I begin? I should tell him I never said a word about any of this to Mel. Only I don't want to defend myself by dumping on my daughter. So, I come at the problem from the opposite direction. "Look, I know how dangerous Afghanistan is. But if you think we talked about me not looking for Seema, well, think again. You *told* me not to go. Like I'm a child."

"Annie." His voice is calm, but the muscle next to his eye is going ballistic. "You wouldn't have the first idea where to look for Seema. You can't just go door to door, asking to speak to her."

"I know that." My voice has a lot of edge to it.

"Glad to hear it. Because you wouldn't last very long." He takes a deep breath. Probably talking himself off the ledge.

Neither one of us says a word. I can feel the anger radiating off him. And churning inside me. I don't want to be mad at Cerelli. How do I fix this?

After a very long five minutes, he lifts my hand, uncurls my fingers one by one, then kisses my palm. "You're not a child," he says. "I was wrong to make you feel that way."

"Yeah, well, I'm feeling pretty bad for yelling at you."

He grins. "You never had any intention of going to look for Seema, did you?"

"That's truer than I'm willing to admit. How did you know?"

"Sweetheart, I've told you before: your face is an open book."

"Not a compliment, Cerelli." Damn, I've got to be careful. Given what just happened, if he gets any idea about the Taliban interview, things will go sideways. Fast. Not to mention that Chris will have my head. And my job. *Keep that secret meeting buried as deep as it'll go.*

"Tell me about Mel's fundraising."

I shrug. "Not a clue. She hasn't said a word to me."

"Then, what was Todd—"

"Oh, I'm sure she told him all about whatever she's dreamed up. And involved me. Like I gave her permission."

"Playing you two off each other? To get what she wants?"

"Basically." I nod. "She's having a tough time with her stepmother."

"She's sixteen. It's a difficult age."

"Especially when her mother's never home." I hold up my hand to stop his protest. "She's a lot like I was at that age. This apple didn't fall far from the tree. But my daughter also has a real humanitarian streak in her. I'm betting she honestly wants to raise money to rebuild that school. And I don't want to quash that."

"Just like her mother. Darya told me your Pulitzer money paid for the original school."

I narrow my eyes. "I had a deal with her, you know. She wasn't supposed to tell anyone." So much for honoring our secret.

"Tell me what you were like at sixteen. Like Mel?"

I laugh. "Oh, Cerelli. What you don't know about teenage girls. I was much worse."

He pulls me against him. "How about you show me just how bad you were."

Milwaukee, Wisconsin

SUNDAY MORNING, AFTER CHECKING in with Marcus and learning he doesn't have anything to report, I catch a flight home and think about my current 'situation' for the entire trip. Yeah, I've got the Afghanistan assignment, but that's it. Chris made it very clear that the investigation will continue. Still, Marcus sounded upbeat. *Not to worry! We'll get this worked out. They'll play ball.* But I *am* worried. What if they won't play ball? What if they out-hardball Marcus and the rest of the company lawyers? Does that mean I'll be stuck in limbo? And just how long will TNN keep me on suspension before they decide to cut me loose? Shit. *Not to worry!* Right.

As soon as we land, I collect my duffel and Uber to my duplex on S. Indiana. All along the street, carved jack-o'-lanterns adorn the bungalows' front porches. Skeletons and black cats peer from windows. Stretchy cobwebs with gigantic black spiders and ghosts made of old bedsheets hang from low tree branches. Give my neighbors a holiday, and they decorate big-time, starting weeks before. A few people are out and about, raking leaves and playing catch. My house, with three small, uncarved pumpkins on the front steps, seems strangely quiet. At least there are pumpkins—thanks to Bonita, my tenant and good friend who helps make my life possible. I knock on the door of her first-floor apartment, but she doesn't answer. Finn, the black lab we share, isn't barking. They must be on a walk.

My Lowepro on my back, I head across the small front porch to the door to my second-floor apartment—the door unlocked and not even closed. I take a breath. Mel is going to have to do better than this. I lug the duffel upstairs, wondering if the inside door is unlocked, too. It is. Trying to tamp down my annoyance, I shoulder it open, drop my stuff just inside, then turn toward the kitchen and scream. Which causes the man in front of my open refrigerator to turn around. Todd. My ex-husband. Emphasis on the "ex," although the fact that he's in my house without permission suggests he doesn't fully grasp his status.

"Annie. Good. You're home. Mel said you'd be getting in today." He shuts the refrigerator door. "There's nothing to eat in this place."

I stare at him. Why should there be any food? I haven't been here for months. There's no point explaining the obvious, so I don't bother. "What the hell are you doing in my apartment?"

He looks surprised. "Like I told you on the phone, we have to talk."

"We *did* talk. That is, *you* talked and expected me to agree with you. Which, I might point out, isn't how co-parenting works."

"Things have gotten worse. Right now, Mel's over at the lakefront with a bunch of Muslims. They've got signs. It looks like some kind of protest."

I palm the air in an attempt to stem the drivel pouring out of his mouth. "There are peaceful protests all the time, especially on the North Shore. What's your point?"

"Annie." He sounds exasperated, as if he's explaining the basics of life to a ten-year-old. "It's like she's obsessed. Who knows what it'll lead to. Not everyone in Milwaukee likes Muslims. What if some right-wing group shows up?"

"If you're so worried, why aren't you at the lakefront watching out for her?"

He crosses from the kitchen to where I'm standing in the living room. "Given the whole Muslim thing, I thought you could probably handle it better."

"What kind of crap is that?"

"Come on, Annie." He takes a step closer and puts his hand on my shoulder. "Darya was your best friend."

I shrug off his hand. More than anything, I want to tell him to leave Darya out of his paranoid delusions. Instead, I take a deep breath. "Which doesn't make me an expert on all things Islamic."

"Well, you know a lot more than I do."

"Look, I'll . . ." I take a deep breath. "I'll text her."

He shakes his head. "She won't answer."

He's right about that. "Okay, I'll take a ride over there in a while. See what's going on. That's all I'm willing to promise."

His hand is back on my shoulder. "Get her out of there. Please? Maybe you could bring her back here?"

There's something else going on. Something he's not telling me. "Why?"

He rubs my shoulder. Way too tenderly. I stiffen. Could Cerelli be right about Todd's feelings? I take two giant steps away from him.

Todd drops his hand to his side. "This whole thing is really stressing out Catherine Elizabeth. Mel has completely changed. She won't even go to church with us anymore."

"I'm kind of surprised. Mel always liked Village Church. It's where she got her start dancing."

He doesn't meet my eyes. "We haven't gone there in years. Catherine Elizabeth's Catholic."

Which means Mel is expected to be, too? This is definitely something we should have discussed. I swallow my annoyance. "St. Robert's?"

"Yeah. But Mel refuses to go, which creates no end of trouble between the two of them. Then, of course, the twins start in. They always want to do whatever their big sister's doing. Or not doing." He sounds done in. "Why does she have to make everything into a battle?"

I assume he means Mel, not Catherine Elizabeth.

He's suddenly looking at his feet, and I know that the next words out of his mouth are going to really piss me off. "Anyway, she doesn't want Mel in the house right now."

"She *what?*"

"Actually, a break would do them both good. Clear the air. You know."

I'm not sure where to begin. "Didn't you tell me Catherine Elizabeth loves Mel like her own daughter?"

"She does."

"I have news for you. Mothers don't kick their beloved daughters out of the house for disagreeing with them. Hell, for any reason." I cross my arms. "And tell me, where exactly is Mel supposed to go?" We both already know, so he doesn't bother to answer.

At least he finally looks me in the eye. "Come on, Annie," he says in the wheedling voice he always used when he wanted something from me. "It'll only be for a while. When things calm down, Mel can come back. Look at this as a chance to spend time with her."

Which is exactly what I'd love to do. But first, I've got to figure out what's going on between Mel and her stepmother. "When things calm down. What the hell does that mean? When Mel finally caves in and obeys?"

"You know what she's like."

"Yeah, I *do* know. She's an incredibly vibrant and creative young woman who dreams big and follows those dreams." And as I well know, Mel can also be sneaky and manipulative and sometimes downright sullen. I take a breath and watch him fight the scowl that's threatening to crawl across his face. "Oh, and in case you haven't noticed, I work." Okay, so my voice is a little sharper than I intended.

He closes the space between us and puts his hand on my shoulder. Then on the back of my neck. Rubbing. That's definitely a caress.

I take another step away from him and growl, "Get your hands off me."

His eyes widen, but he dutifully returns his hand to his side. "Can't you ask for some time off? I mean seriously, they owe you—considering how long you were on this last assignment."

"They *owe* me? That's what you think?" How ironic. Because, of course, I actually do have an unexpected vacation. Six whole weeks. But I seriously don't want to tell him that. To bail out Catherine Elizabeth? Definitely not. *Wait,* I remind myself, *this isn't about Catherine Elizabeth, it's about Mel, who needs a home. And a mother. Of course she'll stay here.*

"Look, I'll be honest." He rubs the lower half of his face—a sure sign something's wrong. "Things are a bit tense at home. Catherine Elizabeth and I . . . well, we're in marriage counseling. The therapist suggested that having Mel stay here could help give us space to work things out." He starts to put a hand on my shoulder, then thinks better of it. "Annie, I need you to step up. Help us out a bit."

His second round of counseling to try to save a second marriage. That bites. I feel for him. "Okay, Mel can stay here. For six weeks. Then, I have to go back to work."

"Thanks. Look, could you stop by the house to pick up her clothes and stuff?"

"I'll talk to Mel and let you know when we'll come."

"This afternoon would be best for us." Before I can figure out what to say, he's moved on. "You're . . . uh . . . seeing Captain Cerelli?"

Whiplash. "I am."

He stuffs his hands into his front pockets. "You really think that's a good idea?"

"How exactly is that any of your business?"

"Come on, Annie. Just because we're divorced doesn't mean I don't care about you. I don't want to see you get hurt."

"Hurt?"

"Don't be naïve. You know what those military types are like. A girlfriend in every port."

I shake my head. "Cerelli's not like that. He's one of the good guys."

"Believe me, I know his type. Don't get involved."

"Stop right there. You do not have a say in my love life." I cross the living room in five exasperated steps and jerk open the door. "I'll let you know when Mel and I will come by to get her stuff. For now, it's time you left before you piss me off even more. Oh, but first. You mind telling me how you got into my apartment?"

He looks at a spot over my shoulder—always a sign that he's lying. "Mel gave me her key."

Except Mel and I agreed that she wouldn't give that key to anyone. She knows damn well that if she does, she loses her privileges to stay here while I'm away. And when she's not getting along with her father or Catherine Elizabeth, staying here is her lifeline. She wouldn't risk it.

I put out my hand, palm up.

"What?"

"Hand over the key. I'll give it back to Mel when I see her at the lakefront."

"You know it's probably a good idea for me to have a key. In case something happens."

I lock eyes with him. "No."

He scowls, then pulls out his key fob, unhooks my apartment key, and drops it onto my open hand.

"Think about it this way," I say, closing my fingers around the worn brass key. "What if you and Catherine Elizabeth came home and found me waiting in *your* house?"

He looks slightly ill at the thought. "Come on, Annie, that's not the same thing, and you know it."

"You got that right." I stamp my foot and nearly cringe at my lack of maturity. "Because that used to be *my* house. *I*, at least, have a claim on it. *You* have no reason at all to be here."

He's out the door and halfway down the stairs when I yell, "And don't do it again!" I slam the door and stomp back inside, wishing I felt a little better about what just happened. I had to stamp my foot?

And that's when I notice the bra poking out from under the sofa. Mel's. She's lucky her father didn't see it. But I do and know exactly what this means. She's back to having boys here despite the no-boys-allowed rule. On hands and knees, I search for more evidence—dreading that I'll find a used condom. Then, pray that she's insisting on condoms. No condom. Instead, I find a dirty glass, red juice crusted on the bottom. Pomegranate juice—her favorite.

I'm heading toward the kitchen, formulating the argument I'm going to have with Mel about boyfriends and cleaning up, when I stop in my tracks. My tiny galley kitchen has been transformed since I was last here. One row of my formerly battered oak cabinets is gone, replaced by open shelving. My favorite pottery bowls and plates and mugs are all on display—colorful and easy to access. The remaining few cabinets and drawers are painted white. New and fresh. With funky black pulls that look vaguely like cameras. I turn in amazement, taking in the potted herbs sitting on the windowsill above the sink. Mel promised to take care of this mini-remodel for me. With help from Bonita. And they came through. Big-time. Amazing what they were able to accomplish with a mere five hundred dollars.

I swing open the refrigerator door and take a look. Except for a few condiments and a bottle of probably flat tonic water, it's empty. Well, Todd was right about that. I add grocery shopping to my to-do list. After I check out Mel's protest on the lakefront. But first, a call to Cerelli to let him know I'm here.

"I'M PRETTY SURE YOU WERE wrong about Todd having feelings for me," I say to Cerelli a few minutes later as I pace around my living room.

"I take it you're home?"

"I am. And what an unexpected surprise I had waiting for me."

"Don't tell me."

I tighten my grip on the phone. "If you're thinking Todd was waiting in my apartment when I got here, making himself at home, you're right."

"And you never gave him a key."

"Correct. He said Mel gave it to him."

"But you don't believe it."

"Not for a minute." I walk across the living room to the window overlooking S. Indiana. Across the street, one of my new neighbors is throwing a frisbee with his kids. "I'm willing to bet he rifled through her backpack and took it."

"Ouch."

"He also took the liberty of putting his hands on me."

"Not a welcome move, I take it. Glad you can fend for yourself. You handled Moose pretty well the other day."

I smile when I think of Moose. "This felt more predatory."

"Don't kid yourself about Moose. He may joke around, but he's lonely. His wife left soon after he lost his legs. She tried. Not everyone can handle it. He'll take anything on offer. And sometimes, letting his hand stay on your thigh a few seconds too long is all the permission he needs."

I close my eyes. Cerelli saw that. Of course he did. The man sees everything. "Damn, that sucks. Well, to his credit, Moose backed off the second I moved my leg. It took a lot longer to get Todd to listen. And I had to remove his hand."

"The man loves you."

"That's where you're wrong." I sigh. "It was all an act. From what he said, there's trouble at home, and he wants my help."

"Let me guess: Mel and wife number two aren't getting along."

"You know, Cerelli, I think you missed your calling. You really could be a therapist or a mind reader."

"No magic to it, sweetheart. It's pretty obvious. Have you seen her yet? Mel, I mean."

"I'm about to head up to the lakefront. It's this stretch of beaches and museums and yacht clubs along Lake Michigan." I wait for him to say he knows, that he's been there. The man's been everywhere. Except he doesn't. So, I continue. "According to Todd, Mel is part of some Muslim protest. He's afraid a hoard of Muslim-hating Midwesterners will swoop down and beat her up."

Cerelli laughs, only he doesn't sound amused. "And he's fucking sending you to protect her?"

"That's the idea. The other part of his plan is for Mel to move in with me for a while." I tell him about Catherine Elizabeth wanting Mel out of the house. Which causes him to emit a noise I can only describe as a growl.

"Sorry, sweetheart, we'll have to continue this later. I've got to run. A meeting and then a PT session."

"Seriously? On a Sunday?"

"Meetings? Always. As for PT, I want to walk without a limp. This is what it takes."

Of course he wants to walk without a limp. I'm betting he's already tired of his desk job at the Pentagon. He wants to get back in the field, as in Afghanistan or another equally dangerous place, as soon as he can. Any limp, any sign of weakness would put his life in danger. And the lives of a whole lot of other people.

"Go! And work on those push-ups."

He chuckles. "Call me?"

"Your wish is my command." I offer an obeisance with a flourish of my hand, which, of course, he can't see.

Another chuckle. "If only I believed that."

8

MY TEN-YEAR-OLD PRIUS GLIDES silently up 794. As I crest the Hoan Bridge, the world turns a million shades of blue. The cloudless sky, bright with sun. The lake to my right, dotted with the last of the sailboats that have yet to be put up for the winter. To the left, mirrored buildings where the city of Milwaukee meets the shoreline reflect the lake and the sky. So much intense, eye-aching, crystalline blue. A perfect autumn day. I can't help smiling.

A mile up Lincoln Memorial Drive, I see a group of about thirty women and teenage girls standing on the grass in front of the yacht club. Not a single *burqa* or *abaya*. But lots of headscarves—blue and green and yellow. One girl with a pastel peach *hijab* is holding a sign that reads: **Meet a Muslim!** The rest are holding bouquets of flowers—what look to be white chrysanthemums and red carnations. I'm guessing this is the protest Todd was talking about, but I don't see Mel. A second look, then a third while I sit at the red light. There's no tall, slender girl with short, peacock-green hair. Maybe Todd got it wrong. Maybe Mel isn't part of this 'protest.' Which honestly doesn't look like any protest I've ever seen.

I turn left at the traffic light and pull into the Colectivo parking lot. Once one of the city's water pumping stations, the two-story cream city brick building has been converted into my favorite coffeehouse. On a day like today, it's mobbed. I luck out and find a just-vacated parking space. The aroma of freshly ground coffee entices me through the door. With nothing to eat in the house, I'm starving and desperately in need of caffeine. It'll be much easier to seek out my daughter if I eat first.

I buy a spicy soy *chai* and a pumpkin cranberry muffin, then carry them out to the crowded patio where a good portion of Milwaukee is spending their Sunday afternoon. And where a black lab who's beyond excited to see me home nearly knocks me to the ground. *My* black lab—Finn—who wraps his front legs around my waist and hangs on for dear life, barking his undying love. It doesn't matter how long I'm away, five minutes or three months, Finn always greets me the same way. I barely manage to set down my *chai* and muffin on the table.

"Sit!" Bonita taps the painted blue metal table and hands me the leash.

Not sure if she's talking to the dog or to me, I pull out the chair, cringing at the sound of iron legs scraping across the flagstones, and plant myself. Finn immediately stops his barking, sits at my feet, and claims my lap for his head. He keeps his eyes glued to my face for good measure. The surest way to make sure I stay put. At least for now.

I nod toward the street. "A good view of the girls."

"I thought so." She smiles knowingly. "Sorry I didn't get in any food for you. I wasn't sure when you'd be home."

"I should've called."

She nods toward my *chai* and muffin. "Those will make you fat."

"Not if you eat half." Nothing, absolutely nothing, makes Bonita fat. She could eat all of Colectivo's muffins and still be just as skinny.

"Since you insist." She dutifully breaks the muffin in two and helps herself to the larger piece. Good of her to watch my weight.

I ruffle Finn's silky ears. He lifts his head and offers his nose to be kissed. Adoration paid and accepted, he circles around and sits with his back to me. Like Bonita and me, he's here for a reason. To keep an eye on Mel. Only I haven't managed to spot her yet.

Bonita clearly senses my inability to recognize my own daughter. "She's the girl with the dark brown hair and purple sweater standing next to the shorter girl wearing the peach scarf. Hard to pick her out now that she's cut off all that green."

I locate the girl with the peach *hijab*, her dark hair peeking out from under the scarf. And then Mel. Five months ago, my daughter's hair was long and colored periwinkle. Then, to spite her stepmother, who had forced her to dye it back to the original brown, she got a buzz cut and dyed it green. Now, it's back to brown. "Her hair . . . it's kind of . . . conservative, don't you think?"

"For Mel, definitely. She had me take her to *Beauty* to get it done. Thomas cut her hair. I think he did a fine job. She likes it, too."

"Thomas is the best." I comb my fingers through my hair, wondering if I should make an appointment now that I've got lots of time available.

Her voice turns sour. "Empress Catherine, though, worked herself into a tizzy. Probably because Mel came to me, instead of going back to that glitzy North Shore salon."

The 'Empress Catherine' bit nearly has me snorting spicy *chai* out my nose. "Why did she go back to brown?"

"Well, I could tell you she's a teenager, and they change their minds every two minutes. But I think it has more to do with her new friend Yasmine."

So, how long has this been going on? And just how serious is this new interest in Islam? My gut churns as I remember Seema's sudden radicalization last spring when she embraced Awalmir's perverted ideas, which weren't Islamic at all. More like medieval Pashtun tribal practices that subjugate women. Seema may have been seventeen, but she was so naïve, so desperate for him to love her, that she believed everything he said. *Stop! That was Seema. And had nothing at all to do with Islam. This is Mel. Two completely different girls.*

Bonita interrupts my thoughts. "Something's bothering her. She's not talking about it—not to me, at any rate. But she's been spending more time in your apartment. Or over at Yasmine's house. That girl's a firecracker. You'll like her. Nice parents. They came over to introduce themselves to me." She raises both eyebrows for emphasis. "To make sure it was okay for Mel to spend a Friday night with them."

"Sounds good. Thanks for taking care of that." I sit back in my chair. Interesting that the parents thought to check in with Bonita, not Todd and Catherine Elizabeth. Or maybe they tried and got rebuffed.

"Your ex has been coming around, too. Said he was checking on the apartment." She doesn't call him by name. Oh, she's pissed.

I tell her about finding Todd in the apartment when I got home. With Mel's key.

Bonita purses her lips. "Something's bothering him."

"No kidding. Her name is Catherine Elizabeth."

"More than that. Do you think he could possibly . . . be carrying a torch for you?"

I laugh. Bonita's only in her fifties, but she has such an old-fashioned way of putting things. Damn, I love her. "Funny you should say that. Cerelli said the same thing. He overheard Todd's call the other night."

She smiles. "You listen to me, girl. That captain of yours, he's a good man. I expect you to hold on to him."

"I'll do what I can."

"How's his leg?"

"Good. Amazing, actually." I take a bite of my muffin.

"You love him." It's not a question.

"I do."

"Have you told him?"

I don't answer.

"It's a simple question, Annie. I'm guessing you haven't. Might be a good thing to do."

"I will definitely give that some serious consideration."

In front of me, Finn rises to his feet, ears alert. It takes a few seconds, then I hear it. The roar of motorcycles. Getting louder. Closer. There have to be fifty of them. No, more like a hundred. At least. The earth beneath my feet vibrates. My heart clenches. The Taliban. On their new favorite mode of transportation: motorcycles. *Oh God, no!*

Pulling on his leash, barking ferociously, Finn calls me back from Afghanistan. Colectivo. I'm sitting outside my favorite coffee shop in Milwaukee. I exhale in relief. But not for long. So frigging many bikes. They look to be mostly hogs. The riders are wearing black leathers, helmets or do-rags, plus heavy, lug-soled Scout boots. The leaders pull up and stop at the red traffic light directly in front of the smiling, flower-holding girls and women.

Normally, I love seeing motorcyclists out enjoying a ride. You can't live in Harley-Davidson country and not love it. But today, not so much. With them stopping in front of the **Meet a Muslim!** contingent, hell, there's just too much that has the potential to go sideways.

Come on! Come on! I sit forward on my chair and mutter to the traffic light. *Turn green!* And to the bikers, *You gents just keep right on going.*

Finn strains against his leash, clearly ready to bolt.

The light turns green, but the bikers' attention is on the girls. Slowly, they pull to the side of the road, parking their bikes diagonally, one right next to another. Then dismount. And start toward the girls.

Before I have time to think, I'm on my feet, Finn's leash in hand. We make our way across the patio, weaving in and around people and tables. Then, adrenaline pumping, I'm dodging cars to cross the street. Finn is running flat out, pulling hard against his leash. My eyes are on Mel. Ahead of me, a huge, muscled biker, who doesn't look anything like a Taliban militant, closes in on my daughter. Black leather is everywhere. I lose sight of Mel and turn in circles until finally, *finally* I see her again. She's smiling at the big, bearded biker, offering him a red carnation.

He's grinning back at her, his beefy, gloved fingers closing around the flower. "Not sure what I can do with this."

"I know just the thing." Her eyes crinkle as she snaps off all but a few inches of the stem and threads it under the do-rag, secure above his ear.

He puts a hand on his hip and poses for his buddies. "Hey, is this cool or what?"

I watch in disbelief as each burly man insists on a flower, then digs out a few bucks and stuffs them into the large coffee can the woman standing next to Mel is holding. A can, I now see, that has a sign: **Help rebuild the Wad Qol Secondary School for Girls!**

One of the bikers asks the woman, "This girls' school, where's it at?"

She smiles. "Afghanistan."

"What happened?"

"It was terrible! The Taliban fire-bombed it!"

"Oh, that's bad." He frowns. "Wad Qol, huh? Anyone die?"

She nods sadly at Mel. "Her auntie. She was the director."

"I hate hearing shit like that. It's just wrong. I did three tours in Afghanistan. And I've got two daughters." Then, he calls the rest of the guys to attention. "Listen up, men! Dig deep!" He pulls a fifty out of his wallet and adds it to the can. More greenbacks follow until the can is overflowing.

"Hope this helps," he says, signaling the men back to their bikes.

I don't move a muscle as I watch their retreat, noting the name of the club scrolled across the backs of their jackets. **Green Knights Military M.C.** Next to me, Finn nuzzles his head against my thigh.

As the bikers roar away, Mel twirls herself into my arms. "Mom! You came!"

"Hey, sweetie." I fluff her hair with my fingers. "Like the hair."

"Really? At first, I was kind of meh." She shakes her head. "Now, I'm pretty much used to the color."

"So, what's all this?" I look around at the women and girls whose bouquets are now seriously depleted.

"Oh my gosh, Mom. I'm so stoked! Can you believe all those guys? We've raised a ton of money!"

"Money?" I ask innocently, craning my neck to look at the sign on the can.

She waves dismissively. "I'll tell you about it later. First, I want you to meet my friend, Yasmine, and her mother."

"Hey!" Yasmine smiles and waves her sign.

"Yasmine. It's great to meet you."

Stepping out from behind me, a petite woman in a flowered silk headscarf holds out her hand. "I am Awa Faqiri, Yasmine's mother." The part Aussie, part Dari accent startles me. "Mel has told us much about you. I have been looking forward to meeting you."

"Annie Hawkins." I stop short, about to say 'Green,' but catch myself in time. Mel's eyes widen, and I realize it's the first time she's heard me say this new version of my name. She smiles and nods, so I guess she's okay with it. "I'm happy to meet you."

"Please." Awa smiles, still holding my hand. "We would like you and Mel to come to dinner this Friday night."

I return her smile. "Yes. That would be wonderful. What can I bring?"

Next to me, Mel gapes. Then almost immediately, suspicion inches across her face. Clearly, she's expecting me to apologize, to explain that I'll be back on the road for another assignment. Which has been the story of her life. But not this time. For once, I'm going to make my daughter very happy.

9

"TELL ME THE TRUTH, MOM." Mel takes hold of Finn's leash as we walk with Bonita to the parking lot. "Are you really going with me to the Faqiris' on Friday? Or were you just being nice? Because if you're going to back out—"

"Yes, I'm going." I'm ready to hang my head in shame. This is what my job has brought me to: my daughter no longer believes me when I promise to do something, anything.

She grins. "For real?" Except then, she stops walking and crosses her arms. "Why?"

It takes me a couple steps before I realize she's not beside me. I look back. "Why what?"

"Mom. Seriously." She frowns. "You hardly ever go to any of my things. Even junior high graduation. So, why are you suddenly willing to go to dinner at the Faqiris'?"

"I've got time off. That last assignment turned out to be a lot longer than anyone planned." No way am I telling her that in the space of twenty-four hours I was suspended, then un-suspended and put on a top-secret assignment.

"Oh my God! Really?"

I hate lying to Mel, not to mention Bonita, so I move on before either one can ask more questions. "Anyway, since I'll be here, I thought you might like to stay with me for a few weeks."

She stares in disbelief. Then lets out a whoop of pure joy and spins in a circle. Determined to keep up, Finn runs frenetically around her, barking his happiness, tangling her legs with his leash. Then, just as suddenly, they both stop, and Mel shakes her head. "No way. They'll never let me."

"Would seem kind of strange for the empress to allow this." Bonita raises a dubious eyebrow.

I do my best to ignore Bonita and focus on Mel. "Actually, it was your dad's idea."

"Are you sure? They've never let me stay more than a night in the past. And C.E. makes even that into a major hassle."

I can't tell her the truth about this either. The fact that her father is pushing her out of the house to make his wife happy isn't something any sixteen-year-old needs to hear. She doesn't press me for details. But she will. Mel unwinds Finn's leash, and they jog after Bonita and me to the cars.

"I'll see you at home," says Bonita as she climbs into her car and slams the door. A sure sign that she'll be around later, demanding a more truthful explanation.

With Finn stretched out and snoring across the back seat, Mel and I drive to the big house on Lake Drive to pick up her clothes and schoolbooks and iPad. My fingers are tightly crossed that no one will be home. That Catherine Elizabeth and Todd will have the twins at a park. Or a movie. I just want them out of the house where I used to live. I don't want to deal with her snarkiness. Over the phone is one thing; dealing with her in person drives me to distraction.

No such luck. I pull into the long driveway leading up to the six-bedroom limestone mansion and park right in front of the ten-foot-tall mahogany double doors. The wrought iron trim accentuates the palatial feel of the place.

Mel shoots me a sideways glance. "You know C.E. hates it when people park here, blocking the door."

"I know."

And there they are—Todd, Catherine Elizabeth, and the twins—framed in the doorway. Like they're posing for the opening credits of a television show. Mel and I climb out of the car. Finn doesn't make a move to follow us, so I crack open the back windows. I'm guessing he doesn't like Catherine Elizabeth any better than I do.

As soon as we get inside, Mel dashes up the grand curving staircase to her room, leaving me in the cavernous, marble-floored foyer to deal with Todd and her stepmother. I take note of the massive arrangement of lilies, spider mums, and roses in a crystal vase on the round table and try to guess how many hundreds of dollars they cost.

For once, Catherine Elizabeth's in a good mood. She smiles the entire time she's instructing me. "Now, you will make sure to get Mel to school every morning. Seven thirty. School lets out at three, except on Wednesdays, when it's early release. She has dance after school on Mondays and Wednesdays. Oh, and I almost forgot, she works on the school newspaper." She laughs. "You'll have to check with her for the days she stays late for the *Ripples* editorial meetings."

I hold up my hand before she can come up with any other places Mel needs to be. "I'm sure she'll be able to get around just fine. She has a car."

"Not anymore." Catherine Elizabeth isn't smiling.

Next to his wife, Todd looks vaguely ill. What the hell? They've confiscated Mel's car? Is this all because of Yasmine?

Mel chooses this exact moment to haul her first load of stuff down the stairs. There's no way she can avoid the tornado of tension swirling in the foyer. She stops midway and stares down at the three of us, her smile fading.

I call up to her. "Sweetie, could you please take your stuff to the car?" I trust she picks up on the unspoken part of the message: *Stay there until I let you know it's safe to come back in.*

She takes one more look at us, then bolts down the rest of the stairs and out. I close the door behind her and pivot back to Todd and Catherine Elizabeth. "I'm afraid I don't understand."

Catherine Elizabeth throws a pointed glare at Todd, which I take to mean, *You better back me up on this.* "It's quite clear. When Mel chose to go against our rules, she lost the privilege of her car."

"Excuse me?" The cutting edge to my voice echoes off the marble floor.

"Annie, we talked about that this morning." Todd puts his arm around his wife's waist.

"Oh, you mean the fact that Mel chooses to have a friend of a different religion?" Todd looks like I've slapped him across the face. Which is precisely what I'd like to do. "Or, could you mean because she's decided not to attend the church Catherine Elizabeth is trying to force on her?"

Finn, bless him, chooses this moment to wake up and start barking.

Catherine Elizabeth takes a step toward me. "You have no right to talk to me that way! Not in *my* house! Todd!"

We both turn to him. He looks seriously unhappy. "Annie, come on. There are rules, and Mel has to know there are consequences when she breaks them."

"Consequences?" I narrow my eyes. "Who the hell do you think will be dealing with these consequences? Not Mel. Me. I'll be the one who has to drive her all over the place."

"Well, it's about time," storms Catherine Elizabeth. "If you'd been around at all the last eight years, we wouldn't be having these problems."

Right for the jugular. *Just let it go!* instructs my inner voice. This isn't about me and my failure as a mother. It's about Mel. "Let me get this straight. Besides Mel having a friend you don't like, are there any other egregious sins she's committed?" Out of the corner of my eye, I see identical seven-year-old faces peering out from behind their parents. They're cute little girls, very cute. I do hope they're paying attention.

Outside, Finn barks louder. A lot louder.

"For God's sake." Todd raises his voice. "She's just a kid. She needs our guidance. She *wants* our guidance, whether she knows it or not."

Where do I begin? "So, what you're saying is that the First Amendment doesn't apply to our daughter?" I know the First Amendment has nothing to do with parent-child relationships. With any luck, they don't realize that.

"This house is not a democracy!" yells Catherine Elizabeth.

Todd tightens his hold on her waist. "That's bullshit, Annie. Sixteen-year-olds don't have any constitutional rights."

Finn's barking escalates to a frenzy. Mel must have let him out of the car because it sure sounds like he's clawing at the front door.

I take a deep breath and speak slowly, quietly. "Do I understand correctly that you want Mel to stay with me for a while?" Even though I want my daughter with me for the next six weeks, I'm giving no quarter. "Am I also right in assuming you want her going to school?"

Now, Catherine Elizabeth looks as uncomfortable as Todd. And a lot angrier. I hold out my hand, palm up. "The keys. The registration. The insurance papers."

"Couldn't you drive——?" Todd pleads.

"No." I smile, but my voice slices through the air like the MK3 knife Cerelli carries when he's on a spec op mission. I keep my hand extended, waiting.

Outside, Finn is still barking. And scratching at the door. I wonder what kind of marks he's leaving. I wonder when the neighbors will call to complain.

"Give her the fucking keys and get her out of here." The woman actually snarls.

Behind Todd and Catherine Elizabeth, the twins' eyes widen.

Once I've got Mel's keys and the paperwork to her car, I open the door and wave her back inside. "I'll help you carry down the rest." Then, inspiration strikes. "Looks like we'll have just enough time to get to Yasmine's house for dinner."

Catherine Elizabeth's sharp inhalation echoes after us.

Mel looks at me, confused. "Mom?" She wisely doesn't say another word until we're in her bedroom. "Mom, Mrs. Faqiri meant—"

I know! I mouth the words, then bring my index finger to my lips. Call me paranoid, but I wouldn't put it past Catherine Elizabeth to have followed us upstairs and be out in the hall listening.

This is the first time I've been in Mel's room since I moved out. I have to hand it to Catherine Elizabeth: she or her interior decorator went all out. Intricate pink and purple flowers twine up the textured wallpaper. A French provincial canopy bed, desk, and dresser make the room look like a showcase.

Mel catches me looking and shrugs. "She decorated when she first moved in. I liked it back then, but . . ."

"Oh, sweetie." I turn around and see several small framed lithographs of ballet dancers warming up at the barre. Walking closer, I make out the signature. Degas. They look suspiciously like originals.

"She gave me those." Mel smiles.

I flash back on Catherine Elizabeth's unending support of Mel's dancing. First, ballet. Then, modern. She was always driving Mel to classes and rehearsals. Not to mention, volunteering to shop for the most gorgeous costumes for the girls to wear in their recitals. And there on the bulletin board is photo after photo of Mel performing. "So, you're saying she's not all bad."

"I guess. Yeah."

Somewhere on the first floor, a door slams. Loudly.

Finn starts barking again.

"Come on." I grab the handle of her suitcase. "Let's get out of here."

Back outside, Finn quiets as soon as he sees us. But he makes sure to stand between the house and me until he's certain I'm close enough to the car to be safe.

"Oops! Almost forgot." I hand Mel the keys and paperwork to her car.

"Mom?" Realization dawns on her face. "How did you—"

"Later." I smile. "For now, let's just go. It's been a very long day, and I still haven't gone grocery shopping yet."

"I can do that. What do we need?"

I hug her within an inch of her life. What sixteen-year-old

actually offers to do anything, much less go for groceries? "You are an angel. And to answer your question, we need everything, absolutely everything."

Finn paws my leg and barks.

"Oh! And dog food." Finn offers me a lopsided grin, and taking one look at the mountain of Mel's stuff filling the back, he hops onto the front passenger seat. Shutting the door behind him, I turn to Mel. "Thanks, sweetie. I owe you big-time."

She smiles smugly. Her way of saying, *Yeah, you do.*

10

FINN PULLS ME TOWARD BONITA'S first-floor apartment. I'd been hoping he'd want to spend the rest of the day upstairs with me. So much for undying devotion. For her part, Bonita insists I bring her up to date on Mel's new living arrangement. Before I can finish explaining, two bright patches of red appear on her cheeks.

"That woman is a piece of work." Then, unexpectedly, she smiles. "It'll sure be good to have our Mel here."

"It will." If only until I leave for Afghanistan.

"When are you going to tell me the rest of what's going on?"

I swallow hard. "The rest?"

"Best I can remember, you've never had this much time off after an assignment."

I palm the air between us. "Let's not go there. At least, not yet."

Bonita offers a curt nod—a temporary dismissal, the emphasis on 'temporary.' I back out of her apartment, knowing full well she won't rest until I tell all.

By the time I finish hauling Mel's stuff up the narrow staircase to my apartment, she's back from the local Outpost natural food store. The girl's got superpowers. What she can do in half an hour takes me at least twice as long. She runs the shopping bags up the stairs and starts loading kale and spinach, cucumbers and apples, oranges and broccoli into the fridge. Soy and almond milk follow. And an organic chicken. I hand her a bag of tomatoes and another of onions. She groans. "Jeez, Mom, you're the one who told me that refrigerating tomatoes and onions kills the flavor. That's what these new hanging mesh baskets are for."

"Thanks." I nod at the baskets. "The kitchen really does look fantastic. Much better. You and Bonita did a great job." Something else I owe her for.

She pulls a bottle of juice out of a bag and turns toward me. "Are you going to tell me what's going on?"

"What do you mean?"

"Why I'm really here."

I think about that for all of three seconds and shake my head. However infuriated I am with her father and stepmother, I'm not about to ruin her relationship with them. "Why don't you tell me about this fundraising thing you've got going on. Looks like you collected a lot of money today."

She pirouettes, her eyes shining. "We did! You heard what Mrs. Faqiri said? Almost five thousand dollars! Add that to what we've already raised, and then the dance next weekend. Mom, I bet we'll have enough to rebuild the entire school."

"The dance?"

"Didn't I tell you? It was Yasmine's idea. Well, mine, too. We're doing a program of Afghan dances. See, Yasmine's in a dance troupe. And I started going." She stops and turns pleading eyes on me. "Please don't tell Dad. Or *her*. They told me I couldn't go. One of their 'rules.'" She makes exaggerated air quotes.

"No worries."

She grins. "Anyway, we were practicing the *Attan*—this really intricate dance—and came up with the idea for the program. You know, as a way to earn more money for the school. All the girls love the idea. So do their parents. And the imam at the mosque. Then, Mrs. Faqiri thought there should be a dinner, too. Like a buffet. All these Afghan foods. We've already sold a ton of tickets. Isn't it great?"

"This is when?"

"Next Sunday. Bonita's coming." Mel looks at me warily, clearly unwilling to ask whether I'll be there. She's used to me bailing on her dance performances. In fact, I haven't seen her dance live in a couple years. Only afterward—the phone videos Bonita records.

"Yes, I will most definitely be there."

"For sure?"

I nod. "Like I told you, I've got a guaranteed vacation. No way I'm going anywhere."

"Yes!" She pumps her fist in the air. "This calls for some pomegranate juice."

What I'd really like is a double Maker's, but I go for the juice. "Please."

She pours two glasses, and we clink.

I love how happy this is making her, that she still believes in me after way too many broken promises. "So, who came up with the idea of rebuilding the girls' school?"

She grins. "Well, I was telling Yasmine and Mrs. Faqiri about the school and what happened. I said, 'Wouldn't it be great if we could do something to help.' And Mrs. Faqiri said we could so long as there's a safe way of getting the money to Wad Qol. Oh, and that there's someone to take charge of the construction."

I know the next words out of my mouth should be 'This is amazing!' But I have a strong suspicion that this project Mel's taken on is heading in a direction that's not going to make me happy. "And who would that someone be?"

She looks at me like I suddenly have two heads. Maybe even three. "Well, you."

"Me."

"Well, yeah. I told Mrs. Faqiri and everyone at the mosque that you go to Afghanistan and places like that all the time. I mean, you do." She nods to make her point. "And, next time you go, you could just take the money and give it to that teacher you told me about. You know, the one who teaches English."

"Gulshan."

"Yeah."

I bite my lower lip.

"What?"

"Mel, you shouldn't have promised I'd do this without asking first." I sit down hard on one of the newly repainted stools at the kitchen peninsula.

"I'm asking you now." I can hear the pleading in her voice.

"Don't you think it's a little late for that?" My voice is way too sharp.

She narrows her eyes. "Well, I would've asked you before if you'd been here." Right for the jugular—just like her stepmother. And her father. The people in my life know exactly what to say to get my guilt churning.

"I know I spend a lot of time away, but . . ." *Stay. Calm!* "It's. My. Job." My voice is most definitely not calm.

"Yeah, well, maybe you should get another job. Ever think of that?" Mel's eyes flash anger. And a large dose of betrayal.

I stare down at the Formica countertop. So many knife marks. It really needs to be replaced. I run my finger along a particularly long scar that I gouged out years ago when Grammy and I were canning tomato sauce. I was chopping onions and garlic. She came in the kitchen and yelled at me for cutting directly on the Formica. Damn, I've made a lot of mistakes. Way too many.

Avoiding Mel's eyes, I climb off the stool and walk the length of the small living room to the bay window. From here, I imagine I can see across the Port of Milwaukee and up Lake Drive to the big house. I retreat eight and a half years to that weekend when Darya and Tariq and Seema came to tell us they were moving back to Afghanistan. Darya to open a school for girls. Tariq to work in a small village health clinic. At the time, I didn't know it was more than that. Much more. That they'd actually be working for U.S. intelligence. I didn't find that out until many years later— after Darya was killed. But that weekend, seeing Darya follow her dream, made me realize I had dreams, too. I had to get back in the field. Back to being a war photographer. Where my heart was. What I was good at. Hell, I'd won a frigging Pulitzer for my images of children in war-torn Afghanistan. I couldn't stay home anymore. Even though the crazy dangerous places I went to scared Todd. Even though I'd be away from Mel for long stretches.

So, I walked away from my husband and my daughter, from that palace of a house. I took a job at TNN and worked my way up.

To what? To a fucking suspension.

Not to mention, never-ending guilt.

I look back at Mel, who's standing behind the kitchen peninsula, chewing her fingernails, waiting for an answer. Maybe expecting me to call her on speaking the way she is. Catherine Elizabeth sure wouldn't tolerate it.

"Do I think about getting another job? Every single day. Sometimes it eats me alive."

"Then quit."

"There's a problem with that."

"What do you mean?"

"I love what I do. For me, it's . . . it's like . . . dancing."

She nearly drops her glass of pomegranate juice.

I don't say a word. I don't have to.

She stares at me, her eyes large, her understanding immediate. "Then you can't stop. You just can't. No matter what. Not even for me." She takes a sip of juice. Swallows. Thinks. And finally, asks ever so casually, "When's your next assignment in Afghanistan?"

I walk back to my stool in front of the kitchen peninsula before answering. "Actually, I've got to be in Kabul in six weeks."

"Seriously? This is frigging fantastic! Wait till I tell the Faqiris."

I hold up my hands, trying to temper her enthusiasm. "I haven't said yes yet. What if Gulshan and the other teachers or the parents don't want to rebuild?"

She laughs. "Of course they want the school. They want their daughters to get an education. Besides, this is the perfect way to honor Auntie Dar. I mean she *was* that school. It's like her legacy."

"Not everyone in Wad Qol wants the school."

She shrugs. "So, you'll have to twist a few arms. Like Auntie Dar did."

"It's not that simple." Just the thought of carrying a lot of U.S. dollars into the wilds of Afghanistan gives me pause. It would be such a temptation for too many people. Especially the underpaid officials at the airport. And the Taliban. "Have you thought of wiring the money?"

Mel shakes her head. "Dr. and Mrs. Faqiri say that's a bad idea.

They've got family there, and every time they wire money, only part of it gets through."

That was exactly my experience the first few times I sent money to Darya. I also checked into NGOs—and other organizations. They wanted to control the money, decide who would get it. My index finger traces a dollar sign on the counter. "So, actually hand-carrying the money in-country is the best way to go." The only way.

"Yeah." Mel holds her breath, pressing her lips together, one beat away from celebrating her victory. The same expression she used when she was four and trying to convince me she was old enough for a two-wheeler without training wheels.

I cross my arms. "Getting money into Afghanistan isn't all that easy. First off, there are limits on the amount of U.S. dollars I can take in."

"How much?"

"Probably around twenty thousand. I'd have to check."

She flicks her wrist. "No problem."

I look up sharply. "How much money have you raised?"

Her smile reaches all the way to her eyes. "About ten thousand. But that's not counting the dance."

I stare for a full count of ten. "That's a lot of money."

She nods happily.

I study my pomegranate juice. Mel's right. Rebuilding the school *is* the perfect way to honor Darya. Something I should've thought of months ago. Being part of this—I should do it. I *have* to do it. For Dar. And for Mel. I'm just about to tell her that when my cell phone rings. Cerelli—calling at exactly the wrong time.

Another ring.

"Mom? Your phone?"

I shake my head. "We need to finish this."

She peers over my shoulder. "That's Captain Cerelli. You should answer." She swipes the phone and hands it to me.

I shoot her a quizzical look as she mouths, *Later*, and heads toward her room. The grin on her face tells me she's sure her victory is complete.

Reluctantly, I turn my attention to Cerelli. "Hi!"

"Glad I caught you. I'm still at the office. Never got to PT."

"Meetings?" I head toward my bedroom. Pushing the door almost shut, I curl up on the bed and wish I were back in Cerelli's condo, nestled in the crook of his arm.

"Endless." I hear the fatigue in his voice. Which is strange. Cerelli is never tired. Or, at least, never shows it. *When he's in the field,* I remind myself. Could it be that this desk job is getting to him?

"Anything you can talk to me about?"

"Sweetheart, you know better than to ask."

I do. And I can't imagine what it's like for an action hero to be stuck behind a desk directing other guys out in the field. Best get his mind off it. "Okay then. It's been quite a day here." I bring him up to speed about what happened at the lakefront. "And get this, bikers showed up."

"So, you got to be Wonder Woman and save the girls?" I can hear the smile in his voice.

I decide not to ruin it by saying anything about the few seconds when I thought the Taliban were riding those motorcycles. "Nope. These were the good guys. The Green Knights."

"A good organization. They've helped a lot of vets, especially those with PTSD."

PTSD. I ignore that, too. "They were great, gave a lot of money to the cause." I bite my tongue and hope he just skips over that slip.

"Then, Mel and I went to get her stuff. She's staying with me for a while." I drop my voice and run through the details. "Catherine Elizabeth is a piece of work."

"How is Mel handling it?"

"I haven't told her that part. Yet. It's kind of hard to know what to say."

"Kid gloves."

"Tell me about it."

"Now, would you please tell me about the fundraiser?"

Damn, I should've known he'd never let that go by.

"Annie?"

There's no point in lying. The man is a pit bull about digging out the truth. "Mel and her friend, Yasmine, and Yasmine's mother—I'm pretty sure she's originally from Afghanistan—"

"I'm not going to like this, am I?"

"I seriously doubt you will."

He exhales. "Tell me."

"Well, you heard what Todd said the other night about raising money to rebuild the Wad Qol School for Girls. Which, I will remind you, I knew nothing about at the time. Now, I do, and it's actually a pretty amazing idea."

"Please tell me you're not thinking what I think you're thinking."

"Just listen. They've already raised quite a bit of money. Thousands today alone. The Green Knights dug deep."

"Annie—"

"There's also a dance performance next weekend."

"They're not expecting that *you*—"

"That is their plan."

"Their plan. Not yours."

"This is where things get sticky. Apparently, Mel has already told them I'll take the money the next time I'm going that way on assignment."

"And that would be in six weeks."

"Yeah." I take a deep breath. "I can get in touch with Gulshan—the English teacher."

"I know who she is. I know her husband, too. Ikrom. But need I remind you that TNN is sending you to Kabul, not Wad Qol?"

"Assuming they want to rebuild and they want the money, Ikrom could drive down and get it."

He's quiet for a long moment. Then, he says, "No."

"What do you mean 'no'?"

"I know you. Once you make contact, you'll want to take the money to Wad Qol yourself. You'll want to be involved."

Damn, he's right. I do want to be involved. For Darya. I want to go back to Wad Qol and help rebuild the school. "So what if I do? I'll go a few days before my start date."

"Annie, you know as well as I do that it won't be a few days. It'll be a few weeks. Remember the last time you told me you'd be there for two weeks?"

I don't answer. I don't need to. We both know what happened. The Taliban firebombed the school and killed Darya.

"It's fucking dangerous over there. Kabul is bad enough. But once you get out in the countryside . . ." His voice is low, so low I can hear his backbone stiffening.

I start picking at a loose thread on my quilt. I'm courting an argument. I should stop now, circle around, and come back to this conversation later. But I don't. "Even in Wad Qol?"

He exhales again. Loudly. He's not going to lie to me either, no matter how much he doesn't want me going. "Not today. Maybe not tomorrow. But the situation is fluid."

"What about Massoud's men? Couldn't they protect me? I mean, after all, this school is for their daughters. Some of their wives teach there." I don't remind him that everyone in the valley credits me with having saved Ahmad Shah Massoud's son and grandson in the aftermath of the Dalan Sang bombing last spring. That the Massoud clan considers me family and have pledged to protect me. I'm warming to my argument. Which is crazy given that half an hour ago, I was practically telling Mel I wouldn't go. I keep on. "They support education for girls. This is the best chance we've got to make a difference in Afghanistan. We *have* to educate those girls. We can't afford to lose another generation to illiteracy." I hear the echo of Darya's voice in mine.

"And I don't want to lose *you*. You're too damn visible. People know who you are. There's a price on your head. I love you, sweetheart. I can't let you go." I can almost feel him cringe as he says those last words. He knows how I'll respond. Especially considering how many times we've argued about exactly this.

I don't let him down. "You can't *let* me go? Cerelli, we've talked about this before. Besides, I'll be in Kabul for work."

"Yeah. I'm not thrilled about that either."

Damn. This is Todd all over again. *Tread lightly!* But I don't. Instead, for the second time this afternoon, I say, "It's. My. Job."

"Annie." I hear the crack in his voice. He's one of the good guys—I know he is—and this must be tearing him apart. Trying to keep me safe but not rule my life.

Silence. I wait for him to say something. Anything. But he doesn't say a word.

So, I talk. "Look, like I've told you before, I can't live with anyone telling me what I can and can't do. I did it once, and it nearly destroyed me."

"I'm not Todd."

I try to take a deep breath. Slow down. Think things through. It's not working. "No, you're not. And you're not in charge of me either."

"I wouldn't do that. I'm just trying to talk reason here."

"*Reason?*" As in, I'm being *unreasonable?* "Look, Cerelli, you don't get to make my decisions. No one does except me."

"Sweetheart." Which is probably the worst thing he could say at this moment.

"Sorry. Never again. I am done."

He's quiet for a full thirty seconds. "I am, too." Quiet, measured, his voice is steel. And it hurts like hell.

Then, the connection's gone.

I push the talk button, but all I get is silence. "Cerelli! Don't do this to me!"

A rustle from the doorway makes me glance up. Mel, her hand in front of her mouth. Her eyes wide. "Mom. Oh my God. I'm sorry. I'm sorry."

"Not now. Please." I bury my face in my hands. The next thing I know, she's climbed onto the bed. Her arms circle around me, hold me close. Then, we rock. Just like I used to do for her when she was a little girl.

Downstairs, in Bonita's apartment, Finn starts to whine. The first-floor door creaks open, and he bounds up the back stairs, the interior link between the two apartments. It takes only a few seconds for him to find us and jump on the bed. A gentle whimper. Then, he props his head on my hip. I look down into his eyes. Loving and also full of worry.

I grab a tissue from my bedside table and dry my eyes. "Okay. Time to tell the truth."

"About Captain Cerelli?"

Another swipe at my eyes, and I shake my head. "Something else." One look at Mel tells me she's not so sure she wants to hear the truth. I take another minute to consider whether or not I should tell her. Because maybe, just maybe, children don't want to know the truth about their parents. But for once, I'm going to be completely honest with her.

"What I'm going to tell you stays here. In this room. It goes nowhere. You tell no one. And I mean *no one*."

She nods. And crosses her heart.

"The real problem, or at least one of the problems, is that I got suspended from my job this week. That's why I've got all this time off."

Clearly surprised, she stares at me for an uncomfortably long moment. "Suspended? Mom? What did you do?"

"After Auntie Dar was killed, I was . . . uh . . . trying to look for Seema, and I . . . well, I did something I shouldn't have."

She looks stunned. "Did you kill someone?"

"No!" Well, I did, but that's a different story. Best to stay focused on the other bad thing I did—pulling a gun on Piera McNeil. "I didn't hurt this person. But she's accused me of some things."

"Like what?"

What can I tell her?

"Mom? What did you do?" she whispers.

Stomach churning, it's all I can do to stay calm. "Everything. And nothing."

She strokes Finn's head, but he keeps his eyes trained on me, clearly worried. "What's going to happen?"

I shrug. "There's going to be an investigation. My boss and Cerel—" I can't say his name without choking up. "They're pretty sure I'll eventually come out okay." I do my best to hide the anxiety that's eating at me. No point dumping that on Mel.

"But you said before that you've got another assignment. In Afghanistan."

"I do. TNN needs me there, but it's a one-off. Afterward, I'll be back on suspension until they finish investigating." I bite my tongue to keep from spilling the truth about my assignment. My *secret* assignment.

Her eyes brighten. "No problem." A sly smile creeps across her lips. She actually looks victorious. "As long as you get your job back, of course."

"No problem? I don't think so."

Finn looks back and forth between the two of us, unsure about the wildly shifting emotions in his people.

"Whaddaya mean? You're already going to Afghanistan. There's nothing keeping you from going a couple weeks early with the money and getting things organized."

"Nothing keeping me? Who's going to take care of you while I'm gone?" Stupid question considering all the times she's slept here when I've been away. Except now, she's living here. I can't imagine the fight with Todd and Catherine Elizabeth if they get wind of this.

She rolls her eyes. "Mom, get real. Bonita's right downstairs. I'll check in with her every day, like I always do."

"We should ask her."

An instant later, Mel is off the bed and at the top of the stairs leading down to Bonita's apartment. "Bonita?" she calls. The clatter of pots in the first-floor kitchen stops. "Is it okay with you if I stay up here while Mom's in Afghanistan for work?"

Two minutes later, Bonita herself is standing at the foot of my bed. "You mind telling me what's going on?"

I fill her in—a sanitized version fit for Mel's ears. But it's clear from Bonita's precariously raised eyebrows that she's got the full picture. She puts her arm around Mel's waist. "You bet I want you here."

"You sure?" I ask.

"Wouldn't say it if I didn't mean it."

"And what about boys?" I ask.

Mel looks sincerely confused. "Boys?"

"As in the opposite sex. *Wanting* sex. I found your bra next to the sofa when I got home today."

"What? But I'm not seeing anyone. I'm off boys—at least until after the fundraiser." She sounds so virtuous that I half believe her.

Head in my lap, Finn covers his eyes with his front paw. He does have a habit of stealing things.

"Remind me to give you back your T-shirt," says Bonita. "Finn brought it down to my place last week. It's a little worse for the wear."

When all else fails, blame it on the dog. "Okay. Back to you being here on your own. What if your father finds out? Your stepmother?"

"They won't."

Bonita raises her eyebrows again.

I shake my head, wondering how long it will take before all this explodes in my face.

Mel isn't waiting for me to say yes. How well she knows that once I start talking logistics, she's getting what she wants. "Say, Mom? You'll take pictures while they're building the school, right?"

"Pictures? Wait a sec. You can't assume they'll be ready to build when I get there. Okay, maybe you're right that they'll want to rebuild, but they've got to draw up plans, and I'm sure there will be a ton of bureaucratic red tape. Besides, I'm only going to be there for a few days."

Mel cuts me off with a major eye roll. "Mom, have a little faith. And take lots of pictures. The people at the mosque will want to see them."

"Anything else?" I'm not at all sure I like the gleam in her eyes.

"While you're over there, couldn't you, like, look around for Seema?"

"Look around? It's a big country. With people who don't appreciate an outsider 'looking around.'" But, to be honest, in the deep, dark recesses of my convoluted brain, I've been thinking of doing exactly that. Even though I did sort of promise Cerelli I wouldn't.

"You could at least *ask*, couldn't you? I mean, who else is going to rescue her? Mom, this is *Seema*."

I put my arms around Mel and hold her close. "That's part of the problem, sweetie. I'm not at all sure Seema wants to be rescued. In fact, she sounds pretty happy."

"You talked to her?" Mel's voice echoes off the walls.

"She texted me."

"Mom!" Before I can shut down her curiosity, Mel grabs my phone and starts scrolling through my texts. Five seconds, and she's got Rahila's text on the screen.

I'm baffled how she got from Seema to Rahila so fast. "How did you know?"

She shrugs. "Her middle name. Rachel? She changed it to Arabic and used it as a pen name for all those stories and plays she used to write. Don't you remember?"

No. I don't remember.

Mel reads the *landay* out loud:

My body is mine,
But my Beloved drinks me like rare, red wine.

Her dreamy smile tells me she likes what she's reading. Then, suddenly, she inhales. Sharply. "Wait. Isn't her *Beloved* the guy who killed Auntie Dar?"

"How do you know that?" Certainly not from me. I've been careful not to tell her any of the horrific details.

Her eyes on the text, she waves away my concern. "I heard Captain Cerelli and Sawyer talking about it at the hospital last summer." She looks up and takes stock of my growing fury. "Mom, chill. They didn't know I was listening. Anyway, that's not the point."

"What's the point?"

She stabs her index finger against the *landay*. "She pretty much says she fucking *loves* him!"

Cringing, I whisper, "Language, please."

"Wait. What if she doesn't know what he did?" Her eyes beg me to tell her she's right.

I don't want to lie, but I'll say what I can to give Mel hope. To give me hope. "That's what I'd like to believe, too. That she doesn't know."

She shakes her head sadly. "You don't really believe that, do you?"

"It's getting harder to believe that she's totally innocent."

"That guy. He must have brainwashed her. It's the only way she'd do something like that. Which means you've got to find her and bring her home."

Brainwashed? It's a possibility I raised myself back in Wad Qol. I still can't bear the thought that Seema knew about her mother's death. And maybe helped kill her. "I'll do what I can. No promises." As I comb her short hair with my fingers, I realize I've made my decision. I'm definitely going back to Wad Qol.

"Say, Mom? Captain Cerelli—he'll call you back. You'll see. It'll be okay."

11

MEL'S WRONG. CERELLI DOESN'T CALL. Not Sunday night. Not Monday. Not Tuesday. Finally ready to talk things through, I call him. And listen to the rings go unanswered. I picture him in a meeting, looking at the incoming call, letting me go to voice mail. I don't leave a message. By the time I end the non-call, I can't decide if my heart is breaking or if I'm mad as hell.

My heart may be a painful lump in my chest, but I can't let it hold me hostage. So, I try calling Gulshan in Wad Qol, whispering a thank-you to Dar for having given me her number last spring. Nothing. Not even the static of an international line failing to connect. I spend Wednesday morning trying to get through. And get nowhere. Finally, I Google the health clinic where Gulshan's husband, Ikrom, works. I come up with a number, but that doesn't get me through either.

What have I been thinking? Dar always waited to call me when she was visiting her aunt—*Hama* Bibi—in Kabul. Because there's no reliable reception in the Panjshir Valley. Not only is it remote, but those confounded Hindu Kush Mountains wreak havoc on ordinary cell phones. Hence, why Cerelli gave me a sat phone last May. My best bet is to call Bibi. She'll be able to reach Gulshan.

I pull up Bibi's phone number and check the time to make sure it's not too late. One thirty here, 11:00 p.m. Kabul time. Borderline. I make the call. At least it goes through. To a busy signal. Which tells me she's awake. Unless it's Uncle Omar on the phone. I wait a few minutes and try again. This time the phone rings and rings, finally going to voice mail. Bibi's voice in Dari, then English, inviting me to leave a message.

LATE AFTERNOON, ONE OF the front doors opens downstairs, squeaking on hinges that need to be oiled. Feet pound up the stairs, and Mel bursts into the apartment.

It's Wednesday. Early release. I do a quick calculation of her after-school schedule and come up blank. I should be able to remember this. "How was . . . dance?"

She drops her pack on the floor, followed by a quilted Lug bag. Her dance stuff, I assume. "Good! Our next-to-last rehearsal before Sunday."

"I thought today was your other dance group?"

She makes her way past me to the kitchen, yanks open the fridge, and pulls out the pitcher of filtered water. "Yeah, well, I quit that group to focus on Afghan dance. And I, uh, didn't exactly tell *her*." She pours a tall glass of water and drinks half. "I mean, you saw how she is. And all Dad does is jump whenever she's pissed off. Would *you* have told them?"

She has a point. Getting on the wrong side of Catherine Elizabeth is unpleasant to say the least, and I only have to deal with her every few months. I watch Mel drink the rest of the water and think about what she could be putting in her body. When I was sixteen, I was sneaking out for beer. Mel is all about water. And not the bottled kind. She refuses to contribute to the destruction of the oceans.

I nod toward her bag. "Is that your costume?"

She puts down the glass. "Wait till you see." She pirouettes across the room and pulls out yards and yards of periwinkle linen, so fine it literally floats through the air. I hear the clinking of small circular mirrors dangling from the hem of the traditional *tunbaan*. The bodice of the ankle-length dress is so richly embroidered in black and gold and green and red that it's almost a tapestry. She holds it up to her chest. "It's beautiful, don't you think?" But she doesn't wait for me to answer. "And here are the pants. I love how they're gathered at the ankle." Whipping off her long-sleeve T-shirt, she pulls on the dress. "Tie the back for me?"

I pull it tight to make the bodice more fitted than most Afghan girls would be allowed to wear. The ballerina neckline looks perfect on her. She grabs her phone and swipes through in search of something.

"I'm kind of surprised Catherine Elizabeth didn't come across this bag. I take her for the kind of mother who snoops."

"Yeah, she does. That's why I keep important stuff at Yasmine's. Or here." She toes off her shoes.

I shouldn't condone her sneaking around, but I'm angry with the woman I've come to think of as the evil stepmother. "Smart girl."

She grins, then ups the volume on her cell and sets it on the coffee table. "This is our final number." She crouches, her back to me, skirt billowed wide around her. Then, as the music begins, she rises slowly, her torso moving in sinuous waves that I can't begin to imagine myself doing. Her arms, graceful and almost boneless, climb through the air in time with the music. She sways as if she has become the music.

Then suddenly, I'm dancing. Not here and now with Mel, but back in Wad Qol with the village girls in the grass next to the Panjshir River. And another time, years before that. In California. San Jose. At Darya and Tariq's wedding in the early '90s. The clans gathered. I'm there, in my own traditional *tunbaan*. *Hama* Bibi grabs my hand and leads me out to the center of the floor with the rest of the Afghan female guests, and Darya, of course, for the *Attan*. Oh, to see Darya dance!

The music ends, and I'm no longer in California. Not dancing with Darya. Mel turns to me expectantly, her eyes shining. "Whaddaya think?"

I wipe the tear off my cheek, hoping Mel doesn't notice. "Beautiful. Do all the girls dance this well?"

She dismisses my comment with a flick of her hand. "That's nothing. I just started learning."

I laugh.

"What's so funny?"

"Oh, to be able to dance like you."

"Really?" She sounds uncharacteristically in need of encouragement.

"I wish you could see how gorgeous—" Bringing my palms together and pressing them to my lips, I blink back the tears that are threatening again. Damn, I mean to be complimenting my daughter, not sinking back into grief.

On the kitchen counter where I left it, my cell phone rings. Hoping against hope that it's Cerelli, I bolt across the room to answer before he hangs up. "Hey!"

"Hello?" A woman's voice. Not Cerelli. I sink in disappointment onto the stool.

"It is Bibi Faludi here. This is Annie? My phone says that I missed a call from you."

"*Hama* Bibi! I'm very glad you called. *Salâm! Che hâl dâred?*"

"*Khub astom, tashakor.*"

It's been months since I last spoke with Darya's auntie, years since we've seen each other, but just this easily, we slide into a conversation in Dari. Mel hovers over my shoulder, struggling to hear Bibi, but her Dari is limited to just a few words, and her frustration is palpable.

"My daughter is here with me. Is it all right if she listens?" I ask in English.

"Of course."

I tap the speaker button and rest the phone on the counter.

"Hello to you, Emmeline." Bibi's voice fills the kitchen. "I have that correct? There is no name like that in Dari, but I have always found it to be quite beautiful. And, of course, it is such an important name."

"*Salâm,*" says Mel, looking confused. "My name's important?"

"Why yes. Emmeline Pankhurst."

"Who?"

"One of the world's great suffragettes. She fought for women's rights in England."

Mel's eyes smile. One sharp nod tells me she likes sharing her name with such a woman.

"You are a dancer, I believe? That is what Darya and Seema always told me."

"Yes." Mel sounds suddenly modest.

I step in. "She is. In fact, she's part of an Afghan dance troupe.

They're performing this weekend to raise money to rebuild Darya's school."

"Oh, what a wonderful thing for these girls to do! I think that is why you are calling me?"

"Yes, as a matter of fact." So far, so good. I give Mel a thumbs-up and go on to explain all the details, finishing with the idea of me taking the money to Wad Qol. "I should be safe there, don't you think?"

"Yes, I think you will be. Of course, one never knows." She's quiet for a moment, probably thinking about the same thing I am: Darya's murder in Wad Qol just five months ago. "When will you come?"

"I have an assignment in Kabul beginning December 1st. I'd like to deliver the money before that and could use your help. I've been trying to reach Bahar Abdulin's parents. To tell them about all this. To make sure the villagers want to rebuild the school. I have a phone number for her mother, Gulshan, but I haven't been able to get through."

"Now I understand. You know, of course, that Bahar is one of my students, and that is the reason you are calling me."

"At an unspeakably late hour. I apologize."

"It is no matter." I picture her batting away my apology with a wave of her hand—just like Darya used to do. "Omar has been on the phone all night. Because of that, I have been awake. Bahar is a lovely girl. Very bright. She will make a wonderful teacher. I will ask her to call her mother. How much money do you have?"

I look at Mel, who shrugs nonchalantly, then says, "Ten thousand dollars."

"Did Emmeline just say ten thousand dollars?" She sounds breathless with disbelief.

I smile. "She did. These girls have been working hard."

"Oh, my. That is a very large amount of money. I will talk to Bahar in the morning. Then, I will call you. Perhaps this Saturday we could converse again?"

"That would be great."

"One more thing, Annie. Your mention of Emmeline's interest in Afghan dance. Do you remember the *Attan* we danced at my Darya's wedding all those years ago?"

"Of course." I nod at the phone. "I was just thinking of it."

"Continue to think about it. That is how I am healing my wounded heart. I remember you and Darya. How beautifully you danced that day."

"Thank you." Another tear works its way out from the corner of my eye.

"Remember that, my child. It will help you. Allah willing, we will talk again soon."

I end the call and turn to Mel, who's staring at me. It's hard to tell if what I see in her eyes is disbelief or admiration. "You danced the *Attan*? For real? Mom, that's not the easiest dance."

I shrug. "It was a special day. I learned it for Dar."

12

MEL LOOKS DUBIOUSLY AT the apple-walnut *roat* I'm carrying up to an English Tudor house on North Maryland Avenue in Shorewood. "I dunno, Mom. A loaf of bread? Is that the best we can do? Maybe we should go buy some *baklava*."

"Just you wait," I say more confidently than I'm feeling. "Mrs. Faqiri is going to love this bread. It may not be as pretty as the loaves Auntie Dar used to make, but if this is anywhere near as good as the loaf Bonita and I tasted, it'll be fine." I ring the bell.

Mel looks ready to press her point—just as the front door opens. Too late.

"Mel! And you have brought your mother. Welcome to our home. I am Firash." He reaches to shake my hand.

"Annie Hawkins." I give him the round loaf of sweet bread sprinkled with nigella seeds. "I know this isn't exactly a dinner bread—"

He accepts the gift with both hands. "In this house, *roat* is the perfect bread for every meal. I thank you. Awa! My dear! Come greet our guests."

Awa Faqiri literally dances into the small foyer from the kitchen, her eyes seeking out the bread in her husband's hands. "Strewth!" she exclaims excitedly, the Aussie slang catching my attention. "Where did you find this? I have looked all over Milwaukee for *roat*. Please tell me you did not drive to Chicago!"

Mel steps forward. "Mom made it," she says way too smugly.

"Truly?" Then, grabbing the loaf from her husband, she leads me into the kitchen. "I must have a taste now. You don't mind?"

I raise my hands. "I hope you like it."

"Both apples and walnuts?"

I nod. "I know it's not the usual recipe. But it's authentic. From my friend Darya's *mâdar kalân*."

She closes her eyes as she chews. I'm pretty sure I hear her humming. "You must share this recipe with me. I insist."

I inhale the aromas filling the kitchen. The national rice dish of Afghanistan, *kabuli palaw*, and eggplant, *banjân borani*. Then, oh, be still my heart. "Is that *qormah- e-sabzi*? Darya and I used to cook that together. This is an absolute treat for me."

She smiles. "I am very glad."

I laugh. "I know it's none of my business, but am I detecting an Australian accent? Mixed with Dari?"

"Too right." She laughs as she arranges food on the platters arrayed across the counter. "Firash and I are both from Kabul, but we actually met at university in Melbourne. Last year, he was hired to teach at university here."

"UW-Milwaukee, I assume."

She nods.

"That must have been quite a move for you."

"It was daunting, yes. But we have such lovely neighbors. And Mel befriended Yasmine, which has been tremendous for all of us.

Now, we are quite settled. Our lives are nothing like what you do, of course—traveling for months at a time. That must be very . . ." She's clearly searching for a word. "Adventurous."

I laugh. "Not always so adventurous. I seem to spend a lot of time waiting—to get in-country. Then, once I'm *in*, it consumes me—in a good way."

She opens a cabinet and reaches for another dish. "You were in Afghanistan recently? That is what Mel tells us."

I'm suddenly on alert, wondering where this is going. "Late last spring, in fact. I was teaching a photography course."

Turning around, she puts the dish on the counter, then leans forward, closing the space between us. "I am not one to doubt your daughter—she's a wonderful girl—but please be honest with me. Mel told us that you have agreed to take the money we are raising to Afghanistan. I want to make sure she didn't just 'volunteer' you as daughters are apt to do."

I open my mouth, but she holds up her hand.

"Firash and I are very well aware of how dangerous it is there. Please, if you really do not wish to do this, tell us. We will find another way to get the money there. Perhaps we will have to wire it after all."

"Mel did ask me." No need to point out that she asked way after she assured the Faqiris I would do it. "As it happens, I'm scheduled to go to Kabul next month anyway. But even if I weren't, this is something that means a great deal to me. Darya is, was, my friend—"

Awa nods. She clearly knows all about Dar.

I hold on to the edge of the counter. "It's important to me to carry on her work. The girls at this school will make a tremendous difference to the future of their country."

She reaches across the steaming platters of food and puts her hand over mine. "That is exactly what I hoped to hear. Firash also will be relieved. Oh! One more thing, if I may be so bold. The donors would love to see the new school. Is there any way you could document the progress while you're in Wad Qol? That is, of course, if you're there while they're building it."

I nod. "I'll likely be there for just a couple days, but I'll do what I can."

"Oh, I didn't mean—it's just that donors do like to see where their money goes."

"Of course." Am I in the middle of a conspiracy or what?

"Thank you."

And before I can point out that she and the girls and the members of the mosque are the ones who deserve thanks, she surveys the serving dishes lined up on the counter and announces, "Now, we are ready to eat."

We carry the dishes into the dining room until the table is mounded with food. The intoxicating aromas have me salivating. I make a quick note to tell Cerelli about this meal, only to remember that he's no longer talking to me. I lock him back inside my aching heart and do my best to enjoy the dinner.

Directly across from me, with Mel on one side and Yasmine on the other, sits the young-ish imam from the Faqiris' mosque. He tells me his name is Nouman, then points to his *taquiyah*, elaborately embroidered with tiny pink and blue flowers. "Flowerbeds." He laughs. "That is my name." Which leads us to go around the table, each telling what our name means.

Yasmine begins. "Mine's easy. Yasmine. Like the flower jasmine." She glances sideways at Nouman. Then at Mel, sitting on his other side. The girls have him cornered. He doesn't stand a chance.

Firash picks up the thread. "I guess my name tells you exactly who I am: perception and ingenuity. What better qualities for an engineer?"

My turn. "Anna. Or in Pashto, *Anaa*, which means 'grandmother.'"

Firash wags his finger at me. "Oh no, you are being too modest. The name Anaa pairs with Malalai. Malalai Anaa is one of the great heroines of Afghanistan. She was the grandmother of our nation."

I look down at my plate, remembering the night I was in Wad Qol, furious with Cerelli for having told Darya about my PTSD. He calmed me down with that story. When I glance up, Mel is staring at me.

"I will go next." Awa smiles. "Another easy one! My name means 'voice.' I guess my parents knew I would always be talking."

"And so, you were blessed with the most beautiful voice." Firash beams at his wife.

I clutch the napkin in my lap. To see such love and devotion. My heart hurts a little more.

We arrive at Mel, and suddenly she's looking stricken. "I don't know what my name means," she blurts out. "It's Emmeline. Totally old-fashioned. But there was another Emmeline who helped get women the right to vote in England."

"It's such a beautiful name!" says Yasmine, reaching across Nouman's plate to squeeze Mel's hand.

"Yes, it is," says Awa, beaming at my daughter. "And I bet there is a story."

"Well." Mel looks at me. "My mom named me for her grammy. She actually grew up living with her."

Nouman is the first to find his voice. "And now, every time I see you, I will think of a mother who loved her grandmother so dearly that she gave her name to you. Allah loves beauty."

"Thank you." Mel is enough of a performer that she doesn't blush.

The conversation shifts to Sunday's dance and buffet. Yasmine is beside herself with how well their rehearsal went.

"Why don't you and Mel show us one of the dances?" says Awa.

"No!" Firash presses his hand to his heart. "I insist on being surprised on Sunday."

The girls giggle. Then, Mel surprises us all. "I just found out that my mom has done some traditional Afghan dancing! The *Attan!*"

All eyes are on me. My blush climbs up my chest to my neck and on to my cheeks. I shake my head to fend off their growing excitement. "Oh, no! Really. I stumbled my way through because it was my best friend's wedding, and she made me promise to dance. I'm not anything like these two." I smile at Yasmine and glare at Mel.

"Mom, that's not true. *Hama* Bibi said you and Auntie Dar danced it beautifully."

My heart clenches a bit more. How that's possible, I'm not sure. Perhaps if I'm able to visit her in Kabul, Bibi will tell me how the memory of that dance has become a blessing for her.

"The *Attan* is our national dance." Awa's eyes are shining. "Did you know it was originally a Pashtun war dance?"

"Really?" Mel looks mesmerized.

Awa smiles. "It has since become a tradition at engagements and weddings. Usually it is the women who dance, but not always. Sometimes men sing love songs to the dancing women." She sighs at the romance of it, making me wonder if Firash sang at their wedding.

"Please, Annie, you will join the girls and dance on Sunday!" Firash enthuses. "And you, too, Awa. I haven't seen you dance in far too long. Since our wedding." The way he's looking at her, I bet he did sing. Sometimes these Afghan men really know how to do it right.

I smile and shake my head again. "Not me, I'm afraid. I want to photograph the dancers, not actually dance."

"Mom! It's just one dance. You can take pictures the rest of the time. Please?"

I hate it when she puts me on the spot. Which she seems to be doing more and more often. "I'll think about it."

Awa smiles sympathetically, the kind of smile one mother offers another when kids are nagging. "Whatever you decide, we must find a *tunbaan* for you to wear on Sunday. All the mothers will wear them, and although we probably won't dance, the traditional dresses will help us remember the days when we did."

"Thank you, but—" I'm just about to refuse Awa's offer of finding me a dress when I catch the look on Mel's face.

Don't ruin this for me, Mom.

"Actually, I have a *tunbaan*. Let me see if it still fits."

Another glance at Mel, and she's not any happier. She's not the biggest fan of my clothes, most of which are admittedly pretty old and not in the least fashionable. Well, wait until she sees this dress—assuming I can get it on. Then, I move us on to another subject. "And please, you must let me help with the cooking."

"*Roat!*" Firash grins. "We have all been sneaking out to the kitchen to nibble. This is what you must bring on Sunday."

WE'RE ALMOST HOME WHEN I hear my cell phone buzz the arrival of a new text. Not Cerelli, I'm sure. But as soon as we're in the apartment, I check.

I walk to the hill outside Kandahar
And see that tonight my Beloved's caravan has not gone far.

Seema. Awalmir is on the move. Without her. Why would she be telling me this?

"'Sup?" Mel crowds behind me.

"Another *landay* from Seema. Or Rahila." I hold up the phone so Mel can read the poem. "I still don't understand why she's texting me with the name Rahila instead of Seema."

"Mom, I told you. It's her pen name."

"I know you said that. But why use a pen name to text *me?*"

She rolls her eyes. "Didn't you tell me that it's dangerous for girls to write these poems? Because they're about love and sex? A pen name would be perfect. That way, if she's caught, she could say she didn't write it." She looks hopefully at me. "Right?"

"You are brilliant."

Mel taps the top of the screen. "Can't you trace her by the phone number?"

"Sawyer and Cerelli have been trying to do exactly that. But last I heard, they weren't having any luck." Of course, I haven't heard anything from Cerelli in six days. Not that I'm counting. I guess it's possible things have changed.

"Why's Seema's boyfriend sleeping in a caravan?"

"Huh?" I read the poem again, and that's when the real meaning hits me. Caravan. A group of people moving together across a desert. The image of a large group of Taliban, traveling in aging, white pickups and on motorcycles, flashes in front of me. My gut clenches. If Awalmir is on the move, along with other militants, they probably have an op underway. An attack. A bombing. Whatever it is, they're targeting someone. People are going to die. Police?

Military? U.S. soldiers? Innocent civilians? God only knows who. I've got to tell Cerelli. He's got to alert Sawyer. The Pentagon, the Afghans. Cerelli may not be taking my calls, but that doesn't mean I can't leave him a message about this latest *landay*.

So, I do.

13

FIRST THING SATURDAY MORNING, Mel leaves for the final dance rehearsal. Which gives me the perfect opportunity to search for my *tunbaan*. I open the lid of the blanket chest at the foot of my bed and breathe in the cedar that wafts up to greet me, then lift out one quilt after another. Each a different pattern. All intricately pieced. And in the corner of each, a stitched dedication. *Emmeline Hawkins Green, born May 20, 1999.* I set this aside to put on Mel's bed. *Anna Hawkins and Todd Green, married November 15, 1997. Anna Rachel Hawkins, born May 19, 1972.* My fingers tighten on the last of the quilts. *Rachel Margaret Hawkins, born August 1, 1944.* My mother. A mother I barely knew. But the quilts, so perfectly made. Grammy's legacy to me and eventually to Mel.

The last of the quilts piled on my bed, I angle out the false bottom to reveal my stash of treasures, securely hidden from everyone in my life. Not even Mel knows what's here. There, on top, wrapped in tissue paper, is the dress I wore to Darya's wedding.

Please let it be in good shape. And not need dry cleaning. I carefully fold back the paper. Antique gold dupioni silk. It's been twenty years since I last saw this dress, and it's more beautiful than I remember. Was the color always this vibrant, this intense? Or have the years given it depth? I trace the twenty-four-karat gold threads shooting through the weave. Tears prick my eyes as I see Darya standing in front of me, insisting that it's Afghan tradition for the bride's family to provide the dresses for the wedding party. Gently, so gently, I run my hands across the fabric. I can almost feel the tiny stitches *Mâdar Kalân*, Dar's grandmother, made with her needle. It wasn't until after the wedding that I learned there wasn't any such tradition. Darya Faludi simply wanted to give me this dress and knew I would never accept anything so valuable.

The magic is in the fabric. Brought from Kabul when the family emigrated, it was part of *Mâdar Kalân's* mother's dowry. Probably close to a hundred years old, it had been in the family for years—too precious to use. I trace the neckline. Simple, plain, no embroidery. It doesn't need any. Besides, the fabric is so fine, I doubt it could stand up to the elaborate needlework that's on most *tunbaans*. It's absolutely beautiful just the way it is. My own wedding dress couldn't compare to this.

Staring at it takes me back to my first day in Wad Qol last May. Darya and I were in my little room when I unwrapped the copper *shalwar kameez* Cerelli had bought for me. Dar was stunned when she saw it. She said something about how much it cost. Well, she would certainly have known. She also said it was much more than the apology I assumed Cerelli was offering. That it was an invitation. My heart clenches. It's been almost a week since our argument.

I stand in front of the cheval mirror and hold the dress up against me. The perfect thing to wear to a dance that will raise funds to rebuild Darya's school, to ensure her life's work continues. Taking this money to Afghanistan is absolutely the right thing for me to do. Anything to continue what my best friend began. *Oh, Dar . . .*

No pity party allowed. I study the reflection of the dress in the mirror. What are the chances it'll still fit? Doubtful. I've gained weight since my twenties. Best find out now. I shed my flannel shirt and jeans and let the dress float down over my head to my shoulders. Possible. But I'll need help with the buttons.

"Bonita?" I call down the stairs. "Could you come up for a minute? And leave Finn down there, please."

Finn barks his protest.

"You've hurt his feelings," chides Bonita as she clomps up the back stairs, stopping suddenly when she catches sight of me. "Annie Hawkins! Where did *this* come from?"

"Darya's grandmother made it for me—for Dar's wedding. What do you think?"

"What I think is you better take out an insurance policy."

"I'm considering wearing it tomorrow for the dance perfor- mance. Mel and Awa are making noises about me needing to be properly turned out." I bite my lower lip. "I don't want to embarrass Mel."

Finn's barking turns into a howl, loud and sustained.

"You won't. Not in this dress."

"Will you do the buttons for me? They're impossible to reach."

Bonita's fingers work their way up my back. "How come you've never worn this?"

I snort out a laugh. "To where?"

"I can think of something you could wear it for. If that man would get his act together."

"Don't go there, Bonita. Things are just fine the way they are." Yeah, right.

She ties the bow at the back and spins me around so I can look in the mirror. "Not bad." High praise from Bonita.

I nod. "Hard to believe it fits."

Finn ratchets his howling up a notch.

"Oh, God. I can't take it anymore." Marching to the door at the top of the back staircase, I throw it open and glare. "Okay. You win. But don't you dare come close to me."

Finn slinks past me, then heads into the bedroom and climbs oh-so-carefully onto the bed where he stretches out across the quilts.

MEL AND I SPEND THE rest of Saturday making loaves of *roat*. Somehow, she's figured out that the traditional recipe calls for walnuts *or* apples. Not both. As a result, despite my extremely authentic and delicious recipe, she insists that at least some loaves have only one filling or the other. Since when did my daughter become so traditional?

We're both molding round loaves on cookie sheets when I ask, "What happened to your hair?"

"What?"

"I really liked the green."

She fluffs her beautifully styled, two-inch-long dark-brown hair and starts in on another loaf. "I needed a change."

I should just accept that answer and let it go. But I can't. After a year of pink and periwinkle and peacock, this is major. "Seems kind of sudden."

Annoyance pulsates off her. She slaps the loaf into shape. "Do you have to know everything?"

I take a step back. "I'm curious. That's all."

"Jeez, Mom, you're beyond transparent."

Okay, so I'm wondering if there's a boy in the picture, despite her assertion last weekend that she's 'off boys.' I'm guessing a boy who isn't crazy about green hair. Even if it was the most beautiful shade of peacock. My thoughts stop in place as I see Mel sitting next to Nouman at dinner last night. Oh, surely not. He's got to be thirty. At least. Besides, any man who wears a flowered *taquiyah* certainly wouldn't object to green hair. Would he?

She finishes with her loaf and takes over shaping mine into a rounder round. "And no, it's not Nouman."

I open my mouth to declare my innocence, but she cuts me off. "He's *old*. Besides, Yasmine likes him."

"Sisterhood. I'm proud of you."

A major eye roll. "I'm so not a feminist."

I raise my eyebrow, about to argue the point, when my cell phone buzzes on the counter behind us. Please, let it be Cerelli. Is that too much to ask? The irony doesn't escape me: I'm ready to argue with my daughter about whether or not she's a feminist while I'm waiting around for a guy to call.

It's *Hama* Bibi. As promised. I press the speaker button and cross my fingers that she's talked to Bahar and Gulshan.

"Annie? This is Bibi calling from Kabul. The plans, they are all made at this end. Gulshan, though, she has a special request."

"Already? You're a miracle worker. What would Gulshan like?" I'm imagining a book or a better cell phone—something from the States that she'd like me to bring over.

"She would like you to come to Wad Qol and stay for a week, or preferably two."

"Oh!" Next to me, Mel is nodding excitedly.

"You are agreeable?"

"Say yes!" Mel whispers with a sharp elbow in my ribs.

I look at her cross-eyed, ready to tell Bibi that I've got to think about this, make arrangements, that I'll be back in touch. I think about Cerelli insisting my 'few days' would become a 'few weeks.' And hear myself say, "Of course!" After all, I've got to respect my hosts' wishes.

"Wonderful! Now, tell me when you will come."

She wants an arrival date? Good God, I don't even have a ticket. Or a visa. A quick calculation. I need to meet up with the TNN crew on December 1st. And now Gulshan wants me to stay a week or two in Wad Qol. "November 15th? Is that okay?"

"That is very good. My husband will be away at a meeting. You will be able to stay a night with me."

"Please. The last thing I want is to inconvenience you. I can always book a room at the InterContinental." I know full well she'll never allow that. Afghans are known for their hospitality.

"No. That I cannot have. It will all be very easy with Omar in Pakistan. Now, I will arrange for a driver to meet you at the airport. And I will have Bahar tell her parents to expect you around that time."

"Thank you."

"Oh, my dear Annie. You are bringing joy back into my life. We will have dinner and the entire evening to visit. The next day, Bahar and her brother will drive you to Wad Qol. Farrakh is his name."

"Aren't they both in school? I can't have them missing classes."

"Please do not worry. This is something they both wish to do."

I raise one hand in surrender. Not that she can see it. "Okay, I will accept gratefully."

"Now, if there is a problem, if you have any difficulties, you will call me. Let me give you a different number." She slowly reads off another phone number.

"Got it." As soon as I hang up, the hair on the back of my neck starts to prickle. As a journalist, I've followed my share of leads into potentially dangerous situations, and I'm getting the same vibes now. Like I've just taken a step down a very deep, dark hole. Maybe it's a good thing Cerelli doesn't know about any of this. He'd kill me. Probably for good reason.

Mel has opened the oven door and pulled out the rack halfway. "How do I tell if it's done?"

I grab the tester from the new utensil holder that came with the kitchen remodel and plunge it into the nearest loaf. "Done." Four loaves come out to rest on cooling racks.

"So, is everything set for you to go?"

"Plane tickets and a visa. TNN can take care of that for me. Then, I'm good to go."

"This is so great! It's really happening." Her eyes sparkle.

The back of my neck is still prickling.

"Okay, back to work!" She shoves a large bowl in front of me and hands me the sifter filled with flour.

"How many are we making?" I nod at the eight loaves cooling on various surfaces around the kitchen. Not to mention the other four now baking.

"More."

"Sweetie, this is a lot of bread. Just how many people will be at this thing tomorrow?"

She purses her lips and does a quick mental tally. "Yasmine says we've sold a couple hundred tickets. So far."

"And it's at the mosque?"

"No." She shakes her head. "The imam thought dancing could be tricky. It's at the high school."

I stare at her incredulously. "Shorewood High School? How did you ever get that to happen?"

She shrugs. "Yasmine and I went to a Board of Education meeting. Dr. Faqiri came with us. No biggie." But I can see from her smile just how proud she is of what she's accomplished.

I cross my fingers that Todd and Catherine Elizabeth don't get wind of this. Or there will most definitely be hell to pay.

14

EARLY SUNDAY AFTERNOON, BONITA comes with Mel and me to the high school. My Lowepro comes, too. This will be one of the few times in years that I'll see Mel dance, and I'm going to photograph every single moment.

The parking lot next to the gym is nearly full. Dozens of women are carrying in pans of food, all carefully covered with aluminum foil. From the aromas, I'm guessing lamb and roasted chicken kababs and *kofta*. And that's just to start. We add our loaves of *roat* to the mountain of covered dishes on the row of tables across one end of the gym. Tables and chairs line the other three white-painted concrete walls. The center of the gym, with its highly polished wooden floor, has been left clear for the dancing.

Awa Faqiri is clearly in charge. When she catches sight of us, she waves us over and points to two garment bags slung over the back of a nearby chair. "Annie, I brought you a *tunbaan* in case you couldn't find yours. And Bonita, I have brought one for you, too."

Bonita shakes her head. "Thanks, but my jeans are just fine."

Awa smiles. "Of course, whatever you prefer."

Standing in front of us, Awa looks truly stunning in her lavishly embroidered dress. Mine will look absolutely plain in comparison. "Thanks for this. I did find my old one. I'll try them both and see which works best."

"Of course!" Her smile lights up the cavernous gym.

I grab the garment bag and, along with my pack, retreat to the locker room where the heat combined with the smell of chlorine from the indoor pool nearly do me in. Not so Mel and the nineteen other girls who are changing into their costumes. They're all chatting and laughing, totally oblivious to the fumes that are burning my throat.

I pull my loaner dress from the bag. Lovely satin and nearly as heavily embroidered as the one Awa is wearing. Where could she possibly have found a dress to fit me on such short notice? A wonderful thing for her to do, but it's really not me.

Mel twirls across the locker room to take a look and pass judgment. "It's nice, Mom."

"It is. But I think I'll wear what I brought."

"Mom—" I know that tone: *Don't embarrass me!*

I unzip my pack, take out the dress that I've rolled in tissue paper, and furl it out in front of me.

Next to me, Yasmine gasps. "Oh, Ms. Hawkins! That's the most beautiful *tunbaan* I've ever seen!"

"Oh, Mom! It *is* beautiful. Where did you get this?"

"This is what I wore when I was in your Auntie Dar's wedding."

"How come I've never seen it before?"

"Because I've kept it well hidden."

Mel takes the dress from me. "Come on! Let's get this on you."

I pull off my T-shirt and jeans and feel the dress float down over my head and into place. Behind me, Mel buttons, then tugs the ties into a tight bow to emphasize my still reasonable waist. I trace my fingers along the scooped neckline.

"Do you have a necklace, Ms. Hawkins?" Yasmine stands back, studying me, then shakes her head. "No. No necklace. This dress is perfection. You really don't need anything else."

Mel nods her approval. Then hands me the loose pants made of the same fragile gold silk, gathered at the ankles.

I look down at my black Keds high-tops. Not exactly the best choice.

"Don't even think about it!" Mel hands me a pair of ballerina flats. "Well, Mrs. Faqiri said she'd have a dress for you to wear, so I packed an extra pair!"

Meekly, I slide on the shoes. Perfect fit.

Looking at myself in the full-length mirror, I feel transformed. How I imagine I would have looked in the outfit Cerelli gave me last spring. An outfit I never got to wear thanks to Seema and Awalmir's rampage through my clothes. But something's not quite right. A moment later, I realize why I feel underdressed. I'm not wearing a headscarf. Neither is Mel. Everyone else is though.

"Is there anything else in the bag?" I ask.

"Like what?"

"Like a headscarf."

"Oh, Annie." Awa is standing next to me, her eyes heavily kohled, her lips a mesmerizing red—far, far, *far* from plain and simple. "This *tunbaan*, it is perfect for you. With your hair. Please, do not cover your hair."

"Well, then." I take a spin in front of the mirror. "Do I look presentable?"

"Oh, Mom! You look gorgeous."

I take it that's a good thing.

IT TURNS OUT AWA IS also the mistress of ceremonies. She approaches the center of the room to thunderous applause from an audience that numbers a whole lot more than the two hundred Mel told me bought advance tickets. I'd put it closer to five hundred. The dancing comes first. The crowd leaves an aisle for the girls in their mirror-clad and sequined dresses, heavy gold necklaces, earrings, and bracelets to sashay into the gym. Then come the boys in white linen *shalwar kameezes* with long embroidered vests to match. A line dance with boys on one side, girls on the other. Couples meet in the middle. The boys set the steps, which the girls imitate. I see Mel cringe when a couple of girls and then a boy go to the wrong lines after their turn. But considering how quickly this performance came together, I think they're brilliant.

Before I realize what I'm doing, I've unzipped my pack and liberated a camera. Then, I'm moving around the gym, weaving my way through the audience, focusing in on the dancers. And seriously regretting my decision to wear this dress, which is creating a challenge every time I want to kneel down. *Please don't rip!*

The dances continue, mostly the girls, led by Yasmine. Dressed in fuchsia, her lustrous black hair peeks out from beneath her matching headscarf. Oh, she's good! Mel is, too, but she doesn't yet *live* the dance quite the way Yasmine does.

To give the dancers a rest, Awa takes the floor, microphone in hand. "Thank you, everyone, for coming this afternoon." She raises her hand in tribute to the packed gym. "I'm sure you all know that on an occasion like this, I cannot possibly avoid singing." Around me, people clap and cheer. "You are too kind," she says before launching into a traditional Dari folk song.

The voice that comes out of this petite woman is dramatic and powerful but also angelic, soaring to the high ceilings of the gym, filling the room. The crowd is on their feet. Many are singing along, their hands clasped over their hearts.

This voice. No wonder everyone laughed at dinner on Friday night when Awa joked about her name. I know this voice. Where have I heard her before? I dig into the recesses of my brain and come up with nothing. Sinking onto my chair, I find myself next to Firash.

"My wife loves to sing." He smiles proudly, then looks at me closely. "You do not know? This is unforgiveable of me. I always assume everyone knows who she is."

I shake my head.

"Perhaps you have heard of her as Awa Sayeed? That was her family name. After we married, she stopped singing professionally."

Of course I know of Awa Sayeed. I had wondered what happened when she stopped recording. Why did she stop? With a voice like that? But I don't ask. Everyone makes her own choice.

Awa's song carries to the corners of the large room. When she quiets the last note, she walks to the far end of the gym to where Firash and I are sitting. She threads her way through the crowd, her hand held out. Not to Firash, to me. *No, please, no.* I start to shake my head, then think better of it. The last thing I want to do is make a scene. So, I take her hand and let her lead me out of the crowd to the center of the room. One quick look over my shoulder, and I see Bonita has her hand protectively cradling my camera. And my Lowepro.

"We would like to end today's performance with a very special dance," Awa announces. "I am sure most of the women in this room know these steps and have danced the *Attan* at least once in their lives. Please join us."

A change of plan—probably hatched after dinner Friday night. I should have suspected.

Awa begins the dance. I follow her steps. Then Yasmine and Mel lead the girls into the gym, and we dance our way into a circle. The beat of the drums is slow to start as we wind our way around and around the room. The tempo gradually picks up as we reach into our imaginary baskets of flowers and cast the blossoms up into the air. One by one, middle-aged women, many of them wearing traditional *tunbaans* and all of them smiling, join the circle. Then, a few older women.

Soon, I'm back at Darya's wedding, following in her footsteps, casting flowers visible only to me. In front of me, Dar looks back and smiles. She's happy. So incredibly happy. To have found Tariq. Her life's partner. Behind me, *Hama* Bibi, in her forties but not yet married, nods to the drummers to pick up the tempo yet again. And then, we are whirling and spinning. Around and around. Hands climbing into the air above our heads, showering flowers onto the audience. Many of the women take off their headscarves and wave them above their heads.

Until finally, after a half hour, we sink to the floor, spent.

It is Awa who helps me to my feet, not Darya. "Never," she whispers in my ear, "have I seen anyone dance the *Attan* with such spirit, such rapture. You became the dance."

I wave her off. "I'm not the dancer in the family."

"Today, you are." She tucks my arm around hers and walks me back to our table where Bonita is smugly checking out the video she just shot.

"That's Mel you recorded, right? Please tell me I'm not on that."

She smiles. "Didn't know you could dance like that. Now I know where Mel gets her talent." Her eyes narrow. "I understand that's a wedding dance. Might be good for you to plan on doing it again. Soon."

Bonita's words stop me in my tracks. "Oh, please."

She mutters something indistinct, and then we eat.

There is no need to worry that Awa will introduce me as the person who's going to take the money raised to Afghanistan, to Wad Qol. "That would be foolish!" she says when I tell her my concern. Firash agrees. As does Nouman.

"Most of the people in this room know why you are here," Nouman continues. "We all want this money to go to Afghanistan to rebuild the school for the girls. We do not want the publicity that might accompany this mission. Or harm you. No. Allah loves peace and beauty, not violence."

"HOW MUCH MONEY DID you make today?" I ask Mel on the drive home.

"A lot."

"What's 'a lot'?" asks Bonita.

"I heard Mr. Faqiri tell Nouman that it was about $20K."

It's all I can do to keep my foot from slamming the brake pedal to the floor. "You mean, twenty *thousand* dollars?"

"Yeeaaah."

Holy shit. "I had no idea. That's amazing." I wonder what the net will be after they cover expenses. Whatever, it's still a hell of a lot of money. I do a quick calculation, adding today's take to last weekend's and the fundraisers before that. We're talking thirty thousand dollars. That I know of. Which complicates things. According to the consul in Chicago, I can take that much into Afghanistan, but I'll have to register the cash in my name with paperwork going to departments throughout the government. I'd been hoping to fly under the radar, so to speak. But I can't see any way around it. If I don't declare it and they catch me, they'll arrest me and seize the money.

I pull up to the stoplight at the intersection of Lake Drive and Lincoln Memorial and look at my daughter. Where did she come from? Where did she get this talent? This vision? I can't possibly tell her about this potential glitch with getting the money into the country.

15

I'M EASING INTO SLEEP when Chris Cardona calls on my cell. "Word on the street is you're heading to Afghanistan two weeks early. Taking a side trip to Wad Qol." No 'hello.' No 'how are you holding up?' Then again, this is Chris. My boss since day one. We've phoned and texted so often over the last eight years that we've cut out nearly all the niceties.

"I take it you've been talking to Kevin? The traitor."

"He's my assistant, lest you forget."

"Is there a problem?"

"Not if you remember to be back in Kabul by December 1st."

"No worries. I'll be at the InterCon with time to spare."

"And do me a favor. According to Al Shabakat, Piera McNeil and her crew will be in Kabul to cover the negotiations. Please make it easier on the legal team and me by staying as far away from her as possible. That goes for anyone who has ever worked for the network."

That's a tall order. Almost every journalist I know does a stint at Al Shabakat. It's like a rite of passage. There's no way I can steer clear of everyone. Then, I catch on. "The lawsuit. You know something?" My heart starts to beat faster.

"There's been progress."

"What does that mean?"

"That's all I can say for now. I probably shouldn't have said that much."

"Chris—"

"Look, Annie, just let it go."

"Let it go? This is my career, my life we're talking about. I've got the right to know what's going on."

"Let's just say it's pretty much been taken out of our hands."

"What the hell does that mean?" I rake my fingers through my hair, catching tangles and pulling at them until my scalp hurts.

"Just between you and me—and this goes no further—the Pentagon is calling the shots now."

"Say what?"

"Sorry. That's all I know."

Or all he can say without putting his own job at risk. Three seconds. That's all it takes for the pieces to fall into place. "Cerelli talked to you and Marcus."

"Annie, you know I can't answer that."

"You just did."

"I'm not confirming anything. But hypothetically speaking, would it be that bad if he did straighten out this mess?"

I count to ten. My free hand curls into a fist. "You know as well as I do what'll happen if Al Shabakat finds out Cerelli's involved, that he gave me—" Damn, I said too much.

"Like I said, it's out of my hands now. I'm just relaying Marcus' message about staying away from Piera McNeil."

"Consider it signed, sealed, and delivered."

"This is serious. Do not mess with that woman. Do not speak to her. If you do, all bets are off."

I let that sit for a good ten seconds. "What if *she* comes looking for *me?* That's what she did back in May. Every frigging time I saw her, she initiated it, stalking me like some kind of paparazzi. Starting at Dubai International."

"And you think this all goes back to you being with Nic Parker Lowe? By the way, I've heard the rumors about you two—"

I grit my teeth. "Nothing is happening between Nic and me."

"Yeah, I know. Nic set me straight that day we met in my office." Chris pauses. "Do you have any idea why this woman has it in for you?"

"You mean other than a crazed obsession? Honestly, I don't have a clue. But you know, she helped herself to my mail at the hotel. She called Mel and got her talking. Then, there she was at Dalan Sang, hovering over the bombing site in a chopper. And Wad Qol, of course."

"I've seen the Dalan Sang video. When were you going to let me in on these other pertinent details?" He sounds happier than he did a few minutes ago. "Let me pass all this on to Marcus. Meanwhile, keep your distance. We're close to putting this entire frigging mess to bed. Do not compromise this investigation."

That sounds a hell of a lot like a warning. I say the only thing I can. "Of course not." He ends the call before I can ask any more questions, before I can tell him Cerelli's theory that Piera was probably using me to get who she really wanted: Cerelli himself. Just as well that I didn't say anything. If Cerelli wanted Chris or Marcus to know that, he would've told them. Maybe he already did.

I'm in a quandary. I should be happy that this whole awful episode with Piera could well resolve in my favor. But Chris as good as told me that it's because Cerelli has gotten the Pentagon involved. Which means even more people know about what I did with that damned Sig. Not that Cerelli himself would ever leak this, but who knows about these other Pentagon types. Or what Al Shabakat might do. If the full story gets out, it could cost Cerelli his career, possibly his life. My career will be toast, too. TNN would probably have to cut me loose, and no other network would touch me. And as I well know, word always gets out.

Besides which, I just can't have Cerelli swooping in to rescue me. The helpless damsel. Incompetent. Beholden. That's a reputation I can't afford to have. And definitely not the kind of relationship I *want* to have with him. Once he starts taking care of me, the next step will be him telling me what I can and can't do. Which he's already tried to do. Damn it, I spent way too many years with Todd telling me to stay home, and it all but killed my soul. I can't let that happen again.

I'm not Todd. Cerelli's voice echoes in my head.

Maybe not. But you're getting too close.

Clearly, it's time for another talk. I glance at my cell. It's late. Even later in D.C. I call him anyway. As I listen to his phone ring, I plan what I'm going to say. Except he doesn't answer. Yet another voice mail message. My calm and rational words go out the window. "I *told* you not to call Chris Cardona. I begged you. But you did it anyway. Stop interfering in my life! Please?" Stabbing my finger against the END CALL button, I drop the cell on the bed.

And immediately clutch my knees to my chest. Oh, God, why did I do that? The man is just trying to help me out of an impossible situation.

Have you considered, observes my inner voice, *that it's not just you he's taking care of?*

Shit! Of course! He's got operatives who are still in-country. And not just in Afghanistan, but all over that part of the world. That's why the big boys at the Pentagon have taken over.

I stare at my cell phone, willing it to ring, for Cerelli to call. *Please ignore my rant! I love you!* I quickly sketch out my apology. Full grovel. But the phone sits forlornly silent.

16

MONDAY MORNING. MEL IS off to school. I roll back into bed, prepared to sleep in. I revel in the luxury until my cell shrieks angrily from my bedside table. It's got to be Cerelli. No one else would dare call me before 8:00 a.m. I shift quickly into apology mode, take a deep breath, roll over, and answer. "Hmm?"

"Annie." Todd's voice. Not a happy sound. Definitely not the intimate and seductive voice of a week ago.

"Todd, do you have any idea what time it is?"

"You should be glad I waited this late to call."

"What's the problem?"

"You know what the problem is."

"Apparently, I don't. Enlighten me."

"Annie, we talked about Mel and that new friend of hers. Jasmin."

"Yasmine. Her name is Yasmine. Faqiri."

"Her name isn't the issue."

"Then, what *is*?"

"Did you see the local news last night? Or the *Journal Sentinel* this morning?"

I sit up and lean back against my headboard, my pillow scrunched behind me. "Not yet. I'm sure you'll tell me what to look for." Coffee. I need caffeine to help me think clearly.

"You're damn right I will. On the news last night, there was a feature story about you and our daughter. You looked like a pair of idiots. As for this morning's paper, just look at the second section, first page."

I close my eyes. Media? Of course there were reporters at the fundraiser. "Idiots? That's pretty strong."

"The two of you were dancing with a bunch of-of—hell, I didn't even know they were allowed to dance." I stare at the phone. Where is this coming from? The Todd I knew wasn't xenophobic. Darya and Tariq were our best friends. Not just my friends—our friends. There were plenty of times that Todd and Tariq went off to play golf while Dar and I did whatever.

"That whole 'allowed to dance' question is debatable. It's more of a cultural thing. Anyway, this was a traditional Afghan dance. It was originally Pashtun, but now it's really considered the national dance. The *Attan*."

"Annie, I don't give a fuck what kind of dance it was. What bothers me is that you violated our agreement and exposed Mel to—hell, you probably *encouraged* her to do this."

The insanity of this conversation finally hits home. "You know, I wish I could take credit for some small part of this, but I can't. Yes, I was there. As were hundreds of other people from all over the North Shore. In fact, I chatted with your next-door neighbor. Jay Taylor, right?"

"Jay was there?" He sounds suddenly defeated.

"With his family. His wife and daughters actually joined in the dancing at one point."

Silence fills the line. I should tell Todd that I'm going to Afghanistan. No worries, though, because Bonita's right downstairs. Mel will be absolutely fine. But I don't. If he calls me, which seems to be happening with greater frequency than I like, his call will follow me to Afghanistan. And once I'm in Wad Qol where reception is less than reliable, his calls will go to voice messages. Where they'll stay, unanswered until I get back to Kabul. Or, with any luck, until I get back to the States. And really, what does he have to worry about? Mel sleeping upstairs and Bonita down is no different than the sleeping arrangement at the big house on Lake Drive. Plus, Finn's here, always on guard duty. At least, that's what I tell myself. I know damn well he won't see it that way. And Catherine Elizabeth definitely won't. Instead, I stab the red button on my cell and quietly end this insane, obnoxious call.

Thank God in a few weeks I'll be going to Afghanistan.

November, 2015
Kabul, Afghanistan

WE'RE MAKING OUR FINAL DESCENT into Hamid Karzai International Airport, and I've got to decide what to do. I'm carrying thirty thousand dollars divvied up in money belts, my boots, my underwear, and the secret compartment of my Lowepro. That's ten thousand more than I can legally bring into the country without going on record. Do I try to smuggle it in? Or declare it all? Either way, there's a lot that could go wrong. They catch me smuggling, they arrest me. I declare it, the Customs officials could easily pocket the money and deny they ever saw it. Once I get through Customs, the Security and Financial Intelligence Unit is likely to hit me up as soon as *they* see the declaration with my name and local address. Then, there's the police. This is a country where every single person wants to take a cut.

Once we land, I pass through Immigration. No problem here. They just want to see my passport and make sure my visa is valid.

Then, I move on to the Foreign Registration desk. Technically, this isn't compulsory, but any foreigner skipping this step runs the risk that an officer from the intelligence service will come looking. Or worse, the police will hassle them on the street, which is sure to end up in having to pay a hefty bribe. In Afghanistan, there's always someone watching.

On to Baggage Claim, where I stop dead in my tracks. There, on the other side of the conveyor belt, is a pile of large, gray Pelican cases. How well I know these hard-sided cases used to transport camera gear. And standing next to the pile is the Al Shabakat cameraman who filmed me in Wad Qol nearly six months ago. I'm sure it's him. He must sense me staring because he suddenly looks up. At me. And raises an eyebrow. Not soon enough, I duck my head, intent on searching for my duffel and my own large, gray Pelican.

This is the last thing I need. Is Piera here with him? Crews usually hang together. Still waiting for my baggage to appear, I notice a couple people come to stand with the cameraman. They're talking quietly, too quietly for me to hear. More than anything, I want to ask this asshole if he's the one who edited the video to make Piera look caring and compassionate and me an insane, gun-toting bitch. But I've missed my chance. Too many witnesses now. I say anything, and it'll just make things worse for me and harder for the legal team or the Pentagon or whoever's handling the 'situation' now.

"Good God! What is taking so long?" Piera's strident voice cuts through the chatter around Baggage Claim.

What are the chances? Of all days to fly into Kabul, I had to pick the same day as Piera McNeil?

My duffel appears in front of me. Then my Pelican case. I grab them and make my way as quickly as possible to Customs. Damn,

I hope she hasn't noticed me. Who am I kidding? By now, her crew has clued her in, and she's focused her laser beam on me. Call me paranoid, but something tells me this isn't the last I've heard her voice.

I get in line at the Customs kiosk, my passport and two very different declaration forms in hand. One acknowledges all thirty thousand. The other claims a little under twenty. There are three people ahead of me. Then, I've got to hand in one form or the other.

Two people proceed through without any problem, which has me leaning toward handing in the form with only twenty thousand dollars declared. Then the man directly in front of me steps up to the kiosk. From what I can see, he looks honest. And Western. The blue jeans, designer leather jacket, and Mets baseball cap are dead giveaways. He hands over his paperwork. Then his passport. Almost immediately, the Customs official starts questioning him. Aggressively. Their voices get louder. And angrier.

I look at the row of clocks on the wall—in particular, the one showing the time in Chicago—and wish I were home. Which surprises me. In all my travels, no matter how fraught with danger, I've always taken everything in stride, never wishing myself home.

An Afghan National Police Officer, holstered gun on his hip, is suddenly at the kiosk. "You will come with me." He bows ever so slightly from the waist.

"Like hell I will! I'm not going anywhere." Definitely an American.

I shake my head. Wrong answer. How stupid can this guy be?

The police officer doesn't ask a second time. He grabs the guy's upper arm and twists, bringing Mr. American nearly to his knees. I hear the whimper. A second officer arrives and takes hold of the other arm.

My turn. Heart pounding, I walk forward ten steps and hand over the form declaring all thirty thousand dollars. I seriously don't want to be arrested. Or jailed. Especially since I no longer have Cerelli to bail me out.

The male officer carefully reads through my declaration form. I pray that he doesn't ask me why I'm carrying so much money.

"Why you have this money?" His words are clipped, but calm. For now.

Judgment time. Calmly and without swallowing too hard, I explain. "I'm here to help build a school." No need to tell him that it's a school for *girls*. Or that the Taliban firebombed the original school five and a half months ago. Who knows how he might respond.

"Where?"

"A village in Panjshir Valley."

He narrows his eyes, then picks up the form, puts it on the counter between us, and points to the line asking where I'll be staying in Afghanistan. "Here, it says you stay with Dr. Bibi Faludi in Kabul."

"Well, yes. Tonight. Tomorrow, I go to the Panjshir Valley." I hope my smile conveys how trustworthy I am. After all, I'm declaring the money.

"Name of village?"

I figure there's no harm telling him this much. "Wad Qol."

"Ah, Wad Qol! This village, I know it. My cousin, he lives there." He smiles and types on his computer. A moment later, he looks back at me, his lips pressed tightly together. "There is school in Wad Qol." So much for the Afghan government's computer system staying up to date.

"We're *rebuilding* the girls' school."

He furrows his brow. "Why?"

I take a deep breath and hope this man is in favor of educating girls. "Their school burned down last spring." No mention of the Taliban or ISIS or truck bombs.

We stare at each other for a count of ten. Then, he pushes the declaration form a few inches closer to me and points to the one tiny bit of white space in the margin. "Write name of person you stay with and full address there."

Does he really need to know this? I've already given him Bibi's info—they know I'm legit. I quickly weigh what could happen if I decline and come up with the obvious answer: jail. I start to write, then stop. Should I put Gulshan's name? Or Ikrom's? A woman's name? Or a man's? Which will cause less trouble? *Hurry up and decide!* Stalling is going to make me look guilty of something. I flip a mental coin and write down 'Ikrom Abdulin, Wad Qol' in print so tiny I doubt he'll be able to read it. Then push the declaration form back to him.

He enters the information into his computer, then smiles. "This is my lucky day! This man, Ikrom, he is my cousin!"

"Really?" I do my best to sound like I believe this unbelievable coincidence.

"You are good friends with my cousin?"

"I've met Dr. Abdulin. Ikrom. I don't know him very well. I'm good friends with his wife."

"What is wife's name?"

He's testing me? "Gulshan. She was the literature and English teacher at the school that burned down."

"Gulshan. She is good woman."

"Yes, she is," I say, mostly because it's clear he expects me to say something.

He taps my declaration sheet. "Please, what is name of organization?"

Ah, he noticed I left that line blank. I think quickly, but all I can come up with is "MEL." I decide it could pass for an acronym and start trying to make up words that would convey what it stands for.

"M-E-L. It is NGO?" He sounds pleased with himself.

Why not? "Yes."

"This is good work they do." He stamps the declaration form, prints out a receipt, and, tucking it into my passport, slides them across the counter to me. "Welcome to Afghanistan."

And I'm through. "Thank you." Picking up my duffel and my Pelican case, I heave a sigh of relief and head out.

In the Arrivals hall, I spot a tall man holding up a card with ANNIE HAWKINS GREEN printed in large block letters. Thank God, *Hama* Bibi came through with a driver. I smile and look up to see Senior Chief Warrant Officer Sawyer in jeans and a leather jacket, full beard and scraggly hair pulled back in a man bun, grinning right back at me. Cerelli's right-hand man hasn't changed one bit since I met him nine years ago.

"Sawyer!" I'm so relieved, I'd love to throw my arms around him. Not exactly the best course of action in this country, though, where public displays of affection are frowned upon. Especially between unmarried people.

He reaches for my duffel. "Ms. Annie Hawkins Green. Good to see you in one piece. And no bad guys in hot pursuit. A nice change."

I tip my head. "Same goes. And it's just 'Hawkins' now. I dropped the 'Green.'"

"The Captain didn't say anything about that."

"Must've slipped his mind."

He raises an eyebrow, which I take to mean, *The Captain doesn't forget anything.* "You got everything?"

"I'm ready to go. Lead the way."

His hand at the small of my back, barely touching, he steers me out of the terminal and over to the parking lot. To an armor-plated Humvee with tinted windows. Not exactly low profile.

I tap the hood. "What's with the military vehicle?"

"Makes for a safer ride."

"You telling me there're problems in Kabul?"

"Always."

I furrow my brow. "Anything in particular?"

"Same old, same old. Thought you'd like to feel safe." He unlocks the doors and dumps my duffel in the back seat. I stow my case, and we climb in.

My Lowepro at my feet, I belt myself in and turn to Sawyer. "How did you draw the short straw?"

"Meaning?"

"This." I laugh. "Waiting around at the airport for hours. Driving me to *Hama* Bibi's."

He presses the ignition button. "Let's just say Bibi Faludi can be very persuasive."

Okay, then. I was kind of hoping to hear that Cerelli had asked him to take care of me. Obviously, that wasn't the case. Still, if Sawyer knows I'm here, then Cerelli does, too. Which drives home his point even more painfully. He knows I'm here but is keeping his distance. *Did you seriously expect anything else?* My inner voice sounds incredulous.

For once, the traffic in Kabul is with us. Amazing, considering it's nearly sunset and rush hour, and the main avenues are crowded with cars. Twenty minutes into the drive, the sun dips behind the

Hindu Kush Mountains to the west, and I hear the *mu'adhdhin* calling the *adhan* for *salat Al-Maghrib*. The men of Kabul hurry along sidewalks and dash across streets on their way to mosques for sunset prayers, snarling traffic. Still, we make it to *Hama* Bibi's apartment in less than forty minutes. Could be a record.

Bibi's apartment building is tall and modern and looks recently built. A ten-foot-high concrete wall encircles it, and armed guards stand at every entrance. There's also a guard by the gated parking lot with Sawyer's name and license plate number on his clipboard. Quite the secure island in the middle of one of the most dangerous cities on the planet. I'm not sure what I was expecting, but it sure wasn't this. Darya never said. Confused, I stare at the compound. Are Bibi and Omar living here because of his position in the government? I shake my head. There's no way politicians can afford to live like this.

Sawyer pulls into the one empty spot, then puts his hand on my arm before I can open the door. "A few welcome gifts, courtesy of the Captain." He reaches under his seat and pulls out a locked steel box.

"Is that what I think it is?"

"It's the Sig you used last spring, yes. Also, the sat phone—minus the bug." He unlocks the box and hands me the gun, ammo clips, and the phone.

The phone I welcome. The Sig and the ammo, well, I would've been happy never to see them again. Still, my heart clenches as I stuff them all into my pack. As much as I don't want Cerelli interfering in my life, I love that he's doing what he can to protect me. Which I realize doesn't exactly make a whole lot of sense. Damn, I'm a mess of contradictions. The only thing I do know is that I've got to find a way to fix things between us.

"One more thing." Sawyer reaches into the back seat and snags a white paper package tied with string. "For your sartorial pleasure."

"Definitely the last thing I ever wanted to see again. Or wear."

"He wants to make sure you're safe."

My heart twinges again. "He told you that?"

"He did." Sawyer shakes his head. "Look, I don't know what's going on between the two of you." He holds up a hand. "And I don't want to know. But I wish you'd both cut it out."

"Yeah, well, I don't know either," I mumble, turning to climb out of the car.

"What's that?" I hear the hint of a laugh in his voice.

"Nothing." I shoulder my pack, grab the wrapped package, and slam the door.

18

HAMA BIBI IS WAITING for us in the marble-walled lobby. Very ritzy. The security guards look on with interest as Bibi wraps her arms around me. "Annie," she whispers in my ear. "I am very glad you are here."

I'm holding her just as tightly. "*Hama* Bibi." The tears pricking the back of my eyes tell me we're both thinking about the person we love, the person who's not here. Darya.

"Well." Her voice a little wobbly, she steps back and clasps both my hands. "Yes." She nods. "It has been a long time since we last saw each other. Much too long. But you look exactly the same."

I snort out a laugh. "I wish."

Her hand cups my cheek. "Some women are fortunate. They hardly show their age at all."

"Your eyes are beautiful," I say, the traditional Afghan way of deflecting a compliment.

We laugh. We've both aged. I know I have, and Bibi looks older than I could have imagined. Deep wrinkles march up the side of her face. Crow's feet gather at the corners of her eyes. But her eyes! They still shine with the keen intelligence that always mesmerized Dar and me. A quick calculation, and I realize she must be in her late sixties.

"Come. We will talk inside the apartment. Senior Chief Sawyer, you will join us, please, for dinner."

He shakes his head. "My apologies, ma'am. I've been called back to base. Besides, I'm sure you two have a lot to talk about. I'd just be in the way."

She sternly wags her index finger at him. "It is always the same answer. Perhaps you have heard bad things about my cooking?"

"No, ma'am." He looks surprised.

"Then, I insist. One day you must allow me to make dinner for you."

He dips his head. "That would be a real pleasure." Handing me the duffel and Pelican case, he salutes his farewell and heads back out to the parking lot.

Bibi reaches to take the duffel from me. I wave her off, letting her carry the wrapped package instead.

"For me?" She smiles, hugging the package to her chest as we step into the elevator.

"Sorry, no. I'm sure it's a *burqa*. Captain Cerelli's way of keeping me safe."

She all but rolls her eyes. "Darya may have told you that my husband would like nothing better than for me to wear the *burqa*."

"She did mention that." I look pointedly at her headscarf and grin. "I take it you didn't agree."

She slices her hand sharply through the air. "Never again. Those years when the Taliban were in power were horrific."

Stepping inside the apartment, my breath catches in my throat. Even having seen the luxurious lobby, I'm not prepared for this large and airy space. Huge windows with sweeping views of the city.

Open concept. Very Western. Very high-end. And very white—the walls, the tile floors, the shag carpets, the modern leather furniture. None of which matches up with the Bibi I remember who loved Persian rugs, antique furniture, and lots of color. This apartment could be in New York or Paris or Tokyo. But to find it in Kabul? I don't know what to say.

"As you can see"—she unwraps her headscarf and shakes out her short, gray hair—"this is very much Omar's taste. Or rather, the designer he hired convinced him that this is his taste."

"It's stunning. And very grand."

"Yes." She laughs, not bothering to hide the sarcasm that coats the single word. "And not exactly what you were expecting, I am certain."

"Well . . ." I slip off my *keffiyeh* and fluff my flattened curls.

She turns to me. "Still, you have the most beautiful hair!"

I laugh. "You should count the white ones."

"Bah! White hairs, gray hairs, they show we have lived."

She leads me down the hall to the guest room, actually more of an office with a narrow daybed where I set down my stuff. Bibi rests her hand on a massive mahogany desk that looks to be an antique. I'm guessing it's hers. Now hidden away where it can't interfere with the new, modern style of the front lounge. "My father's," she says, running her fingers across the top.

I turn in place. It's in this room that I can feel Bibi's spirit. And Darya's. There are books everywhere. The shelves lining the walls are crammed to overflowing. I lean in close to read a few titles. Literature. Poetry. Bibi's books. Not just hers, though. Other shelves are full of books on political science and international relations. Didn't Dar tell me that Omar used to be a university professor? These must be his.

"Wait!" I burrow into my duffel and pull out a slender book of Emily Dickinson's poetry. "For you," I say, handing it to her.

She reads the title and rubs her thumb across the cover. "Oh, Annie. You remembered."

"Twenty years ago, you told me how much you love Dickinson's poems. Since I rediscovered *landays* this past year, I realize how cutting and precise they are, very similar to her work."

"My dear, you always know the perfect gift to bring. Thank you." She reaches for my hand. "As it happens, I do not have any volumes of her poetry. This I will keep in my room to read at night." Sinking onto the daybed, she opens the book and begins to read aloud "Wild Nights – Wild Nights!"—one of my personal favorites—until she looks up at me with a stricken look on her face.

"What's wrong?"

"Oh, my dear. What kind of hostess am I? You must be starving. To travel all this way, and then to listen to an old woman read poetry. Come! We must eat. And talk."

I follow her to the kitchen—a chef's paradise of stainless-steel appliances and a gigantic Carrara marble-topped island that makes me catch my breath. Again. This place is nothing like any other Afghan apartment I've ever seen. There's money here. And it's certainly not from Bibi's salary as a university professor. Or from Uncle Omar's as an elected official.

Bibi opens a zebra wood cabinet and takes out several beautifully hand-painted serving dishes, which she fills with eggplant and meatballs, rice and lamb, and lentils. The aromas have me salivating. Not to dismiss the great food at the fundraiser, but it's been far too long since I've eaten authentic Afghan food in Afghanistan.

"Now," says Bibi, filling a plate for me, "we will eat."

We drift into the dining room—another feature I haven't

often seen in Afghan homes. At least not with this very Western-looking glass-topped table sitting on a base with curved metal legs.

Bibi ignores the place setting on the other side of the table and takes the seat next to mine. "Has it really been twenty years?" She looks searchingly into my eyes.

I nod. "Since Darya and Tariq's wedding."

I watch the cloud pass over her face. "Twenty years. Such a joyous time we had. And now this. Truly a tragedy. But we belong to Allah. It is his will."

My heart tightens. No just and loving God *willed* Darya's death. She was murdered. *Murdered.* I can't say that though. Not to Bibi.

"How I regret that I was not here when it happened." Her voice is sad, her face strained, gray like her hair.

"You weren't here?" Somehow, I didn't know that.

"I was actually in Paris that week. At a literature conference." She cups her hands in front of her mouth, her eyes showing the horror of the thought that clearly just occurred to her. "Oh! Do you think if I had been here, that perhaps—"

I rest my hand briefly on her shoulder. "There was nothing anyone could've done." Except me. I could have chosen not to believe Seema's lies. I could have spoken to Dar and Tariq sooner. *I* could have done something.

"Perhaps Omar could have helped? Not to save Darya's life, but with Seema?"

"I honestly don't think he could've done anything."

Bibi squeezes my hand. "Tell me, has there been any word?"

"If you're asking if anyone has found her or Awalmir, the answer is no. Or at least, I don't think so. I was hoping that you've heard something? Or Omar has?"

She shakes her head slowly. "Me? I have heard nothing. I am

certain if Omar had, he would have told me. But I will ask when he returns home."

Just what I expected. I do my best to focus on the food, to savor a bite of lamb. "You know, it's the oddest thing. Since last June, someone called Rahila has been texting me *landays*. I'm pretty sure it's really Seema. With your expertise in poetry, you might see something I've missed." Digging my cell out of my pocket, I pull up the first poem and hand her the phone.

While she reads, I fork a morsel of *banjân* into my mouth. Oh my God, this eggplant is even better than what Cerelli and I had at *Khosha* last spring. And I thought that was the best I'd ever eaten.

Finally, Bibi reads the poem aloud:

Tell my mother to dry her tears.
The pomegranates will blossom early in the new year.

She turns to me. "Seema wrote this?"

"Possibly. Who else would send me a *landay* with that message?"

"It pains me to criticize anything Seema may have written, but she should know better. This is poorly done."

"What do you mean?"

"It doesn't follow the rules, does it? Of course, it is hard to know because it's written in English, which isn't right either. The count is wrong in both English and Dari. In Pashto as well. There should be nine syllables in the first line and thirteen in the second. And the rhyme feels a bit forced."

"I was wondering if it could be an announcement of a baby coming?"

She nods. "Quite possibly. *Landays* are often about love—with a forbidden lover—but don't usually announce the result."

"It makes me believe that she doesn't know—about Darya."

"Perhaps. It is impossible to know. Has Captain Cerelli seen this? He is more of an expert on this form than I. He also composes some of the most beautiful verses I've ever read." Her eyes seek out mine, clearly trying to read on my face whether I've seen any of Cerelli's *landays*.

My deep blush is her answer. "He *has* seen this one, and said much the same thing as you."

"Then I am in good company." She smiles. I guess Cerelli is the gold standard around here.

"He's seen this next one, too." I swipe forward to the two more recent poems.

My body is mine,
But my Beloved drinks me like rare, red wine.

Bibi scoffs. "Again, the count is not true, and the rhyme, it is lazy. She takes the easy way. This is a pampered young girl's view of love. There is no pathos, no depth." She brings her hand to her heart.

"And here's the last of them. This is the one that bothers me. I sent it to Cerelli, but I don't know if he got it."

I walk to the hill outside Kandahar
And see that tonight my Beloved's caravan has not gone far.

The expression on Bibi's face turns grim. "My dear, you were right to be concerned. As a *landay*, it shows a bit more consideration than the others. Enough that I almost wonder if it was written by the same person. You do not know if Captain Cerelli has seen this?" Her tone tells me I should make damn sure he has.

She reads through the last two poems again. "Did you notice that she uses the word 'beloved' in both of these?"

"What does that mean?"

"It could be that Seema has not yet married Awalmir. We think he is Pashtun. Correct?"

"He is." I nod.

Bibi looks a little surprised at how certain I am. "Well, since that is the case, I find it hard to believe that his parents would allow a marriage between them. I would imagine his people are very tribal. And we know Darya and Tariq did not permit it. I am thinking it is unlikely they are married."

"And here I thought Seema just liked the romantic sound of 'beloved.'" *Landays* are only short poems, but *wow*, they're complicated.

Bibi turns toward me, her eyes gleaming in earnest. "It is more than that. Traditionally, *landays* are poems about romantic love. A Pashtun woman loves a man she cannot marry. As I'm sure you know, Annie, all too often in this country, tribal policy and family alliances determine who will marry whom. It is a business contract, nothing more. Nothing to do with love or romance. Even nowadays. In fact, many Pashtun men see romantic love as violating their code of honor. They believe that a girl who writes verses like these puts a stain on the family. The only way to reclaim family honor, they think, is to kill the girl."

The pieces click into place for me. "So, a *landay* is a cry of separation from her true love."

"A perpetual cry." She smiles. "Well done! I may make you into a literature scholar yet."

"Wait! I remember Darya singing a *landay* to Tariq at their wedding."

"Yes, I heard it, too. A lovely piece."

"They were married."

She shrugs. "There are always exceptions to every rule. And they were Americans by then."

I comb my fingers through my hair. "So, what is Seema trying to tell me? That she's not married?"

"My dear, that I do not know. They could have married secretly. But then, if his family were to find out, they might well be hunting for them to get the marriage nullified, possibly to kill her."

"Seriously?" Does Cerelli know this? Of course he does. Which is exactly why he told me to stay out of it. Not to go looking for Seema. And I won't. Well, I won't do more than ask a few people in Wad Qol, but that's all.

"As I said, there are always exceptions." Bibi smiles. "You do know that Omar is Pashtun?"

I shake my head. No, I didn't know that.

"Of course, by the time we married, his parents were long gone. Still, his brothers and uncle did not object to our marriage. Well, not so much that I feared for my life." Bibi claps her hands together. "Come. Enough of this sadness. Let us talk of happier things. Tell me about Emmeline. I must know everything about the money she and her friend raised."

I tell her about how the girls sold flowers to motorcyclists. Then, about the dance. She stares at me in disbelief when I tell her how much the girls have raised.

"When we spoke on the phone, you said ten thousand dollars. Did I misunderstand?"

I smile. "That was before the dance. The mosque, really the entire town, came together to support this. For the girls of Wad Qol. And for Darya."

For a moment, she cannot speak, but her eyes shine. Finally, she nods at my cell. "Do you have any pictures from the dance?"

"Not on my cell. Sorry." Flipping through the photo gallery to make my point, I'm stunned to come across an actual video. Bonita must have helped herself to my phone and recorded one of Mel's dances. Not for the first time. "Apparently, I was wrong." I lean close to Bibi and press the PLAY button. The music begins. The rhythm of the drums fills the room. But the video doesn't feature Mel. Or Yasmine. It's of me. "This is a mistake," I say, trying to turn it off. "My friend must have been playing a joke on me."

"Please. To see you dance the *Attan* once more. This is good for my heart." Bibi takes the cell from me, then reaches for my hand and holds it tight.

It's not as bad as I feared. In fact, I'm not bad at all. The dress, the *tunbaan*, is what saves me. Thank God I still had it. Thank God it still fit.

"Your dress!" Bibi sighs. "It is beautiful." Then she holds the phone closer. "Oh, my! It is the *tunbaan* that my mother sewed. She used that beautiful cloth from her mother's dowry. I had completely forgotten. And you look as beautiful in it now as you did when you wore it at Darya's wedding."

The video pans around the outside of the school gymnasium, showing the hundreds of people in rapt attention as the dancers twirl on.

"And all these people gave money to help rebuild our Darya's school?" Bibi sounds overwhelmed.

"Charity is one of the pillars of Islam, isn't it?" I say, leaning against her shoulder.

"I would say one of the most important ones."

IT'S AFTER MIDNIGHT BY the time Bibi walks me to the guest room. "This is where Darya slept when she came to visit. Often she would bring Seema with her." She looks away for a brief moment. "Now we use this room as an office and for storage."

I glance around the room. "Storage?"

Bibi smiles. "Omar's boxes would have suffocated you. I moved them into my room so that you could sleep in here more comfortably."

"I'm sure I will."

"Until the morning, then. The young people plan to arrive early to drive you to Wad Qol. Bahar told me her brother wishes to leave by seven o'clock."

"Thank you for making all these arrangements for me."

"Of course, dear one. Now, good night." Bibi closes the door gently behind her.

Finally alone, I set aside the Pelican case, not bothering to unlock it. My gear for the TNN assignment is inside. I won't need any of it until I return from Wad Qol.

Now to organize the rest of my gear. First, I change into my extra-large *Our Daughters, Ourselves* T-shirt. Then, I unwrap the package from Cerelli. Just as I thought, a *burqa*. Periwinkle. It had to be periwinkle? I trace the netted eyepiece. A much tighter weave than my last one, more like a fine mesh. Which will make it that much harder for anyone to see my American face and red hair. Not to mention, harder for me to see out. It's also a much nicer fabric with knife pleats. And, to be honest, the embroidery covering the skull cap is gorgeous. Still, it's a *burqa*. Something I don't want to wear and won't unless I have to. I fold it carefully and, clearing everything else out of my Lowepro, stow it at the very bottom.

I sit cross-legged on the floor, the phone and the gun and the ammo in my lap. Just sit. And wait. If any hallucinations are going to start up, they're going to happen now. While I'm in Kabul, in Darya's room, holding the gun I used to kill Ghazan—the man who was about to shoot Cerelli and me last May. Not anything I care to remember. But it was him or us. There wasn't a choice. I give it five minutes. Nothing happens. Absolutely nothing. Okay, then. I put the phone, the gun, and the clips into my pack.

Next come the small bags of SanDisk cards and batteries and chargers. Everything's where it should be. I tuck it all into the pack. My personal camera comes last, with a smaller lens. I put it in the top compartment for easy access at a moment's notice.

Finally, I make sure the money is where I want it. Half in the secret sleeve at the back of the pack. More in the three money belts I've been wearing. What's left I'll take care of tomorrow, stuffing bills into my boots and bra.

Done. Glancing at my watch, I see I've got all of five hours to catch up on some sleep. I'm pushing myself to my knees when I crunch on something hard. Looking down at the worn carpet, I see the culprit. An SD card. I pull the camera back out of my pack and load the card into the slot. Damn, I'm getting sloppy.

19

HAMA BIBI AND I ARE up before sunrise, lugging Omar's metal boxes from their temporary home in her bedroom back into the guest room. So many boxes, and heavier than I would've thought—each one locked. Neither of us says a word; we just carry and stack them in front of the bookcases.

"Thank you." Bibi's having a hard time catching her breath as she turns off the overhead light. She locks the door, then tucks the key behind the loose baseboard. "I can see that you think this is all very strange."

What can I say?

"It is." She sounds resigned. "No, I do not know what Omar keeps locked away. Government papers is all he will tell me. I have asked him why he does not keep them in his office. He insists that here the security is better."

"Really? That's hard to believe." Even with armed guards down in the lobby, if anyone wanted to get in, it wouldn't be all that hard.

She shrugs. "He may have a point. There was a bombing at the legislative building a few months ago."

"I remember hearing about that. A couple senators were killed?"

"Not senators." She shakes her head. "Members of the *Wolesi Jirga*, the House of Representatives where Omar serves."

I nod. "Omar wasn't hurt?"

"No, *Mashallah*. Since then, he has been storing many documents here." She rubs her hands against the baggy pants of her *shalwar kameez*. "I am quite sure he would not like knowing that you slept here."

"I won't say a word." And given that I'm not likely to see Omar on this trip—or ever—that won't be a hard promise to keep.

"Neither will I." She grins. "And please, there is no need to worry about me."

Her last words take me by surprise. I wasn't worried about her. But now that she brings it up—"Bibi?"

She tries to bat away my question. "It is a long and complicated story."

"I have time."

A minute passes while she considers my invitation. "All right. Since you have asked, I must tell. You may remember that I didn't marry until later in life."

I nod.

"To be honest, I did not plan to marry at all. Then twenty years ago, the Taliban came to power. Suddenly, I could no longer teach at university. I couldn't work at all. It was difficult to leave the house even for food. Omar was a colleague then, and a good friend. His wife had recently passed away, and he took pity on me."

Pity? My eyes grow wide.

"I see what you are thinking. You must understand—those were hard times, and Omar was a good husband, very caring." She smiles coyly. "He was also very attractive. He still is. And as soon as the Taliban were routed from Kabul, he supported me returning to my job."

"A good man."

"Yes, he was."

It's hard to miss that she said 'was.'"

"Until the last few years, when he became interested in politics and saw that the Taliban could possibly return. Now, he is different. He—"

The buzzer in the front room sounds—the concierge calling to let us know that Farrakh and Bahar are waiting downstairs. Whatever Bibi was going to say is left unsaid. She walks me out of the apartment to the elevator.

I kiss her on both cheeks. "Thank you for everything. *Inshallah*, I'll be back in ten days or two weeks. I would love to see you again."

Bibi's arms are around me, holding me close. "Thank you, my dearest, for staying with me. Please call me when you're ready to return. If it is Allah's will, Omar still will be occupied with his meeting." She steps back, her hands clasping mine. "I am glad to find you well. Please remember Darya with love. I know her death pains you. It pains me, too, but we must celebrate her life and everything that she accomplished."

All I can manage is a small nod. Then, shouldering my Lowepro and grabbing my duffel and camera case, I step into the elevator. As the doors close, I hear Bibi's voice. "Do not worry about me. *Khoda hafiz!*"

"And may God protect you," I call back to her, but the elevator doors are already closed.

WHEN THE ELEVATOR DOORS open in the lobby, someone wearing a rose-colored *burqa* rushes forward, throws her arms around me, and hugs hard.

"Ms. Hawkins Green! It is me! Bahar! Do you remember?"

I hug her in turn. "Bahar, it is wonderful to see you! Or it will be when we get to Wad Qol and I can actually *see* you." Bahar in a *burqa*. Probably not so much of a surprise since her mother wears one. But last spring, I got used to this girl in her *shalwar kameez* and a scarf pushed daringly back onto the crown of her head. A school uniform, I remind myself. Maybe she feels that this gives her more freedom and independence, especially in the city?

She giggles and waves forward a young man who looks exactly like her. He has to be her brother. "This is Farrakh."

"*Assalâmu alaykum*," I say.

"*Wa 'alaykum assalâm*." His right hand over his heart, he nods his pleasure to meet me. "Ms. Hawkins Green."

Which is way too formal. I certainly understand the need for Bahar to have called me that last spring when she was my student. But now? "Please, call me Annie?" I smile at them both. "You, too, Bahar."

"Oh!" Bahar is clearly surprised. "Thank you, Annie."

"Your trip, it went well?" says Farrakh.

"Very well, thank you."

"*Mashallah.*" He leans in closer and drops his voice. "As I am certain you are aware, our greetings could last a long time. That is our tradition. But perhaps we should begin our trip to Wad Qol. It could take many hours. I would like to ask if you are agreeable to go to the car?"

"Please." I smile. "That would be most agreeable."

Farrakh leads the way to an aging blue Toyota Corolla with rust eating through the bottom of the door panels. He's clearly proud of having a car, and despite the corrosion, it runs great.

Luck is on our side. It's still early enough that traffic isn't terribly heavy, and we're soon out of the city. I smile at the brother and sister sitting up front. Good of them to let me have the entire back seat. I move my Lowepro to the floor, stretch out my legs, and nearly sigh at the luxury of this much space.

Farrakh turns out to be a cautious driver. At least with me in the car. No speeding. No swerving or rocketing forward to pass other vehicles. Not that there are all that many cars on the road. Just cruising along at a safe clip—a gentle ride that quickly has my eyelids heavy, heavier, and closing.

I'm in a netherworld halfway between being asleep and awake, in the back seat of a car heading to Wad Qol. But, I'm also at *Hama* Bibi's apartment, still mulling over what she said about Omar this morning. *I can see that you think this is all very strange. The apartment—such a beautiful place. Expensive. How can they afford it?*

One moment I'm alone in Bibi's apartment, helping myself to leftover *banjân*. Then, suddenly, I'm no longer alone. There are other people. Not Bibi. She's gone to the university to teach a class. The voices get louder. Men's voices. They're in the lounge. Do they know I'm here? It seems better that they don't know. I scrunch down low in the kitchen, behind the massive island, hoping no one notices me. In this wide-open apartment, that can't last long. Somehow, I'm able to crawl out of the kitchen unseen and make my way down the hall to the guest room.

The door is open. It should be locked.

I slip inside, shutting the door softly behind me, plunging myself into darkness. Wait, there's a light switch on the wall. But where? Starting near the door, I run my hands along the walls until I find the switch.

The small brass lamp on Bibi's desk flares on. Just as I hear the lock click in the door behind me. I freeze, not daring to breathe. They know I'm here. They've locked me in. Taken me prisoner.

Metal boxes. Piles of them everywhere. I shouldn't look in them. That would be beyond rude to pry into Bibi's secrets. No, they're Omar's secrets. But I can't stop myself. The answers are in the boxes.

Even though I don't have the keys, the locks spring open. I lift up the first lid and stare in disbelief, then horror. What the hell am I seeing?

Behind me, the door swings open. Oh, God! Omar has caught me. I try to hide behind the boxes. Peeking out, I see that the man in the doorway isn't Omar. It's Ghazan, his black balaclava rolled up to reveal his brown hair, his full beard, his hate-filled eyes.

"It can't be you. You're dead. I killed you."

"You can't kill me," he sneers. "There will always be others, swearing *badal* to avenge my death." He opens his jacket so I can see the bullet holes. "Count them!" he orders.

I try to count but get to five and lose my way.

"Ten. Why did you shoot me ten times?" He lifts his arm, and that's when I see he's holding a gun, an automatic, and he's aiming at me.

Again, I try to hide behind the boxes, but they're shrinking, getting smaller and smaller.

"This time, *you* die."

I keep my eyes on the gun, waiting for the bullet to come

blasting out. But before he can pull the trigger, the roar of a helicopter hovering outside the apartment distracts him. The rotors are causing the windows to rattle in their frames. Will they hold? Or shatter into millions of tiny pieces?

For some reason I can't fathom, Ghazan doesn't shoot. Now, the building is shaking. I am, too.

Finally, I force open my eyes to see Farrakh and Bahar in front of me. Neither of them the wiser, I hope, that I drifted off. And was almost shot. Trembling from a nightmare that's still with me, that feels way too real to have been a dream, I push myself back up in my seat. What the hell just happened? I rub my arms, trying to warm up and calm down. Please don't let this be PTSD rearing its head. Again. I've been doing so well. For months, there's been nothing. Cerelli's going to be all over me to see a therapist.

That stops me. Cerelli isn't going to say a thing. It's been weeks since I last talked to him. He hasn't returned a single one of my calls, not even my call about Seema's latest *landay*. I need to talk to him. This nightmare means something important. He's the one person who can help me figure out what my subconscious is trying to tell me.

Be honest! I chastise myself. What I really want is for Mel to be right about Cerelli. I want him to ignore the fact that I yelled at him. I want him to call me. I want *him*. My heart sinks. How exactly can I make any of this happen? That confounded helicopter noise is still there. Roaring. Following us. Looking out the window, I see we're already to the river. And it's running high, thundering for all it's worth. The river, not a helicopter. A quick glance at my watch: 10:00 a.m. I've been out for a while. I lean forward and tap Bahar on her *burqa*-clad shoulder. She turns, and I'm talking into the netted eyepiece. "Where are we?"

"Oh, you are awake! Did you have a good rest?"

I smile. "I caught up on some much-needed sleep."

"We just reached the river. Soon, we will be at the checkpoint at Dalan Sang."

Shit. Not a place I want to visit again. My stop there with Tariq last spring was brutal. The bomb. The dead and dying. Why couldn't I have slept through that? I sit back in my seat, training my eyes on the river, willing the sound of the water to wash through me, sluice away my fear. But it's not working. I can't rid myself of this dream about Ghazan. It keeps rattling around inside my head, setting me on edge, as if all isn't right with my world. As if something could be seriously wrong.

A half hour later, we slow down. Just a few vehicles ahead of us at the checkpoint. At first, I glance away, not wanting to see any lingering damage. By the time Farrakh pulls up to the checkpoint, though, I can't help myself. Only there's nothing to see. Everything looks fine. The stone kiosk has been rebuilt. It's as if there had never been a bomb.

A lieutenant asks for our identity papers. Farrakh's and Bahar's don't cause any trouble. But he stops when he gets to my passport and other paperwork, bends down to look into the car, then walks around and opens the back door. "Please"—he gestures with his hand—"you will exit for me."

Stomach churning, heart racing, I climb out. *Let this go well.*

He removes the declaration receipt and my identity card, then, folding open my passport, looks closely at me and again at my picture. "You will kindly remove the headscarf."

In the car, Bahar's gasp is audible. It's unheard of for a man, especially a stranger, to tell a woman to reveal herself. Especially her hair. And I've got a lot of hair—long and red untamable curls.

As Cerelli always says, my hair makes me a very prominent target. But this is an army lieutenant, and I don't want to end up detained. Or arrested. I untie my scarf. He holds the passport up next to my face. And seems satisfied that I match the picture.

"I apologize." He offers a slight bow. "Not many Americans come into the valley."

I can imagine.

"Please, your headscarf." He nods his permission for me to cover myself. "Why are you here?"

I take a second to retie my *keffiyeh*, then explain, "I was here last May when the school was bombed in Wad Qol."

His eyes cloud over, as if he's looking into the distance. Suspicion? Or pain at the memory?

"I was a guest teacher, and I've come back to help rebuild the school." The back of my neck prickles. I've been at many road stops in my day, and it always comes down to one thing: a bribe. And there's definitely the chance he could decide to help himself to all the money.

"These people?" He points to Bahar and Farrakh. "How do you know them?"

Not sure what I should say, I take a deep breath. And thank God, at that very moment, Farrakh steps out of the car and walks around to us. Bahar rolls down her window.

"My sister," Farrakh says in Dari, nodding toward Bahar, "she was one of the girls in Ms. Hawkins Green's class." *Smart move*, I note, *using my last name.*

The lieutenant raises his hand to stop Farrakh and turns to me. "You understand what he says? You speak Dari?"

"Balê."

He raises his eyebrows, then nods for Farrakh to continue.

"Like all of the girls that day, my sister barely escaped the bombing with her life. It has been the dream of everyone in Wad Qol to rebuild this school, but—" He cups his hands, palms up, as if in prayer. "Our village is poor. Ms. Hawkins Green raised the necessary funds in the United States and is bringing the money we need to hire workers. Many men in our village and the valley have no jobs. Now, they will. Our sisters will have a new school, and our families will eat. *Inshallah.*"

I swallow hard. Farrakh is brilliant to frame this entire endeavor in terms of bringing jobs to the valley. I'd focused only on bringing education to the girls. Clearly, though, this undertaking means so much more to all the people of Wad Qol.

"The money?" The lieutenant taps the declaration receipt with his index finger. "You have it with you?"

Both men look at me. Is he asking to see it? Or what? "Yes?"

"Most organizations send the money directly to the government. They do not deliver it in person." His eyes trace my curves, which, thank God, are mostly hidden beneath my bulky Grammy sweater and my loose *shalwar kameez*. Is he going to frisk me? No way. That would really be stepping over the line in this country.

What can I say? Do I let on how this was a good, old-fashioned American fundraiser? Pretty much a bake sale that went viral? Should I tell him about the Faqiris' mosque and Mel? Who would ever believe two teenage girls could raise thirty thousand dollars by smiling at bikers and dancing? Completely improbable.

I'm so lost in trying to figure out what to say that I almost miss the lieutenant smiling and slapping Farrakh on the back. "You are a politician?"

Farrakh shakes his head. "No, I am studying medicine and will return to work in the clinic in my village. We are a doctor short."

"Yes." The tone of the lieutenant's voice tells us he knows the full story. "Tariq Ghafoor saved many lives while he lived in the valley."

Finally, I know what to say. "He also saved lives last May. Here at Dalan Sang."

His eyes widen. "You were here that day?"

I nod.

"You are the American woman who saved Massoud's son? His grandson?"

I look away for a moment, studying the bus that has pulled up on the other side of the kiosk, heading back toward Kabul. Through the windows, I can see one *burqa* after another. Mostly black and periwinkle. Peering, I can see the netted eyepieces pressed against the inside of the glass. Six months ago, there was another bus parked right there when the bomb detonated. I wait, half expecting a great wave of grief and horror to wash over me. But it doesn't. The men are still waiting for me to answer the lieutenant's question. How do I respond to the enormity of that day? I decide not to explain that it was Tariq's doing because that's not how the legend goes. The way the Massoud family tells the story is that I did the saving. "It was a horrible day. My hands. Allah's will."

He smiles his understanding and gives all our papers back to Farrakh. "Please, *Khoda hafiz.*" Then to me, "May God be your guardian." He bows from the waist and moves on to the next vehicle.

Farrakh and I climb back into the car.

"We made it through!" Bahar says jubilantly as we pull away from the checkpoint. She turns around to look at me. "I was afraid the lieutenant was going to take the money."

"Thanks to Farrakh's quick thinking, he didn't!" I smile my relief. Then, heart still racing, I lean back against my seat. No bodies. No blood. No hallucinations. And I'm still a legend.

"Annie?" I glance up to meet Farrakh's eyes in the rearview mirror. "Do you really have the money with you?"

"Of course. Why?"

"Well, the lieutenant is right. Usually, money is wired into the country, although the government takes much of it. May I ask how much money there is?"

Another deep breath. "You need to understand that the main people doing the fundraising were my sixteen-year-old daughter, Mel, and her best friend Yasmine." I go on to tell them about the *Meet a Muslim!* event and the dinner with traditional Afghan dances. I can tell by the expression on Farrakh's face, he isn't expecting much.

"Thirty thousand dollars. U.S.," I say finally.

He slams on the brakes, then pulls slowly to the side of the road, as close as he can get to the sheared-off cliff, and turns around to stare at me. Disbelief distorts his face.

I nod.

He runs his fingers through his hair. "I do not understand. That is a lot of money. More money than everyone in our village together earns in a year. How could two young girls make such a miracle?"

"Well, they had some help. But they were the ones who came up with the idea and convinced everyone else. Even me." I smile.

"Dancing," sighs Bahar. "I remember last spring when we went to the river to take pictures of the village girls. We danced in the grass. That was such a wonderful day." Even though the *burqa* is muffling her voice, I can hear how wistful she sounds. "Did you take pictures of your daughter? When she danced?"

"No pictures, but I do have a video—of *me* dancing." The last thing I want to do is show it again.

"Oh! May I see it?" Bahar nearly shouts her excitement.

"Perhaps you will show me also?" Farrakh seems suddenly shy. He starts up the car. "Let us drive on to Bazarak to buy our lunch. Then, you will please let us see your video."

BY THE TIME WE GET to Bazarak, and then the market, we've agreed to buy kebabs and rice, salad and *nân* to make a picnic lunch farther on. That way, we can all eat together and Bahar can slide her *burqa* back off her face and eat much more easily. Waving away the money I've taken from my wallet, Farrakh heads off to his favorite stand for roast meat and rice. I shoulder my Lowepro and, feeling the full weight of thirty thousand U.S. dollars, join Bahar going in the other direction to search for salad and bread.

The market is bustling with people—men and women and kids. There are so many shops and kiosks selling everything imaginable, from sandals and Western T-shirts to household supplies, cheap plastic toys, and used cell phones that probably work only in Afghanistan. Right now, everyone is hungry for their midday meal, *nân-e châsht*. With all the people jostling against us, I swing my pack around to my chest, which makes me feel a lot more secure. Bahar nods and sticks close to me. We stand in line at the bakery to buy the *nân* first. It's as we're walking away that a cold chill starts creeping up my back.

No! You're imagining things! I upbraid myself. There's no need to be nervous. Only three people here know I've got $30K stuffed in my clothes and pack.

"Just a sec," I say to Bahar and attempt a casual 360-degree turn as though I'm looking for a specific shop and not seeing it. I'm also not catching sight of anyone suspicious who could be tailing me. Just crowds of people milling around us, pushing ahead to buy food.

"Is everything all right?" she asks warily. Clearly, the money I'm carrying has her on high alert as well.

"I think so."

"Here we are." She stops in front of a kiosk with a menu written on a small chalkboard propped up on the counter. "This is my favorite place for salad. We always stop here when we drive back home or to Kabul." We wait in the short line until it's our turn to order.

That's when the hairs on the back of my neck start to prickle. I turn to move closer to Bahar, at least to get my back against the kiosk. But before I can take another step, a hand latches onto my upper arm.

I try to pull away.

The hand tightens its hold, keeping me firmly in place.

I can't even turn to see who it is.

Looking down, I see the thick fingers, dark hairs. A man's hand. On me. This just doesn't happen in Afghanistan. Men do not touch women outside their family. Ever.

I take a deep breath, ready to yell. Then remember that the last thing I want to do is let anyone know that a man is touching me. Especially the police. Who will blame *me* for enticing *him*. Fuck.

The hand squeezes harder on my bicep. I can just imagine the bruise I'll be sporting tomorrow. Then another hand closes around the shoulder strap of my pack. And starts to pull. I will myself to relax, just for a moment. The fingers loosen their grip long enough for me to twist around. And see his face.

Not a face I've ever seen before. Not the phantom from my nightmare. This man is real. Youngish. Early twenties. Sparsely bearded, large nose, dark hair, dark eyes. Just a man who looks like so many other Afghan men.

He tightens his hold again. I can almost feel the capillaries in my skin bursting. Blood oozing. From the smug look on his face, he knows he's hurting me, knows I can't do anything to stop him. That's making him happy. Then, he smiles. He frigging smiles and spits out words in Pashto that I don't understand.

"*Fäshä!*" He says it again, louder. "*Amrikäyi fäshä!*"

This time, I have a pretty good idea he's calling me an American whore. He yanks on my arm. Hard. Like I'm supposed to follow him. Shit! This is one scary, masochistic asshole.

I stop struggling, but he's on to that trick. He doesn't ease up on his iron grip; he just pulls harder, almost dragging me off balance.

When I try to dig in my heels, my position is wrong. In a last-ditch effort, I shift my weight slightly to my left leg and kick out as hard as I can with my right, landing my lug-soled military boot solidly between his legs. Howling, he lets go of me and falls backward. That'll teach him.

Not about to stick around, my attacker hobbles off into the crowd that opens, then closes, around him. Protecting him. They start to point fingers. At me.

I stare after him, but lose him in a few seconds. Who the hell is he?

"Oh, Annie." Bahar is suddenly next to me. "She made the salad fresh for us. It looks delicious." She takes another look at me. "Is something wrong?"

"Did you see that man?" I point into the crowd.

"What man?" She glances at the people gathering in front of us. "There are many men here. Please, tell me what happened!"

More people are turning to look at me. Pointing. Murmuring

in a way that seems ominous. We've got to get out of here. I tuck my hand as best I can under her arm and steer us through the crowd. It's Bahar who senses the mood turning ugly and picks up the pace. Thank God no one tries to stop us. When we're clear of everyone and almost back to the car, I tell her what happened.

"A man *touched* you?" Bahar sounds appalled.

"Who touched you?" Farrakh is back, aluminum trays of food in his hands. He turns around, searching the crowd as if he'll be able to pick out the man.

"A man grabbed Annie! He wouldn't let go, so she kicked him, and he ran off."

"This is terrible!" He hustles us into the car just as two policemen emerge from the masses of noontime shoppers. We don't hang around to see if they're searching for me. Farrakh puts the car in gear, and we're off, heading back to the River Road.

I fill Farrakh in on the details as we head farther east. "It was totally bizarre. He called me—" I stop. I don't want to say the words. American whore. It's too awful and would only upset Farrakh and Bahar.

"Maybe this man thought he recognized you? Could he have remembered you from one of your other trips?" I know Bahar is thinking of the portrait I made of Malalai back in '06 and the ambush I barely escaped with my life. Her timid whisper tells me she's more scared than I am.

"I guess, but I'm pretty sure I've never seen him before today." I try to sound upbeat. But I'm not. Not by a long shot.

"He still should not have grabbed you. That should never happen!" Her whisper gives way to anger.

"It is hard to believe that any man would do this terrible thing because he thought he remembered you." Farrakh scoffs. "No, there must be another reason. Does anyone else know about the money? Could that man have overheard us talking with the lieutenant at the checkpoint?"

I shrug. "Anything is possible."

We drive on, stopping only briefly to eat our picnic lunch. None of us is interested in food. And no one raises the idea of looking at the video of the dance. We just want to get to Wad Qol as quickly as possible. Back on the road again, I look behind us periodically to see if there's a car or a pickup or a motorcycle. As far as I can tell, the road is empty. I'm not the only one checking. I catch Bahar looking over her shoulder. Farrakh is checking the rearview mirror every minute. And driving a whole lot faster.

Wad Qol village

"*MASHALLAH!*" GULSHAN STANDS IN the front room of her house, staring at us in disbelief, her hands cupped in prayer and thanksgiving. "So much money. Is this possible?" She hasn't changed a bit since last spring. Short and stocky with the brightest twinkle in her eyes and the warmest smile.

Bahar sweeps off her *burqa* and dances a circle around me, somehow managing to avoid the floor cushions and low tables, the chairs and shelves stacked with books. Looking around the room, I can't help but smile. It's all exactly the way I remember it from the last time I was here in May. This is a home that is lived in and appreciated. "Isn't it wonderful?" she sings, then grabs her mother's hands and spins her around.

"It is true then?" Gulshan looks to her son for confirmation.

Farrakh nods. "Yes, this is what Annie has told us."

Gulshan turns to me. "My dear Annie. This is more than a wonder. It is a blessing. A very great blessing. And what Bahar says is correct? Your daughter and her friend from Afghanistan raised all this money themselves? For our girls in Wad Qol?"

"With help from Yasmine's parents and the people in her mosque."

"I do not know what to say. I am without enough words to thank you."

"Mother? Without words? That is hard to believe." Farrakh cracks a grin.

"Oh, you!" Gulshan gently cuffs his chin, then turns back to me and pulls me into her arms. "And for you to be here! After what happened last May, I was afraid we would never see you again. And now, to have you in my home. It is too much. *Mashallah.*"

"Mother, please? Some help with these boxes?" The containers of our barely touched picnic lunch balanced in Farrakh's hands look like they're about to topple to the floor.

Bahar, Gulshan, and I rush forward and just manage to avoid colliding with each other. Gulshan grabs the boxes and carries them into the kitchen. "This is good!" she calls over her shoulder. "You will take this tomorrow for the ride back to Kabul."

Just now home from the clinic, Ikrom towers in the front doorway. He hugs both his children and nods to me, his hand pressed to his heart. "Welcome to our home. You do us great honor by staying with us. I am glad that you have arrived safely."

"Papa! Wait until you hear!" Bahar grabs his hand. "Annie has brought so much money with her. Thirty thousand dollars! Not afghanis! U.S. dollars!"

Ikrom's eyes widen. "This money. When will the wire transfer come?"

"There is no wire." Farrakh takes off his jacket and hangs it on a peg by the door. "Annie has brought the cash with her."

Ikrom looks suddenly grave. "All that money? You carried it yourself? Alone?"

"I was afraid you might never get the money if I sent it by wire. And certainly not all of it. Each bank along the way would have helped itself to a share. Not to mention what the government would have taken."

"You did not have to pay anything to bring it into the country? Or at the checkpoint?"

I glance at Farrakh. "There was a moment at Dalan Sang when I got a bit nervous. The guard wanted to see the money, and I was afraid it might disappear. But Farrakh saved the day. And at the airport?" I smile. "I debated *not* declaring it. Then, I worried what would happen if they searched me and found it. In the end, I completed the necessary forms, and it all worked out," I say in a tone that I hope conveys my disbelief. "Oh, and the Customs official recognized your name. He said he's your cousin." I laugh.

Ikrom looks puzzled. "I do not understand. My cousins, they all live here in the valley. They do not work in Kabul."

Coming back from the kitchen, Gulshan cups her hands again, this time over her mouth. She's worried. One glance at Bahar and Farrakh tells me they are, too.

I wave my hand half-heartedly through the air. "Not that I believed him. It seemed like way too much of a coincidence."

"This I do not like." Ikrom sounds more concerned. "The Customs official, did he say my name?"

Did he? I look from Gulshan to Ikrom, trying to reconstruct what happened yesterday. "No," I say finally. "*He* didn't say your name. I did. I mean, he made me write down your name and address as the place where I'd be staying while I'm here." Damn, that guy knew exactly how to play me. I bury my face in my hands for a few seconds, then look up. "I'm sorry. He obviously saw your name and Wad Qol on my declaration form and then acted like this was his home village. That's when he said you were his cousin." And I gave that asshole all the information he needs to come and steal the money.

"You took him at his word," says Ikrom a lot more calmly than I'm feeling. "It is reasonable. Why should a Customs official lie?"

"Because he saw a single woman with a lot of money. And now he knows exactly where the money is. It's all my fault."

Gulshan catches her husband's sleeve. "Ikrom, what can we do? We must put this money in a safe place. We cannot keep it in the house."

Ikrom pulls at his beard. "Perhaps at the clinic?"

"He knows you are a doctor." Could I have screwed this up any worse?

"Please, Annie." Back from the kitchen, Bahar circles her arms around me. "You have done nothing wrong."

"Bahar is right," says Farrakh. "If you had not told this Customs official what he demanded to know, you would probably be in jail right now."

I nod. Absolutely. That's exactly what would've happened.

"Yes." Ikrom has clearly come to a decision. "For now, the clinic is the best place. We have a safe there for medicines. I am the only person who knows the combination to the lock. It is very heavy and bolted to the floor. I will also pay a call on Massoud. He will want to know about this possible danger."

And if I know anything about Massoud, he'll post some of his men in and around the clinic, at least at night. With any luck, everything will be okay. I kneel on the wool-carpeted floor and dig piles of American dollars out of my pack. Then, I look up at Bahar. "Is there a place where I could change my clothes?"

She looks startled.

"A lot of the money is *in* my clothes—" I explain as four sets of eyes grow large and cheeks redden as each person grasps what I'm saying.

Gulshan helps me up. "Bahar, show Annie to your room and—help her."

Bahar leads me down a dark, narrow, meandering hall that suggests there has been one small addition after another to this house. "My older sisters' rooms." She nods as we pass through a couple tiny spaces the size of closets, filled with books and papers, piles of fabric, and a sewing machine. "Most sisters sleep together, but my parents were very kind and built these walls to give us each our own room. Now that they are married, my mother uses these rooms for her projects." We step through a curtained doorway into Bahar's room—small enough for me to stand in the middle and touch each wall. There's only one window, and it's hardly big enough to let in fresh air, much less allow anyone to climb in. Or out. It occurs to me that Gulshan and Ikrom weren't taking any chances with their daughters sneaking out with beloveds. There's just one narrow bed barely off the floor, and my duffel and camera case are resting on top.

I pull off my sweater and lift up my tunic to pull money out of my bra. Then, I start on the money belts I've buckled around my torso. Three of them, extra-large, all stuffed full with American dollars.

Bahar collapses onto the bed in giggles.

"What?"

"I wondered how you could have put on this much weight since last May." She holds her hands in front of her mouth, then whispers, "I thought maybe you were with child."

Then, despite all the stress and anxiety, I laugh, too. More like a snort than a laugh. And I keep laughing while I twist the first belt around to unhook the buckle.

"So much laughing!" Gulshan lifts the curtain aside. "I may come in?" She takes one look at me with the padding wrapped around me, and she, too, starts to chuckle. Silently, at first, then she wraps her arms around herself and laughs out loud. "Oh, my! Annie, I suspected that—"

"Me, too!" Bahar laughs.

Gulshan is the first to stop. "We should not laugh. Having a child is a serious matter. In Afghanistan, a woman who is not married . . ."

For a moment, I remember the last time I was in this house. Last spring, when Tariq and Nic and I were seeking leads on where Seema might have gone, we talked to Bahar, who confirmed my worst fears about Awalmir. A 'seducer' was how she described him then. From the sudden quiet in the room, I'm guessing we're all thinking of that night.

"Has there been any word?" Gulshan has to force out the question.

"She texted me several *landays*. Using the name Rahila."

Bahar sits upright on the bed. "That is the name she always used when she wrote stories."

I nod. "That's exactly what my daughter said."

"Why would she send you these poems?" Gulshan frowns.

I shake my head. "I'm not sure."

"Have you spoken to Captain Cerelli about this?" asks Gulshan warily.

"I have. He says it could be a trap. That they're trying to draw me out."

"Draw you out? I do not understand."

Damn. I shouldn't have gone down that road. But, taking a deep breath, I explain. "He thinks that they've sent me the *landays* to convince me to come back to look for Seema. He's worried that Awalmir and the Taliban might come after me."

"That does not make sense. How could the Taliban know you are here?"

Good point. Then I remember that the Taliban have infiltrated nearly every aspect of life in Afghanistan. Who knows? The Customs official at the airport probably reports to them. "I suspect they know I'm here. And if they don't yet, they will soon. Word will get out. And Captain Cerelli knows that."

Gulshan nods. "Yes, there are ears everywhere. The Captain is probably correct. He is a very smart man. I trust him." She looks like she is asking more than the question I answered, but I'm not willing to go there. Not yet, anyway.

"Have either of you heard anything from Seema?"

"Not a word," says Gulshan, looking down at her clasped hands. "For months I hoped she might try to contact me for help. But there has been nothing."

"I wondered if she might be in Kabul." Bahar speaks quietly. "In fact, one day on my way home from class, I thought I saw her." She shakes her head. "But it wasn't Seema." Her words sink to the floor, taking with them my best chances for a lead.

We're all quiet for a long minute, until I try to unbuckle the second money belt. But it's twisted and too bulky for me to manage. Bahar is on her feet. "Let me help. Oof! They are heavy. This must have been very uncomfortable."

I shrug. "I figured it was the safest place. No Afghan man would—"

Bahar shoots me a warning look. Best not let Gulshan know about what happened at the market. At least, not yet.

Two belts off, one to go. The third has also twisted, and the buckle has managed to jam. Bahar gives it a tug. "Yow!" I yelp when it pinches.

"A minute." Gulshan disappears and returns with a pair of sewing scissors. "It is all right to cut this?"

"Please, yes. I'd like to be able to breathe again." And once the last belt is off, I sit down on the bed. "Wait! There's more." Unlacing my boots, I pull them off and exhale a sigh of relief as I wiggle my toes for a long minute. Then, pull out more wads of bills. I glance up to see a strange look pass between Gulshan and Bahar. Oh, please tell me I haven't broken a cultural taboo. "I'm sorry. I didn't think. The money in my boots."

Gulshan smiles. "No, that is not a problem. We are only concerned that you have taken such risks to help us. In your boots. It must have been difficult to walk. Yes?"

I flex my toes again. "Not so bad. Now." Standing up, I adjust my tunic and slip my sweater back on. It's cold in this back room.

Bahar starts giggling again. "You look much thinner now."

WHEN IKROM AND FARRAKH return from taking the money to the clinic, we sit down to a feast in the lounge. In the corner, the small brazier does its best to warm the room. We sit cross-legged on the floor around a bright-yellow cloth Bahar spreads to protect the colorful woven rugs.

Farrakh and Bahar and I eat like ravenous animals who haven't seen food for a very long time. In our frantic drive away from

Bazarak, we had lost our collective appetite. Now, we're tearing off bits of bread nonstop and scooping up the piping hot lamb and eggplant Gulshan cooked.

Ikrom nods his approval. "Our guest does us great honor."

Oh, please. My mouth full, all I can do is nod until I swallow. "It's all so good."

Gulshan's round cheeks quiver with pleasure. "You like Afghan food? It is not too spicy for you?"

"Not too spicy at all. Afghan food is my favorite."

Bahar looks up in surprise. "But you have traveled all over the world."

"True. But this food is special. It warms my soul. It's what I always eat when I have a choice."

Gulshan presses her lips together to hide her smile. It would not do to show her pride. "Darya once told me that she secretly believed you were born Dari and spirited away to a family in another country. I think she was right."

LATER, BAHAR WINS THE BATTLE of where we will sleep and unrolls a thin pallet on the floor of her room. Much to my dismay, I have the honor of sleeping on the narrow bed, which probably isn't any more comfortable. And it's short—clearly intended for a young child. Or Bahar, who isn't much more than five feet tall.

"Tell me," I ask as she unfolds a blanket. "Do you like being at the university?"

"Oh, yes! Sometimes I feel like I am in a dream."

"What's it like having Dr. Faludi as a professor?"

"She is wonderful—very smart and a good teacher." She looks like she wants to say more.

"And?"

She shakes her head. "No, I should not say."

"Bahar, please. You can tell me."

"It is her husband," she says softly.

Omar? Why on earth is Bahar having anything to do with him? "What about him?"

She clutches the edge of the blanket she's just been smoothing. "He scares me. No, 'scares' is the wrong word . . ." She pauses.

"Bahar?"

"It is a silly thing. One time, Dr. Faludi asked me to stop by to discuss one of my essays. She gave me the address of her apartment. I thought she wanted me to go there. That wasn't unusual because she has met with other students at her home. I must have misunderstood, though. Her husband was there with other men. I could hear them arguing and yelling. But when I knocked on the door, they became quiet."

"What happened next?"

Bahar props her chin against her fist. "A man opened the door. I believe it was her husband. He seemed very angry that I was there. He yelled that Dr. Faludi wasn't there and told me to leave."

"What did Dr. Faludi say when you told her about what happened?"

"Oh, I was very embarrassed. I apologized over my misunderstanding. She was kind and told me not to worry."

Which doesn't exactly answer my question. Still, Bahar has told me enough. There's something going on in that apartment, something Bibi probably doesn't like and is trying to avoid. Or ignore. Political meetings? Omar has become more conservative.

Strike that, extreme. What if he's crossed the line from mainstream Afghan politics to supporting the Taliban? *Get real!* I admonish myself. There's no evidence to suggest that. Still, the anxiety I'm feeling for Bibi tightens around my heart.

Bahar forces a smile. "That meeting, it was not important. I will simply not return to Dr. Faludi's apartment when her husband is there. Please, do not worry."

We strip out of our clothes as quickly as possible. First, I pull on my *Our Daughters, Ourselves* T-shirt, then layer on a tunic. But not fast enough. Bahar catches sight of the bruises on my upper arm.

"Annie!"

I take my first good look at the purpling mess. "Eh. From the man at the market in Bazarak."

"He really hurt you! We should have reported him to the police."

I shake my head. "Remember how the people around us were staring? They seemed ready to blame *me*. They were probably the ones who alerted the police to come after us. If Farrakh hadn't driven away as fast as he did, I'd probably be in jail now."

"That is not right. In Afghanistan, everyone always blames the women for the wrongdoing of men. It is something I want to change." She lowers her voice. "I went to a demonstration with Dr. Faludi. It was for the rights of women."

"That was brave."

"It is what I will teach my students when I become a teacher."

Shivering, I pull on a pair of leggings and my sweater. And long for more of the hot *chai* I drank nonstop during dinner. It helped warm me, but that was hours ago.

"I'm not used to the cold," I whisper as I see Bahar watching me in the light of the kerosene lantern. "I just spent three months in Yemen and Saudi Arabia, where it was very hot." Not to mention that at home in Milwaukee, I've got central heating.

She smiles. "I would love to travel someday."

"Would you ever consider leaving Afghanistan?"

Her eyes widen. "You mean forever?"

I nod.

She mulls over my question. "Many women say they want to leave Afghanistan."

"Yes, especially the educated women."

"They are the very people who should stay. If all the educated women leave, who will teach our daughters?"

"And influence your sons."

"Yes! You understand!" She nods emphatically. "After I finish at university, I would like to travel to see how things are in other countries. The U.S.A. That is the first country I would like to visit—to see how life is different there. Then, I will come back."

"When you do visit, you will be my guest."

"That would be wonderful. I hope I will meet your daughter then. Mel? That is her name?"

"Her name is really Emmeline"—I smile—"in honor of my grandmother, but she prefers to be called Mel."

A few moments later, "Annie?"

"Hmm?" I stretch my feet down under the covers to the bottom of the bed and off the end of the mattress. So cold. I'll never be able to sleep. I roll over and dig into my duffel for a pair of heavy socks.

"That man at the market in Bazarak? Do you think he knew about the money? Could he have been trying to steal it?"

Damn, she's smart. And perceptive. I flop over onto my back. "I'm afraid you could be right. It was strange, though. He didn't just grab my backpack and run." I don't tell her about him calling me a whore. "He knew I was American." And that's bothering me. Maybe it was just a lucky guess. Or maybe Cerelli was right and people, bad people, know who I am. And know I'm here.

"This is what bothers me. Instead of taking your backpack, he grabbed your arm. Afghan men don't do that. Unless . . ."

I don't ask her to finish her thought. We both know she's thinking 'unless they're with the Taliban or ISIS and are kidnapping you.'

With both of us snuggled under the covers, Bahar turns off the lantern. A minute or two later, I can hear her sleep-breathing. But I'm not there yet. My heart hasn't stopped racing. Too much caffeine now coursing through my veins. Too many 'what-ifs' swirling in my thoughts. The man at the market bothers me tremendously. So does the Customs officer at the airport. Even the lieutenant at Dalan Sang is looking suspicious. Then, there's Omar and all his locked metal boxes. His meetings. And *Hama Bibi*. That's two women in the space of less than twenty-four hours telling me not to worry.

Of course I'm worried. Very worried.

21

SUNRISE COMES LATER IN Wad Qol than in Kabul. With the Hindu Kush Mountains towering around us, morning light takes longer to find its way down into the valley. So, it's still dark out when Farrakh and Bahar head back to the city. I stand with Ikrom and Gulshan in front of their mud-brick house, waving them off. But it's freezing in the early morning, and even before the taillights disappear, Ikrom hurries to the bakery for fresh bread while Gulshan and I retreat inside. Where it isn't much warmer. The brazier hasn't been fired up yet and, since I'm guessing the plan is for all three of us to be out for most of the day, probably won't see a match until evening.

"Come," says Gulshan in English, leading me into the kitchen. Functional, with a cooktop of sorts on the wood-fired stove. "You do not mind speaking in English?"

I shake my head. "Of course not."

"It is good for me to practice. Now that Darya is not here, I have not as many opportunities. Ikrom could use some practice, too."

As the English teacher at the school, she probably wants all the practice she can get.

"Now, sit." She points me to the worn oak table in the corner that bears an uncanny similarity to Dar's. I run my hand across the battered top.

Gulshan smiles as she boils water for tea and heats milk in a small saucepan. "You recognize the table. Yes? Tariq made us this gift before he left. He was very generous. Have you heard from him? He is well?"

I trace a burn mark on the table, then look up and meet her eyes. "Physically, he is well, but . . . his soul is tired." This last bit is something Tariq once said to me about Dar.

"Ah." She nods. "Healing will take a long time. For all of us. And for you."

I do my best to wave away her comment.

She laughs and places jars of peanut butter and jam on the table. "Many times, I saw Darya do that! I am afraid you are not nearly as effective."

"What do you mean? I think my wave is just as dismissive as Darya's."

"No." Still laughing, she shakes her head, then bends down to stick a few more pieces of kindling into the stove. "You must tell me, please, what your worry is."

"My worry?"

"Your face is full of worry."

I'm not about to let her in on all my worries. Bibi. Bahar. Cerelli. Not necessarily in that order. So, I say the first other thing that comes to mind. "Farrakh and Bahar. It's a long drive back."

"Bah!" She waves her hand, a perfect imitation of Darya. "Farrakh is a good son and devoted to his sister. He will take care of her." She doesn't probe any further into my worries.

I breathe a sigh of relief. "How can I help you?"

"No." She smiles. "You are my guest. It is my pleasure to cook for you. Please, you would like a fried egg with your *nân?*"

A traditional Afghan breakfast, not the more Westernized version Darya used to make. "Whatever you and Ikrom are having."

"Good. An egg for you as well."

I watch her chop a couple potatoes and peppers and set them frying in an oiled pan. A few minutes later, she adds a can of tomatoes and lets the mixture stew. Finally, she cracks five eggs into the vegetables and finishes the dish with a handful of chopped cilantro. This is when Ikrom fills the doorway, several rounds of *nân* in his hands, a yeasty aroma mingling with the bubbling *shakshouka.* As if they had it timed.

"Sit, sit!" Gulshan takes the breads, setting them to rewarm on the stove, and waves him to the seat kitty-corner to mine. "You had success?"

"Of course! I will tell all after we eat." He crosses the room in three steps and sits, watching as his wife bustles around the kitchen. The gleam in his eyes matches the twitching smile on his lips. This man loves his wife. And isn't afraid to show it. Not always the case in Afghan marriages. Or American marriages, for that matter.

Small bowls of steaming milky tea appear in front of each of us. Then, a bowl of sugar. Ikrom slowly stirs in four teaspoons and widens his eyes when I pass. "Tariq told me you are as good as Afghan. He must be wrong. No Afghan drinks bitter tea first thing in the morning."

"Shh! Such a thing to say to our guest," says Gulshan sternly.

I sneak a half smile. "I am sweet enough. I'm saving the sugar for you."

He roars with laughter. "I save sugar for you! This is good."

Soon, plates of eggs and bread are in front of us, and Gulshan refills our tea. Our conversation is at an end. The only sounds are our lips smacking. I had no idea *nân* with peanut butter and eggs poached in veggies could taste this good. I exhale a soft moan, but apparently not soft enough. Ikrom and Gulshan both stop eating to look at me. I feel the warmth reddening my cheeks and clap a hand over my mouth.

Ikrom is back to laughing, a hearty belly laugh. "You need a husband!"

Gulshan wags an index finger at him but can't hide her smile.

Desperate to shift their focus away from my need for a love life, I ask, "So, what's the plan for today?"

Gulshan looks to her husband, who obliges us by puffing out his chest. "It is all arranged. The men begin work today. They will clear away the debris." He checks the time on his cell phone. "They should be at the school in another hour. Perhaps you two would like to meet them there?"

"And you, Ikrom?" Gulshan asks, refilling our tea *pialas* yet again. "Where will you be?"

"First, I will check in at the clinic. Then, if I am able, I will come to the school."

They both look at me. I look up from my third bowl of tea and smile. "Perfect plan!"

AFTER GULSHAN AND I CLEAN up the kitchen, I retreat to Bahar's bedroom and dig my camera out of my Lowepro.

Take the pack with you! Cerelli's voice, as clear as if he were in the room with me.

Give me a break! You're not even here. Besides which, you're not speaking to me.

Make sure the Sig's in the pack. Loaded.

I'm not going to shoot anyone! I hope I didn't say that out loud.

Annie. I don't want you coming home in a body bag. Take the damn gun!

This is ridiculous! But, cramming my camera back into the Lowepro, I dutifully shoulder my pack. Heavy with the gun and ammo and sat phone. Then, I make my way along the meandering hall out to the lounge.

"You have brought your camera?" Gulshan asks when I meet her at the front door.

"I never leave home without it."

"Good!" She beams. "I was hoping you would take pictures as they build the new school. You will make copies for me? The teachers and the girls, also their parents, will want to see."

"Seriously? You're ready to build the school?"

"Of course! As Ikrom said, today we will clear away what is left from the fire. Tomorrow we will start to build." She holds up a roll of papers. "I have the plans right here."

I put my hand on her arm. "This is unbelievable! You already have plans?"

She smiles coyly. "Darya and I had plans drawn years ago. Our hope has always been to build a new school."

"What about the permits?"

"Permits?" She looks puzzled.

"Permission from the village or the district government saying that you can build the school. Official approval of your plans."

"Permits. A good word. But this is something we do not worry about in Wad Qol." With one deft flick of the hand, she pulls down the front of her black *burqa* over her coat. A few seconds to adjust it, and we're off to the site of the new Wad Qol Secondary School for Girls.

"Have you been there since . . . ?"

"Yes." She sounds so matter-of-fact. "The other teachers and I went back as soon as the debris was cool enough. We wanted to see if there was anything we could save."

"Was there?"

"Not very much. The fire, it was very hot; it burned nearly everything. I did find the safe from Darya's secret closet. That I turned over to Chief Warrant Officer Sawyer right away."

I study her profile. So, she knew. Enough, at least, to go to Sawyer with the safe. Which means she knew about Darya and Tariq's real reason for being here.

She turns to meet my eyes. "Ah, I see that you did not know about Darya's secret."

I shake my head. "Not until after. But it seems like you did."

"It became obvious. Working closely together, I saw things. We never talked about it, and I pretended not to know. That made it safer for everyone, and Darya did not need to worry about danger coming to me."

"I thought we were close. Best friends. Sisters. But I didn't suspect a thing."

Gulshan reaches out from under her *burqa* and takes my hand. "She took great care to protect you. Sometimes I believe she loved you more than anyone. If you could have heard her talk about you. She told us all how you encouraged her, how you paid for the school. She could never have made it succeed without you." She squeezes my hand. "You must know this."

Tears burn the backs of my eyes.

We stop, and Gulshan wraps her arms around me. "Oh, my dear, you must give this sadness up to Allah. Let him help you rejoice in all the wonderful things Darya accomplished throughout her life."

Sometimes I wish I had Gulshan's faith. To put all my sorrow and grief in God's hands would make life much easier. But I don't have that devotion.

"Come. I know what will bring you some joy."

Keeping my hand tucked around her arm, she guides me up the still-sunless, unpaved streets. We pass through the village. Just as I remember it. Mud-brick houses. An occasional walnut tree and mulberry bush, leaves now yellow and gold, their fruit gone for the winter. We skirt the village center with its little shops and kiosks stretching out in a long row. Only the bakery is open this early. The aroma of baking *nân* wraps around me, making me salivate even though I just ate breakfast. A little farther on, we turn off the road and walk up a newly hewn path, trees chopped off low, leaving a line of stumps.

In front of us, a dilapidated, one-story, wooden building. Rambling, with a couple small additions tacked on. There are traces of paint—blue in one place, white in another. Mostly, though, there are large unpainted swaths revealing yellow mud bricks, some of them crumbling. Heavy plastic is tacked over the windows. Looking closely, I see panes of glass that are broken. Several wooden frames are cracked. Except for the newly chopped trees leading from the road to the front door, it looks all but abandoned.

"What is this place?"

"You will see." She pulls a key from the pocket of her baggy pants, a braid of colorful pieces of fabric trailing from the brass hole.

It takes a moment while she jimmies the key into the lock, then she wrenches open the door, and we're finally in. In what? Even inside, I'm not sure what this place is supposed to be. Drafts of cold morning air leak in around the windows. I clutch my arms around me to stop my shivering.

"The maths teacher will come soon to light the fire. Do you remember Iman? She is the other teacher who wears the *burqa*."

"Yes, of course." I'm still looking around the small room. Other than the smallest kerosene stove I've ever seen standing in the corner, there's nothing here. Crossing the room, I push open the next door and see another empty room with yet another door on the far side. I turn back toward Gulshan.

"This, my dear Annie, is the Wad Qol Secondary School for Girls."

"No."

"Yes. And we are very blessed to have this much. Years ago, this was the boys' school. Then, the village built a new school for them, and this was left empty to return to nature. As you can see"—she points to cracked windows and rotting boards—"there is much damage."

"There were a hundred girls at the school last spring. How can you possibly fit them all in these two tiny rooms?"

"There are three rooms. And some of the girls have stopped attending. Their parents became too frightened after the bombing. We have about seventy girls now, and they take turns." She bends down to pick up an old-fashioned piece of slate and holds it up for me to see. "One of the girls left this behind."

"When the new school is finished, will you be able to convince those reluctant parents to let their daughters return?"

"That is my hope. *Inshallah*."

"Let's just hope God can twist those parents' arms."

"Allah works in many ways." I can hear the smile in her voice. "Whoever could have thought we would now have the money to make a building?"

"Darya would have! And she'd be telling us to go build the new school for our girls."

It takes another ten minutes to walk the rest of the way to the burned-down school. I've been bracing for this visit. My first time back since the fire. Since they murdered Dar in front of the burning building. In front of the other teachers. Oh, God. The other teachers—Iman, Maryam, and, of course, Gulshan. They must have been terrified that they were going to be next. To stand there, guarding the girls. What heroes!

The explosion. The fire. Wood splintering. Windows shattering. Cans of kerosene exploding, punctuating the roar of the flames. And the smoke. So thick I could hardly breathe.

This morning, though, nearly six months later, it's quiet— except for a few birds hidden among the golden leaves, serenading us with their early-morning songs. Peaceful. Almost serene.

But I can't bring myself to look at the patch of dirt where Darya lay, covered by her black headscarf with its delicate gold embroidery along the edges. Instead, I walk past the piles of fragrant, new-cut lumber and stacks of plywood and go straight to the school where the mosque-blue door used to be. Where blackened, blistered splinters of wood remain. Using my booted foot to push the wood aside, I step into the wreckage and look over the charred remains. Many of the mud bricks melted. That's how hot the flames were. And what the fire didn't destroy, the rains finished off. The tables and red benches that used to seat two girls each lie unrecognizable amid the ruins.

This I need to photograph. Mel and Awa asked for images of the new school being built. They also need to see the loss.

Slipping my pack off my shoulder, I dig out my camera, loop the strap around my neck, then climb carefully over a blackened wooden beam and into what was once the classroom I shared with Gulshan. Powering up, I compose the first shot and press the shutter. Nothing happens. Instead, a message pops up on the LCD panel.

Check format

I pull up the menu. There's hardly any space left on the SD card. Strange. All my cards should be new. I could just reformat, but that's something I never do. Not without first checking to see what's on the card. Removing the card, I turn it over in my hand. Not the *Extreme Pro 64 GB* I use. Where did this come from? Later. I'll have to go through the images later. For now, I stow the card in my pocket, dig out another, slide it into my camera, and press FORMAT.

Making my way through the jungle of charred wood, Gulshan's desk, and what used to be a cracked blackboard, I'm soon filthy. And wishing I'd worn black. As well as latex gloves. I snap a few shots as I move through the remains of my classroom. Then stop. And squat. And poke at bits of what look to be paper. Picking up one of the larger pieces, the size of my camera body, I turn it over and find myself looking at part of Malalai's face. Her eyes. Frightened. Determined to help me understand what she was trying to say. My Pulitzer Prize-winning photograph of a ten-year-old Pashtun girl, killed for having learned to write. She was writing in the sand to warn me to get out of her village before the Taliban killed me. Only I failed to understand what she'd written until much later—when

I printed the image. The girls had tacked an enlargement of the picture onto the back wall of the classroom. And this is what's left. I lay the scrap of her face on one of the charred tables, take a few steps back, and line up the shot.

The shuffling behind me draws my attention, and I glance up to see Gulshan. "Look what I found."

She comes closer. "Oh! How is it possible that Malalai survived the fire?" I hear the amazement in her voice. "We must save this to remind the students of how we rebuilt the school."

"It's very brittle, just flaking apart."

"I will find a way to preserve this." But looking around, she's clearly at a loss.

"Wait! I've got something." Reaching into the back of my Lowepro, I pull out one of the plastic sleeves I always carry for just this kind of situation. Slipping what's left of the picture inside, I ease it into the secret compartment in my pack. "I'll give this to you when we get back to the house."

I fire off a few more shots and am about to move farther into the ruins of the building when Gulshan puts her hand on my arm. "I came to tell you that the workers have arrived."

Turning toward the yard in front of the building, I see them. At least twenty men waiting patiently to begin demolition. Behind them, a long line of pickup trucks ready to cart away what's left of the school.

I swing my arms wide, embracing the ruin that was once one of the very few secondary schools for girls in the valley. "It's hard to believe all this debris is still here."

"A few people have taken things. And, of course, we removed that horrible pickup truck. Mostly, we have left things as you see."

"Why?"

"Because of what happened. The fire. Darya's murder. People in this area respected her. We were grateful for this school. It is, how do you say, a sacred place?"

I nod. "A sacred place. You said it very well." Walking to the far west corner of the demo zone, I capture a few more images. I'll have to wait until I upload them to my laptop to see if I've captured any of that 'sacred' feeling. But honestly, the place just seems empty to me. Destroyed. There's no life here anymore. No soul. Not even Darya's. And I can't hold back the workers any longer. This place has been sacred and unused long enough. It's time to bring life back to these grounds. "Let's get started."

"They can wait a little longer. We all understand that you need to see this place and find some peace. Come," she says, taking my hand, urging me to follow.

"What?"

"There is something you must see before the work begins."

It takes me all of five seconds to realize we're walking toward the very spot I've been trying to avoid. "No. Please."

"Annie. You must see. This is the way to help you move forward."

I close my eyes for a moment and steel myself. Then, I let Gulshan guide me to the small patch of earth where Darya died. Where I sat next to her, hoping the earth would open up and take us both.

We stop. I'm looking off into the distance toward the glowing golden canopy of walnut trees in the grove where I tried to convince Seema to leave Awalmir. Where a few days later, the girls from the school hid after the bombing.

"Annie." Gulshan gently tugs at my arm. "Here. It was here that Darya died. You must look. She would not want you to keep this pain inside you for the rest of your life. You of all people. Please?"

She's right, of course. I hear Darya storming and stomping around inside my brain. *You idiot! Get on with it! Look! There's nothing left to see here. You're still alive. So, live! Don't you dare waste any more time because of me.*

I force myself to look. Darya isn't here, obviously. The women of Wad Qol took her, washed her body, and wrapped her in a white shroud before Tariq and Cerelli buried her in an unmarked grave. As she wanted. Seema may have accused her of not believing, of not being a good Muslim, but I know better. Darya believed.

"Her footprints, her body will fade to dust. It is what happens to all of us. One day to me. Another day to you. It is the way of all life." Gulshan squeezes my hand as tears stream down my cheeks. "Like you, I will never let her memory fade. Like Malalai, Darya will live in my heart and in yours. Yes? So many girls here will have a chance at a better life because of her. And their children. Their grandchildren. So many girls."

I kneel and scoop up a handful of the dirt where Darya lay, where her blood fed the earth. The dirt now dry, not much more than dust. Opening my fingers, I let it trickle back down to the ground, my tears adding salt.

"More time?" Gulshan asks.

I shake my head, then push myself to my feet. "I have what I came for. What I want most now is to build the new school."

"Good." A split second later, Gulshan launches into action. She organizes the workers. They are free to take anything usable. The burned wood will work well as charcoal, a huge help for cooking and heating during the long winter months. What's left of the mud bricks can be wheelbarrowed into the woods, where they'll continue to break down and return to the earth. Anything else, she tells them, they have to haul to the village scrap pile.

I walk away from the debris, moving halfway across the yard to a spot where I can continue to photograph the men at work. And before my eyes, I see the remains of the front classrooms disappear. Faces and hands and clothes blacken fast as men ferry everything out to the trucks and then to their homes.

Of course they'd want the wood. I picture the stove in Gulshan's kitchen, the brazier in her lounge. Which are probably like the cooking and heating stoves in the rest of the village. The last vestiges of the school will go up in smoke. But at least the villagers will be fed and warm.

"Annie?" Gulshan puts her hand on my arm. "I must go check on the school. Could you supervise for the rest of the morning? I will come back when I can."

"Of course. What if they finish before you get back?"

Her eyes twinkle. "I do not think they will work that fast. They will go home for lunch at midday and return for a few more hours. *Inshallah*, they will finish today. Ikrom will come by at four o'clock to pay their wages and arrange for the work tomorrow. They will wait." She's watching me carefully. "You will be all right with these men."

I let her words settle on me. Then nod. I feel safe. No cold chills charging up my spine. No prickling at the back of my neck. "You go to the school. We'll be fine."

But I didn't count on the director of the boys' school showing up midmorning along with the religion teacher, whose clothes have a decidedly unpleasant odor clinging to them.

The director at least is respectful. "You have brought money from America to rebuild."

It's not a question, so I just nod. Even as I wonder how he knows already.

"Everyone in the village is talking of this."

I nod again.

"I am thinking that you could give part of the money to the boys' school. Or perhaps raise more money. There are many things that we need."

At least he doesn't try to tell me that education is wasted on girls. And he doesn't really demand the money outright. But it still requires more than a nod, and I'm not at all sure what Gulshan would want me to say.

The men continue to work, carting armloads of charred wood to their trucks. "*Mêbakhshêd! Momken ast bogozarom.* Excuse me! Let me by," they say one after another as they wind their way around us.

"Hmph!" snorts the religion teacher, smoothing his grizzled beard. I can't help noticing the bits of his morning's breakfast stuck fast. "All this to educate girls? You ruin them for their husbands." I should've expected the religion teacher would spout this drivel. And he's not done. "You pervert the word of Allah." He crosses his arms over his chest and scowls.

Both men look at me expectantly. Do they honestly believe I'm going to hand over the money to them? Now?

I do my best to sound pleasant. "I understand that Islam values education for girls as well as for boys. And it was a *woman* who founded the very first university. Fatima al-Fihri. Al-Qarawiyyin. 859. In Fez, Morocco." I'm rather proud of this factoid and like to trot it out whenever I can. It makes me feel educated.

Then, figuring this may be the one and only chance I have to make my point, I lean toward the religion teacher. "Doesn't the *Qur'an* command all Muslims, men and women, to pursue an education? I think so." At this point, I might as well go for broke. "In fact, the Prophet Muhammad himself, peace be upon him, used to teach women along with men. Are you actually saying the educated *wives* of the Prophet were 'ruined'?"

His scowl deepens, then he spits into the dirt a little too close to my feet. "You waste all this money. What will happen the next time, when *this* school burns down?" His tone is vaguely threatening, enough to make me squirm. And as he steps closer, another pungent odor wafts over me. Damn, he stinks.

"If that horrible thing should happen, we'll build the school again. And again. As many times as we have to because the girls of Wad Qol and this valley deserve an education." My words sound resolute, but inside I'm quaking. I really should just keep my mouth shut, or at least muster a bit of the diplomatic skill that comes so naturally to Gulshan. She'd know how to handle these two.

The director's frown clearly says he doesn't expect any diplomacy from me. And, if the religion teacher's curled upper lip is any indication, he doesn't either. Finally, they turn to leave. Thank God. But as the religion teacher skirts wide around me, his long, dirty, smelly coat catching the air behind him, he spits out the words, "*Morda-gow.*"

I stare after him. Why the hell is he calling me a 'dead cow'?

22

IT'S DUSK BY THE TIME we finish loading the last of the charred wood into the flatbed of Ikrom's pickup. I stare at the empty space where the Wad Qol Secondary School for Girls used to stand. Gone. Completely gone. Deep inside me, my heart breaks. Again.

I feel an arm around my waist. "You will see, Annie," says Gulshan, tightening her hold. "Soon, the new school will stand here. This building, it will be better. A concrete floor."

"What was there before?" I try to remember but come up with nothing at all.

"Just cement. It was very thin and cracked in many places. The fire destroyed it. Now, we will have concrete. Cement and stone. Very thick. It will be much stronger."

I stare. "How do you know this?"

She grins. "Darya and I talked about how to make things better. We used to dream. Now, our dreams will become real."

I close my eyes to shut out the emptiness in front of me. And to let myself see the new school.

Gulshan gives me a few moments, then tugs at my arm. "Come now. It is getting cold. We will go home."

The three of us pile onto the front bench seat of Ikrom's pickup and head slowly toward the village center. We pass a shepherd herding his small flock of sheep and goats, but otherwise, there is no one on the road. Light glows from inside houses, peeking out from around shutters that are closed against the cold for the night.

"It went well today!" Ikrom sounds pleased with how much the men were able to finish.

"Oh, yes! At this rate, we will have the school built in a few weeks." Gulshan finds my hand and squeezes. "You will stay until we finish, yes?"

"Let's see how fast this goes. I do have to be back in Kabul by December 1st for an assignment." I'm back to thinking about dead cows. "I forgot to tell you that the director of the boys' school stopped by today."

"Good." Ikrom steers the pickup gently around a curve in the road. "I want him to see that people in this village, especially the men, support education for our daughters."

"Well, I'm not sure I convinced him. I know I didn't convince the religion teacher."

"That lazy, old fart!" Gulshan spits out the last word. "I feel sorry for his wife and family. His students, too."

Ikrom turns another corner. "It will be a good day when he is too old to teach."

"He certainly had a lot to say about the girls' school. None of it good. Then, when he was leaving, he said something I didn't understand. I mean, I understood the words; they just don't make sense to me."

"What did he say?" Gulshan sounds wary.

"*Morda-gow.*"

Ikrom brakes in front of their house. "He said *what?*" There's no mistaking the anger in his voice.

"Dead cow. Why would he call me a dead cow?"

"He didn't." In the light of the dashboard, I can see Ikrom's face has turned bright red.

"I misunderstood?"

"No." Gulshan reaches past me to unhook the odd little mechanism that opens the door. "You understood his words. But those words, they have another meaning." We climb out of the pickup and head into the house.

Ikrom looks like he's about to explode, but Gulshan waves him off. "You unload that wood, please? I will take care of this." She sweeps off her *burqa* and hangs it on a peg by the door.

Leading me through the dark of the front lounge and into the kitchen, she explains, "This is something better for me to say. It would embarrass my husband." She takes her time lighting the kerosene lantern and stoking the fire in the stove. Clearly, she needs to figure out what to tell me. I stare at my blackened hands as I lean against the plastered kitchen wall. *What exactly did the old fart say?*

Finally, she turns toward me and bursts out laughing. Not what I was expecting. Then, I get it. After carrying all that charred wood, I must be a complete and total disaster. Not only my hands, but my face, my hair, my clothes. "Oh, Annie! Ikrom will bring in a pail of water for your washing. I beg you to excuse me. I should not laugh. This—what that awful man said to you, it is an insult. A very serious insult."

"You better tell me before Ikrom comes in."

"Yes. This toad, you are certain he said *morda-gow?*"

I nod.

"You understood correctly. Those words, they mean 'dead cow.' But that is also how we say the number '39.' And it means 'prostitute.'"

Not the first time on this trip I've been called a whore. The man in the Bazarak market may have said it differently, but his meaning was the same. There seems to be quite a pattern developing here. "Right before he said that, he also told me I'm perverting the girls of Wad Qol against Islam."

"That I expected he would say. He often said that to Darya and me when we tried to talk sense into him." She sighs loudly. "But to call you a-a . . . That is not right."

"Not to worry. I've heard worse."

"Not from Afghan men, I hope! In this country, we do not insult our guests. It is our tradition to show every kindness. And this? This is not kind." She stamps her foot. "This is not hospitable."

Ikrom appears in the doorway, his expression questioning, clearly wondering whether Gulshan has told me how terribly I've been insulted. Of course, Gulshan and Ikrom have been as well. Clearly, the religion teacher is questioning their morals for hosting and sheltering the likes of me. Ikrom hoists a pail of water with his still-filthy hands, placing it carefully on the stove. "Time for washing, I think?" Gulshan's eyes flash a message, and he turns to go back outside. His stiff nod tells me he's no happier about what the old 'fart' said to me today.

Picturing Ikrom scrubbing down outside with cold water, I push myself away from the wall and move toward the stove. "No need to heat that for me. We'll be waiting forever."

Gulshan studies me, then rummages through a plastic box under the counter for a rag and soap. "You are a good woman. Ikrom is right. We must find you a husband."

I hold up my filthy hands. "Please, I've had one already."

She lathers up the rag and cleans her own hands first, a sly smile creeping across her face. "Perhaps not the right husband."

AFTER DINNER, I GIVE THE plastic sleeve with the charred remnant of Malalai's picture to Gulshan, then retreat to my room to allow her and Ikrom some time to themselves. To be honest, I also want to take a look at the images on the SD card that was in my camera. Digging the card out of my pocket, I upload the images onto my laptop, then scan through them. And don't recognize a single shot.

This isn't my card.

I keep clicking through images. The senior girls at the Wad Qol Secondary School—the old school before it burned. Then I come to a shot of me in profile, looking out a wide window of the classroom I shared with Gulshan. More images of me, all of them candids. Plus, pics of Darya. Tariq in the kitchen at their house. The three of us at the kitchen table eating dinner. I zoom through them, looking to see what else is on the card. Finally, I come to a portrait of a young man, clean-shaven, dark hair with a curl that flops down over his forehead. Moody brown eyes. Full pouting lips. Sexy as hell. Awalmir. The young Pashtun man who was bent on seducing the photographer. In this case, Seema.

Holy shit! I had Seema's SD card in my camera.

I stare at my laptop screen, remembering that I was checking over my gear the night before last in *Hama* Bibi's guest room. Just when I thought I had everything packed away, I found a card. *This* card.

Seema's card.

On the floor.

Which means Seema was in *Hama* Bibi's guest room *after* she took these pictures. *After* the school was bombed. *After* Darya was killed.

My stomach clenches. It's all I can do to keep from throwing up.

Hama Bibi helped Seema and Awalmir get away?

No. Bibi told me she wasn't in Kabul then. And I believe her. The devastation on her face, in her voice, was too real. She couldn't have faked that.

Then, who was in that apartment?

Omar? The only possibility.

Wait! Slow down! This is just an SD card. Okay, so the card was in the apartment. That doesn't mean Seema was. Maybe it was Awalmir. Or someone else entirely who got ahold of her camera. There's only one thing I know for sure: I've got to call Cerelli. Even if he's not talking to me.

MUCH LATER, AFTER GULSHAN and Ikrom have gone to bed and the syncopated snoring from their small room tells me they're asleep, I stick my cell phone in my pants pocket, then gather my flashlight and the sat phone and tiptoe out of the house. Training the light on the ground, I make my way quietly around to the back, careful to avoid the charred wood Ikrom piled here earlier. In the open space behind the house, I take note of an old outhouse and garden beds filled with plants wilted from the cold nights. No chairs, no benches. Unlike Tariq and Darya's courtyard, this doesn't seem to be a place to sit and relax or enjoy drinks and dinner on a summer evening. Maybe that's a Western concept.

I weigh the sat phone in my hand. Was Sawyer right? Did Cerelli really tell him to give this to me? Meaning that he's still looking out for me? Still cares about me? I wish I could believe that. For now, though, all that matters is that I've got the phone. And I have to let Cerelli know about Seema's SD card.

So why is my stomach churning?

Give it a rest! Just call the man and leave a message. It's not like he's going to answer.

I tighten my hold on the phone. *Come on! This is Cerelli. You love this man.*

I tap his number. And wait for the satellite to home in, pick up my call. Finally, his phone rings. And rings. Then nothing. Not even his voice mail. Okay, this has happened before. I give him a few minutes, then try again. Still nothing.

Mel. While I'm out here, I should check in with her. Then, with any luck, Cerelli's line will be clear. It's midnight here, which makes it midafternoon in Milwaukee. I try to remember her schedule of after-school activities, but one day runs into the next. Damn, I should know these things. How did Catherine Elizabeth ever keep it all straight?

I tap in her number on the sat phone. Wherever she is. She probably won't answer anyway. She rarely does.

Two rings, and she's on the line. "Mom? Are you okay?" The worry in her voice stops me.

"I'm fine. I just thought I should let you know I'm here and the money is safe and sound."

She breathes a sigh of relief. "You scared me. When I saw the number—I was afraid something had happened. I mean, it's not like you usually call to check in."

My eyes nearly cross as I remember the series of increasingly frantic calls we exchanged last May. "Well, sorry to worry you."

"Just a sec, okay?" She muffles the phone, but I hear voices in the background. Then, she's back on the line. "Okay. I was in a *Ripples* editorial meeting. We're doing a follow-up story on the fundraiser. Can I ask you some questions?"

"Go for it!"

"So, how did the people in the village react when you got there with the money?"

"Well, I've only seen Gulshan and Ikrom and their adult children. They were all incredibly excited. And the men who were working at the site today are happy because now they have jobs."

"Wow! You mean they've already started building?"

"They have. Which is pretty amazing. Gulshan has plans that she and Auntie Dar drew up years ago. They cleared the site today. Tomorrow, they actually start building."

"This is so great! It's like really happening. You *are* taking pictures?"

I laugh. "What else would I be doing?"

"Back to the money. You got it to the bank, right?"

"There aren't any banks in Wad Qol."

"Then where's the money?"

"No worries. It's safe."

"Come on, really, where is it?"

I think about that for a couple seconds and decide that's information no one should have. Not even the high schoolers who raised the money, no matter that they're seven thousand miles away. "Sorry, that's confidential."

"Give me a break." I can imagine her major eye roll.

"Let's just say someone tried to steal it from me."

"*What?* Did they get any of it?"

"No, he did not. And thanks for asking, I'm fine. A little bruised is all. But no one needs to know where the money is."

She sighs her exasperation. "Get real. They won't be reading my story."

"You never know."

"Talk about paranoid."

"Too many people around here already know about the money. I don't want any more trouble."

"All right. Jeez."

"Any other questions?"

"How'd you keep that guy from stealing the money?"

"Kicked him. Hard. In the *cojones.*"

"Mom, you rock!"

"Yeah, well, I may also have really pissed him off. Let's hope I don't run into him again."

"No worries. He won't risk his junk again. Anyway, back to the school. How long will it take to build?"

I shrug. "Gulshan is saying a few weeks. That seems overly optimistic to me. Still, it's pretty cold here, and the teachers want to get into the new school as soon as possible. They're making do with a run-down shack for now. But sweetie, it really is a shack. There's nothing there. The girls have to sit on the floor, and there's barely any heat."

"Seriously? That's awful!"

"It's awfully cold, that's for sure."

"So, uh . . ." She drags out the words. "You have any idea when you'll be coming home?"

"I head back to Kabul at the end of the month and probably won't be done with my assignment until mid-December. Why? What's going on?"

"Nothing."

"Tell me."

"It's okay, really." But her voice says something is most definitely not okay.

"Mel."

"Dad and *she* found out about you being in Afghanistan."

That was fast. I close my eyes. "How did they find out?"

"Dad came by last night and insisted on talking to you. I finally had to tell him. He went ballistic when he found out I'm alone."

"You're not alone. Bonita's there."

"Yeah, well, apparently Bonita doesn't count."

She's not telling me everything. "What else?"

"I'm not allowed to see Yasmine or her family or anyone from the mosque."

"Fuck them!" Tell me I didn't just say that out loud.

"Mom? I mean I share the feeling, but, well, you know."

"Sorry, sorry. I shouldn't have said that. So, does he want you to move back with them or what?"

"He made me go last night. But let's get this straight. They don't *want* me at all." Her voice cracks.

"Oh, God, Mel, I'm sorry. I just don't understand what's wrong with them. Look, do you want me to call him?"

I can almost hear her thinking. "No. Don't. It'll probably just make things worse." She sounds so resigned. "Anyway, how long . . . no, never mind. It doesn't matter. The school is what's important. Plus, you've got that assignment after. Will you at least be home for Christmas?"

"Count on it." I smile. How did I raise such an incredible daughter? *Hold on! I* didn't raise her. For the most part, Todd and Catherine Elizabeth did the heavy lifting. But their parenting has sure gone to hell over the last six months, and that's got to change. As soon as I get home.

"Say, Mom, have you heard anything from Seema? Or Captain Cerelli?"

"Nope."

"Really? He didn't call? I was positive he would. I mean, he's such a great guy. This isn't like him."

"I honestly didn't think so either."

"Well, what are you waiting for? Call him."

"I have." I swallow hard.

"Did you leave a message?"

"I did."

"Oh, Mom. Something must be wrong."

23

I'M STILL STANDING BEHIND the house, freezing my butt off, wondering what to do about Todd and Catherine Elizabeth, when my cell buzzes against my thigh. Digging the phone out of my pocket, I swipe it on. An incoming text. From Rahila. Also known as Seema.

> *Oh, my Beloved! Separation plants the seeds*
> *Of despair and longing in my heart.*

Oh, tell me about it. I sit down hard on the sawed-off tree stump and read Seema Rahila's *landay* again. Amazing how she's able to capture what's in my heart.

I miss Cerelli. The way he knows what's in my head. And my heart. The way—

Wait! Lest I forget, he's not reading my head or my heart all that well right now. If he were . . . well, damn him for not taking my calls. For not returning them. Yeah, I told him I was done. It wasn't my finest moment, but he didn't have any right to tell me what to do. I think about what his silence means. It's pretty obvious. And equally obvious: I can't force him to feel something for me if he doesn't.

Still, he really does need to know about Seema's SD card. Once again, I tap his number on the sat phone. Then wait for the requisite number of rings before his voice mail kicks in. Or maybe I'll get lucky and Sawyer will answer.

"Annie?" Not voice mail. Not Sawyer. It's actually Cerelli. In the flesh. So to speak.

"Cerelli?"

"I think we've established that." Not the friendliest he's ever sounded.

"I was expecting your voice mail."

"Why?" He seems genuinely confused.

"Because I called before, several times in fact, and you never answered."

"Yeah, well, sorry about that. I'm dealing with some serious stuff. Things are happening. Fast." He sounds rushed, like he'd just as soon finish up this call and get back to rehabbing and meetings and *stuff*.

"Anything you can talk about?"

"Annie." Which I take to mean, *You know better than to ask me that.*

"Right."

"I'm answering now." His voice gentles.

"Okay, then." But I can't get a read on him. Which makes me twitchy as hell.

"You're not in Kabul, are you?" His concern meter has notched up.

"No."

"Good."

"What?" The last thing I expected him to say. "Why?"

"Things here are fluid right now. It's better you're elsewhere."

Here? He's in Kabul? "You're with Sawyer?"

He doesn't answer. Oh, God, this is a conversation I hope never to have again. And now I'm not at all sure what to say. Maybe it would've been better if he hadn't answered.

I try again. "Did you get my earlier messages?" Including the ones when I screamed at you like a maniac?

"Affirmative."

SEAL speak? And here I thought things couldn't get worse. He's obviously still pissed. But I wasn't the only one who said *I'm done*. Yeah, but I *am* the one who told him to stop interfering in my life. Basically, to leave me alone. "Look, I called for a reason."

"Tell me you're okay."

"I'm okay."

"Good. You called because?"

"Because the strangest thing happened. I was overnighting at *Hama* Bibi and Uncle Omar's the night before last."

"Was he there?"

"No. Why? Is that important?"

"Good. Although it may not be important. What happened?"

My head is spinning with all these non-answers. "Well, I was staying in the guest room. Which isn't really a guest room anymore. Omar uses it for storage. Tons of locked metal boxes that Bibi says are full of government documents. Omar said their apartment has better security than his office. Anyway, since he wasn't home, Bibi had me sleep in there."

"And?" Zero to sixty. Cerelli's on high alert. "You look in those boxes?"

"No. Bibi moved them into her bedroom before I got there. I did help her haul them back into the guest room the next morning, but like I said, they were locked."

"Let me guess. You found something *not* in one of the boxes."

"Correct."

"You going to tell me what it is?"

"I thought you'd never ask." I'm trying to lighten this stilted and extremely uncomfortable conversation, but he's not following my lead. "I found Seema's SanDisk card from the workshop last spring."

"You're sure about that?" His voice has gone steely cold.

"Oh, yeah. I was checking my own cards, making sure all my gear was in order, and there was this SD card on the floor next to the daybed. I just assumed it was one of mine and stuck it in my camera. Then today, when I tried to take pics at the school, the formatting was off. I scanned through the images, and bingo."

"Lucky you didn't reformat and lose everything."

"I know. So, why would Seema's SD card be anywhere near that apartment?"

He's quiet for a moment. I've got a pretty good idea that we both know what this could mean. "This goes no farther. I'll check it out."

"Okay. Do you need—"

"Phinneas?" A woman's voice. On Cerelli's phone. "Oh, I am sorry. I—"

The rest of whatever that low, sexy female voice has to say is muffled. But I've heard enough. Too much, in fact. I know that voice. Besides, only two people call him Phinneas, and one of them—Darya—is dead. The other is Fatima, his apparent one-time lover and the owner of *Khosha* restaurant in Kabul. I check my watch to confirm that it's almost oh-one-hundred. So, what's he doing with Fatima this late at night? Oh, hell! I know exactly what he's doing with her.

A moment later, he's back on the line. "Sorry about that."

I can't say anything. The ache in my heart hurts too much.

"Annie? You still there?"

"You're with *Fatima?*"

"Annie. Please, don't." Suddenly, he sounds exhausted. "Something came up that needed my attention."

Oh, I just bet it did.

And that's when the satellite moves out of range. Which is probably for the best because I'm so frigging angry, there's no telling what I would've said. Only that I know I would've regretted it.

I huddle against the cold night air, staring at the sat phone as the pieces of my heart cleave farther apart. Why did I call him? Why tonight? Seema's SD card could have waited. Damn, Mel was right about something being wrong, but it's not the kind of wrong either one of us was expecting.

I wrap my arms around myself and rock back and forth until the cold gets to me. I'm not up for hypothermia on top of everything else. Time to face the reality that's at the other end of the sat phone. And way past time to get to bed. Pushing myself to my feet, I creep around the side of the house to the front. Just in time to see someone dashing up the road toward the school. It's too dark to see much, but I make out what looks to be a puffer jacket. A ski cap. Jeans. Boots. A teenage boy. Probably caught out too late and hoping to make it home before he gets in trouble. Then, training my flashlight on the front door, I see the message the late-night visitor left.

Two numbers in red paint that's running down the door:

3 9

Morda-gow. Whore.

24

KNEELING ON THE KITCHEN FLOOR, I shine my flashlight at the plastic crates underneath the boards that serve as a counter. I'm determined to find something to clean that filth off the front door before anyone sees it. The last thing I want is for Gulshan and Ikrom to suffer insults—or worse—because of me. Slowly, quietly, I ease the crate forward, then lift out one of the plastic bottles. No label. I unscrew the lid and sniff. Whoa! Ammonia. Will it clean off paint? Another bottle. A sniff. A soapy smell. I'll try this first. Grabbing a handful of rags, I push myself to my feet and turn to head back outside. That's when the toe of my boot catches on the corner of the crate, knocking it against another plastic box—upending them both and causing the most ungodly racket. My hip knocks hard against the iron wood-burning stove, and then I land even harder on the tile floor.

Ikrom is in the kitchen in seconds, a two-by-four in his hand, ready to pulverize the burglar who's broken into his house. Gulshan is right behind him, tying a scarf over her hair, then rushing to light a kerosene lantern. Which reveals the complete disaster I've created with pots and pans and bottles of cleaning fluids everywhere.

Sprawled on the floor, I look up, furious as much from the sharp pain shooting down my leg as from having caused my hosts to bolt out of bed. This after losing Cerelli. Again. "I'm so sorry," I manage to choke out.

Gulshan kneels next to me. "Praise be to Allah that I did not leave the soup pot heating on the stove. If it had fallen on you . . . Are you all right?"

Ikrom looks around the kitchen, steps into the lounge, and then comes back. "What is happening?"

Finally, I've got my voice—and my wits—back. "I—I—was outside calling my daughter back in the States." I pause, deciding they don't need to know about the disastrous call to Cerelli. "I heard someone at the front of the house. By the time I got there, he was running away. But the door—" I sweep my hand above the mess on the floor. "I was trying to clean the door before anyone saw it, any of the neighbors."

Storming to the front door, Ikrom is gone only a minute. When he returns, he looks grim.

"What is it?" asks Gulshan, looking from me to her husband.

"A message. I do not want you to see it." He nods toward me, his meaning clear. I am not to tell Gulshan. "Take care of Annie." He takes the rags from my hand, then reaches for the tin can of kerosene.

Gulshan clambers to her feet, ready to help me up.

I put up my hand to stop her. "I can do this." I absolutely refuse to have a broken hip in Afghanistan. It takes some maneuvering, first to my knees, then grabbing hold of a chair for leverage, I work myself up onto my feet. I manage a few tentative, limping steps.

"Not broken," I say with more assurance than I feel. Then loosen my baggy pants and peer down at a bruise that's already black and purple and covering a good part of my upper leg.

Taking a peek herself, Gulshan gasps. "Oh, this is terrible! Come to your room and take those off. I must give you medicine." A few moments later, she is rubbing salve all over my hip and thigh. One whiff, and my eyes start to tear.

"What is that?" Blinking, I nod toward the small, unlabeled plastic container in her hand.

"It is an herb I grow in the back garden. I pound it, then mix in oil and wax. It will break down the bruise faster and help the soreness of your muscles go away. You will see."

Whoa, I can almost feel this stuff working, lifting out the pain. I rub my aching upper arm. "Could I have some more?"

"You also hurt your arm?"

I slip off my sweater, then my tunic, inhaling sharply as I lift my arm over my head.

Gulshan looks accusingly at me. "This is not from falling."

There's no point denying the obvious. "No."

She points to the fingerprints. "Who did this?"

"A man grabbed me at the market in Bazarak. I don't know who he was. I thought maybe he was trying to steal the money."

She frowns as she rubs more salve onto my arm. "I do not like these dangers. It is too much."

"But now the money is safe. And I can feel how much this medicine is already helping." Anything to steer her away from what happened at the market. "You could make a fortune selling this."

She smiles. "Strong is sometimes good, yes? A fortune?" She bats away the idea. "Now, tell me, what was on our front door?"

"Well, uh—"

She helps me pull up my pants, then leans in close. "Do not worry about Ikrom. Husbands don't always know what is best."

I raise my eyebrows. "The number 39."

"That is all?"

"In red paint."

She pats my arm. "It is not to worry about. Ikrom will take care of it."

"I can't help worrying. Your wonderful hospitality . . . my being here brings such an awful insult."

"Bah! Why do you think the insult is for you? This could be for me, for Ikrom. We are building this school to educate our daughters. We know there are people in Wad Qol who believe any education for girls is treachery from the West. Some believe it is heresy. But we will not let them stop us. And I will not let this leg of yours stiffen up. Now, you must walk. Or you will not be able to get out of bed in the morning. Up!" She pulls me to my feet.

I wouldn't dare disobey. For the next twenty minutes, I walk the length of the front lounge, back and forth, until I want to close my eyes and sink to the floor into blessed sleep. But Gulshan won't let me stop. By the time Ikrom has finished cleaning off the paint, I figure I've put in a good quarter mile.

He peeks around the front door and waves us over. Gulshan grabs my flashlight and begins to inspect the door inch by inch.

Ikrom finally takes the flashlight from her. "Not up there! The paint, it was lower down. Here." And he shines the light chest-high.

Finally, she nods. "Yes. You did an excellent job. I can see no paint. It looks like nothing was ever here."

I sigh in relief.

They usher me back inside. Ikrom carefully locks the door, then turns to face us. "You saw who did this?"

"Only from the back. He was running pretty fast."

"Can you tell us anything about him? Was he wearing a coat?"

I call up the figure I saw dashing away. "No, not a long coat. A jacket. In the U.S., we call them puffer jackets. For skiing."

"His hair? Was it long or short? Was he wearing anything on his head? Did he have a beard?"

I close my eyes. "I remember a ski hat. And boots. He was wearing boots. And what looked like jeans." In other words, it could have been just about any male in the village, except the religion teacher. No way he could move that fast. "I'm guessing it was probably a teenager."

From the look on his face, Ikrom seems to agree. "Perhaps you will remember more. We will talk in the morning."

25

FIRST THING IN THE MORNING, Ikrom is called out to the clinic. "A child fell against the stove. The soup pot fell over on him—he was seriously burned," he says as he hurries out the door. His pickup chugs awake, and then he's off, peeling through the unpaved roads of Wad Qol.

Gulshan cups her hands in front of her and murmurs a few words of prayer. From the expression on her face, I can't tell if she's sad or angry or what. "A pot of soup or water. Many children die this way. His family is fortunate to have Ikrom working to save him. My husband is always an optimist. He believes right up until the end that he can save these children." Her message is clear. Most of the children don't survive.

I glance across the kitchen to the wood-burning stove where a large pot of soup now sits. Her other message: I was beyond lucky. I wonder why she decided not to leave the pot of leftover *mashawa* on the stove last night.

"We do our best to watch the little ones, but it is not possible to be always with them, always watching . . ." She smiles sadly, a faraway look in her eyes.

I wonder if she ever had any serious accidents with her own kids.

She shakes her head. "No. *Alhamdulillah.* Such a horrible accident never happened to any of my children."

Somehow, I know she has more to say.

"Many years ago, Ikrom's sister left a pot on the fire. Her little boy—he walked at such a young age—he was curious . . ."

"No!" I whisper.

"The little boy lingered for several days. Ikrom could do nothing to save him. That has always weighed heavily on him. His own nephew. It is the reason why he never gives up."

I PULL ON MY JACKET against the early-morning cold. Gulshan floats her *burqa* down over her coat. Then, we head up the road toward the schools. All along the way, I see the white crystals of last night's heavy frost and the remains of wilted daisies and anemones turned black in small front gardens. When we get to the path leading to the temporary school, Gulshan reminds me, "The men are excavating for the new concrete floor. They must finish this morning because the carpenters will build the forms in the afternoon."

"Forms?"

"The wooden structures that will hold the concrete in place. Do not worry! The foreman knows what they need to do. Come here during the lunch break." Looking at the tiffins she's carrying, I imagine the savory food awaiting me. "And don't let the foreman or the workers get away with lounging. They must finish today. You may need to crack the whip!" She laughs and waves me off.

I walk on to the building site. Just as I'm about to turn up the drive, the man I least want to see comes swaggering down the road. The religion teacher, dressed in a traditional tunic, long vest, and baggy pants. His hand rests on the shoulder of a teenage boy dressed in typical Western fashion—jeans and a puffer jacket. A ski cap. They're caught up in an earnest discussion, and I'm pretty sure they haven't seen me. Yet. I pick up my pace, hoping I can avoid them.

No such luck.

"*Shomâ!*" the religion teacher shouts. Nothing friendly about his glower. Up close, I can see the boy looks exactly like his father. His scowl, though, comes off as more guilt-ridden than anything.

I really don't want to stop and chat, but there's no point in all of us being rude. So, I smile a cheery good morning. "*Sobh ba khaye!*"

"Why you are here?" the religion teacher snarls in Dari.

Which is a pretty ridiculous question, but I force myself to smile. "A lot of work to be done today. We're starting early." I lower my eyes away from their angry faces and see a splash of red on the baby-boy-blue puffer jacket. Paint. I'm willing to bet it's the same red paint that put in an insulting appearance on Ikrom and Gulshan's front door late last night. I'd really like to let them have it. Both barrels. Then I remind myself that I won't be living here long-term. Ikrom and Gulshan will. I won't be doing my hosts any favors by chewing out these two.

"Bah. A girls' school! A waste of money."

I know I should keep smiling, but I just can't let it go. So, I point to the boy's red-stained hands. "I see you have experience painting! Maybe you could help us with the school."

For one second, the boy's eyes light up. I know that look: *Girls!* Then his father's hand claps down hard on his shoulder. "Emad has no time to waste on useless, foolish things. He is too busy studying."

"Except when he's painting doors," I murmur in English.

The boy opens his mouth. Clearly, he does understand English! Another clap on his shoulder gets him back to walking toward the village and the boys' school.

CAMERA IN HAND AND doing my best to ignore the throbbing ache in my hip and thigh, I limp around the building site, taking pics of a few men measuring off the footprint of the new building. They pound stakes into the ground and run twine the entire way around except for the two spots where they lay down half-sheets of plywood. I'm guessing these will act as ramps once the excavation begins. I can't imagine they'll get very far today, not with only five workers here.

Suddenly, the numbers multiply. Twenty more men march up the drive and into the front yard, each with a shovel propped in a wheelbarrow. A few brief instructions from the foreman, and they set to digging, one next to the other, starting at the front of the school footprint. Shovels full of dirt and stones along with an occasional bigger rock land in wheelbarrows that fill quickly. Each man then pushes his barrow up the ramp, across the schoolyard, and into the nearby walnut grove. He dumps the dirt near the trees and comes back to dig some more.

"Twenty centimeters!" the foreman calls to them in Dari. He hurries toward me, his hand out for the roll of plans that Gulshan passed off to me when we left the house. Checking a few calculations, he nods emphatically. "Yes. Twenty centimeters."

I sidle closer to the foreman. "How do they know what exactly twenty centimeters is?" And that's assuming the ground is completely level to start with. Maybe building in these rural areas isn't all that precise? No. This has to be done right.

He nods as if to show he understands but doesn't answer my question and doesn't say anything to the men. Then again, perhaps he doesn't understand. Or he doesn't feel he needs to answer.

I'm not giving up. "Each man could be digging at a different depth." My fluency in Dari doesn't extend to construction vocabulary. So, I pantomime digging, then wave my hand like a roller coaster.

He strokes his beard, then pulls out a tape measure and shows it to me, obviously pleased that he's come up with a solution to appease me. Only, he's got the tape measure, and everyone else has a shovel. He smiles and nods.

I smile and nod. And hope to hell he really does know what he's doing. Because I sure don't.

He doesn't say anything about footings, though.

I do my best to explain the concept of footings. "I'm sure the buildings in Kabul have footings for stability. You know, in case of earthquakes."

"Earthquakes!" Yet again, he strokes his beard as he considers this new idea. And finally nods. "Yes, these footings would be good thing, better for supporting. Yes." He beckons over four of the diggers. Pointing to the four corners, he tells them, "Another twenty-five centimeters." He smiles at me, and I nod my thanks. I'd been hoping for sixty centimeters or deeper, but I'll take what I can get, especially since there isn't anything about footings in the plans.

Maybe I should focus on taking pictures of this project instead of grilling the foreman and the workers on every last detail. No matter that Gulshan expects me to 'crack the whip,' I'm discovering that's not really in my skill set. Me taking pics would probably make all of us a lot happier. Not to mention that Mel and Awa are expecting a full documentary.

I pace around the outside of the deepening and spreading hole, looking for possible images that'll make my fingers tingle with an innate awareness that there's a great shot. Finally, I sense an *interesting* shot. A line of about twenty men in *shalwar kameezes* and *pakols*, backs bent to their work, shoveling in unison. Slow unison. Their wheelbarrows aren't filling anywhere near as fast as they were an hour ago. I move down to the far end of the footprint and fire off a sequence of shots of men digging and throwing dirt that's landing in barrows with incredible synchrony.

The carpenters arrive in the middle of the morning to build the forms that will hold the concrete—the floor for the school. They look a bit surprised that the digging isn't further along. Hauling out long planks of wood and nails, hammers and saws, they get to work. But they can't build more than the form across the front because that's all that's been cleared. I point to the sides, but the foreman explains that they need the sides and back completely excavated before setting in the wooden structures. Of course they do. That's exactly my point. Why don't the diggers work all along the sides and leave the middle and back for later? The foreman smiles and nods, then ambles back to supervising his workers.

We're approaching midday when the diggers slowly wheel their barrows to the walnut grove one last time for the morning. They're making a little progress—about a third of the way across the building site. From what I can see, they have a long way to go.

Despite the work still to be done, they're all slapping each other on the back and grinning at me their assurance that they'll finish by the end of the day. But I know the kind of lunch breaks these guys take. It could easily be two—or later—before they return. And they can't possibly work beyond five because once the sun sets behind the mountains, darkness drops like the blade of a guillotine.

Instead of digging for another fifteen minutes, the men stand around until exactly noon, when they head home for lunch. "You go," says the foreman, pointing me toward the road. "One hour. Then, we continue work. You come back tomorrow. You will see."

I look over my shoulder at the partially dug site. So much work left to do. How the hell can they possibly finish in a couple hours?

26

WITH A SENSE OF FOREBODING churning in my stomach, I head toward the ramshackle temporary school to join Gulshan for lunch. But then, I hear the girls, and my worries stop. I walk faster, and there they are—playing games and giggling in small groups. All of them dressed in brown *shalwar kameezes* and white headscarves. As soon as I turn up the dirt path, they crowd around me, chattering excitedly.

"Ms. Hawkins Green! You will teach another photography class?"

"Please teach all the girls! I want a camera, too."

"You will come back? Next year maybe?"

Hugging each girl in turn, I shake my head. No cameras. Not this trip. Damn. I should've planned another workshop. Brought more cameras. For now, all I can do is smile. "Maybe," I say before I can stop myself. The girls cheer. Next year? Cerelli would absolutely kill me.

Inside the first small room, I find Gulshan and several of the other teachers sitting on the floor close to the stove, which doesn't seem to be putting out a whole lot of heat. Gulshan and Iman both have their *burqas* thrown back over their heads and are hunched over their tiffins, eating. I take off my jacket and am about to shed my sweater when I change my mind. It's chilly in here. Colder than outside. Even with my sweater on, I'm shivering.

Looking up, Gulshan smiles and makes sure I know all of the teachers in the room. I picture them on the first day of my workshop last spring, standing in a line against the back wall of the classroom Gulshan and I shared. A great welcoming committee. That classroom at the front of the school was the target for the bomb-laden pickup. These are the same women who stood vigil around Darya's body. From the looks on their faces, I'm pretty sure several of them are remembering those same moments. But any shadows disappear quickly. They grin their welcomes and shift away from Gulshan to clear a spot for me.

Gulshan pats the floor. "Sit with me. I have your lunch."

I sink cross-legged onto the floor, yelping when my sore hip screams.

"Still, it is hurting?"

"I'm afraid so."

"Tonight, I will apply more salve." She hands me the other tiffin, which I unhinge immediately. The aroma is heavenly. How on earth did she manage to keep this warm? I take a bite of the stewed lamb. Oh, God, it's divine. I've got to wheedle the recipe out of her. When does she find the time to cook like this in addition to everything else she does?

To start my review of the morning, I tell her about meeting up with the religion teacher and his son, our likely culprit, on the way to the building site.

"His grandson," she corrects me. "They took in the boy and his mother after the father died. It does not surprise me that he would push the boy to deface our door. It is not the first time. There were very bad words painted on the door of the old school when we first opened. Darya was never sure who did it. I will talk to Ikrom. He will know how to resolve this problem. I think it is better to let a man take care of this."

"I'm afraid I already made a comment."

She looks at me expectantly.

"I asked the boy to help paint the new school. Since he clearly loves painting."

She laughs. "What did he say?"

"Nothing. Although his eyes definitely lit up at the thought of meeting girls."

"There could be hope for him after all. If I can get him away from his grandfather."

Leave it to a horny teenage boy wanting a girlfriend. Something tells me that in the long run, the girls will win out over his grandfather. I go back to eating. Oh, it's good. Another blast of chilly air makes its way through chinks in the walls, and I huddle an inch closer to the fire.

Gulshan smiles apologetically and points to the stove in the corner. "I am afraid it is not very warm in here. We are trying to save the fuel for the winter months. If it is too cold inside, the girls will not be able to come."

"There's enough money for heat in the new building, isn't there?"

"Oh, yes." She smiles. "For this winter." Her smile fades. "Of course, a school is expensive to operate. There are many costs. The families pay fees, but that does not cover everything. Besides, we never turn away any girl if her family cannot pay. It is too important for all girls to have as much education as possible. We will always need more money."

"Oh, dear." I stop eating.

A stricken look passes across her face. "Please, this is not for you to worry about. Do not think of it. Darya was always writing away for grants. Now, as the new director, that is something I must do."

My thoughts drift back to yesterday—all the charred debris being carted away. Doors and beams, tables and benches, bookcases and window frames. Nothing salvageable. Then, I realize that, except for the bit of the picture of Malalai, I didn't see any books or pencils or papers. There was nothing left. It will all have to be replaced. Another cost.

Gulshan is right—they'll need a constant influx of cash. I should have thought of that when I was back in the States. Mel and Yasmine, everyone was so excited about raising this money. And it *is* a lot of money. But that's just to start. There will always need to be more and more. I seriously doubt the mosque is going to support the school forever. And if I don't get my job back, I won't be able to help either.

Gulshan looks suddenly uncomfortable. "I can see you are worried. Please, do not. You have already been very generous. Without you, we could not rebuild the school."

I take another bite of lamb, still worrying about how to get all the things necessary to furnish the new school. Looking around this nearly empty room, there's a distinct lack of any materials. Just a couple small slates.

"Books," I sigh.

Gulshan cups her hand against my cheek. "Have faith, my friend. Allah will provide."

"I hope you're right. We could sure use some help." In the meantime, I'll give it more thought. I polish off another morsel of lamb and lick my fingers. "This is incredibly delicious! Please, tell me, how do you roast it?"

She smiles coyly. "It is a secret, but a secret all good wives should know. I will show you later."

Later. That sense of foreboding is back, niggling at me. The building site. I can't help wondering how things are going. And I realize I'll feel a whole lot better if Gulshan is with me this afternoon. "Are you done teaching for the day?"

"Why?" She's on the alert.

"I'm just a little concerned that the men aren't working quite as hard as they could."

"Did they finish digging this morning? That was the goal I set with the foreman."

"Finish?" I snort a laugh. "Maybe about a third."

"That is all?" She leans back against the wall. "They were supposed to be done. The carpenters must build and install the forms."

It amazes me how easily she talks about all of this. "The carpenters are there, and they started on the forms for the front. The last couple hours, though, they've pretty much been standing around waiting for the diggers to finish. Everyone promised they'd finish this afternoon—"

"If they are still excavating, how can the carpenters do their work? And that needs to be done *today*. The floor, we pour it tomorrow. Then, the carpenters will return to build the frames. We must stay on schedule!" She looks as frustrated as she sounds.

"Could you come back with me for the afternoon? I honestly think the men will work harder if you're there."

She brushes invisible crumbs off her tunic and pants, then stands. After arranging with the science and religion teachers to cover the afternoon classes, she nudges my foot. "Let us go. The girls will be fine for the rest of the day. I will look for a whip to crack at those lazy men."

We stack our tiffins and head out the door. In the schoolyard, the girls seem surprised to see Gulshan leaving.

"What about our literature class?" two of the senior girls call out.

Gulshan waves. "Today you will have another science and religion class."

The wide eyes and sorrowful faces tell me those aren't favorite courses.

"We will have an extra literature class next week to make up for today."

By the time we reach the site, an hour and a half after lunch began, the diggers are just starting to straggle back. Gulshan stands ramrod straight and folds her arms across her chest. Beneath the *burqa*, her eyes must be blazing. If she actually had a whip, I bet it would be cracking.

She's amazing to watch. Not a word passes her lips. The first workers back take one look at her and sprint to their shovels. They're digging so fast that half the dirt is flying past the barrows. Somehow, word gets back to the other workers who come running up the drive from the village road. No one is taking their time. Except the carpenters, who don't have anything more they can do.

"You know," I say, pointing toward the edges of the footprint, "if the diggers shifted direction and started working along the sides into the middle—" I wonder if the foreman will be more receptive to Gulshan suggesting this idea.

"Yes!" Gulshan beams. "Then the carpenters could set up more forms while the others dig out the middle and on to the back. Annie, you are brilliant." She walks over to the foreman and gently, carefully leads him around to my idea. "I am worried they will not finish the digging. And the carpenters, they will need half the day to finish their work. Then, I remembered that the concrete truck arrives tomorrow morning. What should we do?"

When he comes up with the idea of having the men dig from the sides, working toward the middle, she jumps for joy. "This is a marvelous idea!" She sure knows how to manage these men.

It works. She praises the foreman and his time-saving idea so much that now he'll lose face if the men don't finish both jobs today. She goes on to remind the men that this is a half-day job, making them worry that they won't get paid if the job isn't done. The men listen intently. For a *burqa*-wearing Afghan woman, she's one fierce lady I wouldn't want to mess with.

The men pick up their pace. In a matter of minutes, their tunics are soaked through and their baggy pants are caked in dirt. I'd put away my camera and get in there with them, but as the sun sinks toward the mountains and the temperature drops, my hip is aching more and my leg is stiffening. At least they've cleared the dirt along the sides, and the wooden forms are going in.

By the time the sun is resting its lower rim on the craggy peaks and Ikrom drives up in his pickup, the forms around most of the exterior are finished. But there's still dirt to be cleared from the center. And forms to be built for where the interior walls will go. So, why are the carpenters already loading their equipment into their trucks?

Even though dusk is falling, Ikrom isn't about to let the project fall behind. Telling all the men that he won't pay until the job is done—meaning *done today*—he actually grabs a shovel himself and heads toward the site. The diggers and carpenters stand watching him, mouths gaping. I'm guessing it's something of an insult that one of the bosses has to finish their uncompleted work.

A moment later, a few men ease their trucks closer to the excavation site and turn on their headlights. Then, shovels in hand, the diggers are back at work, clearing out the center. The carpenters are building the rest of the interior forms to anchor in place as the ground is cleared and raked and leveled.

Somehow, in the midst of all this frenzy, Gulshan and I manage to keep from laughing.

Ikrom is just as dirty as the rest of the men by the time they've shoveled the last of the dirt into the final wheelbarrow and carted it off to the walnut trees. The carpenters step forward and finish off their forms in record time.

Before Ikrom hands out the day's wages, he warns the diggers, in words that echo Gulshan's, to be back and ready to work early tomorrow. Personally, I'd do better with a specific time, but the men seem to know what 'early' means. With that, the men head home. Ikrom, Gulshan, and I pile into the pickup for the slow drive back into the village. Scrunched against the door, I cross my fingers that we have a quiet evening. No surprises.

27

THERE ARE NO SURPRISES.

After dinner, Gulshan shoos me into my bedroom, following with the jar of salve. Under her stern eye, I peel off my tunic and pants. We examine the massive bruise on my leg and the bouquet of smaller, still vivid, finger marks on my arm. She seems to feel that her medicine should be working faster. Squaring her shoulders, she rubs in more.

"Maybe it's a good thing I don't have a man in my life," I say half wistfully, half resigned.

Gulshan looks startled. "Why do you say that?"

"He'd take one look at all this and decide I'm too much of a mess."

She smiles. "The man I have in mind for you would never think that."

The man? What man? I stare at her in surprise and not a little dismay. "Are you serious? You actually have someone picked out?"

"I will tell you more when my plans are set."

I hold up my hands, definitely not in surrender. "Please, Gulshan, I'm really not looking for a new husband—"

She keeps rubbing my hip and thigh, her hands warm and strong, easing the stiffness. "A husband could do this for you. And more. It would be very pleasant."

"I'm sure you're right. This is a pleasure I would most definitely enjoy." With Cerelli. I feel my cheeks burning at the thought of him massaging me. Then, I hear the echo of Fatima's voice, and my heart clenches. Has he really moved on? "But some of the other parts of having a husband aren't as nice."

"Your last husband, he was a problem?"

"Todd. His name is Todd. And he sure didn't give massages like this. He also didn't like my job."

"It scared him, yes? You going to places that are dangerous?"

I nod. "That's what finally tore us apart. He wanted me to give up being a photographer to stay home and take care of our daughter."

She stops rubbing my hip and starts in on my arm. "Allah blessed Ikrom and me with four children. For them, I am very thankful. But children take a lot of attention. For me, this was good and proper, but I know that not all women should do the same. I am certain that you are doing what Allah wants for you."

"Really? Sometimes I feel like I've failed."

She laughs. "If we believe that we are perfect, then we are not human. This man I have in mind, he will be right for you. If you learn how to manage him."

"Manage?"

"Oh, Annie." She laughs and rubs harder, as if to drill home her message. "All men need to be managed. Especially the ones who think they are perfect the way they are."

28

I LUXURIATE IN MY BED. No phone calls to upset me. No midnight visitors defacing the front door. Just sleep, deep and blissful. When the aromas of tea and *nân* and Afghan *shakshouka* wake me in the dark of early morning, I feel like a new woman.

Gulshan smiles knowingly when I walk into the kitchen. Even though she's got to be as tired as I am, she's obviously been up for a while, cooking breakfast and packing lunches for all three of us. And here I've been sleeping in like a slug. At least I'm not limping.

"This is so unfair," I protest with a wave toward all the food on the table.

Startled, Ikrom looks up from his bread and egg. "Unfair?"

I wonder if he's ever cooked. "I mean, I should be helping you cook."

Gulshan smiles serenely and points me toward a chair. "You are our guest. Besides, you needed sleep, and that is what Allah gave you last night."

"How is your leg?" Ikrom asks.

"Much better, thank you." I look down at the steaming plate of food Gulshan sets in front of me, then turn toward Ikrom. "Your wife is an excellent nurse."

Gulshan rubs my shoulder. "You will let me know if you need more medicine or massage tonight." It's not a question.

HEADING OUT THE DOOR, Gulshan and I both startle at the sound of a loud engine rumbling its way through the village. It takes a minute to key into what's causing the noise, then all becomes clear when a large truck carrying a concrete mixer and a mountain of bags of cement on its flatbed passes by.

"I know it is expensive to bring a truck all the way from Bazarak, but it is worth it. Do you agree?" Gulshan's frown gives me an inkling of the stress she's under to make sure the money is used wisely.

"Aren't there any concrete trucks in Afghanistan?" As soon as I ask the question, I realize how stupid it is. This isn't the West.

"A concrete truck?" Gulshan stares at me in all seriousness, as if this is something she should have known about.

"A large truck with a huge mixer that turns constantly."

"There is a mixer." She points after the truck heading toward the site. "Ah, you mean a batching truck. Yes, we have those. Hamma Sazaan Company. It is in Kabul. They mix the concrete there and drive it to the site." She shakes her head. "To come all the way here would be very expensive. I am afraid this is the best we can do."

Clearly, thirty thousand dollars doesn't cover everything. Far from it. And the anxious look I see on Gulshan's face through the netted eyepiece tells me I've got to make her feel good about this decision. "You're right. We need the money for so many other things. There's no point spending it all on the floor. Now, let's make sure they do it right." Not that I have any idea how to mix and pour concrete, but I'm willing to bet Gulshan does.

By the time we reach the school, the driver and the foreman have wheeled the mixer off the flatbed. Another truck arrives with hundreds of yellow jerry cans of water. There are also two small mountains of stone, one crushed, the other whole. And bags upon bags of cement. All the makings of concrete.

Thank God Gulshan is here for the entire day. At some point, she's made herself into a building expert. The men could do just about anything, right or wrong—add too much water, not mix in the stone—and I wouldn't know any better. But they won't be able to put anything past Gulshan.

While we wait for the driver and foreman to mix the first batch of concrete and the men to spread stones in the excavated footprint, Gulshan inspects the site. "What are these deep holes at the four corners? I did not see them yesterday."

The foreman hurries over to explain about footings. He's obviously proud of these four additional, slightly deeper holes, and he's holding forth as if they were his idea. An important improvement over the original plans, he assures her. "It will protect the school if there is an earthquake."

"Why have I never heard of these before?" From the doubt in her voice, I'm not at all sure she's convinced.

"The foreman and I discussed this yesterday," I say. "They're part of the building code in Kabul." At least, I assume they are. "And they're common practice in the U.S. They make buildings more stable."

She ponders this new information for a minute, then turns to the foreman. "Yes. This is a good change. I am very thankful that you thought of such a thing."

The foreman swells his chest and struts back over to the mixer.

She leans in close to me, close enough that I can see the twinkle in her eyes. "I see you are learning how to manage this man. He will now do anything for you."

Manage this man? Holy shit! I grab her *burqa*-draped arm. "Please tell me he's not the man you have in mind."

She bursts out laughing. "Oh, my! That is a very funny idea!" But she doesn't say he's not.

Gulshan is amazing to watch. She tests the first batch of concrete to make sure it's just right. I watch as she stirs it with a stick of wood, then scoops up a tablespoon of the gloppy stuff and rubs it between her fingers. After studying the consistency and the color for a full minute—a breathless minute for the driver and the foreman hovering next to her—she finally nods.

The pouring begins.

Gulshan, of course, supervises as the men cart wheelbarrow after wheelbarrow to the forms in the center of the building. They'll work their way out. Once begun, we need to finish today. I glance at my watch. Already eight o'clock. And we've barely started. My heart sinks, but Gulshan doesn't seem daunted. "You will see," she says.

I slip my camera strap around my neck and start prowling the edges of the site, searching for photographs to take. Why Mel and Awa think donors will want to see pictures of a construction site is beyond me. Images of girls in finished classrooms would be a much better option. Not that I'll be here to take those pics. Still, everyone seems happier with me off doing what I do best and leaving them to their work. Gulshan included.

By the time we break for lunch, there are still way too many sections of the slab that need to be poured. And I'm worried. All morning, Gulshan has been reminding anyone who will listen that we must finish pouring the floors *today* to stay on schedule. But so far, no one has done anything to pick up the pace.

When the men return from lunch, they bring a few more workers with them, pushing more wheelbarrows loaded with more shovels and rakes. I photograph workers lining up to take on loads of concrete. Now, finally, they do seem to be picking up the pace. Maybe, just maybe, they'll finish on time.

Eventually the sun starts sinking toward the mountains. There are just a couple hours of light left and a whole lot of the school floor yet to be poured and raked smooth. The foreman keeps taking off his *pakol* and running his fingers through his hair. Gulshan paces. As for me? I'm thinking there's no way it's going to happen.

"We cannot stop," Gulshan says to the foreman. "We must finish today, or the different sections of the floor will dry unevenly. And it will delay the rest of the construction."

He nods and repeats everything to the driver, who looks toward the sun on its downward trajectory and grimaces.

"Can we get more people to help?" I look at all the men lined up, waiting to fill their barrows, and can't imagine how having more men will possibly speed things up. I take more pictures and continue to worry. "We need another mixer." I say the obvious to no one in particular.

The foreman's scowl tells me he's as frustrated as I am.

Gulshan raises a fist. "A trough? Would that work? There's one in the village center where the animals stop to drink."

The foreman calls over a few of the men near the end of the line, and they're off in one of the pickups. I want to believe the shopkeepers will give us the trough, but I'm not so sure. Once it's used to mix concrete, no sheep will drink from it again. And goats? Well, goats probably will. They'll eat and drink anything. I don't know about the donkeys that wander everywhere around the village. They may be as fussy as the sheep.

When the men return with the village trough and more jerry cans of water, the pace of work picks up dramatically. The workers are nearly running to empty their barrows. Others are rolling up their pants legs and wading barefoot into the gelatinous goo to spread the concrete evenly with two-by-four planks of wood.

My fingers are tingling with the shots I'm getting, all the more interesting with the golden side light from the lowering sun, which accentuates the men's puffs of breath as the temperature drops. The cold must be doing quite the number on their feet and ankles.

The next time I look toward the sun, it's reaching down to the mountains. We're now in a race to the finish. More men have shifted over to spreading and smoothing concrete in the forms.

The temperature drops even more. I'm guessing the low forties. Cold enough that Gulshan is fretting about whether the concrete will set correctly. Something about a critical chemical reaction that might not happen.

"Would plastic tarps help?" I ask. "Or blankets? We could drape them over the concrete."

"Yes!" she exclaims, hurrying off to confer with the foreman.

Just a little more daylight. The men work on.

I hold my breath. My heart beats faster, urging the men to pull harder on their two-by-fours.

Once the sun disappears and darkness falls, a few of the workers pull their pickups closer to the concrete slab and turn on their headlights.

The men working in the last section, where Gulshan's and my

classroom used to be, are still spreading and smoothing. Fast, but not so fast that they screw up the job. They want this floor perfectly even for their daughters. No girl will ever trip over a cracked or buckling floor in this school.

Ankle-deep in concrete, the men inch closer to the front of the form until the last two men step out, kneel, and sweep their boards one final time.

Done.

Suddenly, a cheer rises all around me. They did it! They finished. Linking arms, they swing each other through the air, their song of celebration loud and exuberant. Except no one grabs my arm or Gulshan's. I work my way around the circle, capturing image after image of joyful men, their eyes alight with victory, their elaborate dance steps done in bare feet that must be close to frozen.

When Ikrom arrives with the day's wages and piles of tarps, the men cheer again. They must be exhausted and ready to get home to warm stoves and dinner, but they take the time to spread the tarps over the school floor. Bedding them down for the night.

I walk the length of the school, and for some reason I can't begin to fathom, my gut launches into major anxiety mode. Every single person here is thrilled with the work that got done today. But something is eating at me.

Morda-gow! The religion teacher's threat from the other day wafts up from the village through the dark, finding its target. Me. 39. The number painted on Ikrom and Gulshan's door in the middle of the night, when the religion teacher's grandson thought we'd all be asleep. What's to keep him or another disgruntled person from doing the same thing tonight? Here. At the school. I look toward the most beautiful, smoothest floor ever poured. A floor that needs at least a day to set before anyone can stand on it. Without ruining it.

It wouldn't take much to come in the dark of night and run through the still-soft concrete. Or scrawl obscenities. He could easily wreck our floor, our foundation for the rest of the school. A sabotage that would mean starting all over again. And we definitely don't have the money for that.

I find Gulshan and tell her my fear. "Oh, Annie. You are very right to be concerned. There are people in the village who could do serious damage."

We approach Ikrom and the foreman. The few remaining workers gather around us. We need men to guard the site tonight, possibly tomorrow night as well. During the day, there won't be a problem. Plenty of people will be here constructing wooden frames. No one's happy about the thought of patrolling in the cold of the night, then, Ikrom promises double the wages, and everyone agrees to take a shift.

"That was good thinking," says Gulshan as we ride back to the house.

"A waste of money," grumbles Ikrom. "No one will damage the concrete tonight, not right after defacing our door."

"That you do not know." Gulshan sounds determined. "Having men there will send the message that we are on guard. We must always be watching. You know what kind of man the religion teacher is."

Ikrom lifts one hand off the steering wheel. "You are right. He would not ruin the floor himself, of course. He will force his grandson and the boys in his classes to do his bidding. All he has to do is threaten to fail a boy, and he gets what he wants."

Beside me, Gulshan stiffens. "Not always."

There's a story here. I hold my breath and hope she tells it.

She doesn't disappoint. "When Darya first came here to set up the school, that awful man tried to intimidate me through my son Farrakh."

"Seriously?"

"Oh, yes. It was very ugly." She shakes her head. "The old fart was angry about the girls' school. He thought he could threaten to fail my Farrakh unless I stopped teaching at the school."

Holy shit. This guy really is a crazy, nasty asshole. "What happened?"

"Farrakh is like his father—a good man who respects women. He refused to . . ." She seems to be looking for the right word.

"Cave?" I suggest.

"Is not a cave an opening in a mountain?"

I nod. "It's also slang, meaning to 'give in.'"

"That is a good word. Well, when Farrakh refused to 'cave,' that horrible man marked him down in religion class. He gave him a failing grade."

Ikrom slams his fist against the steering wheel. "Farrakh! The best student in his year. The best student in ten years! It was outrageous!"

"What did Farrakh do?"

"My son, he stood up to that toad." I can hear the pride in Ikrom's voice.

Gulshan takes over. "Farrakh appealed to the director. Ikrom went with him. The score was changed. Not as high as it should have been, but it was not a failing mark. This is why you should not think that what happened the other night was because of you."

Possible, I suppose. Not likely. Why would the religion teacher wait all these years to take revenge?

29

AFTER DINNER, IKROM DRIVES back to the building site to check on the concrete and make sure the guards are still there. I retreat to my room and power up my laptop to study the images on Seema's SD card again. More carefully this time—to make sure I didn't miss anything the first time through. Picture after picture of girlfriends, me, her parents. I sure don't see anything that clues me in to where she could be now.

Finally, I come to a series of images of Awalmir, pictures I don't remember seeing before. As much as it hurts me to admit it, he's a good-looking guy. If you like that type. Brooding, moody, seductive. Those 'come hither' eyes. No wonder Seema fell for him. Interesting that he never seemed to smile for the camera. Always this full-lipped pout. I keep looking until I come across one where he *is* smiling. A very scary smile that makes the hair on the back of my neck stand on end. Eyes that pierce through me with their intensity. He looks a lot more like his cousin, Ghazan, at the end of the high-mountain firefight last May—the battle where Cerelli took a bullet in the leg that led to the amputation.

I keep staring at the pic. If I put a scraggly beard and longer hair on him, could he be the guy who grabbed me at the market in Bazarak? No, I'm not seeing it. That guy wasn't Awalmir. Then, why did he grab me? Here I've been assuming it was for the money. That the official at the airport or the officer at the Dalan Sang checkpoint sent someone after me to steal the thirty thousand. But what if that wasn't what was going on? What if the guy was after *me*, not the money? But how did he know I'd be in the market at that moment? And how could he have recognized me? Jeez, I really am paranoid.

Then again, maybe not so paranoid. I scroll back through Seema's photos to a string of seventeen candid shots. Of me. From every possible angle. Then I remember that the SD card housing these images saw the inside of Bibi and Omar's apartment. Whether Seema was actually there or not, someone's hands were on this card, someone saw these images. The card wasn't there by accident. Someone brought it to the apartment for a reason. My skin crawls. This is just plain creepy, especially considering that Ghazan and Awalmir's extended family have called for *Nyaw aw Badal*—justice and revenge. Not just on Cerelli and Sawyer, but on me, too. For the bombing of Khakwali and the deaths of so many in their family. All because I went back to that village to photograph Malalai.

I rake my fingers through my hair. Is any of this possible? Or am I getting seriously freaked by events that could just be coincidental? Yeah, well, that cluster of bruises on my bicep isn't a figment of my imagination. They're very real and still painful.

As much as I don't want to call Cerelli again, he'd want to know about what happened in the market. Can I talk to him without getting upset? I'm still mulling this conundrum when I tune in to the fact that my cell phone is buzzing. A new text.

Even the purest water I must not drink
Lest my Beloved's name, on my lips, be erased.

Oh, Seema. Well done. Such a romantic, even though it kills me to have her wasting her love and devotion on that sick and twisted Awalmir. It's like she's gotten lost in one of her own fairy tales. Except instead of falling for the prince, this time the princess has chosen the villain. All those plays she wrote to act out with Mel when they were younger, Seema was always the princess, leaning over the second-floor railing. Mel was the prince, climbing the staircase to rescue her. I plant my chin in the palm of my hand and conjure up the Seema of ten years ago. When she wasn't writing, she was reading. Always reading.

Seema and her books.

She brought them with her when the family moved to Wad Qol. I can see them now, crammed into the bookcase in her room. What happened to them? Did Gulshan take them when she went to tidy up? Or are they still there, just waiting to be rescued and put on shelves in the new school? Definitely something to find out.

I follow the clatter of dishes to the kitchen, where Gulshan is wrist-deep in a basin of sudsy water. "Here, please, let me." I try to elbow her out of the way.

She waves at me dismissively. "I am nearly finished. Please, tell me what you are thinking."

I straighten. "How can you possibly know I'm thinking something?"

"Oh, Annie." She laughs. "Your face reveals many of your thoughts. You must be careful about that. You cannot let a husband know too much."

I'm about to argue the husband thing. Instead, I just nod.

"Something to keep in mind." Not that there's ever going to be another husband. Or that I could ever control what I show on my face.

"Please, tell me."

I smile. "Books. More specifically, Seema's books. Did you see them when you were at the house? After . . ."

Her eyes light up. "Oh, I did! There were many books. Hundreds!"

"Are they still there?"

"Oh, yes." She stops washing. "Do you think we could—?"

"Why not? I can't imagine Seema's going to come back for them. They're just going to waste."

"Oh, Annie. We must go and look at them."

"Where are you going?" Back from the building site, Ikrom stands in the doorway between the lounge and the kitchen.

"I will explain later," says Gulshan. "For now, how are things at the school?"

"Very good. As I expected. There have been no signs of anyone trying to do mischief."

"That's great!" I may be smiling, but my stomach is still churning with the feeling that something bad is going to happen.

"You mean you didn't see anyone." Gulshan crosses her arms over her chest. "The guards, they are still there?"

"For tonight." Ikrom's voice is firm.

"For tomorrow as well." Gulshan is equally determined.

He frowns. "That would be a waste of money!"

"And what if there is mischief tomorrow night?"

"There won't be. Having the guards at the site tonight has sent a message. We know they won't be there tomorrow. The ones who do damage do not know."

"Bah. All they will need to do is keep their eyes and ears open. They will see there are no guards. They will hear the talk in the village." Arms still crossed, she turns and stalks toward the bedroom.

Throwing me a worried look, Ikrom hurries after her.

This might be a good time to give them some privacy. Back in my bedroom, I grab a sweater, my cell, and the sat phone. "I'm going outside for a few minutes," I say loudly. "I need to make a phone call, and the reception is better in the back garden." I'm sure neither one of them is listening to me. And I thought Afghan wives didn't go against their husbands. Most probably don't. But it's pretty clear who's in charge in this household.

One quick call to Cerelli, I promise myself as I pull my sweater tight around me and head out the door. Once outside, I realize I've forgotten my flashlight. No way am I going back for it—past Gulshan and Ikrom's bedroom. I use my cell's flashlight to help me steer around the pile of charred wood on the side of the house and then into the backyard. In the barely lit shadows, I can see the remains of the gardens. The herbs have mostly succumbed to the black frost. But the tarragon and parsley, the coriander and echinacea are still hanging in there. There's a second, bigger bed with remnants of cucumber and eggplant, peppers and tomatoes. The stalks are blackened and weeping, and a few rotting vegetables litter the ground. Probably great fertilizer for next spring.

I'm just looking at the mulberry bushes lining the very back of the garden when Nasrat Parsa starts to sing a romantic Afghan song. The ringtone Cerelli installed on the sat phone when he gave it to me last May. If I had any doubts about whether this was the same phone I used back then, I don't anymore.

So, *he's* calling me. I decide to keep things friendly, professional. "Hey."

"Hey yourself." Not Cerelli.

"Todd?"

"Glad you still know my voice."

"Of course I recognize your voice."

"I thought I should let you know that our daughter is back with us."

"I see." I wonder how she's holding up to this forced repatriation.

"It's not like we had a choice—with you being in Afghanistan and all."

"I'm not sure I follow."

"Give me a break. You know we couldn't leave her alone in a house in *Bay View*."

"She wasn't alone. Bonita's there."

"In a different apartment."

"You know as well as I do that there's an interior staircase that connects the two floors. How is that any different from Mel being in her bedroom with you and Catherine Elizabeth on the first floor?"

"Because Bonita isn't her mother."

Ah, there's the crux.

"What the fuck, Annie! You said you'd take care of her. A few weeks, a couple months—that's all we asked. And you agreed. Next thing I know, you go running off to Afghanistan. What the hell kind of parenting is that?"

Damn him. He's trying to play on my guilt, make me feel like I've abandoned our daughter. Again. "It's my job. Besides, Bonita is a good friend, and she's looked out for Mel before."

"For a day or an evening. Not for a few weeks." He wants an apology.

There's no way I'm going to convince him that Bonita is probably better at looking after Mel than I am. Best to give him the apology he wants and get him off the phone so I can call Cerelli. "I'm sorry."

"Thank you. When will you be coming home?"

"I don't know yet. It's a fairly long assignment. Probably not till mid-December."

"What's the date on your ticket?" His voice is bordering on angry again.

"Don't know. Kevin probably hasn't booked it yet."

"What?" Definitely not the right answer.

"Todd, in my line of work, things happen. Travel plans change all the time. Rollover fees are a killer. I wait until I know what I'm doing and then get a return ticket."

"Christ, Annie. I'll give you the money to buy the ticket. Just get back here. Now."

We had variations of this same argument all the time when we were married. I should have known this trip to Afghanistan would just lay the groundwork for another fight. But I'm not making decisions for his benefit. "Sorry. This is my job. I'll get there when I can." My voice is quiet, firm. I press the END CALL button. God only knows how he's taking that. At this point, I could care less.

I pace off a square in the backyard, doing what I can to warm up. Damn, my fingers are nearly frozen. So is my butt. The last thing I want is to make another call. I've had enough of crazed men. Cerelli can wait until tomorrow. I stop pacing and weigh the sat phone in my hand. The real question is: can I wait? Cerelli needs to know what happened in Bazarak. Besides, if the Taliban are targeting me, it could be he's heard some chatter. Something I need to know.

I punch in his number. Finally, the connection clicks through, and I hear the phone ringing. In Kabul.

I steel myself to be all business. No emotion. No jealousy.

He picks up the phone mid-ring. "This is Annie?" Not Cerelli. A woman's voice, deep and sexy, purrs across the line.

"Fatima." Holy shit. Things are that tight between them that she's answering his phone? "Yes. I'm here. Look, I need to speak with Cerelli. Finn."

"He cannot talk right now. Please, you tell me. I will give him message."

I don't even want to imagine why he can't talk to me.

A message. Various possibilities career through my mind. *Tell him someone attacked me in the market.* Or *Tell Cerelli to answer his own phone! Tell him I don't want to talk to his once-again lover!* Or, better yet, how I'm really feeling: *Tell him to fuck off!* Immature, every last one of those messages, but accurate.

Instead, I manage to steady my voice despite the pain in my chest as my heart cracks open. "Thanks, anyway. No message."

30

IT'S EARLY MORNING, BARELY light out, when Gulshan and I head to the building site. She plans to be here all day. Thank God. But I'm beginning to wonder when the girls will have another literature class.

"Today, the girls have science and religion again."

I raise my eyebrow. "That's an interesting combination."

She laughs. "It works."

"I'm having a hard time imagining how."

She looks thoughtful. "The religion class balances the sciences the right amount. This way the parents and the imam and the boys' religion teacher do not get too upset. Therefore, they do not interfere. The girls may not have the understanding of biology and earth science that Darya insisted on, but they have some knowledge. I have learned that it is important to balance what we want to teach the girls with what the village is willing to tolerate. It is the best way to keep the school open."

"A very creative solution." I'll definitely have to give this some thought. Especially if I plan to raise any more money. It's possible that Western donors might not be too keen on supporting what is really religion masquerading as science.

When we get to the building site, the three guards from the last shift are wrapped in the tarps and sprawled on the ground, snoring loudly. Okay, I understand that it's been a long night and downright frigid. But these guys live here. They're used to these conditions. Besides which, we're paying them to watch over the concrete slab. I can't imagine how Gulshan is going to manage them.

She sure doesn't sweet-talk them. Instead, she kicks the first booted foot she comes to. The man sputters awake. "For this, I am paying you?" she shrieks. "If I find one single scratch on that concrete, I will pay no one." She stomps over to the next man, who's now sitting up, probably wondering what the hell's going on. Jerking at his tarp, she yells, "We put these tarps on top of the concrete to keep it warm enough to set. If there's a problem, you three will be out of jobs!"

With that, she marches over to the concrete slab and examines as much as she can without actually walking on it. All three men follow closely behind her, trying their best to excuse every mark, even the leaves that have fallen. I'm pretty sure she's looking for footprints that might prove Ikrom wrong, that miscreants really did show up during the night.

Finally, she completes her inspection. "It is good. There is no damage. Now I will test to see how well the concrete has set."

It seems clear to me that the concrete is doing just fine. It's also clear that the men don't know that. They continue to trail after Gulshan, looking more and more nervous as she touches, then knocks on the concrete. Finally, reaching into her pocket, she pulls out some bills and places them into each man's cupped hands. From the relieved expressions on their faces, I can tell she really had them frightened.

"You are one strong woman," I say as the men scurry home for breakfast.

She beams. "Do you think so?"

"You took on those three big, burly guys. Yeah, I think you're pretty gutsy."

"Gutsy?"

I laugh. "It's American slang for brave and strong."

"I was trying to act like Darya would have done. She was the gutsiest of all women."

"Yes." I blink a couple times, then turn away so she can't see my eyes glistening. "Yes, she was."

The foreman is taking his sweet time getting here. I'm beginning to wonder if he's going to show at all when he pulls his truck up the drive. "No carpenters yet?" he calls out his window.

Gulshan marches over to his pickup. I'm right behind her. "The men, why aren't they here?"

The look he gives her says a lot. This is Afghanistan. They'll get here when they get here.

She takes it in without a word, then turns on her heel and marches back to the slab. Passing me, she mutters loud enough that I have to believe the foreman hears her, too. "We will see about that. If they are not here by sunrise, they will not have their jobs."

Wait a sec. We need those guys. There can't possibly be that many carpenters sitting around the Panjshir Valley waiting for work. Unless Gulshan has wall-framing skills in addition to everything else.

I glance at the foreman, his window rolled up again, cozy in his truck. And a lot warmer than we are. I bet that's hot *chai* he's got in that thermos. Well, he's clearly not into sharing, so I do the next best thing to warm up. I walk the perimeter of the slab, doing my own search for marks and footprints. Any signs of cracking or damage. That's when I see the faintest possible handprint at the corner in the far back. I look closer. On one side of the print, I can just barely make out the swirled Dari letter: ڪ. On the other side, an English **A**.

And suddenly I'm back in Bay View. Grammy was living downstairs then, and I had the second floor. Todd and I had split and were finalizing the divorce. I had a week off, which meant Emmy—she was still Emmy then—was staying with me while Todd went off to a ritzy Cancun resort with Catherine Elizabeth. The town was pouring new sidewalks on our block, so Grammy and Emmy and I decided to leave our marks. Emmy pressed her hand into the corner of the slab closest to our front door. Then we each wrote our first initial. E. A. E. Two Emmelines with Annie in the middle. It was there for years, until right after Grammy died and the concrete cracked. The new slab is clean. As far as Mel and I are concerned, it's totally lacking in character.

"What are you looking at?" Gulshan comes up to my side.

I point at the handprint. "You missed something earlier."

She's quiet for a minute. "No, I did not miss that."

"You mean . . ."

"It is a good reminder that two women built this school. The frames and bricks will hide this, but we will know."

"Yes, we will." I squat down and trace the letters. "It's drying fast."

"Yes." She's worried. "I understand it is better to pour concrete in warm weather when it will dry more slowly. If it sets too fast, there is more risk of cracking."

I stare at her. "How do you know so much about building?"

She flaps her hand under her *burqa*. "It was necessary. Back when Darya bought the original building, it was falling down."

I nod. "Yeah, I saw the pictures. I'm kind of surprised it lasted as long as it did."

"She put me in charge of restoring the school. I studied how to make concrete and pour it, how to frame the walls and lay the bricks, how to anchor windows and hang a door. Everything."

Is there nothing this woman can't do? "So, if the carpenters don't show up, you'll teach me, and the two of us will build the frames."

She mulls that idea for a few seconds, then shakes her head. "That would take too much time. The carpenters have much to do before the bricklayers come."

The pickups pulling up the drive catch our attention.

"The carpenters." The relief in her voice is palpable.

"And the sun still isn't above the trees. Their jobs are safe."

After a short discussion with the foreman, the men set to work. They've clearly decided to build the sections of the frames separately, laying them flat on the ground as close as possible to where they will eventually stand. A couple hours into the morning, the job site looks like a 3D project that's still in the 2D phase.

I take up my usual job, prowling for images to capture. I do hope Mel and Awa appreciate this. The real image I want would be from high above, looking down when the entire frame is built and ringing the slab. I'd need a helicopter, of course, or better yet a hot-air balloon, which gives a smoother ride and is better for camera work. Neither one is likely to happen.

For now, I focus on the men at work. Their backs bent, heads bowed, and their hands—big and muscular, thick-fingered and battered. I photograph the bruises, the grizzled hairs, and the missing fingernails as saws shorten board lengths, hammers pound nails, and frames come together. What else have these hands built besides this school? I envision boys' schools. Mosques. Homes. Shops. Besides hammers and nails and levels, what else have these hands held? The *Qur'an?* Their wives? Their children? A pencil and book? An AK-47?

"Ms. Hawkins Green! Ms. Hawkins Green!" Two schoolgirls are running up the drive, smiling and waving. When they get closer, I tune in to the fact that they're not wearing the school uniform of a brown *shalwar kameez* and a white headscarf. Because they're no longer in school. Instead, one has on a light-blue scarf, and the other is wearing yellow with fuchsia flowers. And both scarves are modestly covering all their hair. No locks hanging out to attract the attention of boys who might happen past.

Still, I recognize their faces. Wiin and Chehrah. Two of my favorite students from last spring. As budding photographers, they tended to take shots of pouting girls trying to look like Western fashion models and actresses. They weren't quite as adventurous with their camera work as Bahar and Seema, but they brought amazing energy to the critique sessions after our photo shoots around the village.

I walk over to meet them. "Did you both pass your exams?"

"Yes!" They burst out laughing. "Just barely."

Wiin steps forward to hug me, then keeps her arm around my waist. "Both Chehrah and I studied very hard with Bahar. Every day, we worked, and she helped us all she could. But we are not as smart as her."

"Bahar is brilliant! Even smarter than Seema—" Chehrah looks stricken. "I am sorry. I should not . . ."

I glance from one to the other. "Please! Tell me. Has either one of you heard anything from Seema? Do you know where she is?"

The girls share a look. "No," says Wiin. "People in the village don't talk about her because . . ."

It takes me a few seconds, then I get it. Seema brought dishonor to her family, and people here want to bury her memory, lest any of her shame rub off on them. Clearly, I'm not going to learn anything, so I change the subject. "So, what're you two doing now that you're out of school?"

Another look at each other, and they beam. "We are both getting married!" Wiin squeals with delight.

"I am getting married first." Chehrah sashays proudly forward and grabs my hands. "In two weeks."

"And who's the lucky man?" I swallow my sigh of disappointment and churn through a litany of 'if onlys.' If only they'd taken school more seriously, if only they'd studied harder, if only they'd had any interest in going to college. With the education they got from this school, these two girls had a chance to do something more with their lives. Such a waste! The women and girls in Afghanistan need to become doctors and teachers if there's going to be any hope of progress. Then, I remember all the photographs of high school boys with dreamy eyes both these girls turned in. This was clearly what they wanted. Damn, I hope this is a conversation I never have to have with Mel.

"You didn't meet him. He is older and was away working in Bazarak when you were here." She grins broadly. "I will move there right after we are married."

"Chehrah, I'm very happy for you." I turn to Wiin, whose arm is still circling my waist. "Tell me about your future husband."

Wiin is suddenly a bit hesitant to talk about her beloved. Chehrah pokes her friend with her elbow. "Tell her! It doesn't matter anymore. Bahar should have stayed if she wanted him."

Oh, no, not that cute boy I saw in the market on one of our field trips. He was flirting like crazy with Bahar. I kind of thought they might be sweet on each other. Now, her best friend has the boy?

Almost as though Wiin can tell what I'm thinking, she whispers, "I have not told her yet, but I promise I will. Please do not say anything to her mother."

I glance quickly over my shoulder to Gulshan standing by the wooden frames, watching us. Something tells me she already knows Wiin's secret. I have the feeling Gulshan's aware of just about everything that goes on in Wad Qol.

"You see, he did not do well on his exam either. He did not go to university. And we have known each other since we were babies. Like with Bahar. We all grew up together. After Bahar left, well . . . Our parents are all very happy. I will tell her. She will understand."

I hug her against me. "Yes, you should tell her." I have to wonder if Bahar will understand. Then I remember her whispered confidence the night we shared her room. *I went to a demonstration with Dr. Faludi. It was for the rights of women.* Maybe this boy isn't all that important in her life anymore.

After the girls leave, promising to visit again, I make my way back over to Gulshan. And wait for her to ask the question I know is uppermost on her mind.

Gulshan gets right to the point. "Did Wiin tell you she is engaged?"

"Oh, yeah. She promised to tell Bahar."

"Bah!" A dismissive wave.

"You don't think she will?"

"Bahar could have studied with any other girl, but she chose to work with Wiin because they were good friends. And because of that, Bahar's score was a little lower than it should have been. Wiin's was good enough for her to pass. That was a surprise to all of the teachers and to Wiin. This boy, he promised to wait. Bahar thought she had an understanding."

"The boy. Is he working?"

Gulshan smiles. "You did not recognize him the other day? I guess it would have been hard. Everyone was covered in dirt."

"He was one of the diggers?"

"Yes." And that one word tells me that deep down, Gulshan isn't all that upset to see the boy marry someone besides Bahar. "Do not worry about my daughter. *Inshallah*, she will find the path Allah wants her to follow."

"Chehrah is also getting married soon. And then moving to Bazarak."

Gulshan shakes her head sadly. "That is a bad match. Good for the parents. I have heard that the man paid a large dowry. It is not so good for Chehrah, I believe, although he has given her beautiful gold and silver jewelry. I have to wonder why they must marry this quickly."

"You mean . . ."

She nods. "That is what I hear. She is a beautiful girl and lively. But to marry this fast? That is not a good way to begin. It is not only that. She will be a second wife."

A second wife? I am so not good at sharing.

31

WHEN WE RETURN FROM LUNCH, the carpenters are already back and working hard. Only four more hours to finish all the frames. Tomorrow and the day after, they'll raise them, one after another, anchoring them to the slab and to each other—assuming the concrete is sufficiently hardened. Then to the roof. After that, they'll close in the outer walls and the roof with plywood. Once that's complete, we'll be ready for the bricklayers.

"When do the bricks get here?" My mind is still on the incredible roasted eggplant in yogurt tomato sauce Gulshan prepared for our lunch.

"Tomorrow." She smooths the front of her *burqa*. "Late in the morning."

"But the carpenters still have a ways to go. We won't be ready for the bricklayers for a few days, right?"

Her eyes twinkle through her eyepiece. "I want to make sure the bricks are here when we need them."

"Let's hope."

We walk among the carpenters and inspect their frames. "You

are working very fast! This looks perfect!" Gulshan says again and
again to each team. The men dip their heads in appreciation until
we pass, and then, when they think we're not looking, slap each
other's shoulders.

After Gulshan compliments the last team, she turns to me
with a smile. "Are you ready to take a walk?"

"Is that a good idea?" I nod toward the men.

"Bah." She waves away my concern. "They will continue working
and finish today. Besides, we will not be gone that long."

"Where are we going?"

"Why, to Darya's house, of course. I want to take a look at
Seema's books." She pulls her hand out from under her *burqa* and
holds up the key.

I grin. "Let's go!" I take a step toward the drive.

"First"—Gulshan links her arm around mine—"we will speak
with the foreman. He needs to know we will return in exactly one
hour."

"Gulshan, we'll barely be able to walk there and back in one
hour."

"Of course. I know that. But he does not know where we are
going. I want everyone to *expect* us back any minute."

FROM THE OUTSIDE, DARYA AND Tariq's house looks exactly
the way it did six months ago. I can almost imagine that it's May
again and I'm the first one home from school. Seema and Darya
will be following soon.

Gulshan unlocks the front door and pushes it open. Inside, it's
like a deep cave—heavy with inky darkness. For a second, I hesitate,

listening for the voices of the people I love. Why did I ever think this was a good idea?

Yeah, well, you did, so get on with it! My inner voice cuts me no slack.

Digging my flashlight out of my pack, I flick it on. In the shadows and the cold and the silence, the lounge feels much bigger than I remember. The rugs are still here. The low sofas. The cushions on the floor. The photographs I took of Seema and Mel over the years are gone, though—the empty frames propped against the interior wall. I can just make out the dusty outlines where the frames used to hang.

Gulshan opens a couple windows and shutters to give us some light. Then, sweeping her *burqa* back off her face, she turns toward me. "So much life this house used to have. Now, it is empty and sad."

"It is." I nod. Then, my mind wanders down the hall to the bedroom I slept in when I was here. The last time I saw it, my clothes lay slashed in the middle of the floor. Awalmir's doing, I'm sure, with Seema's help. My thoughts shift direction and venture into Darya and Tariq's room, then Tariq's study. All trashed. Tour complete.

"Okay, let's take a look at those books." I lead Gulshan back through the cold darkness to Seema's bedroom.

She edges past me and crosses the room to open the casement windows, then the shutters. Sunlight streams into the room. I turn in place, taking in the furniture and the belongings Seema left behind when she fled with Awalmir. It all looks exactly the same as when I last saw it. The desk. The books. A few photographs tacked to the walls. This girl had so many dreams and so much potential. I can't imagine what went wrong. I run my fingers along the dusty edges of her shoulder-high bookcase. Still crammed full, one row of books hidden behind the other. A treasure trove in English and Dari and Persian. Probably more than what the rest of the girls and the school have all together.

I take a book from the shelf and riffle through the pages, then hand it to Gulshan. "What do you think?"

"I think Allah has answered our prayers."

"Maybe Seema and her love of reading helped a little."

She reaches for another book and carries it to the open window. Then she's back for another. Finally, she helps herself to my flashlight and kneels in front of the shelves, her fingers trailing along the titles printed on the spines. "These are wonderful. The girls will be very happy to have them. But . . ."

"What?" I sit cross-legged on the wool Persian rug and reach absentmindedly past Gulshan for a book from the lowest shelf.

"Is it right for us to take these?"

"Like I told you before, I can't believe Seema will come back for anything in this house. Certainly not for books. Let's remember who her *beloved* is—a man who has declared *jihad* against all things Western, including girls getting an education." I shake my head with such fury that I can almost feel my brain slamming against my skull.

"Truly, this I cannot understand." She examines yet another book. "Ah, Persian poetry. Captain Cerelli gave her this. Yes, he would want this book to come to the school." She sets it aside to take back with us today.

I slide out a book from the middle of the shelf. Turning it over to read the title, I have to smile. *Little House in the Big Woods.* A book I gave Seema when she was about eight and going through her Laura Ingalls Wilder craze. As I leaf through it, my fingers start to tingle—the sensation I get when I've lined up a really great shot.

Which I'm not doing now. It must be the cold. So, I flex my fingers, then rub them, anything to warm them up. But the tingling keeps on. Because, I realize, it isn't the cold.

Sweetheart, what are you looking for? Cerelli's voice. And not particularly welcome.

I do my best to shut him out. Giving my thoughts free rein, I find myself back in *my* room when I was seventeen. Folding and folding secret messages from boys, love notes I didn't want Grammy reading. Once I got those notes small enough, I was able to hide them inside the bindings of my favorite books. Very handy hiding places.

I know Cerelli and Sawyer searched the house. But did either of them check the bindings?

I crack the book in my hand and stare down the gap between binding and pages. Empty.

I check the rest of the *Little House* books. Nothing.

From the row behind, I try *Little Women*. And there is Seema's treasure. A tightly folded bundle of rough white-lined paper that I pull out oh-so-carefully. I've seen this paper before. Months ago. This is the paper Awalmir used to write the *landays* that seduced Seema away from everything and everyone she knew.

"What have you found?" Gulshan leans forward and shines the flashlight on the paper in my hands.

"I don't know." Unfolding it, I stare at the tiny swirling letters for ten long seconds before I realize that I can't read it. Definitely not in English. It doesn't look like any Dari words or phrases I've ever seen. Pashto? I can say a few things in Pashto, but my reading and writing abilities are nonexistent. The numbers, though, are Arabic. Could be phone numbers. Or a code. The only thing I can tell for sure is that this isn't Seema's handwriting. I'm not sure it's

Awalmir's either. It doesn't look quite as rough as I remember his being.

Gulshan plucks the paper from my hand and studies it. "This is mostly a list of names and phone numbers. There are also Pashto words that I cannot understand." She hands it back and looks at me quizzically. "Why would Seema have such a thing hidden in one of her books?"

My heart sinks as the all-too-obvious answer stares me in the face. She was hiding a contact list for Awalmir. Or something like that. It's clear what I have to do, even if it means talking to Fatima again. Well, if she answers this time, I'll definitely leave a message.

"I need to call Cerelli and let him know what we've found."

Gulshan nods. "Yes, that I think you should do. I will gather a few of the books to take with us now. Later, Ikrom can help us pack up the rest."

I push myself to my feet, grab Louisa May Alcott, and head toward the front sitting room. Before I can dig out the sat phone, Nasrat Parsa's singing announces an incoming call.

I answer with a generic, all-purpose "Hi." And hope I sound reasonably friendly.

"Annie. I got a message you called." All business. Not a hint of friendliness.

"I didn't leave a message." I tone down the friendly, then open the front door and step outside for a little more privacy. Something tells me I'm going to need it.

"Fair enough. But I know if you call, you've got a good reason."

"Well." So, this is where things stand between us. And really, what could I expect? I haven't exactly been on my best behavior either. "Yeah, I did have a reason."

He waits a couple beats. "You going to share?"

Really poor choice of words, Cerelli. No, I'm not going to share *you*. Not that I probably have that option anymore. I swallow hard. Okay, then. All business. "Actually, there are two reasons. You sure this is an okay time to talk? I'm not interrupting?"

I can almost hear his brain putting the pieces together. "Please believe me, this isn't what you're thinking."

"Not going there, Cerelli."

"Look, things are happening here that I can't talk about. Just trust me a little longer, sweetheart. Then, I promise I'll tell all."

"All?"

He exhales his frustration. "You know what I mean. Now, what's going on that has you calling me at midnight and not leaving a message?"

"I called last night because I looked at the images on Seema's SD card again."

"Tell me."

"Okay, this probably sounds crazy, but while I was here last spring, she took a lot of pictures of me. Candids, that I didn't know about."

I can imagine him shrugging. "Where are you going with this?"

"Well, there was a little episode at the market in Bazarak the other day. Farrakh and Bahar were driving me to Wad Qol, and we stopped to get lunch."

"And?" I can almost see him ramming his fingers into his hair, trying to contain his frustration over how I'm drawing this out.

I tell him the rest, including the part where the guy grabbed me. When I finish, Cerelli doesn't say a word. Silence stretches between us. In fact, I'm thinking we've lost the connection when he finally speaks. "You okay?"

"Bruised, but okay."

"Good." His relief morphs to fury. Zero to sixty. "You were in Bazarak days ago. When the fuck were you planning to tell me about this?"

"I did call you." Okay, I didn't call to tell him about *that*.

"Yes, you did. And caught me right in the middle of—" Goddamn, Todd was right. A woman in every port. What the hell have I been thinking? I clench my fist and bite down on my knuckle to keep from screaming. Cerelli continues, "Right in the middle of something that I'll explain when I can."

"But it's not what I think it is."

"No, it's not." He pauses for a count of ten. "The SD card. Your theory is that Awalmir or someone held on to it because there are pictures of you. And now that they've got an even better idea of what you look like, there are tangoes out searching for you."

Listening to him actually say what I've been thinking makes me realize how ridiculous the whole thing is. "I thought it seemed like a pretty amazing coincidence. That's all."

"It is. And I don't like coincidences. I'll do what I can to check it out. You said there was a second reason you called?"

"There is. I'm here at Darya and Tariq's with Gulshan. We thought we'd help ourselves to Seema's books for the school."

"Good idea." His voice is a bit friendlier.

"I found something. Hidden in the binding of one of her books."

"*Seema's* books? Hell! I searched them myself."

"You must be losing touch with your teenage-girl self."

"Hate to say this, but I've only got a couple minutes left. What did you find?"

I describe the paper, the handwriting, and the numbers as succinctly as I can. "Gulshan looked at it, too. She says it looks like a list of names and phone numbers. Probably written in Pashto."

"Read me the numbers."

I do. "Well?"

"I think Gulshan's right. Any way you could send that to me?"

It takes me a few seconds before I remember my cell phone has a camera. "I'll text you a pic. Does that work?"

"You're not only beautiful, you're brilliant."

Okay, then. I'm betting he recognized one or more of the numbers. "So, this list is important?"

"Oh, yeah."

"You going to tell me why?"

"Sweetheart."

"I take it that's a no."

"I'll tell you what I can when I see you. Look, I'm sorry for everything that's been going on. Just trust me a little longer. Please." I hear a distinct pleading in his voice.

"Yeah. Okay." My lack of belief is audible.

"I'll call you tomorrow."

And then he's gone, leaving an open line between us. I punch the END button, then jam the sat phone into my pack and swing it onto my shoulder, ready to be gone as well. First, though, I follow through on my promise. A quick snapshot of the list I found in Seema's book, then I upload it to a text and hit SEND. What are the chances he'll ever tell me what any of this is about? Slim to none.

I turn to find Gulshan standing in the doorway, *burqa* still pushed back over her head, a maternal look of extreme disappointment distorting her face. "I am sorry, Annie, I could not avoid. You were speaking quite loudly. I heard most of what you said."

I fling up my hands. "He's maddening. I thought he loved me. But then, I called the other night, and *Fatima* interrupted us. At one o'clock in the morning. He was with her. *With* her. Then, when I called last night, she answered. *His phone.*"

She nods. "And you do not know what to think."

"Oh, I know exactly what to think." Tears well behind my eyes, and I quickly bury my face in my hands.

"Annie." Her voice is soft and comforting, as if she's talking to one of her children. The next thing I know, she's prying my hands away from my face. "Captain Cerelli is a good man. An honorable man. You need to listen to what he has to say."

Not what I want to hear. I look away from her, toward the sun that's about an hour from sinking behind the mountains. I'd really prefer no one see the purplish orbs around my eyes. To say I'm an ugly crier is an understatement.

"Come." She hands me a pile of books. "We have stayed far too long. The foreman and the carpenters will be missing us."

Not likely.

32

FOR ONCE, IKROM DOESN'T NEED to go to the clinic at the crack of dawn. Gulshan puts him to work piling plastic crates and a kerosene lantern into the bed of the pickup, and the three of us drive to Darya and Tariq's house to load up the rest of Seema's books.

As soon as we arrive, Gulshan is all business. She hands Ikrom and me each a couple crates and opens the front door. Again, the cold and dark push us back, then Gulshan lights the lantern, and any ghosts that might have been lurking vanish. She leads the way down the hall with Ikrom and me following behind. But Seema's room is far too small for three people, so flashlight in hand, I take myself to Tariq's study to see if there are any books left from Awalmir's rampage. Anything we could use at the school—for the science classes maybe.

Shining my light around the room, I can see the desk and the bookcases. As far as I remember, there was nothing left to salvage. Now, I see I was wrong. There are a few books sitting on shelves.

I train the flashlight beam onto the spines of thick tomes.

Handbook of Surgical Technique. Textbook of Surgery. Current Surgical Therapy. No good for the school. The clinic could use them, though. Setting them aside for Ikrom, I move on, trying hard to focus on the titles. But I can't help thinking about Tariq. He spent a lot of time in this room. Almost a decade. Reading. Studying. Staying up to date with medical research. It's been six months since he left, and I can't picture him here at all. Can't hear him. In fact, when I saw him in Boston a few months ago, he was a shadow of his former self. Completely gray. Drawn. Thin. So many lives lost.

The creak of the safe door swinging open breaks the silence. I spin around and imagine Awalmir's greedy fingers stuffing dollars and afghanis into a backpack. Then passports. *That's all in the past,* I remind myself. No Awalmir. The door must have opened on its own. From down the hall, I hear the murmur of voices and the slap of books being packed into crates.

Back to Tariq's books. *The Kite Runner. A Tale of Two Cities. The Book of Rumi.* Perfect additions for the school. I hug the *Rumi* to my chest. Darya's book. A twin to mine. How many Saturday nights during college did we stay in and read his poetry to each other?

Gulshan's and Ikrom's voices are getting louder. I poke my head out the study door to see each of them carrying a crate heavy with books. "Is there any space left?" I hold up the *Rumi.*

"You have found more books?" Gulshan calls out as she exits the front door. In a moment, she's back, joining me in the study.

"Not many." I point to the piles on the shelves. "Some that would be terrific for the school. And a few that should be in the clinic." I direct the beam onto the front cover of one of the medical books.

"Yes!" This is from Ikrom, crossing the room to scope out the books. "I know my friend Tariq would want these put to good use."

We finish carrying the rest of the boxes from Seema's room and load them into the flatbed. I look back at the open door. "What about the bookcases?"

"Oh! Do you think . . ." The note of surprise in Gulshan's voice is audible.

"Absolutely. And not only the one from Seema's room, the bookcases from Tariq's study, too." I'm sure Dar would insist we take them.

Ikrom nods slowly. "Yes, Tariq would want these things in the school and the clinic. We will take the one from the back room now and come back later for the rest."

The bookcase is heavier than I expected, but Ikrom and I maneuver it up the hallway and into the back of the truck. Gulshan locks up the house, and we're off—heading back into the village. When we reach the turn-off to the building site, Ikrom veers to the left and up the slight incline, cruising past the line of pickups parked along the verge.

As Ikrom pulls to a stop, I sense the wrongness of the scene in front of us. The carpenters should be working, even in the low morning light. They're not. Everyone is standing around, arms crossed, staring in the direction of the concrete slab. Gulshan reaches past me, unlatches the mechanism that functions as a handle, and all but shoves me out. Tumbling out after me, she hits the ground running, her *burqa* billowing behind.

It's not until I'm right on top of the damage that I see it. Our beautiful wooden frames, finished yesterday and left overnight to install today, are in ruins. My heart literally sinks in my chest.

Gulshan stalks among the frames spread out on the ground, examining each section in minute detail. The carpenters walk with her, pointing out breakage and stamping their feet in anger. So much wasted work! So much wood destroyed! I bring up the rear, cringing at the axe marks, the splintered wood, the show of hatred. Can we possibly save any of this wood? And when the hell will the carpenters be able to build more frames? Which is exactly what Gulshan wants to know.

"When? When can they rebuild these?" The fury coating her voice makes me realize that part of her anger is directed at the foreman and Ikrom, who last evening convinced us there was no need to waste more money on hiring guards. No need at all.

The foreman is doing his best to negotiate with the carpenters, most of whom are shaking their heads. I catch snippets. *Another job. Not enough lumber. Another delivery will take days.*

Really? There's that much work in the valley for carpenters?

As Cerelli would say, it's all too much of a coincidence. He wouldn't believe these guys. And neither do I. I'm more than willing to bet they know something about what happened here last night. They probably got wind of how much money I brought for this project, and they're looking for more pay. A lot more pay. Not that we can accuse them of sabotage, of course.

Oh, hell! I walk over to the nearest carpenter and point toward the hammer he's holding. Everyone stops talking and stares as the man, startled, hands over his hammer. Ikrom follows my lead. Soon, the two of us are standing next to a splintered frame, assessing what we can save. And honestly, the damage could be worse. At the first frame, we figure we can reuse at least half the wood. Plus, it doesn't need to be rebuilt from scratch. Still, taking apart the frames and rebuilding them will require a lot of time. Best start now. I kneel down and start knocking frames apart. Ikrom swallows a grin and does the same.

Not three minutes later, my carpenter is hovering next to me, reaching gingerly for his hammer. And taking care to stay clear of actually touching me. Pushing myself to my feet, I brush the dirt off my pants and stroll back over to where Gulshan is still deep in conversation with the foreman and the head carpenter.

"I will pay an extra day's wages if they finish rebuilding and installing today." Gulshan has dug her feet into the dirt and crossed her arms over her chest.

"Impossible!" The head carpenter turns to walk away. "And where is more lumber? We need more lumber to rebuild."

I nod my agreement. From what I can see with what's left over, we'll need maybe a third more lumber. And that's just for the walls. Then there's the roof . . .

Gulshan steps closer to the carpenter. Her head tilts back so she can look directly into his eyes. She's all of a couple inches from him. Way too close. He steps back. Bad move. I can feel the victory pulsing through the *burqa*. "We will order more wood now! It will be here by lunchtime."

The foreman pulls out his cell phone and walks toward the carpenters, who are disassembling frames to assess what's needed.

The head carpenter glances at me, then back at Gulshan. "My men will rebuild today and tomorrow and install the day after. Then one day for the plywood."

I was right. They all want more money. And there's not a damn thing we can do about it. Might as well just suck it up and pay. Even though she's not looking at me, I nod my approval.

Which she somehow manages to see. She points toward me. "The boss agrees to your request. *If you finish on time.*"

I have the good sense not to snort out a laugh. And let's hope none of the rest of the workers hear about this, or they'll want more, too. No telling what kind of sabotage could happen.

Neither one of them moves. Not an inch. They're locked in a stare-down. Finally, he nods and looks away. A deal. He heads off to tell his men.

"Someone must drive to the mill for the lumber." The foreman is looking at *me*.

Gulshan slices her hand through the air. "They can deliver."

He shakes his head. "The truck already left with today's delivery."

I exhale my disappointment.

Luckily, Ikrom is back and claps his hand on the foreman's shoulder. "Good. We can go. We will need both trucks, I think." He's already steering the foreman toward their pickups. He leans closer and says something I can't make out. Whatever it is, the foreman is suddenly eager to get on the road and all but leaps into his vehicle.

"What was that about?"

Gulshan waits another minute for the trucks to leave, then chuckles softly. "Those two know they made a big mistake last night by not having guards. They believe that going to get the lumber will put everything right. Bah!"

It never ceases to amaze me how well she can read her husband. And the foreman. "You *will* forgive Ikrom, won't you? Eventually?"

She turns toward me. "Of course I will. But he does not need to know that yet." She raises her index finger in lecture mode. "That is how you manage men. Keep them wondering what you will do next."

I clap my hand over my mouth. This woman knows her way around. "I just remembered. The crates! And the bookcase in the back of Ikrom's truck."

"Yes. They will have to stop first to unload everything. That is our bonus." Her smile is so broad I can see it through her netted eyepiece. "Now, while Ikrom and the foreman are busy getting more lumber, we will arrange for men to stand guard tonight."

"I think that's a very good idea."

33

THE SUN IS DIRECTLY OVERHEAD, but Ikrom and the foreman aren't back from their lumber run yet. The carpenters are getting antsy, looking over their shoulders at us, wondering when they'll get to break for lunch. Finally, Gulshan takes pity and heads over to tell them to go, with a sharp warning to be back within the hour. The men don't waste a second. They gather their tools and race toward their trucks.

It's at that very moment that my sat phone erupts with Nasrat Parsa's melodious voice. Cerelli. He promised he'd call today.

"Hey." I pitch my voice as low and sexy as I can make it. I can't compete with Fatima, but with any luck, I'll take his mind off her for a little while. Even though he swore that whatever I think is going on between the two of them isn't. Yeah, well, we'll see. Pending his promised explanation. And I really hope I can believe whatever he tells me because I want to get back on track with him.

"Annie?" Not Cerelli.

I swallow hard. "Todd?"

"Annie, uh, wait a sec?" He doesn't wait for an answer, just presses the phone against his chest. I'm all set to hurry him through whatever he's got to say when he comes back on the line. "Sorry. That was the police officer just leaving."

"Police?" My heart drops a little farther in my chest. "What's going on?"

"I don't know any easy way to say this. Mel is missing."

Missing? My heart stops. Just stops. I don't breathe. *Missing.* "What?" I'm not sure if I say the word out loud.

"She's missing. And now the police are saying they can't put out an Amber Alert until they confirm she's actually been abducted. What kind of crap is that?"

I close my eyes, try to keep myself calm. This isn't Seema all over again. It isn't. It can't be. "What exactly does *missing* mean?"

"She's missing!" Catherine Elizabeth yells into one of the extensions. "She's missing. What do you think that means?!"

"That's what I'm trying to find out." I'm really struggling to stay calm, to keep my voice under control.

"All I know is she wouldn't be missing if you weren't in Pakistan or wherever you are. Mel is a problem child, and you're always traveling, leaving us to deal with her."

I grit my teeth, determined not to take the bait. Except I can't help it. "I'm in Afghanistan."

"Well, pardon me! But that's hardly the point. Why are you there building a school anyway? You should be *here*, dealing with her . . ."

From seven thousand miles away, I hear crying. Catherine Elizabeth is *crying*? About Mel?

"Catherine Elizabeth. Please." Todd's voice. Gentle. "It'll be all right. You'll see."

"The police won't even *look* for her." Her sobs get louder. "This is exactly what I've been afraid would happen. It's just like that girl in Whitefish Bay."

"What girl?" I ask quietly, hoping to steady Catherine Elizabeth and move this conversation back to where it needs to be: on Mel.

"One of the seniors. Her family goes to St. Robert's, too. A good family."

"You mean Cassie Richards?" Todd again.

"Yes. She started seeing that Muslim boy, and the next thing her parents knew, she was attending a mosque and wearing a headscarf. Then she insisted on wearing that black robe—I don't know what it's called."

"An *abaya*?" I whisper before I can stop myself.

"Oh, for God's sake," she snaps. "What does it matter what it's called!"

"You're right. It doesn't matter."

"Cassie ended up running away with that boy. The last I heard, they went to Syria to be part of ISIS." She's back to crying. Harder.

"Are you sure about that?" Todd sounds like he doesn't quite believe what he's hearing.

"Yes! That's what her mother's best friend told me after church—just last week."

I listen to the silence filling the line between us and count to ten, desperate to get back to Mel. "So—"

"I know you don't believe me, but I love her. She really *is* my daughter. I'm terrified about what could have happened. I-I . . ." Her weeping drowns out the rest of her words.

Listening to Catherine Elizabeth cry and Todd not saying a word is quickly pushing me over the edge. "Could one of you tell me what happened?"

Catherine Elizabeth is the one to answer. Still teary. "I don't know. She didn't tell me before she took off." Even when she's crying, she really does have the most acerbic voice. Fingernails on a blackboard. Why the hell can't she just get off the line and let Todd and me deal with this?

"You actually saw her before she left?" My voice climbs at least an octave.

"You're putting words in my mouth. That's not what happened."

I notch back my voice, force myself to calm down. "Then please tell me what did happen. I'm trying to understand."

"Yesterday morning, I reminded her to come right home after school. No more working on the school newspaper or dance rehearsals or hanging out at the library with *that girl*. Home."

I want to know why they're punishing her like this. But that argument can wait.

"Then, she told me to *eff* off. I will not stand for that in this house. Maybe you—"

"Catherine Elizabeth." A low warning from Todd.

"After she said that, I took her cell phone. There have to be consequences for such unacceptable behavior, or she won't learn. Then, she said the f-word again! That's when I took her car keys and told her she had to walk to school." She dissolves into more tears.

"Did she take anything with her?" Kudos to Todd for asking a totally reasonable question.

"Her backpack, I guess. I didn't notice. I was busy with the twins, getting them in the car and to school."

"In other words," I say as calmly as I possibly can, "the last time you saw her, she was on her way to school."

"That's what I said." I can picture Catherine Elizabeth tightening her hold on the phone, her eyes red and swollen from so much crying. "Then she never came home last night."

"Last night?" I do a quick calculation and realize for the first time that it's 3:00 a.m. in Milwaukee. Oh, God. She could be anywhere. I decide to pretend Catherine Elizabeth isn't on the extension and talk to my ex. "Todd, have you spoken to Bonita?"

"First thing. Bonita says she hasn't seen her."

Yeah, well, Bonita could be parsing her words. She might know damn well Mel's upstairs, but because she didn't actually *see* her . . .

"What about Yasmine?"

"Do you have a phone number?"

I decide to be as literal as Bonita. "Sorry, I don't." I *do* have one for Awa, though, which will be the first call I make after I hang up. Even if it is three o'clock in the morning there.

"Look, Annie, I don't know what's going on here. You need to fly home now. Today."

"It's not that easy—"

"Did I hear you right?" Catherine Elizabeth erupts again. "Mel is *missing*. If you had any feelings for her, you wouldn't be there in the first place."

That's the button Mel's stepmother shouldn't have pushed. Somehow, I manage to keep my voice low, but the steel in it scares even me. "Don't you dare presume to judge my feelings for my daughter." And I end the call.

I refuse to allow myself to believe Mel has been abducted.

Which means she probably ran away. Not good. In fact, it's pretty bad and could get her in a hell of a lot of trouble. With Todd and Catherine Elizabeth and with the police. And me. Consequences that I'm sure haven't occurred to her. Still, it's a whole lot better than being abducted. Or missing. Now, it falls to me to see if I can track her down. Which borders on the ridiculous. If *they* can't find her, how the hell am *I* going to?

Fingers crossed, I try Awa Faqiri first. And apologize profusely when she answers.

"Annie! You are calling from Afghanistan?" Bless her, she sounds wide awake and happy to hear from me.

"I am."

"The school? Have they started building yet? No, they couldn't possibly build right now. Winter must be starting where you are."

"Oh, they *have* started. I'll tell you all about it when I get home. The real reason I'm calling is because I just had a frantic call from my ex-husband. He says Mel is missing."

"But she was just here for dinner."

"Do you have any idea where she went afterward?"

"It wasn't very late when she left. Firash offered to drive her home, but she wanted to walk."

"Do you happen to know if she was going to the house in Shorewood?"

Awa doesn't answer immediately. "That's where I assumed she was going. I am sorry, Annie, I simply don't remember. This must be very difficult for you being so far away."

Finally, a woman who understands. "As you may have guessed," I say, "Mel isn't getting along with her stepmother. Or her father."

I can actually hear her sympathetic nod. "Yes, she has mentioned that there are problems. I wonder if perhaps some of them are because of her friendship with Yasmine?"

"I'm pretty sure that's part of it, although I don't understand why."

"Yes, well, they aren't the only people who don't appreciate having Muslims in this country or their town. I must say, Firash and I are very proud of Mel for defying her father and stepmother. Pardon me. I shouldn't say that, but we love Mel and respect how she holds to her principles."

"Unfortunately, she will learn that there is a price to pay for going against their wishes." I may have an incredible daughter, but I'm afraid she's just screwed up her life big-time.

"Please, Annie, if you think of anything we can do to help, call."

"Thanks. I will. Now, I need to make some more calls to see if I can track her down. They've already reported it to the police, and I want to resolve this whole thing before anyone gets arrested." Or worse.

"ANNIE." BONITA ANSWERS THE PHONE much in the same terse way as Cerelli. I wonder if that's the reason I love them both so much.

"Hi, Bonita. I'm sure you can guess why I'm calling."

"Todd called you, didn't he?"

"He did."

"He called here first. Asked me if I'd 'seen' our girl."

"And have you?"

"Of course I have. She's upstairs asleep."

Thank God. "But you told him you didn't."

"I said what she asked me to say. That stepmother is toxic, and I figure Mel needs an adult standing up for her right about now."

I want to laugh, but I groan instead. "Slight problem. Todd and Catherine Elizabeth have brought in the cops."

"Stupid man." She snorts her displeasure. "Sorry, Annie, I know you used to be married to him. But only an idiot would marry Catherine Elizabeth. Anyone with two eyes can see what a bitch she is. She's sure been doing a number on our Mel."

Somewhere in the apartment, Finn barks his agreement.

A moment later, I hear steps pounding down the interior staircase a third of the way around the world. And then my daughter. "I heard the phone. Is that Mom?" A second later, she's on the line. "Please don't make me go back there, Mom. Please. She's horrible! A total bitch."

"Tell me about it."

"It's not just that she took away my phone and the car. Mom, she ordered me not to have anything to do with Yasmine. My best friend. Then, she made me quit dance. And *Ripples*."

"Sweetie, here's the problem. They called the police and reported you as a missing person."

"*They what?*"

"Well, they're stupider than I thought." This, from Bonita. I can see her standing head-to-head with Mel, sharing the conversation.

"Stupid or not, Mel, you've got to let the police know you're safe. And they're probably going to insist you go back."

"No." Mel doesn't take even two seconds to answer.

"No?"

"I'm not going back. I can't. She'll kill me."

"Probably. Although from the way she was talking tonight, I think she does love you."

"Yeah, right."

"Annie, there's something Mel's not telling you." Bonita sounds serious. "I thought this might blow up, so I took her to see your divorce lawyer this afternoon."

Damn, Bonita's smart. "And what did Tricia say?"

"Well, this was before we knew about the cops, of course."

"Of course."

"I told her I want to live with you, Mom. I asked for you to have full custody."

Holy shit. I feel my legs wobble. Going down. I sink to my knees in the dirt. Mel's sixteen. Which probably means any judge would give a lot of weight to her preference. As for living with me full-time, though, that's not good. I mean, I've got a job. Assuming I get permanently reinstated. And my job requires a hell of a lot of travel.

Stop! Just stop! This is Mel. My daughter. I'll make it work. Somehow. I've got to. "What did she say?"

"Well . . . I'd say it's not looking so great." It's good to have Bonita's down-to-earth input. "She pointed out that you're away a lot of the time, and the judge probably wouldn't go for that. Especially if those assholes, pardon my language, fight it. And you can be sure Catherine Elizabeth won't take this lying down."

"You think?"

"Oh, yeah. No way on God's green earth is she going to want any child support money going out of her greedy little hands. Or having her hoity-toity friends talking about them losing custody."

"True." I'm letting the thought of Mel moving in with me on a permanent basis settle in my brain. "So, short of me having to give up my job and foregoing child support, are there any other problems?"

Bonita barks out a laugh, which sets Finn yipping. "She did point out that you don't have two dimes to rub together, what with you giving away all your money."

I wave away that thought. "Oh, that."

"Yeah, missy, *that*. It's all well and good for you to give up your job, but how would you pay the bills?"

"Eh, practicality can be overrated." What am I saying? That I'll just give up my job? A job I'm suspended from at the moment— despite my upcoming Kabul assignment. That's not going to sit well with any judge. Not to mention, if the judge finds out I pulled a gun on Piera McNeil, all will be lost. And what's the likelihood of Todd's attorney or the judge asking if there are any outstanding or pending judgments against me? Pretty damn good.

And despite my bravado, there's no way I can go jobless. Could Mel really live in my apartment basically on her own for long stretches of time? Even with Bonita downstairs?

"Annie, you still there?"

"Yeah." I cringe at how defeated I sound.

"You should call Tricia. She said she'll need to talk with you."

"I bet she will."

"Wait. You haven't heard everything yet." The tone in Bonita's voice suggests something big is coming. "She wants to discuss naming me temporary guardian. That way, Mel could stay here, at least until you get back."

"Please, Mom?"

I pick up a handful of dirt and watch as, bit by bit, it slips through my fingers and back to the ground. "Bonita, are you sure about this? I mean, this is huge."

"Wouldn't have offered if I didn't want to do it." Her voice turns suddenly gruff.

"Bonita."

"Annie. I want to do this. Let me."

I take a deep breath. "Okay. I'll call her. She can talk to the police and possibly get Todd to back off. Oh, I have just one more question for now. Mel, how did you get home from the Faqiris' tonight?"

"Um, well—"

"That's on me," Bonita interrupts. "I thought you'd probably be okay with Mel using your car for a while."

"Of course," I hear myself saying while all I can think is: car insurance. Another call I'll have to make—to my insurance agent to make sure she's covered on my policy. That can wait. I hang up all set to punch in my lawyer's number when I notice the carpenters streaming back to the building site. Lunch is over already? Then, I see Gulshan trailing behind them, my familiar lunch tiffin in her hands. And bringing up the rear: two pickups loaded down with new lumber. Finally, something's going right today.

Before I can eat, I've got to call Tricia, even though I'm sure she won't welcome hearing from me at four in the morning. I pull up her number on my cell, then tap it into the sat phone. And wait. And wait. No connection to the satellite overhead. I try again. Still nothing. Damn it! I've got cops out searching for my daughter and an attorney I need to talk custody strategy with. I should also call Todd.

On the chance that for once my cell will get an international connection, I try. Nothing. I sink back on my heels. There's no help for it. With any luck, this is just some sort of temporary glitch with the satellite, and everything will be back in alignment soon. For now, I stuff the phones into my pack and turn to Gulshan.

"I brought you something to eat." She points to the blanket she's spread on the ground. "First, you must tell me what has happened. I can see that you're very worried."

"Oh, you have no idea."

34

I SHOULD BE INDOORS HELPING Gulshan with dinner, but instead I'm sitting on the tree stump in the dark behind the house, staring at my sat phone. Clearly, what I hoped was a temporary glitch isn't. The phone has stopped working. I can't get a connection. It's dead and done. As expected, my smartphone isn't getting me an international connection either. Which means I can't call home. Can't talk to my attorney. Or the police. Can't rescue Mel from her angry father and stepmother. I'm effectively incommunicado. Which normally would be a good thing. I don't have to listen to all the insanity swirling around Milwaukee. On the other hand, my daughter needs me. If I don't ride to the rescue, she could end up in front of a judge in juvie court.

Damn!

Finally, it occurs to me to try Cerelli on my smartphone. Which, fingers crossed, just might work in-country if I can catch a ping off a tower or a passing satellite. I pull up his number and tap. Ten seconds later, the man himself is on the line.

"Annie?"

"Hey."

"Are you all right?" I hear the worry in his voice.

"Fine. But the sat phone isn't."

"What happened?"

"Don't know. It's just not working. The best I can figure, it might need a new battery? Honestly, I don't have a clue."

"I'm sorry, sweetheart." He sounds frustrated. "There's not much I can do about replacing it right now. I'm in kind of deep."

In? In what? I don't ask. For once, I decide that if he could tell me, he would. "Look, is this an okay time to talk?"

He waits a beat. I can tell he's trying to read my mind, decide what it is I want to talk about. "I told you before, there is nothing, absolutely nothing, going on between Fatima and me. Nothing that should worry you. Or make you jealous." He's smiling.

What the hell? "Do you want me to be jealous?" Is that what all this has been about? Some weird macho need for me to . . . I shake my head. That just doesn't seem like Cerelli.

"Every man has his fantasies, and God knows I'm no saint. But I've come to realize you don't do jealousy well. So, no. I don't want that at all." His voice is definitely warmer, friendlier.

"Good answer." And I mean it. I feel like I'm finally getting back the Cerelli I love.

"I do what I can. Now, tell me why you called. Or was it just to let me know about the sat phone?"

"Partly." A gust of cold air finds its way around the side of the house, and I huddle deeper into my jacket. "I was supposed to call my divorce attorney this afternoon, and that's precisely when the sat phone gave up."

"Your attorney?" Trust Cerelli to go straight to the heart of the matter.

"It's a very long, very complicated story."

"Can you give me the abbreviated version in case we get cut off?"

I fill him in on the main plot points, starting with Catherine Elizabeth's insane demands that Mel end her friendship with Yasmine. Then I explain about Mel sneaking back to my apartment—which has been reported to the police as 'missing' but is really 'running away.' As a finishing touch, I tell him that I'm trying to renegotiate custody from seven thousand miles away.

Cerelli shifts into lawyer mode. A complete transformation. "Meanwhile, you need to get your attorney to talk to Todd and to the police to keep Mel out of juvie. I take it you're also thinking you want to have Mel living with you on a more permanent basis."

"I knew there was a reason I love you."

"Do you?"

"What?"

"Love me."

I don't wait even a heartbeat. "Yes."

"You've never said."

"I know. Kind of unforgiveable."

"Not unforgiveable. I was willing to wait."

"Well, I do. Love you. I wish you were here. I'd rather be saying this in person."

"Soon. And I love you, too. But you already know that?" I like the slightest bit of a question mark he inserted.

"Unlike me, you've definitely said it. And you make it clear. Most of the time."

"Annie—"

"Yeah, I know. Nothing for me to worry about."

"Exactly. Now, about Mel."

I take a deep breath. I can't believe I'm going to ask Cerelli to do this. "I was . . . uh . . . Look, I know this seems like a major contradiction after everything I said before, but I was wondering if you could help me clean up this mess? Please?"

"Tell me what I can do." I hear the laugh in his voice. He's probably also shaking his head in disbelief.

"I need you to call Tricia—my lawyer—and tell her I'm fine with Bonita having temporary custody until I get home. And have her call the Shorewood police. And—"

"I've got the picture. And yes, I can do that. One lawyer to another. And I assume you'd prefer that the footage Piera's cameraman shot never sees the light of day?"

"Yeah, that would be good." The time has most definitely come for me to be officially grateful that he's cleaning up my previous mess, the one I made when I lost my temper with Piera. He deserves an apology. Full grovel. "Thank you for taking care of this and . . . for dealing with the Sig fiasco. And I'm sorry . . . for all those awful things I said. I really am. Truly." But I still don't want you trying to control my life.

"I know, sweetheart. And I promise not to run interference in your life. At least, I'll do my best not to."

"Thank you." My voice is little more than a whisper. "This would be so much better in person."

"We'll be together soon. You can thank me again."

"What do you have in mind?"

"No worries. I'll think of something. Now, if you'd just give me that phone number?"

I do. And as much as I don't want to end this conversation, just when we've gotten back to a good place, I know I have to so he can make those calls for me. I have the feeling that *being in deep* could demand his full attention sometime very soon.

35

IT'S NOT QUITE SUNRISE, but the carpenters have beaten us to the building site. For the second day in a row. The foreman is already here, too. The three of us listen to what the guards have to say about their night's work. No vandalism. They thought there might have been a couple teenage boys intent on doing more damage but were able to chase them off. One of the guards lifts his rifle and aims toward where the building will soon be.

"Pow! Pow!" He laughs.

Oh, God, I hope he didn't shoot at anyone. That won't help the school's reputation. Not at all.

Gulshan links her arm around mine and pulls me close. "This is very good. I worried last night that there might be more frames destroyed and that the carpenters would have to start over *again*. Or that they might not come back today."

"Bah!" I wave my hand through the air. "Of course they're back. They want all their extra pay."

She catches my hand. "I think Darya may have been right. You are Afghan."

I grin. "So, when do the bricks get here?"

"This morning. There are also men coming to help unload the truck. Today will be a good day, *Inshallah*."

BY LUNCHTIME, THERE STILL aren't any bricks.

"This is strange." Gulshan says as we pace down the drive to the road and back. For the third time. "The company promised to deliver the bricks this morning. They are very reliable. I am not sure what to do. We have men coming this afternoon to unload them." She grabs my arm. "We need those bricks here, now!"

"Maybe the driver ran into traffic?" I keep my voice calm and upbeat.

She's not buying it. "There is never much traffic on the River Road once you are past the checkpoint."

"Maybe he had a flat tire? Or the truck broke down?"

Gulshan doesn't even pause to consider these possibilities. "This is *Jawid*." She says his name like I should know who he is. "If he could not make the delivery on time, he would call the company. He would also call the foreman." With that, she hurries over to see if anyone has heard from Jawid.

I go back to lining up more shots. Walnut leaves scattered around the handprint Gulshan made a few days ago—soon to be covered by wooden frames. I can't help touching the concrete, just to test how well it's set. It is set. As in hard. I knock on the surface. Rock-hard. Damn these cold nights. I hope it's not setting too fast.

Looking up, I see the puzzled expression on the foreman's face as Gulshan gesticulates with her hands. I study the black tent that's enveloping my friend. She's wonderfully energetic and vibrant, and no man ever gets her down. And yet, she wears the *burqa*. More than that, she's committed to wearing it, and not just so she can have greater freedom to move around, more independence. This is her way of showing her faith, her devotion to Allah. Not something I could do or would want to do. But I sure admire her strength and commitment.

She's heading back over to me. I pull up my last shot and show her. "Ah!" she gasps at the image of the handprints with yellow walnut leaves overlapping them. "This is very beautiful. You will make me a copy?" She wags a finger at me. "I really should look at all your pictures."

I nod toward the foreman. "Did you learn anything?"

She sighs. "He called the brick company. They loaded up the truck yesterday. Jawid left before dawn this morning. He should have been here by now."

"He's coming from Bazarak?"

She nods.

"And no one has heard anything about a delay?"

"No." I can see how troubled she is.

"Could he have stopped at a village along the way? For lunch and a nap, and the time got away from him?" I know how these Afghan guys are. Even though jobs can be hard to come by, they sometimes have other priorities.

"No." She shakes her head. "Jawid, he was the driver when we restored the first school building. He is the company's best worker and very reliable. He would not do that. Unless he is injured." She looks thoughtful. "There are too many motorcycles on the road, and those drivers can be reckless. Perhaps one of them cut right in front of him. Perhaps there has been an accident."

"So, how about we have someone drive toward Bazarak. They can check the road and see if Jawid has broken down."

"Yes! I'm sure they will find him. *Inshallah*."

I look around at the carpenters hurrying to finish the frames in the few hours of daylight we have left. No hope of installing them today. The foreman now has a hammer in hand and is hard at work. "It seems like we're the only two not working. Can you drive?"

"I am sorry, but that I cannot do."

Really? There's something this wonder woman actually can't do? "Well, I can. And I've got an international driver's license."

We head over to the foreman, and somehow Gulshan makes a convincing argument that it would be better for him to stay at the site while we go in search of Jawid and his truck. He looks astounded for all of ten seconds, then glances around to count the number of frames still needing attention and hands over his keys without question. Amazingly, he doesn't ask if either one of us can drive. Trusting soul.

I snag the keys, stuff the camera inside my pack, then climb behind the steering wheel. This pickup has rust spots over the wheel wells and has obviously seen a lot of miles, but when I key on the ignition, it hums. Clearly, this is the foreman's baby. *Please*, I beg the universe, *don't let anything bad happen while I'm driving*.

We cruise through the nearly empty village awash in a blaze of yellow walnut leaves and the deeper gold of mulberry leaves. A few shepherds are herding goats and sheep along the road. We pass the village shops, doors closed against the late-autumn chill and no wares on display out front. Then, we cross the bridge over the Panjshir River.

"Right?" I ask, looking toward the west.

"Yes. That would be the way he would have come."

I turn onto the river road, heading into the afternoon sun. Gulshan was right: there's virtually no traffic. We pass just one car.

Then, a few motorcycles. She's right about the motorcycles, too. The riders go way too fast, zigging and zagging across the road when there's no need to. Male braggadocio. Accidents waiting to happen.

There's nothing that looks remotely like a large truck with a flatbed full of mud bricks. That would be kind of hard to miss. Something starts to niggle at me. Deep down. And suddenly, I'm not feeling good about this search. Not good at all. I slow the pickup. "I don't think we're looking for a truck."

Gulshan shakes her head. "I do not understand."

"I'm not quite sure myself."

A way-too-familiar chill starts inching up my back. Slowly at first. Then faster, until it rockets the rest of the way to my skull. The skin on the back of my neck prickles. I check the rearview mirror, then the side mirrors. No one's behind us. I've been through this before, though—way too many times. As much as I don't want to believe it, my body's picking up on something or someone out here. And I don't think it's PTSD. I check the mirrors again, searching, searching, but see nothing.

I slow the pickup more. "Can you look along the side of the road while I drive?"

She's on it. Scanning as well as she can. "The bank drops off sharply along here." Which means that being in a vehicle, even in this lane so close to the river, we can't see all the way down the slope.

I drive a little farther, then pull as far to the side of the road as I can and stop.

"What are you doing?"

"I'll climb down the bank and check."

I scramble over the boulders, thanking Allah for my lug-soled military boots. Twiggy mulberry bushes claw at my jacket and pants as I wend my way past them. At one point, my jacket gets hung up on a dried-out branch until I manage to pull it away. Scowling at the small tear in the nylon, I keep making my way over the rocks until I'm almost at the river's edge. I peer west, looking for a truck that could have veered off the road to avoid a collision with a motorcyclist. Nothing, except more boulders and golden mulberry bushes. And a bend in the river. Turning around, I look back the way we've come. Same story there. Looking down at my feet, I'm saddened by the amount of litter—empty soda cans, crumpled foil packets, and a lot of cigarette butts, obviously thrown from passing vehicles. Even here.

Back in the pickup, I drive another mile, then scramble down the bank again. Still nothing. Climbing up to the road, I look toward the west, my hand shielding my eyes against the sun.

Gulshan rolls down her window. "Can you see anything?"

"No."

"Annie, this could take us days."

"I know." The prickling on the back of my neck is getting stronger. Someone is out there, watching us, waiting for us.

You mind telling me what the hell you're doing out there? Cerelli's voice. *Has it occurred to you that you could be walking into a trap?*

He's right. Being out here is stupid. We should turn around and drive straight back to Wad Qol. Let the police handle it. Are there police in Wad Qol? Instead, I say, "Just a little farther. If we don't find anything in the next few minutes, we'll head back. I don't want the foreman to worry that we've stolen his truck."

"If we don't get back soon, he will come looking for us."

Which might be a really good thing. Gulshan and I could use a couple big and burly men right now. I drive another mile. Park. Climb down, holding aside the mulberry branches before they can snag my jacket again. And, oh shit, this time I do see something.

A scrap of purple cloth hung up on a dead mulberry branch with particularly grasping tentacles.

Not purple, periwinkle. Cerelli's voice again. *Did you happen to notice the blood? Like I said before, this could be a trap.*

He's right. Cerelli's always right. The back of my neck is cold, the hairs prickling ominously. Someone could be lining me up in the sights of his rifle. Why the hell did I come out here? And leave the Sig in my pack?

I do a slow 360. Still nothing. Glancing across the road, above the sheared-off mountain face, I see the mulberry bushes are growing thick, the golden leaves providing excellent camouflage for anyone who decides to hide there, to aim a gun, to pick off a hapless photographer way out of her element. I scan the bushes, blazing brilliantly in the rosy late-afternoon light. No glinting metal of a rifle. At least, not that I can see.

I allow myself one minute to examine the scrap of cloth. Coarse. I'm guessing from a *burqa*. It's also spotted with a red that looks a lot like blood. Blood that's too bright to be very old. Out here longer than a day or two, it would already be fading. I decide not to climb farther down to the river and instead pluck the cloth off the dead twig and carry it back up to Gulshan in the truck. Relieved to be moving.

"Is this what I think it is?" I hand it to her through the open window.

"A *burqa*."

Which I knew, of course. In Afghanistan, only a woman would wear clothing made from fabric this coarse and scratchy. Not to mention, this color. Hearing her say those two words, though, all but slams me back down the bank. I round the truck and climb in. Then, grabbing my pack from behind the seat, I dig down to the

Sig Saur at the bottom. Pulling it out, I ram in a clip, make sure the safety's on for now, then bed it carefully between my legs.

"A gun?"

"I don't plan to use it, but it's probably a good idea to have it out and ready."

"Annie?"

"Yeah?" I turn to look at Gulshan.

"There is evil out here. I can feel it." She folds her *burqa* up over her arm and brings her hand to her heart.

"I feel it, too." I cup my hand around the nape of my neck. "You mind if we go back to Wad Qol? We'll tell the police, and they can come out here."

She shakes her head. "There are no police in the village."

"Then I'll call Cerelli and ask him what to do. First, we need to mark this place. Even though I didn't see anything else down there except for the scrap of cloth, this is where they'll need to start looking."

I slide quietly out of the truck, tucking the gun into the waistband of my pants. This time, I shrug out of my jacket and stuff it behind my seat. Too many layers to get past if I have to draw the gun. My sweater will cover the bulge. Making my way along the flatbed, I spy a few pieces of lumber, long and narrow. The foreman probably helped himself to it from our site. I grab a one-by-two. Then, finding a good-sized rock, I do what I can to hammer it down between the narrow space of two abutting boulders.

And manage to pound my left thumb in the process. "Damn!" I yell as the rock falls to the ground.

A moment later, Gulshan is next to me, holding the wood and pounding with the rock. Two more whacks, and she seems satisfied.

"Yes, this is good. Unless someone takes it." She's still sensing the evil of this place.

So am I. And I want to get out of here as fast as possible. But first, I reach down and grab an old paper coffee cup on the ground next to my feet. Gross, but sticking it upside down on top of the one-by-two might help make our marker more distinct.

A few seconds later, we're back in the pickup. Gulshan is gingerly holding the Sig with two hands, pointing it toward the windshield, and I'm making a three-point turn to get us the hell out of Dodge.

THE SUN IS SINKING BEHIND the Hindu Kush by the time we get back to the building site. The frames are done, lying flat on the ground around the concrete footprint. It's too dark to inspect the work. Tomorrow's job—before the carpenters erect them and anchor everything in place. Gulshan will want to make sure everything is rock solid. For tonight, these big and burly men look completely done in. They want to go home to dinner and bed. Ikrom is already here, handing out the day's wages. The first shift of armed men are ready to start their guard duty.

When I pull to a stop, the foreman charges over and yanks open the driver's door. "My truck!"

I hand him the keys. "Your truck drives like a dream, and you are a saint—" I bite my tongue. Islam doesn't have saints. But they recognize Christian and Jewish prophets, don't they? Whatever. I'm honestly too tired and too upset to care about being politically correct.

Still angry, the foreman keeps yelling. "Where is Jawid? The bricks!"

"We did not find him or his truck!" Gulshan yells back, then slams the pickup door and stomps her way over to the foreman until she's standing *burqa* to massive, jacketed chest. Way too close for a woman and an unrelated man. Clearly, she's not happy with him yelling at me.

Ikrom calmly pays the rest of the workers, then comes over to join us. He seems pretty relaxed in the face of this argument between his wife and the foreman. Despite how close they're standing, he doesn't separate them. The foreman finally realizes the impropriety of their situation and takes a couple steps back.

Gulshan raises a triumphant fist. "We did find *this!*"

I peel back her fingers and help myself to the small scrap of blood-spattered periwinkle cloth.

"What is this?" The foreman takes his volume down a notch, but it's clear he's still seething.

"Probably a piece of fabric torn from a *burqa*," I say.

"I send you out to find Jawid and the truck." The foreman is back to yelling. "You come back with a tiny bit of cloth. What kind of craziness is this? This is what happens when women try to do a man's job!"

Ikrom trains his cell phone flashlight on the scrap in my hand. "These spots, they are blood?"

"I think so." I tell him where I found the cloth and how the twigs tore at my own jacket. "It's clearly fresh. Probably from today. Early this morning. Any older and it would be faded and windblown."

"You believe this is connected to Jawid and his truck disappearing?"

Disappearing. The word stops me. I glance over at Gulshan, but it's too dark now to see past her netted eyepiece, to get any idea what she's thinking. "Look, we didn't see any evidence of Jawid or the truck. This could have something to do with him. Or nothing at all."

"Then, why do you bring this back?" The foreman is beside himself.

"Because it's highly unlikely that a *woman* in a *burqa* would be climbing over boulders along the side of the road. Especially a woman dripping fresh blood."

The foreman stiffens his shoulders. "Jawid does not wear the *burqa*. A black leather jacket, that is what he wears. And blue jeans. Always. He never dresses like a woman."

"I'm sure you're right." I'm struggling to keep my voice steady and low and reasonable. "But something happened out on the River Road."

"We both felt it," says Gulshan, her voice back to normal volume.

"Felt? *Felt?*" The foreman walks a few steps away from us, then back, right up to Gulshan, his face thunderous.

And this time, Ikrom puts his hands on his wife's shoulders and gently eases her an acceptable three feet from the man. Looking at me, he asks, "What did you feel?"

I really don't want to get into cold chills and prickles on the back of my neck, but all three of them are staring at me. They clearly expect me to say something. "There was someone out there. Watching us."

"A man stopped to help you?" The relief in Ikrom's voice is palpable.

"Not exactly." I'm still hedging.

Gulshan steps closer to me. Like an Afghan soldier. *Shohna ba shohna.* Shoulder to shoulder. Except her shoulder is quite a bit lower than mine. Her voice is firm. "He was hiding nearby, watching us."

I take over. "He could have disguised himself by wearing a *burqa*." I keep it vague. Given what happened last spring when Awalmir—or maybe it was his cousin Ghazan—blew up the Dalan Sang checkpoint, killing a whole lot of people, then escaped in a periwinkle burqa, this could well be a repeat of a strategy that worked. Cerelli kept this detail quiet, though, so I'm pretty sure he doesn't want me telling the story now.

The foreman laughs. Uproariously. Ikrom laughs, too. Both of them are bent at the waist, hands on their knees. "A man in a *burqa*!" They've obviously forgotten that Jawid and his truck with all our bricks are missing.

I clench my fists. Standing next to me, Gulshan hisses. We're both pissed.

The two men keep laughing.

Gulshan and I throw quick glances at each other, then stalk angrily over to Ikrom's pickup. Once we're on the far side, out of view of the men, she hands me the Sig. "I almost wish I had the nerve to use this."

36

BY THE TIME WE GET back to the house, I've decided to call Cerelli. Not something I particularly want to do when he's *in deep*. But he needs to know what's going on. Gulshan agrees.

Smartphone in hand, the Sig in my waistband, I make my way around to the back garden. Even though it's still early evening, it's already cold. The guards out at the construction site are going to freeze tonight. Crossing my fingers that Fatima doesn't answer the phone, I place the call.

He answers on the first ring. "Annie."

"Hey."

"I'm glad you called." He does sound glad. His voice has that warm, wrap-around-me tone that makes my heart sing. "Look, I talked with your lawyer, and she's dealing with the cops. She's reasonably confident she can convince them not to file charges against Mel. Or Bonita."

"Shit! It never occurred to me that Bonita could be in trouble."

"She interfered with a police investigation, sweetheart."

"But she never spoke to the cops. It was Todd who called her."

"Good point. Although it might be a little too fine a difference for Todd."

"What do you mean?"

"The bigger problem is that your ex is contesting the custody hearing. From what I understand, his exact words were 'Hell, no.'"

I sit down hard on the tree stump. "I guess I should've expected that. They wanted Mel to stay with me for a while, not forever." My voice sinks to a whisper. "What can I do?"

"Your attorney plans to run with it. She got an expedited hearing in the judge's chambers in a couple days. Mel and Bonita will be there. Todd and Catherine Elizabeth will be there, too, with their counsel. Given the circumstances and Mel's age, the judge will almost certainly talk to her without them in the room."

"Will the judge actually give any weight to what Mel has to say?"

"Definitely. She's sixteen, not six. And from what I understand, she's a straight-A student. Right?"

"She is."

"I don't think any judge is going to look kindly on a dictum of not being friends with a Muslim girl. Oh, by the way, Yasmine and Awa have agreed to attend. Whatever the judge rules will only be temporary. Once you get back to Milwaukee, he'll revisit the custody agreement in full."

I look up to the heavens and mouth a silent *Alhamdulillah*. I owe so many people. "Thank you."

"Now, you okay?"

I take a deep breath. "I think so." My words sound shaky. Even to me.

"Talk to me."

"This is going to seem pretty crazy, but our bricks didn't arrive. The bricks for the school, that is."

"Things can be slower in Afghanistan. A lot slower."

"That's what I thought. But everyone here seems pretty worked up about it. They called the company in Bazarak, and the owner said the truck should've gotten here this morning."

"You happen to know the driver's name?"

"Jawid. Don't know his last name."

"Fuck."

"Yeah, that's pretty much the reaction Gulshan, Ikrom, and the foreman had. And, well . . ."

"And, what?"

I close my eyes. Should I tell him? He's going to get pissed off.

"Annie." His voice is getting firmer.

"Okay. Look, all the workers were really busy, trying to finish building the frames this afternoon." The frames that were destroyed two nights ago, but I don't tell him that.

"And?"

"Gulshan and I thought Jawid's truck could've broken down. So, we drove west along the River Road, looking for him." I pause, waiting for him to explode. But he doesn't.

"Find him?"

"No. But I did find a scrap of what looks like a torn *burqa*. Periwinkle. With fresh blood on it."

"That all?"

"Yes. No. If I'm being completely honest—"

"I would appreciate that."

"While we were out there—Gulshan and I—well, I felt like someone was watching us."

He's treading lightly. More than anyone, he knows about the PTSD that I've promised to deal with but just haven't gotten around to yet. "Any hallucinations?"

"None. Just cold chills running up my spine. That awful, prickly feeling. But get this, Gulshan felt it, too. She's calling it 'something evil.' And she's right. That's exactly what it felt like."

It's a long twenty seconds before he says anything. I can almost see him ramming his fingers through his silvering hair. The muscle at the corner of his eye spasming. Doing his best not to yell. Finally, "Are you all right?"

"I'm good. This is just a bit unnerving. Especially if Jawid is as great a driver as everyone says."

"Oh, he is. Believe me. One more thing. Is Ikrom worried? The foreman?"

"They don't seem to be. After we told them about what we saw and felt out on the road, they laughed. Hard. Couldn't stop."

"You're saying they were acting like typical men?" I can hear the smile in his voice.

I smile, too. "In a word. Yes."

"You tell them about what happened last spring? With Awalmir and Ghazan?"

"No."

"Good. Don't."

"So, what should we do? We need bricks. And I'm worried about what might have happened to Jawid."

"Let me see what I can turn up. And you might want to get Gulshan or the foreman to order more bricks."

I sigh. "That will seriously deplete the $30K."

"How much?" His voice goes up a notch.

"Thirty thousand. Dollars."

"Are you fucking telling me you brought thirty thousand dollars into Afghanistan?"

"Well, yeah. But I did it legally."

"You *registered* the money?" He's getting closer to losing control. "Which means everyone from Kabul to Wad Qol knows about it. And wants to put their hands on it. And on you."

"That's become pretty evident."

"Annie, why the hell didn't you tell me it was this much money? I would have helped you, gotten it in through military channels—"

"Yeah, well, you weren't exactly answering my calls, were you?"

"No." One syllable that tells me exactly how upset he is. I'm guessing that this time, he's pissed at himself. "That won't happen again. I promise. Look, let me get on this. I'll call you back."

"Thanks," I say—for his promise to always take my calls and for his help with locating our driver and the bricks. "Oh, and by the way, did you ever get a chance to talk to Bibi about Seema's SD card? Or Omar?"

"Bibi says she knows nothing about the card, and I believe her. As for Omar, he's away. In Pakistan. According to Bibi, he's been spending a great deal of time there."

"How convenient."

"You said it. I've dealt with him in the past, though, and he's always been straight enough."

"You trust him?"

"Not for a minute. But I can usually tell when he's lying. Which he often does. Omar Mohaqiq likes to play both sides of the political spectrum. Survival instinct probably. When the Taliban take control again, he doesn't want his head to roll."

"Where I come from, we call that hypocrisy."

"Yeah, well, there's plenty of that going around. But so far, it's not a crime. Meanwhile, things here are fluid, which is why I'm in Kabul."

"And you can't tell me more than that."

"That would be affirmative." Despite the SEAL speak, his voice manages to wrap itself around me, and for the first time today, I actually feel warm. The same way I feel when he writes me a *landay*. Which reminds me of Seema's most recent texts.

"One more thing?"

"Shoot."

"Seema Rahila sent me another couple *landays*."

"Anything like the last one about her beloved's caravan?"

"Not really. This is more the 'cry of separation.' How upset she is at being apart from him."

"You're wondering why she'd send them to you."

"Yeah. But it's more than that. These last two? They're really lovely. They speak to me in a way the others haven't. And that's kind of bothering me."

"How?" His voice is suddenly sharp. "How are they different?"

I've definitely got his attention. "Hard to say. They seem more mature than the earlier ones. Actually, a lot more mature. And well crafted. I showed the first couple to Bibi when I stayed with her. She was pretty dismissive, said they seemed like what a seventeen-year-old girl with no life experience would write. And when I compare them to the more girlie ones I *know* Seema wrote last spring, these latest two seem like they were written by a different person." As soon as the words are out of my mouth, taking shape as mist in the cold night air, I feel the heat of awareness charge full bore up my spine.

"What did you just say?"

"Like they were written by a different person."

"Can you read them to me?"

Half a minute later, I've pulled up the first text and read it aloud.

Oh, my Beloved! Separation plants the seeds
Of despair and longing in my heart.

Then, the second one.

Even the purest water I must not drink
Lest my Beloved's name, on my lips, be erased.

"Fuck, Cerelli. Someone else *did* write them. There's no way Seema could've gone from what she wrote last spring to these. And I'd bet the pot she didn't write any of the *landays* she supposedly sent after she went missing."

"Read them again, would you?" I hear Cerelli scribbling as I slowly read each poem. "Thanks. Got 'em. That's good work, sweetheart."

"And it all means . . . what?"

"That someone wants us to think Seema is writing to you. They want you to believe she's alive. To draw you out. Me, too. You be careful. And Annie?"

"Yeah?"

"Promise me you'll keep the Sig with you."

"Got it with me now."

After I end the call, I replay Cerelli's last words. *They want you to believe she's alive.* Oh, God. That's as good as saying that he doesn't think she is. I jam my phone into my jacket pocket and shiver against the cold.

On the road out front, I hear the rumble of a small truck, most likely a pickup. It seems to idle briefly, long enough for me to wonder if it's the foreman stopping by with news for Gulshan about our brick truck driver. Or maybe it's the religion teacher's grandson back for round two of painting our front door. Then, whoever the driver is, he revs the engine and takes off.

No way I'll catch him, so I take a few moments to figure out what I'll be able to tell Gulshan and Ikrom about my conversation with Cerelli. Finally, I settle on the simple truth: Cerelli's concerned about Jawid and will look into what's going on. Meanwhile, it looks like we've got to spend a whole lot more money for another order of bricks. And who knows how long that'll take. Or what it'll do to the budget.

Heading back to the front of the house, I let my thoughts settle on Cerelli. It feels like we're back on track. Or at least getting there. That warm and sexy voice makes me want to get naked and crawl into bed with him. Except I *heard* Fatima the other night, and her voice wasn't exactly cool and business-like. Wait, he assured me. And he promised there's nothing going on between them. Do I believe him? Trust him? I sure want to. But he has yet to explain what he was doing with Fatima in the middle of the night.

Standing in front of the house, I train my flashlight on the door and heave a sigh of relief. No new **39** in red paint. Ikrom and Gulshan will be pleased to go a couple nights without any more defacing insults.

But just as I'm about to climb the one step to the door, I glance down and stop with my booted foot hovering in the air. A scream claws in my throat. Just as quickly, the air is sucked out of my lungs. Blood covers the stoop. More blood is splashed on the lower half of the door. All I can do is pound on the door while I stare at the severed head on the step.

His mouth locked open. In a shout never heard.

Eyes once wide in terror. Now sightless.

37

"IT IS JAWID." IKROM STANDS in the doorway, blocking Gulshan's view. "Go back inside. This is not for you to see."

Gulshan doesn't back down. "Annie, she is all right?"

I'm feeling pretty woozy, but when Ikrom glances at me, I nod.

"Annie will be in soon," he says sternly. "Now, go!"

I think I hear Gulshan's slippered feet pad away. Except that's not possible. The rugs would muffle her footsteps.

Ikrom examines the head. "Did you see anything?"

"Nothing. I was behind the house, on the phone with Captain Cerelli. Just at the end, I heard a truck."

"Yes! I did, too. A pickup."

"It sounded like it stopped here."

"Perhaps. I will take this to the clinic now. I want to see if I can learn anything."

"An autopsy?"

"No, we do not have the equipment to do more than a very general exam. But I would like to look more closely. Will you and Gulshan be all right for a few hours?"

I know Gulshan will say yes. And I do have the Sig, digging into my flesh. "We'll be fine. Should I tell her about, uh, this?"

He nods. "I will call the foreman myself. For now, I want you both to stay inside the house. The shutters must remain closed and the door locked. Do not open it for anyone except me." He runs quickly into the house to grab a yellow plastic bucket from the kitchen and a pair of latex gloves. Then, he carefully lifts the head and eases it in. "Jawid, he was a good man, a faithful man." He's about to climb into his pickup when he turns toward me. "Do not let Gulshan come out to clean up this mess. I will do that."

IT'S LATE, NEARING ELEVEN O'CLOCK, when Ikrom gets home. We hear his pickup puttering down the road and pulling up to stop on the far side of the house. A minute later, there's a knock at the door, and Ikrom calls to Gulshan. Locking the front door behind him and taking off his jacket, he settles onto his seat at the kitchen table. He looks grim as he nods the sad news to us. "On my way to the clinic, I stopped by the foreman's house for a second identification. It is as I thought. Jawid. Then, I went to alert Massoud. Jawid was his cousin. I thought he should know what happened."

"The blessings from Allah and mercy be upon him," Gulshan whispers. Then, "Your dinner. I have kept it hot for you."

"Not yet. First, I will clean the step."

"No." She places a hand tenderly on his chest. "I will do that. You must eat and rest."

"I'll help." I lift my jacket off the peg by the door.

Ikrom raises his hand to stop us. "Annie, could you please call Captain Cerelli about this? You still have the scrap of cloth?"

I nod. Picking up my cell phone, I precede Gulshan outside. No way am I going to let her be out here on her own, scrubbing down the door and the step—a ready target for whoever's driving around in that pickup.

"Please, let me help you," I plead as Gulshan kneels in the dirt. "It will go much faster with both of us working. I'll call Cerelli after we finish."

Holding up her scrub brush, she smiles. "I only have this one. You call the Captain. I will clean. Then, we will both be finished." She tightens her headscarf—no *burqa* at this time of night—and scours her front step while I call Cerelli for the second time tonight.

"Annie?" He's breathless. And worried.

"It's been—" My voice cracks. "A long night."

"What happened?"

"We found Jawid. Actually, he was delivered to us. Here. In Wad Qol." Hand on the gun in my waistband, I pace back and forth in front of the house, my eyes trained on the road, determined to stay alert for anyone who might happen along.

"Don't tell me."

"Yeah. He's dead."

"You?" I'm guessing he's asking if I'm the guilty one who found the body.

"When we finished talking earlier, I heard a truck stop in front of the house. And then I found his head—" Again, my voice cracks.

"That's all? Just the head?" His voice is incredibly gentle.

"Yeah." I stumble through everything else I know, jumping from point to point and probably not making a whole lot of sense.

"Sweetheart, listen to me. Is Ikrom with you now?"

"In the kitchen."

"Let me talk to him."

I reach over the still-bloody step and push open the freshly washed door, almost hitting Ikrom, who's standing just inside eating his dinner. I should've known he'd be hovering nearby. "Cerelli," I say, passing him the phone.

Gulshan finishes scrubbing while I stand guard. The Sig is in my hand. Safety off. With a final swoosh of her brush, Gulshan stands, and we retreat into the house. My hands hurt like crazy as they begin to warm, burning as if red-hot needles are pricking into them. Then, I look at Gulshan's. After twenty minutes of scrubbing with ice-cold water, her hands look horribly red and sore and cracked.

A few minutes later, Ikrom hands Cerelli back to me.

I walk to the far end of the lounge, my steps in rhythm with the pain pulsing in my fingers. "Keep the Sig with you at all times. Please." Cerelli's in full military mode.

"It's that bad?"

"To be honest, I don't know what it is. Yet. I'm heading to Bagram. I'll call you as soon as I know what's going on. In the morning, no matter what. Promise me you'll keep your cell with you, too."

"Will do." All I really want to do, though, is sleep. "And . . ."

"What?"

"Please take care of yourself." Probably a stupid thing to say. I doubt SEALs ever think of themselves first. Still, I imagine him quirking a grin.

"And you do whatever Ikrom tells you."

Not the right thing to say, but I let it slide and hope Cerelli will have something positive to tell us in the morning.

38

I LIE IN BED, MY FINGERS curled tightly around the Sig. The cell phone is next to me, under the covers, within easy reach. I can't risk closing my eyes. It's not that I'm afraid whoever killed Jawid is going to break into the house and try to kill me. Gulshan and Ikrom and I made sure every shutter was locked against the night. Both doors are bolted fast. And the one window in my tiny room is too small for any man or woman, probably any child, to wedge their way through. Still, I feel like a giant wave is building and about to crash over me. A tsunami of bloody hallucinations.

Finally, beyond exhaustion, I close my eyes. Just as I feared, I see Jawid, alive and behind the wheel of his truck, driving along the River Road toward Wad Qol. His radio is playing romantic Nasrat Parsa music or maybe a talk program with teenagers calling in *landays*. They give first names only —theirs and their beloveds'— sending out love messages to someone waiting, listening, hoping to hear the right name, the right voice. Praying a brother, father, uncle, grandfather doesn't hear, doesn't make the connection, doesn't seek vengeance for the dishonor to the family.

I open my eyes to erase the vision. But I've got to sleep. So, hoping my mind won't notice, I ease my eyes closed again. It's no good. I'm back with Jawid out on the road, driving along the edge of the Panjshir River.

Maybe he sees a rusting white pickup in the rearview mirror. Then, out of nowhere, there are motorcycles heading toward him. Two—one on each side of the road. Or maybe more—four, six—spanning across the road.

He honks the horn. The cyclists don't stop. They just keep heading toward him.

He leans on the horn, but still, they do not stop.

Jawid must wonder why in the name of Allah they don't move over. The fear of crashing the truck, hurting these riders, seizes his gut.

He glances again in the rearview mirror. The pickup is still behind him.

Can he see who's driving? That scrap of periwinkle cloth. From a *burqa*.

He sees a flash of periwinkle and realizes a woman is driving the pickup. She's close. Too close. He can't possibly let a woman be involved in an accident.

What else can he do? He has to stop the truck.

But not quickly. He can't ram his foot against the pedal, not with the heavy load of bricks he's carrying. Do that, and the flatbed would jackknife. Bricks would go flying. Right through the windscreen of the pickup that the woman is driving. They would kill her. The last thing he could ever do is harm a woman.

He taps the brakes to slow the truck. Slower. Slower. He's determined to prevent an accident. To spare the life of the woman in the *burqa*.

The long truck grinds to a stop.

In front of him, six, no eight, motorcycles have stopped, arrayed from one side of the road to the other. What kind of dangerous game are they playing? Jawid glances in his rearview mirror. There is the pickup and the woman; she is bent over the steering wheel. He wants to check on her before he lets loose on the crazy cyclists.

No, wait! First, he takes the keys from the ignition. He's a careful man. He would bury them deep in his pocket. Then, he opens his door and swings down to the ground.

As soon as his feet touch the pavement, an arm is around his neck.

What next? What does Jawid do? If I'm guessing right, Jawid is a big man, and strong, so he might throw an elbow into the abdomen behind him, hard enough that the arm around his neck loosens briefly. Just long enough for him to turn.

Again, he sees the flash of periwinkle. The *burqa*! The woman from the pickup.

Now, he's confused. A woman who is this strong? Then, he sees she has a knife.

His eyes must grow large. His bladder lets loose. Is he even aware of the warm pee running down his leg? Of the acrid odor of ammonia?

The woman presses the blade against his neck. Cold and sharp. Then orders him to the side of the road and down the embankment. When she speaks, it's a man's voice that comes through the netted eyepiece. Deep and gruff and sneering. Does Jawid realize what is about to happen?

Does he yell? Maybe. Maybe not. What's the point of yelling when there's no one to help?

A kick in his back. His kidneys groan in pain. He falls to his knees on a boulder.

This is where it will be.

No. Two sets of hands yank him to his feet and push him farther down the bank, through the mulberry bushes, laughing as the twigs scratch his face. Down to the river's edge.

Jawid tries to peer through the netted eyepiece of the periwinkle *burqa*. "Why—"

Blood. There is so much blood, splattering over the boulders.

A wave of blood.

I struggle to surface through the giant wave, then force open my eyes. Even with the darkness around me, I see the knife, huge and glinting in the morning light of the sun as it slices its way deep across Jawid's neck.

My scream sticks in my throat as the man whips the periwinkle *burqa* over his head and off, rolling it into a ball, his clothes, his face, his beard blood-free. The man looks like Ghazan. No, it can't be. Ghazan is dead. Awalmir, then. It is Awalmir.

"The keys aren't in the truck," I imagine one of the cyclists calls down from the road.

Awalmir looks at the body sprawled in front of him and scowls. Then he rolls back the sleeve of his tunic and plunges his hand into a blood-filled pocket, where he finds them. Another few steps to the river where he washes first the keys, then his hand and arm.

A cyclist pulls out a plastic garbage bag.

No more! Imagining all this in my mind's eye, it's too much.

I curl my legs to my chest and wrap my arms tightly around my knees. If I make myself small enough, maybe they won't see me.

Quiet! Quiet! I bundle my screams in my chest until Awalmir climbs into the truck and drives it down the road, farther into the valley. The pickup follows behind. Then the motorcycles. They head farther up the valley, east, where they will hide until the deepest, darkest hour of the night.

39

CERELLI CALLS EARLY IN THE morning when it's still dark. I grab my cell and swipe it on.

"Sweetheart," he breathes into my ear.

It would be a nice way to wake up if I hadn't just managed to fall asleep. If I were certain he meant it. If a nasty little worm in my brain weren't burrowing deeper, reminding me that Fatima is keeping a bed warm for him in Kabul. "Cerelli?"

"Who else calls you at this time of the morning?" His voice is warm and cozy, but there's an undercurrent of something ominous just below the surface.

"Actually, no one."

"You get any sleep?"

"Not really."

"Nightmares?" he asks gently.

"Not exactly. More like anxiety. And horrific speculation about what happened on the River Road yesterday."

"Would it help to tell me?"

"It might. Look, can you give me five minutes to dress and get outside? This is a small house, and I don't want to wake Gulshan and Ikrom."

"Call me back in five."

I pull on pants, my sweater, and my jacket, plunge bare feet into my boots, but leave my *keffiyeh* behind. There's no one to see me out behind the house. Besides, I'll be outside for ten minutes max.

I'm easing my way along the side of the house when I realize I've left the Sig inside. Remembering Cerelli's caution about always keeping the gun with me, I think about going back for it. But all that in and out of the house could wake Gulshan and Ikrom, and they need their sleep.

I settle on the tree stump and tap Cerelli's number. Three seconds later, he's back on the line. I tell him about the crazy speculation I came up with last night in the depths of my fear and anxiety. Every last detail. Crazy, but way too real.

Cerelli listens. Like he always does. Even when he was interrogating me on the USS *Bataan*, accusing me of all kinds of horrible and completely untrue things, he was always a good listener. After I finish, he doesn't say a word. A minute goes by. Two minutes. Three. I let him sync all the pieces together. Damn, he's taking a long time. Maybe I *am* crazy. It takes a pretty loosely wrapped mind to come up with the story I just created. When I get home, I absolutely have to get help.

"It fits."

"You think?"

"In your speculation, did Awalmir drive east or west?"

Holy shit. He really does believe me. This was just a product of my crazed imagination.

"East or west?"

"East."

"Which means that for these guys to do anything that makes an impact, they'll have to drive back west. To Kabul."

I pull my jacket tighter around me. "You know, it's a little freaky that this is your only lead."

"Did I say it's my only lead?" He sounds grim.

"You've got something else?"

"Sorry to say, I do."

"You gonna tell me?"

"We found Jawid's body about an hour ago. He was hung up on a fallen tree about a hundred yards downriver from where you set up the roadside marker. That was good thinking, by the way."

"Thanks. I managed to pound my thumb with the rock I was using."

"Ouch."

I close my eyes and wish for once that I were religious enough to know a prayer for the dead. A blessing. Jawid certainly deserves one. I end up repeating what Gulshan said earlier: *Upon him are blessings and mercy from Allah.* "So, what's next?"

"I've got to find that truck before this fucker kills anyone else."

"Good plan."

"Look, just keep your eyes open and be aware. You might also try living in the moment and not your imagination." He waits a couple seconds. "Sorry I had to wake you this early. There's something else you need to hear."

"And that is?"

He growls into the phone. "The whole damn country knows you're here."

I'm way too tired to make the quick connection he expects. Finally, taking my time, I manage to say, "You mean because of that guy at Customs?"

"Oh, I'm sure he's passed the word on to a few people who'd like to get their hands on the money you brought in. But no, I mean the media—newspapers, television—has gotten wind of you being in-country and why. And they're all running the story."

"What're you talking about?

"You ever hear of a newspaper called *Ripples*?"

"You mean the school paper Mel writes for?"

"You got it in one."

"What does that have to do with—anything?"

"Did Mel just write a feature about raising money for the Wad Qol school? Maybe under the name 'Emmeline Green'?"

She's writing under the name Emmeline? Which is totally off the point of what he's asking me. I try to remember my last phone call with her. "She asked me a couple questions."

He groans.

"What?"

"There's a story from your daughter's school newspaper that's gone viral. And I mean *viral*. It's all over the internet, and most of the cable news networks are airing it. Especially Al Shabakat. Your favorite person is hyping this for all it's worth."

"No! Not Piera."

"Sorry to say, yes. You didn't happen to run into her in Kabul, did you?"

"I saw her cameraman in Baggage Claim at the airport. Then heard her. But *run into her*? As in talk to her? No. Chris made me promise to give her a wide berth, and I have. Isn't she supposed to do the same?"

"That's not the way she's running with the story. *My good friend Annie Hawkins Green told me all about rebuilding the Wad Qol Secondary School for Girls.*" He does a great falsetto. "She's providing lots of details, all of which she probably picked up from Mel's article. Or flat-out fabricated. The woman's out to get you. And me."

"You? How so?"

"She infers you're working for me. Any idea how she could've come up with that?"

"Not a clue."

He makes a sound akin to a growl. "Look, I'm sure Mel is thrilled to have her story picked up. But I sure as hell don't like seeing your face plastered everywhere—and I mean *everywhere*. Especially given how recognizable you are. In the picture, not to mention in person."

"Fuck." I'm not big on having my picture taken, although I'm not as obsessive as Cerelli. Still, I feel a whole lot more comfortable *behind* the lens than in front of it. Suddenly, I flash on Bonita sitting at the table in the gym. Her arm claiming my camera. Her smile smug. She definitely recorded me on my cell, which she could easily have borrowed from my Lowepro. I'm betting she also snapped a few pics of me with my own damn camera. As a favor to Mel.

"Fuck, indeed." Cerelli is literally growling. "Every tango in the country knows exactly where you are."

"Oh, God."

"And need I mention *Nyaw aw Badal*?"

"No, let's not go there. The *Ripples* article doesn't say anything about revenge, does it?" I shudder at the fear in my voice. And suddenly, my anxiety is back in full force. Could this be the reason why the Taliban approved me for the interview coming up in December? They may have 'guaranteed' our protection but really mean to follow through with Ghazan and Awalmir's call for *Nyaw aw Badal*.

"No, it doesn't use that exact word. But Mel gives a lot of

background. Why you're in Wad Qol, that you were there last spring, and what happened to Darya. She also makes mention of nine years ago. A little girl named Malalai."

I bury my face in my hands. "No. I swear to you I never talked to her about any of this. Ever."

"The fact that the picture was on the front cover of *Time* was probably enough. Unfortunately, *Ripples* ran that picture alongside the one of you."

"In other words, any insurgent with half a brain can easily connect the dots. And those guys aren't stupid."

"All of which means you've got one giant target on your back. That head in front of the house last night? It's pretty clear someone knows you're there."

Great. Just great. What the hell am I supposed to do about this? I'll be a sitting duck out at the building site. And putting every other worker there as well as Gulshan and Ikrom in danger.

"Annie? You still there?"

"Yeah." My voice is tiny and scared. "Did Mel mention Seema in that article?"

"No. Thank God for small favors."

"At least they don't know I'm looking for her." I bite my tongue as soon as the words are out of my mouth.

"Are you?"

"Nothing more than asking a few people if they've heard from her." I'm positive the muscle next to his eye is pulsing in anger and frustration.

"Let's hope the people you asked have kept it to themselves." He exhales noisily. "Look, I got through to Chris Cardona and managed to get them to pull the story. The other cable news stations are still running it."

"Of course they are. Piera would love to see me go down." I decide not to ask if Chris happened to mention the status of the investigation.

"Sweetheart, listen to me. I need you to get to a safe place. These guys are serious and escalating. Any chance Ikrom and Gulshan ..."

A noise on the side of the house takes my attention away from whatever Cerelli is saying. The wind blowing through the leaves? No. This doesn't sound like wind. More like footsteps. Heavy footsteps. Running footsteps.

I've just processed the thought that no one except me should be back here when the cold barrel of a gun presses against the side of my head just above my ear. I'm still holding the phone when someone else grabs my wrist and wrenches it behind me. I groan in pain.

Someone takes my cell.

"Cerelli—" But instead of an answer, I hear the quiet ping of my cell being turned off.

A thick cloth with the faint odor of gasoline is forced into my mouth. I gag on the filth and manage a few grunts.

Then a blindfold wraps tight around my head. Too tight.

I throw my elbows. But don't connect with anyone.

I kick. And find only air.

My attempt to scream comes out sounding like a grunt.

Then I hear the almost inaudible click of a safety being disengaged.

"Quiet," hisses a voice into my ear. "You make noise." He drills the barrel of the gun against my head.

Hands tighten on my upper arms. There must be more than one of them, but how many? They walk me around to the front of the house, one of them periodically kneeing the backs of my legs when I drag my feet. All is quiet inside the house. No smell of the wood fire burning. No aroma of breakfast cooking. Gulshan and Ikrom must still be asleep.

Unless. Oh, God! Did these fuckers go into the house first before they came looking for me? Please, no. Please let Gulshan and Ikrom be alive.

Again, I try to scream. But all I manage is another muffled grunt.

The gun barrel presses harder. I can barely breathe.

Behind me, another hard kick to the back of my knee nearly knocks me off my feet.

Someone grabs my other wrist, wrenching it behind my back. Crunching both wrists together. Something sharp cuts into my skin. A zip tie?

A hand on my shoulder jerks me to a stop. Hands under my armpits. Lifting me off the ground. Flying through the air, I land hard on metal. The bed of a pickup? My already bruised hip cries out in pain.

Hands on my ankles, pulling them together. I try to scrabble away, but they drag me back. Another zip tie, this one around my ankles, way too tight. I groan again, as loud as I can. But no one comes to help.

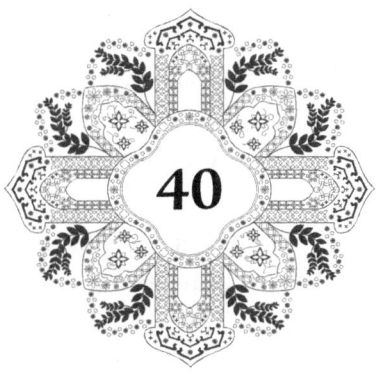

40

WHEN I WAKE UP, my head is *thunking* against something hard. Again, and again. Until I feel like it could explode. I force open my eyes but can't see. Or breathe. What the hell is in my mouth? I'm desperate to pull it out, but my hands are tied behind me, tied with something that's cutting sharply into my wrists. Panic tightens my chest. And vomit burns in my throat.

What the fuck is happening? *Think!*

I'm in Afghanistan, the Panjshir Valley. I know that. Wad Qol. My thoughts try to squeeze past the pounding in my head. Gulshan. Ikrom. I'm staying in their house. But this sure isn't their house. Wherever I am is frigging cold. And hard. I stretch my fingers down and manage to touch whatever I'm lying on. Metal. Another jounce. The back of a pickup.

Please let this be a hallucination. A nightmare. I struggle to wake up.

But I'm already awake. It's not a hallucination.

They've got me.

The very thing all journalists from Syria to Afghanistan fear most. Taliban? ISIS? Please, please let it be the Taliban. I might, just might, stand a chance with them. They've been known to release the occasional journalist after a few months. Probably not when they've sworn *Nyaw aw Badal* on them, though.

ISIS? I don't stand a chance.

Why now? Is it the thirty thousand? They kidnap me and demand a ransom?

I try to remember what happened. But my head is pounding, pounding, pounding. Pushing with my feet, I gain enough traction to angle myself into the corner of the flatbed, enough that I can wedge my shoulder onto what feels like a folded tarp and prop up my head. That eases the constant knocking against metal. And the pain.

Somewhere nearby, I hear ringing. A cell phone.

That's it. My cell rang. Early, early. It was still dark. I went outside to talk. Cerelli. I was talking to Cerelli. What did he want to tell me? Can't remember. Cerelli! He was on the line when they took me. He must know they've got me. He'll find me.

Hold on. He's in Kabul. Hours away from Wad Qol. And who the hell knows where they're taking me. No way they're going to hide out anywhere close to the village. Too many people there know me.

Then where *are* they taking me?

I start to tremble. God, I'm cold. My feet, my hands are numb. And I'm scared shitless.

Stop it! Yes, my worst nightmare has happened. Is happening. This is real life. *So, deal with it. Figure out how to get away.*

I try wriggling my hands behind my back, except I can't budge them. No room for me to twist either hand. To slide one out. Or my ankles. I can't move them either. I can't even feel them.

The truck slows. Now what?

Do whatever you have to, sweetheart. Just get out of this alive!

What should I do? Pretend to be unconscious? Or throw myself at them and do what I can to fight?

The truck slows some more. Turns. We head downhill. Dust rises in the air, into my nose, making me sneeze. The acidic taste of vomit again.

Almost as soon as we stop, I hear voices. Male. Speaking a language I don't understand. Pashto? The tailgate clunks down, and I let myself go limp, waiting for my moment to launch into action. Hands grab my ankles, drag me to the end of the flatbed. A faint *plink*, and my ankles are free. I'm sore and aching and still numb, but when hands under my armpits lift me to my feet, at least I can stand. Am I crazy, or are these hands gentler?

"Come." One word in Dari, but I hear the accent. I'm pretty sure it's Pashto. A hand is at my elbow, on my jacket, gently guiding me. He cautions me to step over the threshold. And then we're inside. Where it's warm.

I can smell the packed earth under my feet, the mud bricks of the walls. Musty. And the faint aroma of something delicious. Soup? I sense the men crowded into the room, their bodies shying away from me. I smell their sweat, their testosterone. So much frigging testosterone. The hair on the back of my neck stands on end.

Do not give in to fear! Keep hearing and smelling and feeling. Be ready to run when the chance comes. My inner voice this time. Not Cerelli's.

We don't stop in this room where it's warm. He leads me farther back into the building. My shoulder slams against a doorway. Then, I'm in another room. Where it's colder. I feel it closing in on me.

Finally, I hear another voice. Female. In pain. "Auntie?"

Seema? Oh my God! Could it really be her?

They remove my gag first.

Desperate to pull air into my lungs, I take deep, rasping breaths. Trying to breathe. At long last, I can talk. "Seema? Are you all right?"

"Auntie! Is it—" A groan of pain. Then a whimper. "Oh, please help me! Please!"

Someone behind me unties the blindfold. I peer into the darkness, unable to see a thing. Off to the side, a lantern flickers.

I turn, looking around the room. Now, I can make out shutters closed against the outside. It takes another minute, and finally, my eyes land on Seema. On a thin mattress, pushed into the farthest corner of the room. She's clad in a black *burqa*, half sitting, half curled over on herself. She groans again. Louder this time. I take a step toward her and nearly fall. I'm slowly getting the feeling back in my feet, but not enough.

I limp to the mattress and lower myself down next to her. "Seema?" I'm about to ask her what's wrong when she hunches forward and groans, hands on top of her swollen belly.

"My wife. You save her," says the bearded man behind me. A respectable distance. He's careful now not to touch me.

I glance back at him. Full lips that once pursed in a sexy pout, dark hair that once fell in a cute curl over his forehead, driving the senior girls at the school wild for a day or two. Until they decided he was too scary to be attractive. I'm face-to-face with Awalmir.

From the look on his face, he's scared. Scared for Seema.

He shakes his head in despair. "This." He sweeps his hand through the air above her.

"How long has she been like this?" I struggle to maintain my calm. It won't do Seema or me any good if I lose my temper.

"I don't . . ." Again, he shakes his head. What does that mean? He doesn't understand what I'm asking, or he doesn't know the answer?

"She needs to be in the clinic," I say as forcefully as I can. "We must take her. Now."

"No! No men doctors. You save her."

Seema reaches for me. "Auntie, please. I want my mother." The words climb hoarsely out of her mouth.

I glance up at Awalmir. He's watching her writhe beneath the black *burqa*. "I'm not a doctor," I hiss. "Or a midwife. She needs medical attention."

"You save Massoud's son and grandson. You save my son. And my wife."

Instead of fighting any longer, I say the first thing that occurs to me. "My hands." I turn so he can see they're bound.

Out of the corner of my eye, I see the silver flash of a blade. A *snick* behind me, and my hands are free. Still numb. I look down at them—wrists that are gouged and bloody. I flex my fingers, rub my wrists, trying to massage back some feeling. Awalmir lets loose another torrent of Pashto at the man standing by the door. For Seema's sake, I hope he's saying this isn't the way to treat a woman. What's more likely, he's yelling that he needs me alive. For now.

"You save them."

"I'll do what I can." *Damn it!* I want to shake my fists at the ceiling. *If you really wanted to save her, if you really loved her, you'd take her to the clinic. Even if you just dumped her at the front door.*

"Auntie?"

My heart pounding, I lean forward and cup my hand against her cloth-draped cheek. I turn back to Awalmir, frantically trying to figure out what to do. How best to save Seema. How to escape if I get the chance. But first, Seema. "Please, I must have you all out of here. I need to remove her *burqa*." I pass my hand over her belly. "I need to examine her."

He furrows his brow.

"I need to see." I lift the hem of the *burqa* and start to slide it up Seema's leg.

He doesn't say anything for a long thirty seconds. Is he seriously going to issue a ruling on whether or not I can take off her frigging *burqa*? Finally, he nods. "Yes. My son live. My wife live. Maybe you live."

Most of the men have returned to the front room when I call to Awalmir. "Wait! How far along is she?"

"Far? She there. You see."

"How many months? Pregnant?"

He turns to the other man still in the room. They whisper, and when Awalmir looks at me again, I see that he understands. I also see his worry. "Seven months. Early."

"Way too early," I mutter. Then, "Seema needs to be in the front room, near the stove, where it's warm."

He strains to understand what I'm saying.

I point to Seema. Then to the doorway leading to the front room. The warmth. "Stove." My voice is louder than it should be. Demanding.

"No! Men there." He points again to the mattress. "This good." He nods, satisfied.

"I need hot water. And a clean cloth." I'm pleading now. *You bastard! Give me a fighting chance to save this girl.*

"No water. For women to get."

"Then, give me a bucket, and I'll go get water."

He just stares at me.

"A bucket," I repeat and then do my best to pantomime the shape with my hands. The look on his face tells me I'm not succeeding.

Finally, one of the other men, who's been standing in the doorway, brings in a cloth. One single cloth. That looks like a headscarf. A very dirty headscarf. God only knows where he found it. I can't imagine when anyone last lived here. The house feels empty, abandoned, even with all the men I can hear in the front room. Awalmir takes the cloth and drops it in front of me. Then points to my hair. And leaves the room.

41

"I'M SORRY, AUNTIE," SEEMA whispers. In the front room, the chorus of male voices reminds me, and probably her, that they're right on the other side of the wall. If we can hear them, they can certainly hear us. And it's clear she doesn't want to be overheard. "Please don't be mad. I told Awalmir that you saved Massoud's son and grandson. I thought you could help me."

I slide across the mattress to her. "No worries, sweetie. I'll do whatever I can to help you get this baby born." *I'm also going to help you get out of this hellhole and away from these militants. And that includes Awalmir. Whether you want to go or not.*

"What did you do to save that baby?" Her voice is so muffled by her *burqa*, I can barely hear her.

"Honestly, not that much. The mother had some contractions and pushed, and the baby was born."

"Were her contractions bad like mine?"

"Yeah. Pretty much."

"Is it going to get worse? Hurt more?" She gulps back tears.

"Seema, how long have you been like this? In labor?"

"I don't know. We've been here for about a week. In the beginning, I was fine. Then, Awalmir and the other men went out for a long time." She claps her hand over her mouth. "I wasn't supposed to say. Please don't tell him I told you."

I pull her closer, cradling her against me. "I won't. I promise." But I'm willing to bet I know exactly where they were—stopping Jawid's truck on the River Road. "And that's when your contractions started? While he was away?"

"No. Last night. After they came back."

I have no idea what time she means or what time it is now, so all I can do is guess. Twelve hours ago? Not too bad. Then again, not good. She shouldn't be in labor in the first place.

"That baby lived, didn't he? I mean Massoud's grandson."

I root for her hand beneath the mountain of black cloth, and finding it, entwine my fingers around hers. "Yes. Yes, he did."

Another contraction. Seema groans heavily as she pushes her back against the wall for a long minute. When it passes, she starts to cry and whispers, "I don't think my baby will live. I'm afraid he's already dead."

"Seema."

"No, really. He used to kick all the time. But he hasn't for a while."

"How long ago did the baby stop kicking? Can you remember?"

She squeezes my hand. Hard. "After we got here. A few days ago. I don't remember." She holds my hand on her belly. For a very long time. There's no kicking. No tumbling. No movement at all. "You see?"

"Shh. Sweetie." I want to keep her calm. She needs to save her energy for when the contractions get really bad. "The baby could just be sleeping."

"Oh, Auntie. I don't believe that. He's been kicking hard up till now. All the time. He wouldn't sleep this long." She shakes her head. "I'm scared he's dead. What are we going to do?"

"What we're going to do is make sure you have this baby."

"No, that's not what I mean. If he's dead, the baby, I mean . . ." She takes a deep breath. "Awalmir will do something terrible."

Well, he has done terrible things. Which I don't want to get into right now. Instead, I opt for the failsafe, "You don't really believe that."

"You don't understand. Sometimes he gets very angry . . . and he . . . uh . . . goes crazy."

I try to wait for her to tell me in her own time, but I can't. "What does he do?" I'm not whispering anymore.

Suddenly, the men in the other room stop talking. So do we. For a good five minutes. When they finally start talking again, a deep rumble of Pashto that I don't understand, she whispers, "Please, we have to be quiet. One of them speaks English."

So, Awalmir has one of his men spying on Seema. And me. "What does he do when he gets angry?" I'm back to whispering, barely louder than a breath.

"He . . . hurts me."

What the hell can I say to that? I seriously don't want to imagine what he's done to Seema. Or what he'd do to me. So, I don't even try. We just sit there in silence, listening to the raucous voices in the next room. But there's something I want to know. "Seema? Before, when Awalmir was here, he called you his wife. Are you married?"

She nods. "Right after we ran away, he took me to an imam. And we signed the papers."

Married. It seems like she's telling the truth. But something's off. Why am I having a hard time believing Awalmir would go through with a legal ceremony? *She is a fool. A plaything. Awalmir, he will tire of her soon.* That's what Awalmir's cousin said last May. Scratch that. Fornication is a sin, and a Taliban man would be sure to marry a woman first. Of course! That's exactly what Awalmir would do. Besides, he can have up to four wives. When he tires of one, he can divorce her. Easy enough.

"Auntie?"

"Hmm?"

"I need to ask you something."

I hug her to me. "Sure."

"Is my mother still mad at me?"

My heart clenches. *Oh, Seema.*

"I need her. Oh, Auntie, I'm so scared. I want her with me."

My arm tightens around her shoulders. What she's just said answers all my questions about whether she knew what happened last spring. Whether she was involved. I let the silence grow until I feel her shoulders trembling. It takes me a few seconds to realize she's crying. What can I possibly say? "No, sweetie. She's not mad." I can feel my own tears welling, but crying isn't going to help either one of us.

"Auntie?"

I press the backs of my hands to my eyes.

"He did something horrible, didn't he?"

"Yes. He did."

"That day . . . the explosion . . . the smoke. He came to the house and told me to get in his truck. He and the other men went into the house for a while. When they finally came out, Awalmir had my backpack and some of my clothes. And we drove away."

I hold her close and let her talk.

"He blew up the school, didn't he?"

"Yes, he did."

"And my mother?"

I kiss the top of her head through the filthy *burqa* that reeks of sweat and dirt.

"I overheard the men talking. He-he k-k-killed her, didn't he?"

I can't bring myself to say yes. Not now. Not with her in labor. Instead, I rest my cheek on top of her head and hum. No words. Just the melody of a silly song I used to sing to her and Mel when they were little girls and upset about something or other.

Her tears aren't silent anymore.

All I can do is hold her and rock. Until her cries quiet to a whimper. "How could he? My mother!"

"I know, sweetie. I know."

"My father? Is he—"

"He's fine. Home in Boston. And missing you terribly."

"Oh, Auntie. I've made such a mess. I thought . . ." Whatever else she was going to say drowns in her tears.

I hold her tight. "Crying is for later." Something Darya once said to me. "For now, let's just focus on getting this baby born. Okay? Here's what I need to do. I have to lift up your *burqa* so I can see—"

"No! You can't. There are men in the next room. If anyone except Awalmir comes in here . . ."

"Seema, listen to me. I have to examine you." And that's when I stop. My hands are filthy, caked in dirt and dust. I can't possibly touch her or birth a baby. Somehow, I've got to convince Awalmir to get me water. Or at least have one of the men go with me while I haul water back. Even if it's cold, it's better than nothing. "But first, I'm going to see about getting some water."

She holds tight to my hand. "Auntie, please don't leave me. Please. I can't do this myself. I'm scared."

"Five minutes. I'm just going to get water. I'll come back. I promise." I squeeze her hand and push myself off the mattress. And wish to hell I hadn't made that promise. What if I get the chance to run?

I'm halfway across the room when I remember the headscarf. Dirty. Probably bug-infested. Not anything I want to wear, but maybe if I cover my hair and put on my best 'humble woman' act, I can persuade the bastard to let me get water.

Hair covered, I'm almost to the door when I see a plastic bucket tucked away in the corner. When I pick it up, the reason for its being there becomes all too obvious. Seema's toilet. Although right now, there's just a slop of urine in the bottom. If they don't have another bucket, this will be easy enough to clean. If they've got soap. Soap. Right.

I stop in the doorway to the front room, bow my head, and clear my throat. Almost immediately, the man closest to me drops the *nân* he's eating and jumps to his feet, ready to—what? Tie me up again?

From his place near the stove, Awalmir grunts, then takes a mouthful of soup from the bowl he's holding, slurping and chewing and smacking his lips. Which I guess is as close as he's going to get to saying, *What can I do to help you?*

Not sure exactly how to show humility, I bow my head lower and dip my knee. Then hold up the bucket. "Please? I need water. For the baby."

That gets his attention. "My son?"

I shake my head. "Not yet. I need water to clean Seema. If not—" I glance up to see him frowning. He's not sure what to do. But I can see that he's desperate for his son to be born. Alive.

Finally, he nods. Then kicks the foot of one of the younger men, sparsely bearded, sprawled across the floor. He scowls at being ordered out. Grabbing what looks an awful lot like an AK-47, he jams the barrel against my lower back. Much to the amusement of the others.

A military assault rifle. And I have no doubt this guy knows how to use it. I'm a pretty good shot myself. Yeah, and what are my chances of wresting the gun away from him? Probably zero to none. Besides, could I actually leave Seema behind? Do I even need to ask the question? No, I can't leave her. So, this foray for water isn't my chance to escape. It's my chance to reconnoiter the area, to try to figure out where I am.

Bucket in hand, I push open the door and hear the squeal of the rusting hinges. After the darkness inside the house, stepping outside into the bright daylight makes me squint. Late morning? Early afternoon? I'm not sure. Taking a moment to let my eyes adjust, I start uphill toward the road. Just as quickly, the gun barrel is rammed against my lower spine, causing me to stumble. Still, I've managed to see the narrow road and the thick stand of pine trees. Almost alpine in feel. I take a deep breath, relishing the fresh air, although it's cold, colder than in Wad Qol. We must be at a higher altitude. I listen, but hear nothing. No neighbors working outside. No vehicles on the road. No donkeys braying or goats bleating or roosters crowing. In other words, we're nowhere close to Wad Qol. In fact, we're nowhere close to anyplace or anyone.

Another hard poke of the gun, and I turn toward him, really seeing him for the first time. Damn, he looks familiar. I've seen him before. Where?

One of the workers at the school? No.

Dalan Sang? No.

Then, I've got it. Holy shit. The market at Bazarak. The guy who grabbed me. Whose gonads I kicked.

I do my best to look innocent. He scowls and tips his head in the opposite direction, toward the back of the house. And I limp in that direction. I figure the limping and a little foot dragging are a good distraction. If he thinks I'm too weak to try to escape, maybe he'll let down his guard.

Once we're behind the house, I notice the pickup, its bed full of yellow plastic jerry cans. Gasoline, I'm betting. There are motorcycles, too. And, what the hell? A flatbed truck with tarps partially covering its load. Bricks. And now I know what happened to Jawid's truck. There are enough vehicles back here for a major attack, all of them well out of sight just in case anyone happens by on the road. But what are they going to do with a truckload of bricks? I look closer. The load looks intact, but why are there so many bricks piled next to the truck?

You're outside now. Look for weak spots! Any way you could break out! Cerelli's voice.

Easy for you, Cerelli. You train for situations like this. I bet SEALs take each other prisoner. Go for days without eating or sleeping. Drink your own urine. And still manage to outsmart your captors.

Just do it! I don't know where you are, sweetheart! I need you to help yourself.

Okay, then. A quick look back at the house, and I see a tiny addition built off the side. Not the stronger mud bricks used on the rest of the house, but wooden, with what looks like a rusting sheet of metal for a roof. I see a small window with shutters close to the roofline. Another quick look. A one-by-four nailed across. Definitely something I need to check out. And then what? With all these militants around, there's no way I'll be able to get to that tiny room and climb out the window. Even if I do manage to get the board off.

Don't discount any possibility!

We walk downhill, not too far, until we come to a small pond. Very small and not very clean. The water is covered with decaying leaves. Seriously? This is almost worse than no water at all. He grunts and points his gun toward the pond. The message is clear. It's this or nothing. I kneel next to the water's edge and dip the bucket, then slosh water around and around and hurl it off to the side. Then do the same thing again. I'm ready to rinse it a third time when the butt of the gun stops me, pressing against my abdomen.

Looking up, confused, I take in his sneer as he pulls back the gun, then rams it against my belly. Hard. A second time. Even harder. Falling onto my side, I wrap my arms around myself and gasp for breath. Deep, wrenching gasps. *Don't cry!* But I can't help it. Tears spring to my eyes before I can stop them.

He gives me a minute, then he's back to poking me with his gun barrel, ordering me to my feet. The last thing I want to do. My hip is aching. Now, my stomach. God only knows what he's broken inside me. It's all I can do to push myself to my feet to retrieve the bucket. To fill it. I do the best I can to avoid the scum floating on top and manage to pick out a few dead leaves. Bucket full, I drag my way back up the path, each step painful. Finally, I round the house and reach the front door. Which is, of course, closed. And there on the ground, pushed close to the house, a pile of one-by-fours. If I could just manage to grab one and swing it . . . Yeah, right, I'd get a quick bullet square between my eyes.

I stand there and force myself to look toward the higher peaks of the mountains. The Hindu Kush—it has to be. And with the sun still overhead, it must be about noon. It hardly seems possible that I've been held prisoner for eight hours.

Cerelli? Are you out there looking for me? Or do you just think my phone went wonky this morning?

Gulshan? Ikrom? A huge lump forms in my throat, nearly suffocating me. God, please let them be alive. Unhurt. Looking for me. Ikrom would've talked to Cerelli. And Massoud. Are his men combing the area?

And Seema! I want to yell to the universe. *I found Seema. She's alive!*

Behind me, my guard is getting impatient, poking his gun against my lower back. And not making a single move to open the door.

Scope out the door! Cerelli again. *Could you get out this way?*

Heavy, but old. It's clearly been here a long time. Wide planks running top to bottom that are gray and starting to splinter at the ends. A rope hangs from a hole at about doorknob height. No obvious lock. Could be that I've found a way out. If the militants are willing to all fall asleep at the same time and let me tiptoe over their bodies. Right. Unlike Cerelli and his men, I'm not a ghost. They might be able to sneak out without anyone noticing. I'd make way too much noise.

I catch sight of a window next to the door. Shuttered. With one-by-fours nailed across them.

Sighing, I grab the rope and pull open the door. The hinges repeat their rusty squeal. A push from behind, and I stumble across the threshold. Against all odds, I manage to hold on to the bucket but slosh water over the man stretched out closest to the door. He kicks his lug-soled boot hard against my calf, which nearly sends me sprawling. Catching myself, I turn toward him. I am so tempted. But kicking back or dumping the bucket of putrid water over him would be suicide, at best.

What I really want to do is find a metal pot to heat this water on the stove. But one look at the scowling faces around the room tells me this isn't an option.

"Thank you." I bow my head and carry the water into the back room. Behind me, the men guffaw for a full count of sixty, clearly amused at having forced my humiliation.

IT TAKES A FEW MOMENTS for my eyes to adjust again to the darkness of the room. Finally, I see the mattress and the mound of black *burqa* in the corner. Seema isn't moving. Could she be asleep? Then, I hear the soft whimpering. In the next room, an amused laugh drowns out her cries of pain. I tamp down my urge to demand Awalmir do something. Take her to the clinic. Let her get warm. She could die back here in this cold filth, and those assholes would just go on eating and having a jolly time. Awalmir's laugh drowns out the others. Getting ready to celebrate his fatherhood.

I park the bucket of water on the dirt floor next to the mattress, then lie down next to Seema, curling my body around hers. Wordless, she threads her hand out from under the *burqa* and finds mine. Once again, I rock her and hum every song I can think of. Eventually, her whimpering eases into soft snores, and I let her be. She needs the sleep more than a sponge bath with filthy, cold water.

The men are back to talking—louder now. I pick up on the more serious tone in their voices, and although I recognize the occasional Pashto word, it's not enough to figure out what they're talking about. But then, I start to hear words that do seem familiar.

Klinik. Could be 'clinic.' I think that's Awalmir talking now. Could he actually be planning to take my advice and get Seema to the clinic?

Then someone else says *khazina roghtun,* and for a second I'm lost. Wait! *Roghtun* is a lot like the Dari word for 'hospital.' A few minutes later, in the middle of a long rant, I'm pretty sure it's Awalmir who says the words *khazina däktara*. He follows up with *zeshantun*, and they all laugh.

Okay, I'm going out on a limb here. I'll bet he's talking about a women's hospital and women doctors. The last word, though? *Zeshantun?* I flat-out don't know what that means. And where does any of this get me?

They keep talking. The kind of talk that takes me back to Yemen, when we managed to spend a few days embedded with the Houthi. The commanders gave us incredible access, even—amazingly—to a strategy session for an attack to rout AQAP out of their stronghold in the south. That's exactly what this sounds like. The tone, the seriousness of their voices. Oh, God, Awalmir's not softening on the idea of taking Seema to a clinic. He's planning an attack. A truck-bomb attack? That's why Jawid's truck is sitting out back.

My still-aching stomach tightens. They're going to bomb a clinic. Ikrom's clinic in Wad Qol?

I think back to my last conversation with Cerelli. He seemed pretty sure Awalmir would be heading back to Kabul. The women's hospital in Kabul? The *maternity* hospital. That's got to be one of the softest targets in the entire country. All those women giving birth. Newborn babies.

My thoughts veer away from Kabul. We're in alpine country. Which means the northern end of the valley. What if Awalmir's target isn't in Kabul, where Cerelli and his team and the Afghan forces would be expecting him to strike? Where they're probably gearing up for a counterattack. What if it's here? Oh my God, what if it's the maternity hospital in Anabah! The last place anyone would expect the Taliban to hit.

42

THE ROAR OF ENGINES startles both Seema and me awake.
So loud, I can feel the mattress, even the ground, vibrating. Then,
closer, the sound of hammering. *Hammering?* What the hell is
going on?

I quickly assess my injuries. Not too bad. My hip is still sore,
and my belly aches, but it's a little better. The hammering keeps on.
At the door, I think. Are they really nailing those frigging one-by-
fours across the door?

Seema erases any doubt. "They're locking us in."

"Seriously?"

"I tried to run away a while back. So now, whenever they go
out, Awalmir makes sure I can't do it again."

"Why?" I ask, not sure I really want to know the answer. "Why
did you try to run away?"

She bows her head. "Oh, Auntie! I did something stupid. I
didn't mean to, but I burned his dinner, and he got really mad.
So . . . he-he . . . beat me. To teach me a lesson, he said. Maybe I
deserved it . . ." She's crying again. "I've tried so hard to be good . . ."

I gather her into my arms. "Oh, sweetie, no woman ever deserves to be hit. Ever."

"I know that. I really do. No matter what he says." She sounds defeated. "Anyway, that's why I ran away. Except I didn't get very far before he found me. There's no escaping Awalmir."

The hammering stops, and now the entire house shakes as first the pickup, then the motorcycles, and finally the big flatbed truck drive up the incline to the road. Then they're away, the roar of their engines eventually fading. The start of their operation. Are they really going to blow up a women's hospital? Oh God, of course they are! That's why Awalmir wouldn't take Seema to the hospital. And that's why they're using the truck, why they removed the bricks from the center of the stack on the flatbed. If anyone stops them, it'll just look like a load of bricks. But they've fucking hidden explosives inside. Enough to make a mega-bomb. Big enough to destroy a very large hospital. And kill a lot of people.

And here I am, nailed inside a house with Seema. They've made damn sure I can't stop them.

There's no escaping Awalmir. "We'll see about that, Seema. Let's figure out what we can do to get out of here!" Pushing myself off the god-awful mattress, I help Seema to her feet, and we move silently into the front room where it's a bit warmer. Interesting that they thought to leave the fire burning in the stove. And the lantern lit. Or maybe they just forgot.

I head to the door and, in the quiet, listen to make sure they haven't left anyone behind to stand guard. But I don't hear a thing. No breathing. No shuffling of booted feet in the dry leaves. No coughing. Just silence. With any luck, they've all left. I push hard against the door, but it doesn't budge. Not even an inch.

Looking around the room for anything that could help me

break out, my eyes light on the small pile of sticks and charred wood next to the stove. And a shovel. I go ahead and stoke the fire until it's pouring out heat, making the room much warmer, which will be good for Seema. And the baby. Staring at the piece of wood in my hand, I allow myself ten insane seconds to consider setting the front door on fire. And quickly quash the notion. There's no controlling fire. Flames would jump overhead to the beams, and the roof would crash down on us. If we haven't already died of smoke inhalation. Having seen the school burn last May is more fire than I need in a lifetime. I shove the piece of kindling into the stove.

That's when I notice the pot of rice, cold now, and some partially eaten scraps of *nân*. Not much, but it's something, and we both need to eat. Or we won't be good for anything.

Seema adds the pieces of bread to the rice pot and sets it on the stove. "It's disgusting, eating their leftovers, but there's nothing else."

There's also a jerry can behind the stove. I drag it out, unscrew the top, and sniff. Water, I'm pretty sure. It's got to be cleaner than what I hauled back from the pond. I pour a little onto Seema's hands. Then she does the same for me. And we scrub. More water. More scrubbing. Until our hands are clean enough to cup some water to drink.

Drink. Eat, although the food is barely warm.

We've just finished when Seema clutches her belly and sinks onto one of the filthy blankets on the floor. "Oh, it hurts!"

I grab another blanket and spread it over her, then hold her hand until the pain subsides. "I think I should examine you—to see how far along you are."

"No! Not here. What if they come back?"

"Stop worrying! We'll hear them way before they get here."

She doesn't answer right away, but finally pulls her *burqa* up and over her head. "Okay." We both look down at the pants of her *shalwar kameez*. Reddish-brown. They're caked in blood.

She sees me looking. "Is there always this much blood when a baby is born?"

"Birthing a baby can be pretty messy." I try for reassurance, but seeing Seema like this, I can't help remembering Nazira last spring at the Dalan Sang checkpoint after the bombing, when she gave birth to her son. And died doing so. Just like then, this is way too much blood.

Together, we ease Seema's pants down and off. Her legs are hardly more than sticks. Like Darya, she's petite, but this is painfully skinny. Has he been starving her? How has she managed to carry this baby as long as she has? I pour water onto the headscarf and sponge off as much blood as I can. Then, try to examine her. But even with the light from the stove and the lantern, I can't see much.

Sitting back on my heels and pulling my sweater tighter around me, I feel a hard clunk against my hip. My flashlight! I took it with me when I went outside to call Cerelli early this morning. Exactly what I need.

She lies back, and I direct the beam. Oozing blood. But as best I can tell, there's no head crowning. I don't understand. Seema's been having contractions for hours, but there hasn't been any progress. My shoulders sag.

"Something's wrong. Isn't it, Auntie." It's not a question.

I don't know what to say because she's right. Something should be happening by now. Then, suddenly she's bending forward and groaning loudly with a contraction. A mighty contraction that makes my heart ache for her. I hold tight onto both her hands and watch more blood stream out from between her legs. Why isn't this baby coming?

Spent, she lies back on the rug. "Please, Auntie, tell me the truth. I'm going to die, aren't I?"

"Sweetie, every woman feels like she's going to die when she's in labor." And I don't have any idea what's going on or what I should be doing. Some help here, Darya? God? Please. I can't let this girl die.

I curl up next to Seema, my arm under her shoulders. She rests her head against me. Another contraction, and then, somehow, she manages to drift off to sleep. She needs the rest. So do I, even though I should be trying to find a way out of here. But damn, I'm tired. So tired. My eyes are burning, blurring. I can barely focus. Five minutes rest, then I'll get to work breaking us out of this prison. I close my eyes, only to see Awalmir's bearded face, his yellowing teeth, his hate-filled eyes.

I open my eyes. And there he is, scowling down at me.

Fuck! I blink. He's here. He's really here!

How could I have slept through the roaring return of the pickup and the motorcycles? And the men prying the one-by-fours off the front door that's just a few feet away from where Seema and I were sleeping?

And now, he's inside. The others must be right behind him. What can I possibly do against all these men?

Heart pounding, I reach for the Sig, only it's not in my waistband. There, on the rug. My fingers close around my gun. Except it's not a gun. It's my flashlight.

Awalmir follows my glance, sees the flashlight, and sneers. Two steps, and he wrenches it from my hand. Holding it up, inches from my face, he laughs. "It is good. To have *Badal*. I kill you now. Then, I wait for your captain. I myself called him on your cell phone. I told him we have you. His life for yours. He will come. I know this. And he will find you dead. Then, I kill him, too. It is just."

"No, please. Don't do this. It doesn't solve anything. I have to help Seema."

He points at the black *burqa*-draped figure next to me. Motionless. "Look at her. My wife is dead. My son is dead. Because of you. I will have justice and revenge."

"Please!" I hold up both my hands. "I have a daughter, waiting for me at home."

"Western whore! You should be at home taking care of your child. You should not be bringing godless Western ways to my country." He laughs and, lifting the gun, looks down the barrel, sighting me.

Point-blank range. He can't miss.

I brace myself against the shot. Waiting for the bullet to rocket into my body, to rip me apart. Then, *No! I won't let him shoot me. Not like this.* I leap to my feet and charge toward him, ready to claw out his eyes. I scream. And scream. And scream.

Screams jolt me awake.

The room is empty, except for Seema and me.

Not my screams. Seema's.

43

SEEMA'S SCREAMS ECHO AROUND ME. One touch to her forehead. She's burning with fever. And still bleeding. I pour water onto the bloody headscarf and bathe her but can't tell that it's helping.

Enough time wasted. I've got to get us out of here. But how?

I feel the mouse climbing across my pants leg before I see it. He dives for the crust of bread on the blanket. Snagging it with his tiny teeth, he scurries across the front room.

My stomach roils at the thought of mice climbing over us in search of food. Then I pause. Mice! Could it be going back outside? I grab my flashlight and follow. But he's long gone.

Seema cries out again. Yet another contraction.

I have to find a way out, or she'll die. We'll both die.

I try pushing the front door again, but there's still no budging it. Taking a small step back, I ram my shoulder against the weathered boards and come away in pain. Where did he nail the one-by-four? Probably at the level of the rope. Sitting on the floor, I lift my legs and kick at the bottom half, as low as I can manage. And hear a creak. Doing my best to ignore the pain in my hip, I kick again, but make no progress.

The shovel by the stove. I try that, slamming it against the lower part of the door. Nothing.

I try the windows in the front room. The shutters aren't budging. *Damn it! There's got to be a way out!*

Flashlight in hand, I retreat to the back room. Another window. I push. It's solidly shut, too. Barred from the outside.

I sweep the flashlight beam along the floor, into corners, searching for anything that's been left behind, anything that could help me break out of here. Nothing. Then I see the curtain hanging from the ceiling. Filthy, tattered. When I push it aside, there is the small room built onto the side of the house. I aim the flashlight at the ceiling. It's the rusty sheet of metal I saw from outside. And there, close to the roofline, is a window. Maybe six feet off the floor. I can touch it, but there's no way I can hoist myself that high. Plus, it's small. Probably too small for me to climb out. Even if, by some miracle, it's not nailed shut. I consider that possibility for all of one second. No, I definitely saw a one-by-four across this window when I was out by the pond. But I don't have any other choice. I've got to break out of here.

Another sweep of the flashlight, and I see four heavy-duty plastic crates piled two by two with a wide board balanced on top. At one end are several plastic bowls nested one inside the other. Next to them, a spoon and a knife. A kitchen. I flash back to Gulshan's kitchen. The same crates, two by two. A board balanced on top. Not terribly clean, but it's not the filth that's niggling at me. Who's been cooking? Afghan men aren't known for their culinary skills. Which leaves Seema. And now I know what's eating at me. Why she's even here. To cook.

Seema groans, snapping me out of my pointless speculation

and back to getting us out of here. I clear the bowls and utensils off the quasi counter. This will put me a good thirty inches higher. If it holds my weight. I retreat to the front room and grab the shovel. One giant step up, my hip screaming, and I'm at the height of the window. No glass in the frame. I push at the shutters. No give.

The shovel is fairly heavy. Not good enough to ram through the front door, but maybe it'll do the job on these shutters. I grab the handle and aim the blade at the lower part of the shutters, right where they meet in the center. Pulling back as far as I can, I ram the blade against the wood. And hear a creak. Another smash against the wood, and a few chips fly back past me.

Progress!

I ram the blade again and again. My shoulders ache, but I can't stop. I've got to get us out of here.

A chunk flies past me, just missing my face. A warning to be more careful. I can't afford to lose an eye.

Finally, a loud crack. One of the shutters sags down in the middle. Another assault with the shovel, and a large piece of the shutter drops away outside. I've got a hole in front of me now. Just big enough for me to stick my hand and arm through.

I've earned a one-minute break—to give my shoulders a rest. Leaning my forehead against the interior surface of the shutter, I startle when Seema groans. "Auntie!"

I step backward, ready to run in and check on her, and, losing my footing, fall against the wall. My legs collapse under me. The board shoots off the crates, landing hard against my thighs. The crates tumble one off the other in front of me. But I'm good. Except for my hip. And Seema is quiet again.

I rebuild my scaffold and climb back on. The shovel once again in my hands, I ram it against the edge of the hole I've opened, hoping that's the weak spot Cerelli's been telling me to go after. It works. And now, the chunks of wood are flying outside instead of back into the house, into my face. I've blown out all of one shutter and loosened the wooden crosspiece. My shoulders and arms are tiring. I can feel the burn in my muscles. I need another break.

"Auntie! Help me!" I climb down and run to check on Seema. Another contraction. This one is bad. More blood. A lot more blood. Oh, God, how much more blood can she lose? I shine my flashlight. No progress.

Back to my hole. The cold night air rushes in at me. For the first time, I can see the sky and realize with a sinking heart that it's lightening to gray. Another hour or so and it'll be dawn. Which means Awalmir and his band of murdering insurgents will return anytime now. That's enough to get me back to ramming and pounding. I drive the shovel blade into the cross board again and again. If I can detach that, I'll be set.

There's movement. The board is loosening. And then, finally, mustering all my strength, I push the board out. The nails are out of the window frame.

Now, I work on the other shutter, pushing, levering. It's opening. The shutter is prying the other end of the board out, away from the window frame, away from the house. One final push with the shovel blade, and the second shutter falls to the ground.

I've got an empty hole in front of me. If I'm lucky, I'll be able to squeeze myself through and out. But not from this position. I need more height. I jump down from my scaffold, set the board aside, and pile all four plastic crates one on top of the other.

Seema screams. Not a groan. I bolt to the front room. She's rolled herself into a tight ball. I kneel next to her, take her in my arms. God, she's small.

Soon, Seema, I'll have us out of here. I'll get you to a clinic or a hospital. We'll get that baby born and save you.

And exactly how am I going to get her out of here? Yeah, I've created an escape route. For me. A pregnant girl who's been in labor for who knows how long isn't going to be able to climb up to that window, much less jump out of it and fall however far it is to the ground. What have I been thinking?

Seema is quieter now. Whimpering. I cradle her in my arms and try to figure out what to do. I could go for help. Bring a man back with tools to break down the front door. Except by the time I get back, it's likely Awalmir will be here. And none too happy to find I've broken out. And Seema near death. The baby dead.

How can I do this?

There's only one way I can think of, and I've got to move fast. Awalmir's been gone a long time. He'll be back—a whole lot sooner than I'd like.

I settle Seema again and tuck the blanket around her. Back to the kitchen. I pick up the shovel and use it to balance me as I hoist myself up the stacked crates.

Only to fall back as the crates tumble.

Four crates are impossible. I try three, with the fourth in front as a step-up. Then, grabbing the shovel, I stretch myself up. And I'm there. My head and shoulders are out the window. Hauling myself back inside, I debate heaving the shovel out the window. My only tool. But I'll need it to work my way back in through the front door. There's nothing for it. I've got a plan and have to go with it. I hurl the shovel, making sure to throw it far enough from the house so I don't fall on it and kill myself. Then, checking to make sure I've got my flashlight in the pocket of my sweater, I say a little prayer and hope for the best.

Sweetheart, sometimes that's all you can do.

Yeah, well, let's hope I don't break my neck. I turn away from the window, placing my back to the wall. Hands above my head, I reach out and grab hold of the metal roof. The edge is sharp. I can feel it cutting into my palms. But I can't stop now. Clenching my teeth, I hoist my shoulders and chest out the small window. I have to maneuver myself nearly onto the roof so I can get my torso and then my butt out. It's slow going, but finally, I'm sitting on the windowsill.

Now what? I've got to land on my feet. Land on my back, and I'll lie there broken, waiting for Awalmir to return and slit my throat.

Easing my right leg up, I manage to thread it up and out the window. Definitely a move I'll never be able to make again. Not in this lifetime. With my right leg dangling out the window, my hands holding onto the edge of the roof for stability, I'm able to twist and shift. My hip yelps in pain, but I get my left leg out. Now, I'm perched—facing forward—on the sill. Seconds from being out of my prison, I risk taking one hand off the roof to shine my flashlight down to the ground to see what awaits me.

A ten-foot drop. Perfect leg-breaking height.

Go for it! Cerelli's voice. *You're strong. You won't break your leg.*

You can't possibly know that.

Trust me!

I jump.

Landing on soft knees, ignoring my hip, I let myself roll. To a stop. Not too far from the shovel. The air is cold on my right shin. Looking down, I see my pants are torn. I touch my fingers to the skin—wet, bleeding. I don't have time to deal with a banged-up leg. I push myself to my feet. Take a couple steps. My hip isn't happy, but at least nothing's broken. Or sprained.

Another minute to catch my breath, then, shovel in hand, I limp around to the front of the house.

The sky has lightened enough now that I don't need my flashlight to see the boards nailed across the front door. Two of them. The fucking bastards! Just the adrenaline I need. I try ramming the shovel against the older part of the door. Despite their age, these planks prove so much more solid than the shutters.

I look at the cross boards themselves. They're nailed into the doorframe, which juts out an inch from the mud-brick wall. I figure there might just be enough room for me to force the shovel blade between the end of the board and the brick, and then lever the plank forward. I go for the upper board first. The blade fits, and the long handle juts away from the house. It's harder than I thought. I dig my boots into the dirt, take a deep breath, and slowly push the shovel handle inch by inch back toward the house.

I almost weep when I hear the first creaking of nails pulling out from the doorframe. I keep at it, levering the board until all the nails on the left side are out. Then, I take hold of the one-by-four itself, walking it away from the house until it cracks. I push more until there's another crack. It's off.

A deep breath, and I look down at the middle of the door. The other board. My heart sinks. Then, I glance up at the ever-lightening sky. Once again, I wedge the shovel between the board and the brick wall. And push against the handle. A crack. Almost there. Except the crack I hear isn't the board. It's the shovel handle, cracked just above the shaft.

Keep at it! Cerelli's voice, urging me on.

My hands tighten around the broken shovel. *Damn it! This isn't going well.*

Another look at the sky. I've never dreaded the coming of dawn as much as I do right at this moment. I've got to get this frigging board away from the door. Now.

I grab hold of the handle shaft and, with all the strength I can muster, push it toward the mud-brick wall. It's slower going than the first time. I keep pushing, and finally, *finally*, I hear the squeak I've been waiting for. The nails are letting go of their hold. The board is moving forward. The nails are out. And the shovel is done. I pull at the board, but it's not moving enough to let me open the door. I'm not sure how much more I can do. My shoulders are just about dead. I can barely feel my hands.

And I still don't have Seema out of the house.

Doing my best to steer clear of the nails, I wedge myself between the door and the plank of wood right at my lower abdomen. Then I walk it forward, leaning with all my strength against the wood.

It's tough going. At first, nothing happens. I take a break, a step backward, and the board slaps against me. Hard. I bend over the wood, trying to catch my breath and hold back the tears.

No stopping! I remind myself, listening for the roar of the pickup truck and motorcycles that could be churning their way up the road. *Do it!*

Despite the twinges of pain clawing in my belly, I get back to pushing and keep at it until I hear the cracking of wood. The doorframe is actually splintering. The crossbar and the entire frame are pulling away. Good enough.

I've got clearance, enough to open the door.

Seconds later, I'm back inside, kneeling next to Seema. "Sweetie."

No answer.

I feel her forehead. Hot.

"Please, sweetie. I need you to help me. We're leaving."

That seems to rouse her. "Leave? No. Stay. Awalmir." She's too weak to fight me.

"Seema? Please? I'll carry you, but I need you to hold onto me. Your arms around my neck."

She doesn't say anything, doesn't do anything. Her arms stay limp by her side. She's not even groaning.

I put my hand against her chest. Still breathing, but shallow. I pull down her *burqa* and slip my jacket on her. Grabbing one of the blankets, I drape it over my shoulders, then lift her into my arms. She's tiny, and I'm strong. But with my wonky hip and my aching shoulders, I won't be able to carry her for long.

44

UP WHERE THE DRIVEWAY meets the road, I have to decide which way to go. West? Or east toward the cresting dawn? East. I'm pretty sure that's downhill where I'm more likely to find people who might, God willing, help us. I breathe in the cold alpine air. This high up in the Hindu Kush Mountains, the light from the rising sun will reach us earlier than down in the valley. A mixed blessing. The sun will warm us, and I'll be able to see where we're going. Which means anyone passing by will be able to see us, too. And help us. Or hand us back over to the Taliban.

I walk as fast as I can. Which isn't very fast at all. Seema is dead weight in my arms. *Please wake up!* I long for her to circle her arms around my neck, to wrap her legs around my waist like she and Mel used to do when they were little. I want to let my thoughts stay with the girls when they were young and playing, but I can't risk losing myself in memories. I have to stay alert, focused on the here and now. Or run the danger of Awalmir taking me by surprise. Killing us both.

A small puff of condensed air wafts up, hovers, then dissipates.

She's still alive. The baby, though. I haven't felt a thing from the baby. I try not to think about that. It's Seema I have to save. Seema. And me.

We can't have gone more than a half mile when I hear the rumble of a vehicle approaching from behind. I'm ready to bolt off the road and try to hide behind the trees, but I'm too slow. The truck is on us before I've done more than step to the side of the road. I turn enough to see that it's a white pickup. Like Awalmir's. Then I see a periwinkle *burqa* peering at me from behind the cab.

I freeze in place.

The white pickup pulls next to me and stops.

Clutching Seema closer and trying to shrug the blanket around us both to shield her from prying eyes, I see three periwinkle *burqas* in the flatbed, leaning forward. Silently.

The passenger window lowers, and the driver leans across.

I close my eyes briefly. Please, God.

The Tajiks and the Afghans are the most hospitable people in the world. Cerelli's voice. This could still be the miracle I need.

"*Mêtawânêd bâ man komak konêd?*" I ask.

"*Balê*," he says with a smile that reveals several missing teeth. "*Amrikâyi?*"

I nod. "Yes."

"I help you," he says in English. "What is trouble?"

English. He speaks English! And he's not going to kill me. At least, not right now. My ability to speak Dari suddenly vanishes, and I switch to English. "We've just escaped from the Taliban. They've been holding us captive."

From the corner of my eye, I see the three *burqas* rear back. The driver looks behind him, back up the road.

"I don't know when they'll come back. This girl is sick. With child. I need to get her to a clinic. Please. *Roghtoon-e-zanäna*. A women's hospital."

"*Balê*." He nods and turns off the ignition.

The women are out of the flatbed in an instant, taking Seema from my arms, then gasping when they look back at me. I look down and see the front of my *shalwar kameez* saturated in blood, then feel myself start to get dizzy. So much blood.

Head down until the wave passes!

I reach for the side of the pickup to steady myself.

One of the women takes my hand. "You hurt, too."

"No, no. I'm fine."

I climb into the back of the truck, and the women lift Seema into my arms. As soon as we're settled, the women huddle around us, sheltering us from the cold wind that's picking up. The truck chugs to life. We're off. The driver is on a mission now, careening down the mountain to the valley. He'll get us to the hospital. And far away from the murderous Taliban.

I pull the blanket close around Seema and me, against the wind and the snowflakes that are beginning to fall. Then shut my eyes.

THE PICKUP JERKS TO a stop. I open my eyes to a large, modern building with tall, red letters spelling out HOSPITAL in Dari and English. My eyes widen. A hospital! Like this? In Afghanistan?

"Anabah. *Roghtoon-e-zanäna*," says one of the women next to me.

Anabah. This is where Darya and I planned to come after the photography workshop last May. And now, here I am with Seema. Dar! We've got to make sure she lives.

A small crowd of women in pink *shalwar kameezes* and gray

headscarves are waiting in front of the doors. For us? How could they possibly know we'd be coming? Within seconds, they launch into action, lowering the back flap and lifting Seema from my arms. I watch them lay her on a gurney, and then they're wheeling her quickly across the walkway and through the metal and glass doors.

The blanket still wrapped around me, I inch forward until I can slide out of the flatbed. "*Tashakor!* Thank you!" My hand over my heart, I say it over and over to each of the women and to the driver, who's now standing outside the pickup.

Waving away the wheelchair, I turn toward the hospital, only to find a microphone in my face and who else but Piera McNeil blocking my way. Her intrepid cameraman is recording. "Well, look who's here. Annie Hawkins Green. The caped crusader."

Desperate to tell the doctors what I know of Seema's condition, I put up my hand to ruin the shot and do my best to skirt around her. She's not giving way.

"You really *do* show up in the most unusual places. A spec op anywhere in Afghanistan, and there you are."

Doing my best to tune her out, I turn abruptly and head in the opposite direction. But Piera matches me step for step, her frigging mic way too close to my teeth.

"I'm sure my viewers will be very interested to know you're here—"

I push away her mic but don't say a thing. Let her viewers see how she's going after me. Maybe TNN's legal team can go after *her*. Once more, I try to reverse direction, but there are too many people out here now. I can't get past, and I'm desperate to find the doctors. "Get. Out. Of. My. Way!" I yell. So much for not talking, but I've *got* to help Seema.

A hand reaches around and grabs my wrist. I look up to see a nurse nodding at me. She drags me past Piera, and into the hospital.

"Seema!" I say. "Please! I have to speak with the doctors."

She shows me into an office with a table and several hard, plastic chairs.

"You sit?" She smiles. "Doctor come soon."

The doctor arrives almost immediately, before I have time to organize my thoughts. With no interest in the usual obligatory and lengthy exchange of greetings, she parks herself on the edge of the desk and peppers me with questions.

I tell her what I can.

Seema Ghafoor. Just eighteen. About seven months pregnant. Contractions for twenty-four hours that I know of. No progress. And a hell of a lot of blood.

Then, she's gone. I hear her shouting orders for an ultrasound and to ready an operating room.

Ultrasound.

A women's hospital.

A maternity hospital. Awalmir's target. I'm sure of it. They wouldn't have holed up so close by for an attack in Kabul. Wait! What did Piera say? A spec op?

Before I can stand up to chase after the nurse, to warn her about the attack that could still happen, a different nurse—this one, American—hurries into the room. I tell her.

"No worries. The Taliban never got all the way to Anabah. The coalition forces bombed them. I heard they used a drone. It all happened about ten kilometers from the hospital, but the explosion was so loud, we could hear it."

"Did they get everyone? What about the head guy? Awalmir?"

"Sorry. I don't know." She looks at me closely. "How do you know his name?"

My shoulders sag in relief. "He's been holding us captive. We escaped after they took off last night. I was so scared they'd bomb this place or the maternity hospital in Kabul, then come back before I could get us out. They would've slit our throats."

She stares at me—her mouth frozen agape. A moment later, she's back in charge with a friendly smile. "Let's find you a more comfortable room. Then, I'll take a look at your hands."

I glance down at my hands and inhale. Audibly. They're a mess. Scraped and bloody with splinters sticking out at all angles. Long gashes, with red lines starting to inch ominously up my arms. Now that I'm starting to warm up, I can feel it all. Needles and pins and splinters. My hands hurt like hell. So does my belly. Thanks to that asshole with his AK-47.

"Please. First, tell me how she is. Seema."

Her smile turns grim. "From what I heard, it's touch and go. A thready pulse. They're prepping her now for a C-section."

I slump against the back of the chair. Defeated.

She leans forward, a hand on my shoulder. "We have outstanding doctors here. Probably the best in the country. Don't give up hope."

I'm having a hard time tracking what she's saying and realize I'm fading fast. "Please. I need to get in touch with some people. To let them know we're here. Captain Finn Cerelli and Dr. Tariq Ghafoor."

"Did you say Dr. Ghafoor?"

"Yes." I nod toward the door. "Seema is his daughter. She's been missing since last May."

She stares at me, her eyes widening in astonishment. "You're

Annie Hawkins Green, aren't you? The entire valley is looking for you."

Suddenly light-headed and dizzy, all I can manage is a slurred "Really?"

She looks at me more closely, but I can't quite make out her face. "Wheelchair!" she calls into the hallway.

My gut is cramping more. That water in the jerry can. Oh, God, what parasites have I got growing in me? I lean forward, hoping to lessen the pain, and that's when I see the pool of blood at my feet.

45

Anabah, Northern Panjshir Valley

I OPEN MY EYES to the rosy light of sunset streaming into the room. A hospital room—that much is clear. Slowly, slowly, it all comes back to me. Seema. The baby. Awalmir killed by a drone. Or maybe he's on the run. But what's wrong with *me*? Why am I in a bed and feeling like hell?

"Annie. Sweetheart." The voice I most want to hear. Warm. Loving. It wraps around me. "Welcome back to the land of the living."

"Cerelli?" I turn my head, and there he is, sitting on a blue plastic chair by the side of my bed. "How did you get here so fast?"

He quirks a half grin. "Not that fast, I'm afraid."

"What do you mean?"

He holds up two fingers.

"Two hours?"

"Try two days. You've been out for a while."

I stare at him in disbelief. "I've been asleep for two days?" I try to sit up but don't get very far before the cramping in my belly forces me to lie back down. "What's going on?"

He leans forward and cups his hand over my wrist. Which is when I notice my left hand is wrapped in gauze bandages and is three times its normal size. I look at my right hand. Same thing. And they're both throbbing. I remember how cold it was up at the house. Colder when I was carrying Seema down the road. Cold enough to snow. I didn't have any gloves. By the end, I couldn't feel my fingers, my hands. Not even the horrible splinters.

Frostbite. *No. Please, no.* Tears well in my eyes. They've had to amputate my fingers. I'll never hold a camera again. Just kill me now.

Cerelli stands and hovers over me. "Listen to me, sweetheart. It's not what you think. I promise, you've still got all your appendages. Much to the doctors' disbelief, I should say. But those splinters were bad. Dirty. There are also some serious cuts. You've got a nasty infection. The docs are concerned about sepsis." He points to the IV drip running into my left arm. "Antibiotics. Heavy duty. And fluids to deal with your dehydration."

I can't begin to wrap my mind around splinters causing this much trouble. "I'm not going to lose my fingers? My hands?" I sound ridiculously weepy.

"You're not." That half grin again. But looking into his eyes, I see a profound sadness he's not able to hide.

"Seema. Tell me she's still alive. Oh, God, please don't let her be dead."

He looks away toward the window, then back, as if bracing to give me the bad news. "She's fighting hard, holding her own."

"I need to see her."

"Later. When you're doing better."

"*Now!*"

He holds up his hands in surrender. "I'll talk to the doctor, but no promises. You're in pretty bad shape yourself."

"How bad?" My voice suddenly a whisper.

"Bad enough that I'm worried."

Worried? Cerelli? That scares me. "What about the baby?"

"A C-section. A little girl."

I start to smile.

"Stillborn."

Now, I look away. Cerelli rubs my forearm. "There was nothing you or anyone could have done. Seema had placenta previa. The placenta was almost totally blocking the cervix. There was no way that baby could have been born without surgery. Tariq says it's rare for a girl her age, but not unheard of. He says you saved her life."

"Tariq is here?"

Cerelli nods. "He flew in early this morning."

My brain is still pretty fuzzy, but I remember one thing Tariq and Cerelli need to know. "Tell him—he has to know this—Seema guessed that Awalmir killed Darya, but only recently. She didn't know before. She wasn't part of it. Back at that horrible hellhole, she told me she was scared that Awalmir was going to hurt her if she didn't have a boy."

A cloud of anger passes over his face. "You can tell Tariq yourself. He'll be in to see you later."

"That's allowed?"

He grins. "He's a doctor."

"The nurse told me about the drone attack. Did you get them? Did you get Awalmir?"

Cerelli shakes his head. "Don't know. There were reports of at least one runner."

"Oh my God! If it's Awalmir, he could come here. For Seema."

He puts his hand on my shoulder. "Hold on. We don't know who it was. And if it *is* Awalmir, this is the last place he'd come."

"You didn't see the way he looked at her. In some weird, perverted way, I think he really did love her."

"He was beating her, Annie. She's got a lot of nasty bruises."

It's all coming back to me now. My tears are welling. "I tried, Cerelli. But until they left, I couldn't do anything besides scope out where we were, look for ways to escape. Then I heard them talking. Pashto. I picked up on a word or two, enough to know they were planning to blow up a women's hospital. And there wasn't a fucking thing I could do to stop them."

He wipes away my tears with his thumb. "You did good. Really good. Against terrible odds, you saved Seema's life. Not to mention *your* life. I couldn't have done better."

All good news. Well, mostly. When I lock eyes with him, I still see sadness.

"What aren't you telling me?"

He leans close to kiss me. A gentle kiss. On the cheek. "Why don't you rest now? We'll talk more later."

"Tell. Me. Now."

He sits on the edge of the bed and cups a hand against my cheek. "You sure?"

I stare at him. In five seconds, a thousand horrible possibilities run through my mind, and I stop at Mel. No, no, no. "Not Mel," I whisper.

"Not Mel." He smiles. "She's fine, just waiting till you feel better to call."

"Then . . ."

"Sweetheart, Seema wasn't the only one to lose a baby."

"What? Who?"

"We did."

All I can do is stare at him. Words come to my lips but go unsaid. This makes no sense. A baby? I was pregnant? Then I remember the pool of blood at my feet in the office where I met with the doctor and the nurse. *My* blood? Another cramp seizes me.

"The doctor says you were about six weeks along."

I count back to my days and nights with Cerelli in October. "Oh, God, I'm so, so sorry. I didn't know." It was early. Barely a baby. "If I'd known . . . I would never . . ." There's no holding back the tears now.

"Shh." He wipes his thumbs across my cheeks but can't begin to keep up with the flow. "Can you move over a bit?"

I ease across the mattress, and in ten seconds, he's stretched out next to me. He wraps his arms around my shoulders and holds me against his chest. And big, bad, brave SEAL that he is, he cries with me.

THE NEXT TIME I wake up, the curtains are drawn, Cerelli is gone, and the American nurse is checking my vitals.

"You're awake! How are you feeling?"

"I'm . . ." Cerelli telling me about the miscarriage comes flooding back. Only six weeks. I'm sad, but honestly not sure what to feel. It's hard to mourn a baby when I didn't know I was pregnant. When it wasn't even a tadpole. Still, it could have been. Cerelli's and mine. I was responsible for keeping it safe, and I failed. *No! That way madness lies. Don't do this to yourself!*

"Could you eat a little dinner?"

With the thought of food, a wave of nausea washes over me. I shake my head.

"How about flatbread and tea? Think you can manage that?"

Defeated yet again, I shrug. "Okay. I'll try."

She smiles. "Exactly what I want to hear." She starts toward the door, then turns back. "I just wanted to tell you that we're all sorry you had to deal with that reporter, Piera McNeil, the day before yesterday. Especially considering how sick you were. She can be pretty intense."

"Oh, yeah."

"She's not all bad, you know. Yes, she can drive us crazy, but she raises a ton of money for the hospital."

"Seriously?"

She nods. "She did a documentary on the hospital a couple years ago, and ever since, we've had improved cash flow. Enough to buy a second ultrasound machine."

All I can do is stare at her.

"So, although she can be really intrusive, we mostly put up with her. Still, she shouldn't have gone after you like that. Word is that your husband took her down a peg, if you know what I mean."

"My husband?"

Her eyes sparkle. "Why didn't you tell us Captain Cerelli is your husband?"

WITH MY HANDS WRAPPED in gauze, I'm fumbling a piece of dry *nân* to my mouth when Cerelli strolls into the room. The bread falls back onto the plate.

"You're walking."

"Have been for a while."

"No, I mean you're really walking. As in normally. No limp."

He chuckles. "Hang around me long enough, and you'll see me limp. Guaranteed." He nods toward the plate and my partially eaten bread. "Can I help you with that?"

"I feel like a baby." We lock eyes. And damn it, I feel tears pricking. "I mean, an idiot."

"Sweetheart, I know what you mean." He sits on the edge of the bed, picks up the *nân*, and tears off a bite-size piece.

I open wide, then chew. "This is weird."

"You have to eat if you want to get out of here."

"Huh?" I open again.

"The doc says you're looking thin."

"You mean, if I eat this, they'll discharge me?"

"Weeellll. There's also the little matter of the infection you've got going because of your hands. Another infection, too. In your gut." He doesn't mention the miscarriage. He doesn't have to.

"Aha!" I point my gauzed hand at him. "You lied to me!"

"Never." He's doing his best to look truthful and innocent, but he can't hide the twinkle in his eye.

"Get real, Cerelli. You almost never tell me the truth."

He looks wounded. "I never lie about the important things."

"Such as?"

"Loving you."

Well, that shuts me up. For a minute. Then, I'm right back at him. "I hear you had a little run-in with my favorite person."

"Piera McNeil." Just saying the name makes him scowl. "Word travels fast."

I take a deep breath. "And? Tell me!" Then, I add, "Please," for good measure.

"The reason I spoke to her had nothing to do with you."

"Seriously? But she was horrible to me when I got here. And the nurse told me—okay, then, what *did* it have to do with?"

"I'm in the middle of an operation, and her interference could have caused a lot of problems."

"Wait. I thought you already took out the truck bomb."

"We did, but the op is ongoing. If Piera ran that story, it would most undoubtedly have tipped off the militants who're still out there. Not to mention, you could've been in danger. More danger." He puts his index finger against my lips to stop my protest. "And Seema."

Okay, then. The man knows how to shut me up.

"And your nurse was right. There was also the matter of how she went after you."

"Cerelli—"

"There were lots of witnesses, and your driver actually recorded the entire incident on his cell phone. Piranha, right? That's what you call her?"

I nod. "And?"

"The driver's video is now with the Pentagon attorneys. And Marcus. The cameraman handed over his copy, reluctantly. Al Shabakat has been digging and discovered that some rather broad editing has been going into Piera's stories for far too long."

In other words, she's been making things up wholesale. Lying. An ethical line that journalists absolutely do not cross. I press my lips together. Be gracious. Humble. Appreciative. "Thank you." I watch his eyes gentle. He was actually worried I'd go after him. Both barrels. "You know, the nurse told me that Piera isn't all bad. She raised money for this place."

"Don't go soft on me. The truth is she got other people to give money."

"But—" He's right. Besides which, Piera put a whole lot of lives at risk. Including Cerelli's. And mine. As well as my career. "Holy shit," I whisper. "My job. I'm supposed to meet the crew in Kabul."

"Annie—"

"What's today? The date?"

"November 26th."

"I've got to get to Kabul." I try to throw off my cover but only manage to wrap it around my gauzed hands. Tight. The more I fumble, the tighter the cloth binds. Until all I can do is lie back in total frustration. And cry. Damn, I couldn't hold a camera if my life depended on it.

Cerelli wipes my cheeks. "Listen to me. I've already called Chris."

I open my mouth. "My job," I whisper.

"Your job is secure. I've got it on good authority from both Chris and Marcus. And Chris has already replaced you on this assignment."

I watch him untangle my hands from the sheet.

"Chris also said to tell you that the secret assignment has been cancelled—given the circumstances."

I keep my eyes on my gauze-covered hands. "He told you that, did he?"

"Annie, I've known about that interview for weeks."

I meet his eyes. "But how?"

"Trust me. I've known."

Of course he's known. He's running operatives everywhere. One of his sources undoubtedly told him.

"So, did Chris tell you when I'm due back on the job?"

"They've got you on medical leave at the moment. The docs here figure you should be back in the game by late December."

"Okay." I say the word with way too much doubt and uncertainty. Glancing up, it's clear that Cerelli heard it, too. I watch him debating whether to ask.

He does. "You want to tell me?"

Do I? I'm not sure myself what's upsetting me about the thought of going back to work. I try to push back my hair, but end up slugging myself. He smiles his sympathy and gently pushes my hair away from my face, his eyes clouded with curiosity. And worry. And then he waits. Which he's much better at than me.

More tears are welling, and it's all I can do to keep them from streaming down my face. "I don't know."

He takes hold of my gauze-wrapped hand.

"When Chris suspended me, I thought it was the worst thing that could've happened—the end of my career, my life. Now, I just don't know. Do I even want to go back? Maybe I do. But I'm not sure the *drive* is still there—" I swallow hard. "Save me. I'm blathering."

"Sweetheart, you've just been to hell and back. There's no need to make a decision now."

"But see, in the past, 'hell and back' was part of the adrenaline rush. Documenting the conflicts, the people living through war. Surviving. Getting to go home so I could go back into the field. It's different now. I—" My eyes meet his, the uncertainty I'm feeling reflecting back at me.

"I repeat: now is not the time to decide." He moves his hand down the covers until it's resting on my belly. He knows. He really knows. "Not when you're in a hospital bed. Later. We'll take some time, talk it through."

"Thanks. You're good at this, you know, Captain."

He grins, then leans forward and gently kisses me.

I start to respond with a great deal more passion, only to have him pull back. "Later. I promise. For now, are you up to seeing a couple pictures?" He pulls his cell phone out of his pocket and clicks into the gallery.

"Okay."

The wariness in my voice makes him glance up for a moment, but he's quickly back to swiping through pictures. When the one he's after slides into place, he enlarges it, then holds it up for me to see. "Is this the house where Awalmir was holding you and Seema?"

I shudder. "I'm pretty sure. Yeah." It's a pic of the front of the house, the door hanging from its hinges, cracked one-by-four planks dangling to the side. He swipes to the next pic. The wooden addition at the side. I can just make out a few large chunks of shutters strewn across the ground. Then, I look at the little window. From this perspective, it seems awfully high up. Definitely more than the ten feet I estimated.

"You want to take me through what happened?"

"Do I have a choice?"

"Not really."

Memories of the last interrogation he put me through, almost exactly nine years ago on the USS *Bataan*, surface. "You know, the last time—"

He leans forward and kisses me again. Still not the passionate kiss I'm longing for, but we're getting there. "I'll be gentle. I promise."

"From the beginning?"

"Please."

"Okay, then. It was early when you called, and I didn't want to wake up Gulshan and Ikrom—" I stop. "Are they all right? I can't believe I didn't—"

"Hey. Deep breath. They're fine."

Thank God! I breathe deep, which doesn't exactly help the pain and cramping in my belly. "So, I was outside, talking to you, and suddenly there was a guy holding a gun to the side of my head."

Cerelli's face shows no emotion, except for the muscle at the corner of his eye that's pulsing like crazy. Looking into his eyes, though, I see rage. I'm guessing a little bit of that rage is directed at himself for having failed to protect me. Even though that wasn't his job.

"I honestly didn't know if you heard what happened next. Or if you thought the call got dropped."

"I heard." The devastation in his voice makes my heart ache.

I tell him about the endless ride in the back of the pickup, then being shoved into the unheated room with Seema. I tell him everything right up until when the militants left on their mission to blow up the maternity hospital. "I didn't know which one. Kabul or Anabah."

"They were on their way to Anabah. Which is what we guessed. We got lucky."

Another deep breath to erase my mental images of how things could've turned out if Cerelli hadn't gotten lucky.

"And after they left?" He's not letting up.

I swallow hard, struggling with this next part. I don't want to remember Seema's hemorrhaging. Her pain. Her terror. My fear. Tears are welling behind my eyes. God almighty, I'm hormonal.

"Please?" He lays the back of his hand against my cheek.

He really is being gentle.

"I, uh . . . well, they nailed us in before they left. One-by-fours. Across all the shutters and the front door."

He nods, but I see how that muscle next to his eye is spasming again. This is taking a toll on him. He honestly doesn't want to hear what I went through.

Knowing this, it's hard to look at him, to see the pain he's enduring. So, I look at a spot over his shoulder. "I tried, but I couldn't get out the front door or either of the lower windows."

"Used your shoulder as a battering ram, did you?"

My eyes are instantly back on his, and what I see lifts my spirits. A glint of humor. "How do you know? Ah! Took a little peek at me?"

"Oh, I did. And I didn't like what I saw. You're black and blue all over. Please tell me they didn't beat you."

"No. Other than when my unconscious body bounced around the bed of the pickup, oh, and when one of them rammed his gunstock into my abdomen—" More tears well in my eyes.

Cerelli leans close, rests his forehead against mine. Neither one of us says a word for a very long time. Finally, he sits up. "You up for telling me the rest?"

Not really, and from the look in his eyes, he's expecting me to say no. But the sooner I get through this, the sooner I can start moving forward. "Yeah, I just want to finish."

He nods.

"As I'm sure you've already figured out, I went for that upper window in the little addition." I fill in all the details of how I smashed my way out.

"Then, you jumped."

"Yeah, well, it's not like I had a choice. It was almost dawn by then. I was terrified they'd all come back and find me. But I managed to break back *in* through the front door to get Seema. It was the only way I could carry her out."

That stops him. "You carried her? All that way?"

"Well, until the pickup stopped and gave us a lift." I see the fear mounting in his eyes. All I can do is shrug. "I heard the truck behind us, and to be honest, I just gave up."

He leans forward and kisses me again. This kiss isn't sweet or gentle. This kiss tells me everything he's feeling. Everything.

Later, he tells me what happened to the house. "After Sawyer searched the place and shot these pics, he took care of it."

"You mean?"

He nods.

Sawyer does like his C-4.

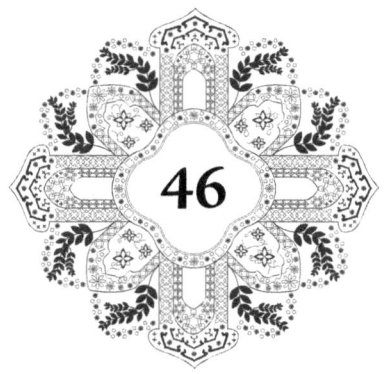

46

CERELLI'S STILL THERE, HIS hand on my arm, when I wake up again. "Good." He smiles. "You've got a call coming in."

I hold up my hands. "Could be a challenge to deal with a phone."

He holds his sat phone next to my ear.

"Mom! Finally. Are you okay? Captain Cerelli said you're in the hospital."

I catch Cerelli's eye. He shakes his head, which I take to mean he hasn't told her about the miscarriage. "I'm okay. Just dehydrated. And bruised. They're keeping me for observation."

"He said you rescued Seema. For real?"

"Yeah, I did."

"Way to go! Mom, you're a hero."

"Hardly." Climbing out a window to save your own life doesn't qualify.

"Does she know about what happened to Auntie Dar?"

One quick nod from Cerelli.

"Yeah. She does now. But she didn't know back in May when it happened." No one could fake the grief and horror she showed when she pieced it all together.

"That's what Uncle Tariq said."

"You talked to Uncle Tariq?"

"Yeah. And to Seema."

I glare at Cerelli. No one bothered to tell me that Seema's conscious and talking?

He shrugs.

"Sweetie, I need to talk to you about something else."

"Okay . . ." She sounds wary.

"The custody hearing, the police, your father."

"Oh, that." I can just see her waving her hand through the air to dismiss that drama. "That seems like so long ago. Well, first of all, Ms. Knight, your lawyer, is *a-ma-zing*. First thing she did was get me my own lawyer. We all met with the judge. *In chambers.* That way C.E. wasn't shitting about all this being public."

Cerelli raises an eyebrow and swallows his laugh.

"Language, please. And what happened?"

"Well, Dr. and Mrs. Faqiri and Yasmine were there, too. And Bonita, of course. The judge asked all of us questions, then asked me where I want to live. I said with you. And Bonita said she'd be my guardian when you can't be there because of work. As soon as I said that, C.E. started crying. But Dad, he didn't say anything."

"Bottom line?"

"We won!"

This is good. For Mel. And that's what's important. The rest, I'll figure out. "We'll celebrate when I get home, okay? Listen, have you talked to your dad?"

"Yeah. He called, and I couldn't not answer, even though both my attorney and Ms. Knight said I should wait a while, let things settle down. Mom, he's really sad."

"Of course he is. He loves you, sweetie. Catherine Elizabeth does, too."

"Could of fooled me."

"They do."

"Yeah, well, I sure don't fit in his life right now." I notice she doesn't include C.E. in that statement.

"Look, don't give up on him. Or her. Okay? Oh, and Mel, before you hang up. About that article in *Ripples?*"

Cerelli raises both eyebrows.

"Mom, Captain Cerelli, he, uh, kind of talked to me about that. I'm really, really sorry. I honestly didn't know it would cause problems."

"Yeah, well. . . I was wondering. Is there any way you could set up a GoFundMe page? And publicize it through your paper? Turns out, we lost a truckload of bricks for the school, plus vandals wrecked the framing. Anyway, we need more money."

"Oh!" I hear the relief and excitement in that single syllable. "I already told Captain Cerelli. Didn't he tell you?"

I shoot another glare at Cerelli, who has the grace to look a little abashed. "No, he didn't happen to get around to that."

"Oh." Mel puts a whole lot of meaning into that syllable. "Anyway, Dr. Faqiri went ahead and set it up, and we've got tons of money coming in. And get this: Captain Cerelli told Dr. Faqiri that *he* can get the money to the school. No fees or bribes."

"Sweetie, that's amazing! You and Yasmine really nailed this." I notice that Cerelli suddenly seems preoccupied with needing to adjust his pants leg over his prosthesis. I wonder when he was planning to tell me about his new role as courier for the school.

Despite Mel's excitement, I'm fading fast, struggling to keep my eyes open.

"And Mom? About Captain Cerelli? We need to talk."

That wakes me up again. "About what, exactly?" Don't tell me my daughter is going to give me advice on my love life.

"Jeez, Mom, don't be such a dork." And she ends the call.

Or maybe Cerelli does. His thumb is definitely on the END CALL button.

I try to snag his arm with my bandaged hands. Which really is pretty dorky. "Something has me just a little confused. I'm hoping you could clear it up for me."

He looks ever so slightly uncomfortable. "Sorry I didn't tell you about the money. I thought Mel would want full glory points."

I put my gauzed mitts on either side of his head. "It's a wonderful thing you're doing. For the school. And for Mel. Thank you."

"I'm doing it for you." His lips are less than an inch from mine.

"Even better. Although that's not what has me confused."

"Then what?"

"The nurse referred to you as my husband. Did I miss something?"

He laughs. "Best way I could come up with to stay in your room. Now, move over."

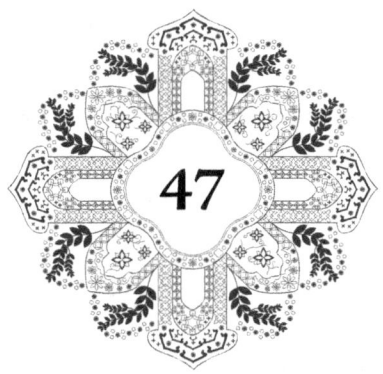

47

IT'S DARK WHEN I NEXT wake up. Out in the hall, voices murmur and shoes squeak, then move away. My hands are back to throbbing, and the IV in the crook of my elbow is getting really annoying. I reach for Cerelli, but the other half of the bed is empty, the sheets cold. My bodyguard has finally taken a break.

I need a break, too. No matter what Cerelli and the doctor and nurses say, a slow walk to the toilet a couple times a day does not suffice. If I don't get up right now, insanity is a real possibility in my very near future.

Swinging my legs off the side of the bed, I reach for the IV stand to steady me but end up crashing it against the headboard. The clatter echoes throughout the room. I freeze in place, waiting for a nurse or Cerelli himself to charge through the door. But no one comes.

I inch my butt off the bed, plant both feet firmly beneath me, and snake my non-IV arm around the stand. And now we roll. Not to the toilet. I'm determined to find Seema's room and check on her myself.

The lights in the hall are dimmed, and thank God no one's

around to hustle me back into bed. I check the two rooms next to mine. No luck. But when I move on to the third door, I come face-to-face with Tariq just leaving the room.

"Annie." He's still thin and gray, but not quite as hunched over into himself. And he's smiling, all the way to his eyes. But then, he takes note of my hospital gown and bandaged hands. "I think you should not be out of bed."

"Probably not. But I'm desperate to check on Seema. How is she?"

"She is making an amazing recovery. Physically. Her spirit, I think, will take much longer to heal." He glances away for a moment, clears his throat, then looks back at me. "My dear friend. There is no way I will ever be able to thank you enough for bringing Seema back to me. You saved her life, and you also saved mine."

"I think we'll all heal now."

"Having Seema at home will help me enormously, although . . . Darya . . ."

"Tariq, I—" My voice cracks. "Darya—"

He places his hand gently on my arm, barely touching me. "Darya would not be happy to see us like this. When we moved back to Afghanistan, we talked about such a possibility, one of us dying. She insisted that I go on with my life. That is what she would want. We must honor her wish."

"I know." I decide not to mention that she's recently been haunting me, ordering me to get on with my life.

"We will talk more tomorrow. For now, I have kept you standing far too long. Captain Cerelli and the nurses will be angry with me. You must rest. Perhaps the chair next to Seema's bed would be a good place for you to sit for a few minutes." He raises an index finger in lecture mode. "Then, you must return to your room."

I grin. "Thank you, Dr. Ghafoor."

He opens the door, and there is Seema's too-thin body curled on the bed. Quietly, quietly, I slip into the room, rolling my trusty IV stand alongside. Damn, the wheels are noisy.

"Auntie?"

I stop dead in my tracks. "Seema. I'm sorry! Did I wake you?"

"No. I've been awake." Her voice sounds stronger than I expected. But scared. "It's hard to sleep here. What if Awalmir comes? He'll be furious that I lost the baby."

I feel for the chair next to her bed and sit down harder than I expected. "No, sweetie, he wouldn't dare come here."

"That's what my father said. And Captain Cerelli." She shakes her head with determination. "But they don't know him like I do. He *will* come. Like I told you, I tried to escape once before, and he found me. He'll find me again, and he won't let me go this time either." There are all kinds of emotions coating her words. Fear. Sadness. And probably a whole lot of guilt. Plus, she must be as hormonal as I am.

"Listen to me. Captain Cerelli doesn't even know if Awalmir's still alive. He was probably killed in the explosion."

"No. He's still alive. I know he is." She's quiet for what seems like a long time. Only the occasional sniffle tells me she's crying. "You know, I really did love him. In the very beginning. And he said he loved me. I believed him. But then he . . . How could I have been so stupid?"

"I think he did love you." In his own strange and twisted way. "I saw the way he looked at you back at that awful house. He was truly worried." Although maybe it wasn't Seema he was worried about. Maybe it was his son.

"Do you really think so?" She hiccups.

Why am I telling her this? Because it's exactly what she needs to hear. She's already lost too much. "I do. But I also think love should feel good. It shouldn't hurt. Not the way he hurt you."

"I just want to go home. To the U.S., with my father. Except that my mother . . . she won't be . . . I-I feel horrible about what happened to her. And to the school. Oh, Auntie, how could my father ever want me to be with him again? He says he does, but he must blame me for everything that's happened. He must."

"He doesn't blame you. He's happy that he didn't lose you, too. He loves you, sweetie. He does. Believe me. That's how it is with parents and their kids. The love doesn't stop."

She tries to smile, but the sniffles betray her. "Will you stay with me?"

"Of course. Until you fall asleep, my Seema. Would you like that?" I drag my chair closer to the side of the bed and lay my gauzed hand next to her. Somehow, she finds a way to hold on.

I must doze off, too, because the next thing I know, the door to Seema's room creaks open. Likely Tariq ready to corral me back to my room. Or a nurse coming to check on Seema. I hope this is the American nurse. She's way more likely to let me sit here a bit longer. Pushing myself upright on my chair, I turn toward the door, ready to offer a completely implausible reason for being in Seema's room.

It's not Tariq. Not a nurse.

Stepping away from the door, Awalmir pulls an automatic from inside his jacket and trains it on me. "Seema!" he hisses. "Wake up! We go now."

Next to me, Seema tightens her hold on my bandaged hand.

"Seema!" Awalmir's voice is louder now. His eyes dart around the room as if he's looking for a nurse or a guard who might be hiding in the shadows. Skirting the perimeter of the room, he closes in on Seema's bed.

I glance at her. Her eyes are still closed, and she's not moving, but I know she's awake, listening. When I look back at Awalmir, he's pointing his gun at me. Between my eyes. From just a few feet away. There's no possible way he can miss.

"Seema!" he says again, glaring at me. "Why she not wake?"

"She's very sick. The doctors have her on sleeping medicine."

"My son? Where?" His gun is steady.

Keep him talking. No wobbles. Don't let him know that I'm frigging terrified. "The nursery," I say in English, not Dari, banking on his poor language skills. Maybe this will delay things—until help can get here.

"What is nursery?"

"A special place for babies who are very small. Too small to live on their own. The doctors have him in an incubator." None of it's true, but he has no way of knowing that I'm lying. God help me if he demands I take him to the nursery. Would he actually take a baby boy? A baby who's not his? A son who never was?

"Incubator? What is incubator?"

"A machine to help him breathe." I take a few deep breaths to illustrate my point.

"Why he need this?" He's shouting now. "You hurt my son!" He steps closer. The gun can't be more than three feet from my face. Why the fuck isn't anyone coming to help?

For just a moment, he looks at Seema. With his left hand, he grips her shoulder, jostles her. "Seema! You wake! We go now!"

That split second of looking at Seema is exactly what I need. I'm on my feet, grabbing my IV pole. With my bandaged hands, I can barely keep my grip. But I hold fast, slamming the pole as hard as I can against his right arm.

"*Fäshä!*" he yells in surprise as the gun clatters onto the floor.

Then, suddenly, Seema is out of bed, scrambling across the floor, her hand closing around the stock of Awalmir's gun.

I hear the scream, Seema's scream. "You killed my mother! I won't let you kill my Auntie!"

But I don't hear the shot. Or feel the blood spattering me.

Lights flood the room.

Uniformed men with guns drawn surge through the door.

I sink to the floor and hug my legs to my chest. And I rock. Is any of this real?

"Annie?" Cerelli is next to me, gathering me into his arms, holding me tight. Tight enough that it feels real. "God almighty. You're so fearless, it terrifies me."

48

FIGHTING MY WAY OUT of a drug-induced sleep, I open my eyes to someone in a black *burqa* sitting on the blue plastic chair next to my bed. Real? Or am I hallucinating? I look at the hands clasped in her lap. Chapped and raw. I know those hands.

"Annie?"

"Gulshan!" Please let her be real.

"You are all right?" She sounds doubtful.

I push myself up so I'm sitting. "It's been a rough week, but I'm better now. Wait! How did you get here?"

She sweeps her *burqa* off her face. "Ikrom drove me, of course."

"Ikrom's here, too? Can he come in?"

"He is conferring now with Tariq and Captain Cerelli. They say you have an infection in your hands?"

I hold up my gauzed mitts. "As you can see. It's been pretty bad."

She holds up a small, round jar. "I brought you medicine. A salve I make for infections. The doctors probably will not approve." Her eyes twinkle. "This is the real medicine that will make you better. Shall I put some on your hands now?"

"The bandages."

"Bah! Bandages are meant to come off!" In an instant, she frees my hands and gently, oh so gently, rubs her salve into my skin.

I can't bear to look.

She keeps massaging. A feather touch. So light, I could be imagining it. When she's done and the bandages are on my hands again, she puts the lid back on the jar and sets it on the small table next to my bed.

"How often should I use it?"

"Just a little bit. Two times a day. Have Captain Cerelli rub it gently all over your hands."

"Captain Cerelli?"

"Of course! Who else?"

Of course. I rest my eyes for just a moment to think about that.

When I wake up again, the chair is empty. But looking at the bedside table, I see a small, round jar.

49

TWO DAYS LATER, THE bandages come off my hands. I stare at the ruin in front of me. My fingers and hands, still swollen and scraped, are riddled with a slew of reddened puncture marks and purple bruises and deep gashes now sutured closed. I'm about to lose it, but when I look up, the doctor, my American nurse, and Cerelli are all smiling.

"Much better," says the doctor. "Truly remarkable. And no sign of sepsis. You heal well. I'm discharging you on one condition."

I'm back to looking at my fingers, trying to flex them, not at all happy with how stiff they are. Not to mention how much they hurt. "Anything."

"You will see your regular doctor as soon as you get home." She turns to Cerelli. "I am putting your husband in charge of that."

My husband? I'm ready to object—vehemently—then I see Cerelli's raised eyebrow. "I'll see to it," he says, barely swallowing his laugh.

A few hours later, with the afternoon sun bearing down, a nurse pushes my wheelchair to the helipad where our U.S. Navy chopper is waiting to take us to Bagram. "I don't need a wheelchair," I mutter.

"Humor them," says Cerelli. "They like doing things like this. It boosts morale."

When we reach the helicopter, I'm ready to climb on board, then think better of it. I decide to boost Cerelli's morale by letting him lift me up. The power in his arms never ceases to amaze me. Losing a leg hasn't diminished his upper body strength one iota. Probably increased it.

They've already loaded Seema in her wheelchair on board. Without her *burqa*, she looks impossibly tiny and frail. She's still hooked up to an IV, but she's smiling, clearly happy to be going home to the U.S. with her father.

Cerelli slaps the side of the chopper and circles his index finger in the air, then climbs aboard and rolls the door shut. A minute later, the rotors are roaring. Then, we're lifting into the air. With the cheers of the hospital staff sending us on our way, we turn and head southwest—the length of the valley.

It feels like barely a half hour later that we're descending and then circling. We can't possibly be at Bagram already. I shoot Cerelli a quizzical look. He crooks a lopsided grin and points out the porthole. Looking down, I see what will soon be the new and better Wad Qol Secondary School for Girls. The walls are up, and they've started on the bricks. The roof is framed in and the plywood sheets in place. It looks like there's even a front door. And lined up in front of the school are the workers and Ikrom and Gulshan, all the teachers, and a whole lot of girls in brown *shalwar kameezes* and white headscarves. Waving. They're all waving.

"Sorry, sweetheart. We don't have time to land, but I promised Gulshan we'd do a flyover."

I wave back from the little porthole, although there's no way they can actually see me. And then my tears start leaking again. Even though I'm smiling. On the other side of the chopper, Seema's waving, too, clearly excited to see the new school. A new beginning.

"Hey!" says Cerelli as he wipes away my tears. "I thought—"

"I'm happy. Really. It's wonderful to see the school, everyone. I'm just so fucking hormonal."

A UNIFORMED OFFICER AND a couple medics meet our helicopter when it touches down at the Bagram airfield. "Admiral Cerelli, sir. Lieutenant Fightmaster reporting." He salutes sharply.

Admiral? What the hell? He got promoted and didn't tell me? I've been sleeping with an admiral and didn't know? When I get him alone, he's gonna hear about this.

"Lieutenant." Cerelli returns the salute. "At ease." Then, he offers his hand. "Congratulations on the promotion, Fightmaster. Well deserved."

"Thank you, sir." The lieutenant's cheeks redden, making the freckles across his midwestern farm-boy nose all the more prominent. He turns to me. "Ma'am, if you and the rest of your party would follow me?"

"My stuff?" I say, looking at Cerelli. "Any chance . . ."

"A duffel, camera case, and backpack are already on board, ma'am," Fightmaster says with great efficiency. "Your gear, too, sir."

"Thanks, Lieutenant." Cerelli touches my arm. "There are a couple things I have to do. I'll be with you in thirty."

IT'S A GOOD THREE HOURS later, and Cerelli's still not here. In my seat at the front of the plane, I'm starting to get antsy. Looking behind me, I see one of the medics and Tariq hovering over Seema. The other medic sits a few rows ahead of them. He glances up at me and waves. Subtle. Other than that, the plane is empty. A military jet. Smaller than a troop transport and much nicer. Hard to believe the military sent this for us. Then, I remember that Cerelli's an admiral now. I'm guessing the top brass get more luxury.

Finally, I hear movement and turn to see what's going on. Bibi Faludi is walking up the aisle with Cerelli behind her. He looks past her toward me and shakes his head, which I take to mean, *I'll tell you later*. Bibi sits mid-plane, and the medic is on his feet and moving to a seat just opposite. When Cerelli waves me over, I make my way down the aisle and kneel on the seat in front of Bibi.

She reaches for my hands, but catching sight of my battle wounds, doesn't touch me. Instead, she smiles. "Thank you for saving my grandniece. You were right to believe in her. For this, our families will always be grateful. *Alhamdulillah*."

I decide to pry. In a roundabout way. "I'm so glad to see you again. I was afraid I'd have to leave Afghanistan without getting the chance."

"Ah, you are wondering why I am on this flight."

Apparently, I wasn't as subtle as I thought. "Well, yes."

"Tariq will need my help. Seema has a long road ahead of her. We all do."

I almost would've believed it if she'd looked at me when she said that instead of at Cerelli. As if checking to make sure she'd said the right thing. I look at him, too. And except for the slight pulsing of the muscle next to his eye, he's wearing his poker face. Which means something is definitely going on.

More movement in the aisle. "Ma'am. Admiral, sir. We're ready to take off." The lieutenant nods toward our seats.

Before I can push myself to my feet, Bibi catches my sleeve. Leaning forward, she whispers, "*Adâlat.*"

At least, I think that's what she says. It's not a Dari word I've ever heard.

Back in our seats, Cerelli takes the seat belt from my fumbling hands and fastens it for me. The engines roar into action, and the jet backs around onto the runway, taxiing down to the far end. Then, the engines go into turbo drive, and we rocket down the runway and into the air. I'd forgotten how steeply military jets climb right at takeoff. No slow and steady for these guys. The jet circles toward Kabul, and pressing my forehead against the porthole, I see an eruption of fire on the horizon. A bombing, I'm sure of it. My heart clenches. *Please, let it not be the maternity hospital.* Moments later, before I can bring it to Cerelli's attention, it's out of sight. I tell him about it anyway.

He doesn't say a word. Which tells me he definitely knows something about what I just saw.

"What's going on?" I ask.

"Annie, there are bombings all the time in Kabul."

"Right. Quite a coincidence that this one happened just as we're flying past." And I know Cerelli doesn't believe in coincidences.

"Not to change the subject, but I've got a present for you." He hands me a small camera. "It seems Sawyer has untapped videography skills."

I shoot Cerelli a suspicious glance, then lean against his shoulder and press the PLAY button. The new school comes into view. Cupping my hand in front of my mouth, I don't know whether to laugh or cry. The building is so big and beautiful. And now, I'm getting a much better view than I did from the helicopter. The exterior walls have bricks going about two-thirds of the way up. The windows are definitely in place. The camera zooms in on the unpainted front door where Gulshan is standing in her black *burqa*.

"Annie, you will join me for a tour?" She points to the door. "A bright color, no? Blue. Do you agree? Perhaps the religion teacher's grandson will paint it for us?"

"Great idea!" I laugh. As if she can hear me.

Gulshan steps through the doorway and stands for a moment in the center hallway between two classrooms and points. "This room. Do you remember it?"

"My classroom! And there are walls. Real walls." I close my eyes and hear the senior girls shrieking with laughter as Seema's image of Bahar and Wiin and Chehrah flashes on the sheet I draped across the blackboard as a makeshift screen. "*Che Bahaaal!*" Wiin called out that afternoon.

Gulshan stands in the center of the empty room. "As you see, Annie, we do not yet have tables or chairs or a blackboard. Captain Cerelli told me he will bring more money for us to buy everything we need. Mel and Yasmine have given us a miracle. As I told you, Allah would answer our prayers, and he has."

"It's beautiful!" I say to the video.

Gulshan walks toward the far wall. "The windows now are much bigger. We will have more light. And there is insulation. This we never had in the old school. It will be much warmer in the winter. Many more girls will want to come to learn."

And at that, the screen fades to black.

I nestle against Cerelli. "You've already seen this?"

"I have not. Sawyer said it was a gift for you."

"Thank you. It's a wonderful gift. There are a whole lot of people back home who will love watching this." I let that happy thought sit between the two of us for all of one minute until I remember that I'm sitting next to an admiral. "We've got to talk."

"Yes, we do." He picks up my hand, gently, as if he's holding a feather. "I meant what I said before. Fatima is very happily married to her husband, whom she adores."

Not the conversation I intended for us to have, but it's a good idea to get this out of the way. "Then, why were you in Kabul? With her? At one in the morning?"

"Fatima works for me."

I turn toward him and stare in disbelief. "She's—"

"Yes." He nods, then puts a hand on either side of my face so I can't look away. "And I made a mistake. A long time ago. We slept together. Once. Something I never did with any other operative. For good reason."

"And?"

"I told you before, I'm not a saint."

"Yeah, well, neither am I. So, what happened?"

"We agreed we weren't good together and broke it off. She met Samy and married him."

"Then, why did you come to Kabul? Especially after arguing with me? I thought—"

"I know what you thought. And I couldn't tell you any different. Not when you called. Sweetheart, you know what kind of work I do. There are things I can't tell you. But please believe me, I would never hurt you."

The lieutenant is standing in the aisle next to Cerelli. His cough sweeps Fatima's ghost away. For good, I hope. "Admiral, sir, the pilot requests your presence in the cockpit."

Cerelli's on his feet with the speed and agility of a man who has two working legs. Truly impressive. And he's back in less than five minutes, walking limp-free down the aisle to Bibi. I can't hear a word. All I can do is watch Bibi nod, then close her eyes. Cerelli doesn't move. When she finally looks back at him, I could swear her lips form the word *tashakor*. A few more words, and then Cerelli is sliding back into his seat next to me.

"Omar Mohaqiq is dead."

"Oh my God! Uncle Omar? What happened?"

"Best the National Police can figure out, there was a gas leak in the apartment building."

"And?" I flash on the explosion of fire I saw.

"The entire building is in flames."

"Was anyone else killed? Hurt?"

"The authorities say everyone else is accounted for. And safe. *Alhamdulillah*."

I glance behind me again. Bibi looks calm. No crying. No wailing. *Tashakor*, she said. Almost as if she already knew. "I should go to her."

He stops me with his hand. "Not now."

Another quick look. "She's not a grieving widow."

"No, she's not." Clearly, he's not going to tell me what's going on. Or, he can't.

I'm pretty sure I know part of it, at least. That SD card I found in their apartment. Seema's card. Either she was in the apartment after Darya's murder or Awalmir was. Somehow that card got to Omar. Bottom line: Omar was involved.

I look back at Bibi again. Eyes closed, she looks tired, but serene. I know she was involved with whatever happened to Omar. Cerelli was, too. And Sawyer. But how they did it, I doubt I'll ever know.

Cerelli catches me looking. "One thing I *can* tell you, and this goes nowhere."

He's got my attention.

"Those last two *landays* Rahila sent you?"

"Yeah?"

"I asked Bibi about them."

"She's the expert."

"They definitely piqued her curiosity. Especially given the SD card you found in their apartment."

I hold my breath.

"She did a little investigating. Got into a couple of Omar's locked boxes." He looks at me like he expects me to connect the dots.

And suddenly, I do. "Holy shit! She found copies of the *landays*? *Omar* wrote those *landays*?" I lock eyes with him. "Or if he didn't write them himself, he copied them from someone."

"From Bibi herself. *She* wrote those last two *landays* to Omar years ago—before they married. In fact, before his first wife died." He pauses as I absorb the meaning behind his words. "She also found copies of the *landays* Awalmir purportedly wrote to Seema, including the one left in the house last May when they fled."

"But it was in Seema's handwriting."

"Back at the hospital, Seema admitted that Awalmir gave her the text and told her to copy it."

I try to clench my fingers into a fist, but they're still too swollen and sore. "I knew she couldn't have written that. Not on her own."

Cerelli grins. "Might be a good idea for the men in your life to listen to you more carefully."

Then the full impact of Omar having written that particular *landay* hits me. Hard. "Wait! You're telling me that Omar—he knew Awalmir was going to kill Darya? *Her own uncle?*"

"Annie." Cerelli's arm wraps around my back and pulls me against him.

"And he sent the rest of the *landays* trying to draw us out. You and me. To kill us." I bury my face against his chest as the wave breaks over me. Until some of the horror passes. Until I'm able to make sense of my crazy thoughts. And that's when I finally put all the pieces together. "It was more than that, wasn't it?" My voice trembles with fury. "Omar was running the whole fucking operation. *He* was the uncle Awalmir told Seema he was working for—back when he first met her last spring. Omar didn't just *know* what Awalmir and Ghazan planned to do. He *ordered* them to do it. Omar was behind everything."

Cerelli doesn't tell me I've got it right. He doesn't tell me I'm wrong either. I roll my mental video of the last couple weeks and finally freeze-frame at Darya and Tariq's house. Seema's bedroom. The list of names and numbers I found in the binding of *Little Women*. "That list I found. It was important, wasn't it? That was the link between Awalmir and Omar you needed." But there's something else. I can see it in Cerelli's eyes.

"Tell me what I'm missing."

"Annie—"

Omar. Awalmir. My job. Chris Cardona telling me they needed me for this job . . . "Oh my God. The Taliban approved me to be on the crew for the secret interview. Me. They were going to kill me. Weren't they?"

Cerelli makes no effort to answer.

I exhale loudly. "How about a simple 'yes'? Just this once?"

"Sorry, sweetheart." Cerelli reaches for my hand, twines his fingers gently around mine. "But there is one thing I can tell you. What Bibi said to you an hour ago? *Adâlat* is Dari for 'justice.'"

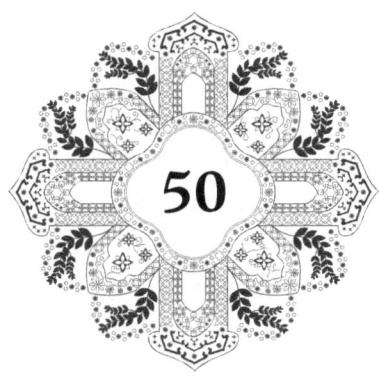

50

HOURS LATER, CERELLI JOSTLES me awake. The lieutenant is standing in the aisle with my dinner, doing his best not to look at me sleeping on the admiral's chest. I push myself upright, keenly aware of how wet I've left Cerelli's shirt—from tears and drool. Damn, I'm a mess.

As soon as the lieutenant moves on to the other passengers, Cerelli's back on task. "Did I answer all your questions? Before?"

I'm pretty sure he doesn't mean about Omar. It's Fatima he's referring to. He wants to make sure I'm good with where things stand. "Except one."

He looks puzzled. "What did I miss?"

"Telling me you made admiral."

He stabs his fingers through his no-longer-quite-so-short military haircut. "To be accurate: Rear. Lower Half. It's a desk job. Mostly." There's just the slightest downturn of his voice on those last three words.

"Close enough. It seems like everyone knew but me."

"Weeellll." He ducks his head for a moment, then looks back

at me. "Promotions like this can take years. If they happen at all. It came through faster than I expected."

I snort a laugh. "That's your reason for not telling me? Cerelli, that's seriously lame."

"I wanted to settle something before I told you."

"What are you talking about?"

"Annie, this isn't the way I had it planned, sitting with you next to the cockpit in a military plane. But the time is now. I'd get down on one knee if I still had it. I was hoping you'd give some thought to marrying me."

I sit silently, staring at him for a full count of ten seconds. "Did you just propose?" Talk about blindsiding me. "Isn't this kind of sudden?"

"In my line of work, it's best to move fast." He cups his hand against my cheek. "Yes, I did just propose. And I promise, I'll take another shot at it when we get home. A much more romantic shot. Unless you turn me down flat now."

I stare in total disbelief. "I don't get it. What the hell does this have to do with you getting promoted to admiral?"

That telltale muscle next to his eye is pulsing again. "I figured a woman like you might object to marrying an admiral."

"Valid point. You know me well."

"I was hoping to ask before you found out about the promotion."

"A bit deceitful, don't you think?"

"For a good cause." The muscle is nearing a full spasm.

"Cerelli, you have the worst tell."

That surprises him. "I do not."

"That muscle at the corner of your eye?"

He grins. "Only you."

Time to put him out of his misery. "About this whole admiral thing?"

"Yeah?"

"I might be able to make allowances. But first, there are a few things I need to know."

"And those would be?" He looks wary, probably thinking I want a full list of ex-wives, former affairs, every woman in every port. Which is actually the *last* thing I want. What I *do* want goes to the heart of who this man is.

"How is an admiral going to cope with not being able to tell me what to do?"

"I'm sure you'll let me know when I step over that line. You always have before. Besides, I've got Mel on my side, and she seems able to get away with ordering you around."

"Mel knows?"

"I asked her first."

"Totally unfair advantage."

"All's fair." He grins.

I narrow my eyes. "Okay. Next question. Why did the Navy send an admiral to Afghanistan to clean up whatever this latest mess was?"

He shakes his head. "Won't work, sweetheart. I'm still not going to tell you why I was there. Anything else?"

"One last question. For now. How the hell are you going to manage a desk job?"

He nods. But he's not grinning anymore. "You finally got to it."

"Hard to see you behind an oak desk."

"Mahogany."

"Hardly the point, Cerelli."

"If I tell you, will you say yes?"

"I might." I put my hand flat against his chest. "But if you don't tell me, it's a definite deal-breaker."

"What if I compose another *landay*? Would that work?"

"I'd like that, too," I say in all seriousness. "For now, though, just answer my question."

He's still not smiling. "A desk job isn't what I signed up for. I don't know if I can handle it."

"Seriously?" This man is a SEAL. All Navy. And he knows *everything*.

"Seriously. I don't know."

"Cerelli?"

"I'm baring my soul to you."

"I'd expect nothing less."

"It could be a rough ride—for a while."

"I like riding with you. But"—my hand is back on his chest—"I need to do some solo riding, too." I pick up his hand, turn it over, and kiss his palm. "You may not be aware that I'm dealing with this PTSD thing."

"Are you?"

"Okay, what I should probably say is that I've done my best to avoid dealing with it, but the time has come for me to get serious. And I sure as hell don't want to dump damaged goods on you." I lock eyes with him. "I love you too much."

"So? Your answer isn't a definite 'no'?" I can see the question in his eyes.

"I need some therapy time." Just saying the word makes me shudder. "I'm hoping you'll be willing to wait." What the hell am I doing? "Please?"

He wraps his arms around me and pulls me close.

"My heart holds fast for my Beloved,
More beautiful even than rubies from Badakhshan."

"For me?" I blink back the tears pricking my eyes. Good tears.

"For you. Sorry I'm a syllable short. I'll make it up to you. I promise."

"I'll hold you to that."

Glossary

There are two official languages in Afghanistan: Dari (often referred to as Afghan Persian), spoken by 77% of Afghans in the west, north, and northeast of the country; and Pashto, spoken by 48% of the populace, mainly in the southeast. There are more than forty additional minor languages and many dialects. Dari is written in the Persian form of Arabic script; Pashto is a modified form of Arabic script. The Dari and Pashto words included in *Double Exposure* are transliterated into English script based on Nicholas Awde's *Dari Dictionary & Phrasebook*, Nicholas Awde and Asmatullah Sarwan's *Pashto Dictionary & Phrasebook*, and *Dari/Pashto Phrasebook for Military Personnel*, compiled by Robert F. Powers, (Dari Editor) Edris Nawin, and (Pashto Editor) Subhan Fakhrizada. Many words have multiple variations in spelling in English. Most words and phrases are translated within the story or their meaning is made obvious in the context.

Abaya – A simple, loose overgarment, essentially a robe-like dress, caftan, or coat that covers the whole body except the head, feet, and hands. Usually worn with a *hijab*.

Adâlat (Dari) – Justice

Adhan – The Muslim call to ritual prayer, typically made by a *mu'adhdhin* from the minaret of a mosque.

Alhamdulillah – "All praise and thanks to God."

Amrikâyi (Dari) – American

Anaa (Pashto) – Grandmother

Asr – The midafternoon obligatory prayer

Assalâmu alaykum. Wa 'alaykum assalâm. – "Peace be unto you." "To you peace." This is a Muslim greeting with many variations in spelling.

Attan – Originally a Pashtun folk dance performed in times of war or at engagement announcements, now considered a national dance

Baklava – A sweet dessert made with phyllo dough, honey, and nuts

Balê (Dari) – Yes

Borani banjân – Sliced, sautéed eggplant served with garlic yogurt sauce

Burqa – A long, loose garment covering the body from head to feet, concealing even the eyes and hands, worn by many Afghani Muslim women in public. Wearing a *burqa* is cultural and is not required by Islam. Some Muslim women see the wearing of the *burqa* as a way to show modesty. Others see it as a mandate by Taliban men to oppress women.

Chai – Tea

Chalau (chalaw) – A traditional Afghan stew made with lamb and rice, seasoned with garlic and cayenne

Che Bahaaal! (Dari) – "Cooool!"

Crikey! (Aussie slang) – An expression of surprise

Däktara (Dari) – A doctor who is a woman

Fäshä, Amrikäyëy (Pashto) – Whore (American)

Hama (Ama) – Aunt (father's sister); in Dari, Pashto, and Arabic, there are different words to specify how an aunt or uncle is related to an individual—for example, father's sister as opposed to mother's sister.

Hijab – A headcover worn in public by many Muslim women

Inshallah – "If Allah wills it."

Kabuli palaw – A lamb and rice dish for special occasions

Keffiyeh – A Bedouin Arab's kerchief, worn by men as a headdress and popular among Western journalists and photographers in the Middle East

Khoda hafiz – "God protect you." Literally: "May God be your guardian." A common way to say goodbye

Khazina däktora (Pashto) – A doctor who is a woman

Khazina roghtun (Pashto) – Women's hospital

Khosha – A popular restaurant in Kabul

Khub astom, tashakor. (Dari) – "I am well, thank you."

Klinik (Pashto) – Clinic

Landay – A two-line poem with twenty-two syllables, traditionally composed and sung by Pashtun women

Mâdar Kalân (Dari; var. *Mâdar-bozorg*) – Grandmother

Maghrib – The sunset obligatory prayer

Mashallah – "What Allah has willed." Used to express appreciation, joy, praise, thankfulness.

Mashawa (Dari) – Afghan vegetable and barley soup

Mêbakhshêd! Momken ast bogozarom. (Dari) – "Excuse me! Let me by."

Mêtawânêd bâ man komak konêd, lotfan? (Dari) – "Could you help me, please?"

Morda-gow (Dari) – Literally means "dead cow." It also means "39," and in Dari slang, it means "prostitute" and "pimp."

Muezzin (var. *Mu'adhdhin*) – The Muslim official who summons the faithful to prayer five times a day

Nân (Dari) – Bread

Nân-e châsht (Dari) – Noon meal or lunch

Nyaw aw Badal (Pashto) – Justice and revenge (part of the Pashtunwali Code)

Pakol – Soft, round-topped cloth hat worn by Pashtun, Tajik, and Nuristani men

Piala (Dari) – Small bowl used for drinking tea

Qormah-e-Sabzi (Dari) – Spinach stew, flavored with olive oil, lemon, cilantro, green onions

Roat or Roht (Dari) – Afghan sweet bread

Roghtoon-e-zanäna (Dari) – Women's hospital

Salâm! Che hâl dared? (var. *Hâl-e shoma chetor ast?*) (Dari) – "Hello! How are you?"

Salat – Islamic mandatory prayers performed five times daily, facing the direction of Mecca

Shalwar kameez – Traditional trouser loose at the waist and narrowing to a cuff at the ankle, worn with a long shirt or tunic, worn by both women and men

Shohna ba shohna (Dari) – Shoulder to shoulder, as soldiers stand next to each other

Shomâ! (Dari) – "You there!"

Sobh ba khaye! (Dari) – "Good morning!"

Taqiyah (Arabic) – Muslim skull cap

Tashakor (Dari) – "Thank you."

Tiffin – A round, metal lunchbox. In India, it also refers to a light meal or a midday meal.

Tunbaan – A traditional Afghan tribal dress, also known as a Kuchi tribal dress

Wolesi Jirga – One of the two houses of government in Afghanistan, equivalent to the U.S. House of Representatives

Zezhantun (Pashto) – Maternity hospital

Author's Note

The U.S.-led coalition forces drove the Taliban from power in November 2001, but the Taliban regrouped and, for the next twenty years, launched terrorist attacks throughout Afghanistan. Using car and truck bombs, they targeted Kabul University and destroyed hundreds of girls' schools. Hospitals were another soft target. In May 2020, the Taliban attacked Ataturk Maternity Hospital in Kabul, killing mothers and newborns. Using undercover agents, the Taliban also successfully infiltrated all levels of the Afghan government ministries, universities, businesses, and aid organizations. This "peaceful" takeover facilitated the actual takeover of city after city across the country at breathtaking speed, with the final toppling of Kabul.

Like millions of people around the world, I watched in horror on August 15, 2021, and the days that followed as the Afghan government crumbled and the Taliban returned to power. As expected, they immediately shuttered girls' schools and launched vicious attacks of retribution against any Afghan who worked with the coalition forces, government, military, and police. Thousands of Afghan nationals fled the country this past autumn, many leaving with literally the clothes they were wearing, to countries where they now live as refugees and hope to restart their lives. Many millions more Afghans could not escape and continue to suffer as I write this.

Double Exposure is a work of fiction with its roots set firmly in the reality of what Afghanistan was in Autumn 2015, nearly six years before the Taliban regained control. My goal in this novel is to highlight the struggle of women and girls for education, for health care, and for a say in determining their lives. Although Annie Hawkins took the money raised by Mel and Yasmine to rebuild the Wad Qol Secondary School for Girls, there are actual NGOs that have helped build girls' schools and provide educational opportunities for girls and women: Women for Afghan Women, Women for Women International, Global Fund for Women, and Malala Fund. There are also organizations helping provide health care for Afghan women and girls: Doctors Without Borders and the amazing medical staff at Anabah Maternity Centre and the Anabah Surgical and Paediatric Centre in Anabah District, Panjshir Valley, Afghanistan, which is a training center for doctors throughout Afghanistan. As always, a portion of the proceeds from the sale of *Double Exposure* will go to support girls' and women's education and health care.

January 9, 2022

Double Exposure Discussion Questions

1. Annie is suspended from her job for having aimed a gun at Piera McNeil. In what ways does this leave Annie morally compromised?

2. Annie and Cerelli regularly keep significant secrets from each other. How does their secret-keeping affect their relationship?

3. Annie's PTSD continues to be a problem for her in *Double Exposure*. What impact does this have on the story? Why is she reluctant to deal with it?

4. Annie's daughter, Mel, is a secondary character who plays a major role. How do her actions affect the events of the story?

5. During Annie's stay in Wad Qol, she and Gulshan become good friends. In what ways are these two women similar? In what ways is their friendship surprising?

6. *Double Exposure* explores the relationships of four married Afghan couples: Awa and Firash Faqiri, Bibi Faludi and Omar Mohaqiq, Gulshan and Ikrom Abdulin, Seema and Awalmir. How do these marriages differ from one another, and how do they reflect the complexities of Afghanistan?

7. The rebuilding of the Wad Qol Secondary School for Girls encompasses this novel. What does this endeavor mean to the different characters?

8. Although *Double Exposure* is a work of fiction, it is grounded in the reality of Afghanistan in Autumn 2015. Based on what you know about the events of 2021, what are some of the events and situations in the novel that could have really happened?

9. In what ways do *landays* drive the plot?

10. What are the different meanings that the characters attach to the *burqa* in this novel?

11. What did you learn about Afghanistan and Afghan culture by reading *Double Exposure*?

Jeannée would love to join your book club discussion! Please contact her at jeanneesacken19@gmail.com.

Acknowledgements

Myriad thanks to . . .

Shannon Ishizaki, who gave Annie Hawkins and Finn Cerelli a home at Ten16 Press. Lauren Blue's editing crystalized the novel and made it so much better. Kaeley Dunteman's perfect cover design works on so many levels. Josh McFarlane created a beautiful chapter graphic that found its way onto the cover. Veronica Davis-Quiroz, Sean Malone, and Jenna Zerbel all make 259 South Street a wonderful publishing house.

Ann-Marie Nieves, publicist *extraordinaire*, who works miracles to get *Double Exposure* into readers' hands.

Heba Elkobaitry, who refined my portrayal of Islam and insisted I create a bigger role for Seema Ghafoor. She was right.

The Penny Loafers—Judy Bridges, Sara Rattan, and Maura Fitzgerald—who made me dig deeper, write leaner, and kept me laughing.

Nancy Backes, who believed in this novel from the very beginning and offered critical insights, especially with backstory. Elizabeth Jonas made sure the characters felt real and the story flowed. Jennifer Rupp offered invaluable help to the plot exactly when I needed it most.

Debra Thomas, Laurie Buchanan, Maggie Smith, Tahmina Nadir, Patricia Sands, and Kathryn Gauci, who all cheered on Annie Hawkins Green. Patricia Sands set me to tap-dancing when she posted that Annie is "my new favourite badass woman."

Roi Solberg, who knew no bounds when it came to supporting Annie and Cerelli and literally flew halfway across the country so we could talk in person instead of on Zoom.

My husband, Michael Briselli, who took time from his own writing projects to read mine and shared my disappointment when we had to postpone photo shoots for yet another year.

And finally, the many wonderful readers, podcasters, bookstagrammers, and book groups who loved *Behind the Lens* and recommended it to friends. I hope you enjoy *Double Exposure* just as much.

Photo © Agnieszka Tropiło

A former English professor at Rochester Institute of Technology, Jeannée Sacken is now a photojournalist who travels the world, documenting the lives of women and children. She also photographs wildlife and is deeply committed to the conservation of endangered species. When not traveling, she lives with her husband and three cats in Shorewood, Wisconsin, where she's hard at work on the next novel in the award-winning Annie Hawkins series. Follow Jeannée at jeanneesacken.com.